Louisa Heaton is a married mother of four—including a set of twins—and lives on an island in Hampshire. When not wrangling her children, husband or countless animals, she can often be found walking her dogs along the beach, muttering to herself as she works out plot points. In her spare time she read a lot and crochets. Usually when she ought to be doing something else!

Ann McIntosh was born in the tropics, lived in the frozen north for a number of years, and now resides in sunny central Florida with her husband. She's a proud mama to three grown children, loves tea, crafting, animals—except reptiles—bacon and the ocean. She believes in the power of romance to heal, inspire and provide hope in our complex world.

HEALED BY HIS SECRET BABY

LOUISA HEATON

BEST FRIEND TO DOCTOR RIGHT

ANN McINTOSH

MILLS & BOON

First Published in Great Britain 2020
by Mills & Boon, an imprint of HarperCollins*Publishers*
1 London Bridge Street, London, SE1 9GF

Healed by His Secret Baby © 2020 Louisa Heaton

Best Friend to Doctor Right © 2020 Ann McIntosh

ISBN: 978-0-263-27975-7

MIX
Paper from
responsible sources
FSC® C007454

This book is produced from independently certified FSC™ paper
to ensure responsible forest management.
For more information visit www.harpercollins.co.uk/green.

Printed and bound in Spain
by CPI, Barcelona

HEALED BY
HIS SECRET BABY

LOUISA HEATON

MILLS & BOON

For all the lovely staff at Staunton. xxx

CHAPTER ONE

Hey, you.

So, this is it. My final wish. And I'm sorry I'm asking you to do this, but I truly have no one else. You're the only one I trust, and you've always been there for me, and now I'm asking you to be there again. But this time it's for Tori and that way you can't say no!

I never told her father. You know why, and it was the right thing to do at the time, but as I get closer to going I can't help but think of my darling little girl having no one in the world she's related to. I've been there. I've done that. And it's a lonely place. She'll have you, her godmother, but...she has a father out there and he could be amazing!

So, I'm tasking you with this. Find him. His name is Cole Branagh and he's a doctor. A GP. And if he's a doctor then surely he cares about people? I'm hoping he has a good heart. I'm hoping he can be everything she needs.

I want you to find him, and if you think he's a good man then let him know about Tori.

I need you to find her daddy.

I know you'll make the right decisions.
Much love to you, always and for ever,
Skye xxx

LANE PUT DOWN the note and exclaimed, 'Why are you making me do this?'

She went to scrunch it up in frustration but then stopped, thought better of it, and instead stared with defeat at the Liberty Point Surgery, a small general practice nestled in the village of Bourton-on-the-Water. As if just staring at the building long enough would make this whole sorry mess disappear.

He was in there. Cole Branagh.

Dr Cole Branagh.

The man who'd slept with her best friend when he really ought to have known better than to take advantage of a woman whose inhibitions were in question because of her alcohol intake.

Lane knew *exactly* what type of man he'd be. A charmer. A user of women. The type to hang around in bars looking for lonely easy pickings. This Cole Branagh bloke had got *exactly* what he wanted from Skye and nothing more.

Just like Simon.

And here she was, sitting in her car, feeling trepidation about going in there because a man like that wouldn't want to know about his dead one-night stands, or babies they didn't know they'd fathered. Men like that didn't care.

Lane had uprooted her own life just to find this slime ball and have her theories proved right! Surely this was going to be a waste of time? Skye had told Lane all she needed to know about this Cole Branagh!

It had been quite easy to find him on the internet. Liberty Point Surgery's website helpfully had a staff page with a smiling photo of each member of staff and a short paragraph explaining a bit about who they were. Probably to make them seem human.

Who would want to have a go at medical receptionist Mary when they knew she knitted hats for the preemie babies up at St Luke's?

Cole was the only one who had no photo and his paragraph was missing. There was just his name and a list of his qualifications.

Dr Cole Branagh, BM, MRCGP, DGM, DFFP, DRCOG

Such an impressive array of letters. She'd had to look them up to see what they meant. Bachelor of Medicine. Member of the Royal College of General Practitioners. Diploma in Geriatric Medicine. Diploma of the Faculty of Family Planning. Diploma of the Royal College of Obstetrics and Gynaecologists...

She'd laughed cynically at those last two. This man who knew so much about the best way to have a baby, was a man who had *no idea* he had an eight-month-old daughter. Wasn't *that* ironic?

Sighing with irritation, she folded Skye's letter and slipped it back into her bag as she stared once more at the surgery building, delaying for just a few more moments. It looked quite nice, as surgeries went. Modern. Redbrick. It even had hanging baskets filled with flowers in glorious pinks and greens.

She'd been lucky they'd needed a temporary healthcare assistant. Lane had registered with an agency in order to get the post there and her mum had stepped in to babysit

Tori whilst she discovered if this Dr Branagh could be trusted to know that he had a child.

She flipped down the visor to see the photo she'd tucked there. It was of her and Skye. Tori's mother was blowing out the candles on a birthday cake, with one arm around Lane, wearing a silly paper party hat. It had been taken just one year away from a diagnosis that would change everything.

'I can't believe you're making me do this, Skye,' she said out loud. 'Who am I to be judge and jury?'

You're Tori's legal guardian, that's who. It was as if Skye's voice came to her. *You made me a promise. On my deathbed. You can't break it!* She could almost hear the devilish chuckle in her friend's voice.

No. She wouldn't break it. She'd sworn it, holding Skye's hands, squeezing them tight as her best friend in the whole wide world had taken her final breaths.

She'd almost lost herself afterwards. The intense grief had pulled her towards an unimaginable darkness.

She and Skye had been friends for ever. Since infants' school. Skye had seemed strange to Lane at first. Someone without a mum? Or a dad? But they had bonded instantly and stuck by each other's side through everything.

Until the very end.

Only baby Tori had kept Lane going. Going through the courts to get official guardianship. The little girl laughed and smiled just like her mummy! Tori was all she had left of Skye. And now she had to decide if some man—*whom she didn't even know!*—could be a father to that precious little girl. That some sleazeball from a bar would have to be in their lives.

It wasn't fair.

She hated him already. But Skye, bless her heart, had

thought that he deserved a chance to know his daughter. That he deserved a chance to show that he could be a good man and a good father.

'He'd better be some kind of unbelievable saint,' she said out loud to the photo. 'That's all I'm saying.'

Five minutes later, she was walking inside the surgery, headache brewing, with her backpack over her shoulder, trying to look as if she wasn't an undercover spy on a secret mission, but just an ordinary agency healthcare assistant, ready to start her new posting.

But when she got inside, she saw a crowd of people huddled around a person lying on the floor, and her instincts immediately kicked in.

She dropped her bag. 'Let me through! I can help!' she said as she barged her way through, pushing and shoving, desperate to give assistance.

Only she burst through to the front of them to see a woman lying on the floor, looking up at her with curiosity, whilst kneeling beside her was a very handsome man who had clearly been in the middle of some kind of demonstration.

'Hi,' he said, one eyebrow raised in question.

Lane glanced again at the 'patient'. A woman who seemed to be totally unhurt, with a big smile on her face. A woman who was conscious. Breathing. Absolutely fine.

She could only blush as around her one or two people chuckled. 'What—what's going on?' she stammered.

The man smiled. 'First aid demo. I'm showing our patients how to put someone into the recovery position.' He pointed at one of the walls. 'There are posters.'

She followed his finger and noticed that every wall, and even the door through which she'd walked, had a large poster on it, stating that all were welcome to attend an emergency first aid demo to be held at the surgery today. A demo that would be run by Dr Cole Branagh.

How had she not noticed? Had she been so absorbed in trying to look normal?

Lane swallowed hard and turned back to face the man who had now taken the hand of the 'patient' and was helping her gently to her feet.

Tori has his eyes.

He didn't look anything like the charming Lothario weasel she'd pictured in her head. Annoyingly, he had the audacity to be extremely handsome, and she could understand how Skye might have fallen for his charms. The females all around him seemed to be gazing at him with appreciative eyes and he clearly thrived on their attention. Their *adulation*.

He was probably used to having women throw themselves at his feet.

Well, not me, Dr Branagh.

'Right. Okay. Sorry I interrupted.' She grimaced and turned away, trying to control the heat flaming in her cheeks, and pushed back through the assembled throng to get to the reception desk, where she introduced herself in a low, embarrassed voice. 'Lane Carter…agency HCA.'

The woman on Reception was Mary, knitter of preemie hats—she recognised her from her research—and she smiled at her. 'Oh, yes, we've been expecting you. You're in Treatment Room Two. This is your card for the computer.' She passed over a temporary locum ID card that hung from an NHS lanyard. 'Let me show you where everything is.'

Cole stood in the small staff kitchenette, making himself a cup of tea. He was feeling great. The first aid demo had produced a great turn-out, with more people attending than he'd expected. He'd taught them how to deal with choking, adult CPR and baby CPR, and putting a person into the simple recovery position.

He smiled as he remembered the young woman who had interrupted his demonstration. He liked it that she'd been eager. Keen to help. And the look on her face when she'd realised it was a demo had been priceless!

As if his thoughts had summoned her, she suddenly appeared in the doorway of the kitchenette. She stopped when she saw him standing there. Just briefly. Then she came in to grab a mug out of the cupboard.

'Hello, again,' he said, holding out his hand. 'We didn't get to introduce ourselves earlier. The name's Branagh—Cole Branagh.'

Weirdly, she seemed to hesitate, as if she didn't want to shake his hand, but then she did, and smiled a greeting that wasn't quite genuine.

'Lane Carter,' she said.

He felt a little puzzled. Was she upset at being so embarrassed that morning? He didn't want her to be. Anyone could have made the same mistake.

'You're our agency HCA?'

'Yes.'

'Thank God. We certainly need you after Shelby's mad dash to Scotland to be with her father. Heart attack,' he added, just to clarify. 'Your being here will lighten the load for the nurses.'

It really would. They'd been overwhelmed since Shelby had left, having to take on her workload, too. It had been causing some real problems for the poor receptionists, who were taking the flak from disgruntled patients, because they couldn't get an appointment for weeks.

She grabbed a decaffeinated teabag from the box and popped it in her mug. 'Good. I hope I'll be of some *real* help.'

He smiled, assuming she was referring to that morning's mishap. 'I'm sure you will be. You certainly seem raring to go, and we need that around here.'

She turned from him and poured hot water into her mug. 'I always do my best.'

'Good. Well, maybe I'll see you later?'

Lane nodded. 'Definitely.'

He grabbed his own tea and left the kitchenette, feeling a little odd. Something hadn't been quite right with their conversation, and for the life of him he couldn't pinpoint what it was. Lane Carter had seemed...*tense.* Which was odd, because normally he was great at putting people at their ease.

Perhaps it was first day nerves and she just needed some time to feel comfortable?

Yes. That had to be it. She'd be fine.

He had no doubt that she would fit in very well once she got comfortable with her surroundings. And perhaps, someday, they'd find themselves hoping that she'd never leave at all.

'The name's Branagh—Cole Branagh.'

My God, did the man think he was James Bond? Did he lean on bars, drink in hand, twinkle in eye, as he said that? Charming women with his suave introduction, his bespoke suit and those twinkling blue eyes? He probably had a sports car in the car park.

He had no cares in the world at all! Here he was, living his best life, women at his feet, whilst *she* had been through the worst loss ever, had had to turn her entire life around and was now caring for *his* child, whilst he swanned about in his expensive tailored clothes and shiny shoes?

It was unfair. It was wrong.

Lane put her mug of tea down on the desk and noticed that on the screen it told her she had a patient waiting for a blood test. She pressed the button to call her in, and whilst she waited for her to arrive got out the equipment she'd need. Just a turquoise vial for the warfarin test. A needle, vacutainer, swab and tourniquet.

The patient arrived and sat down. 'You're new.'

'Yes, my name's Lane, Mrs Downing. Can you confirm your date of birth for me, please?'

Mrs Downing confirmed it, and even added her address.

'Thank you. Now, you're here to have a blood test. Do you have your yellow slip?'

The yellow slip came from the anti-coagulation clinic at the hospital, so that it would go back with the blood sample to Pathology.

'Yes, lovey, here you go. You might have a bit of a hard time of it, though. My veins aren't very good.'

Lane smiled and grabbed the tourniquet. 'Let's take a look, shall we?'

She cast her gaze over both her patient's arms and decided to pick the left, which looked more likely to give her a successful blood draw. She tied the tourniquet.

'How does that feel? Not too tight?'

'No, it's fine—you go ahead. I won't look, though.'

'As long as one of us does, hey?'

Lane smiled and palpated the patient's arm, finding the median cubital vein almost immediately. She swabbed the area and let it dry.

'Sharp scratch coming...' She inserted the needle, added the vial to the vacutainer and the blood began to flow. 'There you go. No problem.'

Mrs Downing still wasn't looking. 'Have you done it?'

'Yes. Got it first go.' She removed the needle and added a cotton swab. 'Press here for me.'

'It's done? Oh, you *are* good! You can do that again; I'll have to ask for you next time. I like all the nurses here, but the one I saw two weeks ago gave me some horrible bruises trying to find my veins. I was black and blue!'

Lane tried to give a sympathetic look but didn't want to say anything detrimental about nurses—it just wasn't right. No one tried to hurt a patient on purpose. It would have been no one's fault.

She scribbled Mrs Downing's details onto the vial and popped it into the bag with the yellow slip, then checked to make sure her patient's arm had stopped bleeding before she put on some tape to hold the wadding in place.

'Leave that on for an hour or two. No heavy lifting, okay?'

Mrs Downing smiled and winked. 'I'll give the gym a miss today, then, lovey. Am I all done?'

'You are. Have a nice day, Mrs Downing.'

'You too, lovey.'

Lane popped the blood sample into the collection box and cleaned down, ready for her next patient. He hadn't arrived yet, so she took a sip of her tea, thinking about the chick magnet in the next room.

Dr Branagh's consulting room was right next to hers. He was mere feet away. Just a wall between them. And she held a secret that would bring his well-ordered life crashing down in an instant.

Tori's arrival had made Lane change her entire life,

so she wondered if she ought to feel sorry for him? But then she decided not to. No one had ever felt sorry for *her*. Simon hadn't even considered her feelings. All he'd been able to think about was himself. His own happiness.

Well, Lane had to consider *Tori's* happiness. That poor little girl had lost her mother for ever, and she would not introduce her father into her life until she knew she could trust him not to ruin it even further. Simon, and even her own father, had taught her that when the going got tough or complicated, most men bailed out.

What if Cole was no good?

What if he was reckless?

What if he had no idea how to look after a child?

What if he walked out on Tori after only a few weeks?

What if he's married already?

That thought made her chew on a fingernail.

What if Dr Branagh had a *wife*? Lane would be causing problems for her, too. What if he already had kids? They'd have a new half-sister…

And suddenly, as if her thoughts had summoned him to her room, there he was in her doorway, stethoscope draped casually around his neck, smiling his charming disarming smile and looking at her with those gorgeous baby blues.

'Hey, do you have a moment? I need a chaperon.'

She blinked. Nodded. Looked to see if he had a ring on his left hand. He didn't.

'Of course. I'll be right in.'

'Miss Thomas? I've brought Lane in as chaperon. She's our new HCA. So if you'd like to go behind the curtain and remove everything above the waist and let us know when you're ready…?'

Cole's patient nodded and stepped behind the curtain, pulling it closed behind her. As he waited, he took a moment to re-read the notes from his patient's last few consultations, then he smiled at Lane.

'How are you settling in?'

She still looked a little uncomfortable. First day nerves again?

'I'm all right. Trying to remember how to use the computer system.'

'Have you been away from general practice for a while, then?'

She didn't get to respond as his patient was calling out from behind the curtain. 'I'm ready.'

He indicated that Lane should go first and then he stepped behind the curtain with her, pulling it closed behind them.

Miss Thomas was here because she'd had a double mastectomy and was worried about the healing of her wounds. From what he could see, the left incision was healing nicely, but the right one appeared to be weeping, and it hadn't adhered the way it ought to.

He donned gloves and took a closer look. 'Any pain?'

'A little. But I was told that would be normal anyway.'

He palpated the skin around the wound. It didn't feel hot, but there was still some residual swelling from the procedure.

'I think we ought to take a swab to be on the safe side, and I'll put you on some antibiotics in the meantime— just in case. Lane, could you pass me a swab from over there, please?'

Lane rummaged in a drawer and pulled out what he needed before passing it over.

'This shouldn't hurt, but let me know if it does.'

He gently touched the end of the swab to the weeping wound, trying to make sure he got a good sample to send off to the lab. He capped it off when he was done.

'There you go. You can get dressed now.'

He held back the curtain for Lane to pass through and then closed it again, so that his patient could get dressed in privacy.

'Do you need me for anything else?' Lane asked, not really looking at him, but at some point just over his right shoulder.

Why did he get the feeling Lane was keen to get away from him? *Had* he embarrassed her this morning? Thinking back, he didn't think he'd said anything terrible to her. Perhaps he should take a moment to apologise to her when he could? Because he really didn't want there to be an atmosphere between them. She seemed uncomfortable, and there was something about her discomfort that made him feel he wanted to take it away. People normally felt relaxed and easy-going with him.

Lane had soulful eyes. A deep, mesmerising blue. Almost sorrowful—as if she'd been through a terrible loss. And, having been through a dreadful loss himself, he wanted to make her feel better. Give her a reason to smile.

'If you wouldn't mind taking the swab to the sample collection box in the foyer...?'

It was all he could think of to say. Any other words stuck in his throat. Now was not the right time. He had a patient and they were both professionals.

'And if you could add a note to the patient's file to say that you chaperoned?'

She nodded and took the swab. 'Of course.'

And then she was gone, just as Miss Thomas threw back the curtain and emerged fully clothed once again.

Did the room seem a little dimmer with Lane gone? *How ridiculous! It's probably just the morning light.*

Cole smiled at his patient and began tapping at his keyboard to request a prescription for her. He was back in work mode and he'd stay that way until lunch.

Lane dropped the swab into the sample box and took a moment to breathe in the fresh air coming through the open front doors of the practice. That poor woman... A double mastectomy! Had she had preventative surgery? Or had she actually had breast cancer? She'd seemed so young. Her own age. But whatever had happened she was surviving. Perhaps it had been caught early and the doctors had had time to do something about it and save her life?

Lane hadn't expected to be so shocked by it. To be this close to cancer again and stare it in the face. She'd tried to remain impassive in the room, but behind her eyes she'd been fighting back tears, thinking about Skye.

And Dr Branagh had been so nice. Considerate. Interested. And so good with his patient! Not that that should be a surprise, but to see him being so attentive and helpful... Would he have been that way with her best friend? Had Skye made a mistake in not telling him about her pregnancy? Or was this just his work persona?

Lane didn't know. She was used to misjudging men—to having them pull the wool over her eyes and deceive her, making her think one thing when another thing was happening. And it had been agonising to be in close quarters with Cole, knowing that she knew something about him but couldn't tell him. Not yet.

Would there ever be a good time? What was the perfect time to tell a man he was father to an eight-month-old he hadn't even known existed?

And once she told him about Tori he'd want to meet her, surely? Any decent father would. Any decent man would want to do the right thing. And he could make a claim to her in the courts. Skye had never really made it clear whether she wanted Lane to share Tori more officially with Cole, or whether she just wanted her daughter to know her father.

What if he could fight her legally to take Tori away? The thought made her shiver. Goosebumps prickling her skin and she rubbed at her arms to make them disappear.

She headed back inside, knowing she had work to do. She updated Miss Thomas's notes regarding the chaperoning, and then managed to get through an ECG, a double ear syringing, three B12 jabs, two suture removals and a whole host of hypertension checks before lunchtime rolled around.

And suddenly there Cole was again, looking at her weirdly from the kitchen doorway as she nuked her lunch in the microwave. She could feel his intense gaze upon her and she felt unnerved by it.

'Can I help you?'

He frowned, his arms crossed. 'I wonder if I could have a quick word with you? In private?'

He knows! Oh, God, how did he find out?

She swallowed hard and followed him to his consulting room. He closed the door behind her and asked her to sit down in one of the chairs the patients would normally use. She thought he'd sit behind his desk, but he didn't. He grabbed his chair and pulled it out so he could sit across from her, as an equal.

A smile formed upon his face. 'I just want to say that

I hope I didn't embarrass you this morning. It wasn't my intention, and in fact I was very impressed with how you came forward to help.'

Relief flooded through her and the heat she'd felt surging into her cheeks slowly began to drain away. She half laughed. 'Ah, yes… That.'

'I just feel that you're not very comfortable with me, and I don't like that, so if I did anything wrong at all, I apologise.'

Damn it. He's being nice. And respectful.

'No, it wasn't that. It isn't that. No.'

'Then is it first day nerves? I'd like to help if I can. We're all really nice here. We look out for each other and lift each other up—we've always got each other's backs.'

Seriously? Why can't he be an ignorant idiot?

'No, it's not that. It's…'

It's because of who you are. What you did. And how it changed everything. If it hadn't been for you my friend could still be alive, for all I know.

If Skye hadn't met this man, hadn't got pregnant by him, then she might have survived the cancer by having it treated it earlier, instead of continuing with her pregnancy.

'It's nothing. I'm sorry if I made you think that way.'

She tried to sound genuine, look him in the eye, but it was hard. She'd spent months *hating* this man. His very existence, his sleeping with Skye, meant that her best friend's life had been changed for ever—as well as her own. The repercussions had spread out like ripples on a pond. And the way he was looking at her now…

His gaze was intent, and his appraisal made her self-conscious. Those blue eyes of his—so like Tori's—were hypnotic, and they sparkled with a light that she found mesmerising. He was a very attractive man. Short, closely cropped dark brown hair, broad shoulders, and a genuine smile that was warm and inviting.

If she'd been the one to meet him in a pub then she had to reluctantly admit to herself that she would have been enthralled and drawn to him too.

But she couldn't let that happen.

Eventually he nodded, as if he were going to accept her answer for now, even though they both knew it wasn't over.

'Okay. Well, I don't want to keep you from your lunch. We don't get long and I've got a home visit to do.'

It was a relief to be dismissed. 'Right. Okay. Well, I'll see you later this afternoon.'

'What kind of cake do you like?'

She was at the door, her hand on the doorknob, and his question seemed to come from left field. *Cake?*

'I'm sorry?'

'It's my turn to buy cake for everyone, but as you're new I'm happy to get your favourite. What is it?'

She stared back at him, trying to work him out, trying to see if he really was as nice as he seemed to be...

'Lemon drizzle?'

He beamed a smile. 'That's my favourite, too.'

She smiled back at him and felt something lurch in her heart. As if a part of the wall around it was beginning to crumble. The wall she'd so carefully constructed before coming here.

Damn.

She'd only wanted to come here to assess him, tell him the news, and then work out a new 'normal'.

She'd never expected to *like* him.

CHAPTER TWO

THAT WEEKEND LANE decided to take Tori to the bird park just outside Bourton-on-the-Water. Tori loved birds. She especially loved Peter, the macaw parrot that Lane's mother owned, so she was hoping that she'd enjoy the bird park. It would be a welcome outing for both of them. Lane in particular had found her first week at Liberty Point Surgery quite stifling.

Not because of the work. That part was easy. It was because of Dr Branagh and her conflicting emotions surrounding him. She'd spent ages hating a man she'd never met, and now she'd observed him, both with and without patients, and considered him likeable and charming, helpful and kind. And the rest of the surgery staff couldn't sing his praises highly enough! None of it melded with the way she'd thought of him over the last year. She'd pictured a dark, almost mythical figure, cruel and selfish and probably heartless. A man like all the rest—out for what he could get and damn the rest of the world.

Only he didn't seem like that at all. Perhaps he'd never been like that. She was feeling bad for having misjudged him. There were always two sides to a story and she'd never thought to find out his.

'Lane!'

She turned to see who was shouting her name and who should it be but Dr Cole Branagh himself. Looking delightfully casual in a slim-fit checked shirt and jeans? Her heart skipped a beat and she felt her cheeks flush.

'Dr Branagh! What are you doing here?' She skilfully turned Tori's pushchair in the other direction, so that she was facing away from the man who was her father and was instead looking at the flamingos.

'I'm here to support a patient. They're having a Keeper for the Day experience and his parents invited me along.'

Oh. That seemed reasonable.

'That's nice of them,' she said.

'I delivered this boy in the back of a car. He was born with Down syndrome and I've been his doctor ever since. It's his birthday today and he wanted to spend it cleaning out birds. What can I say? The heart wants what it wants.'

She smiled back at him, but her heart was racing and her mind was running through a whirlwind of thoughts and concerns, trying to find a safe topic to talk about and tossing unsuitable ones back into the maelstrom of her mind.

He was less than a metre away from the daughter he didn't know he had. His life could change in a moment. Would he know the second he saw Tori? Would he suspect? Now she knew him a little better, she couldn't help but see him in his daughter.

The heart wants what it wants.

Yes. It did.

She swallowed and tried not to blush. 'Well, I won't keep you…'

'You're not! He'll be busy for the next hour or so. They're taking him to the hatchery, so I've got some spare time before they need me back taking photos.' He waved his mobile phone at her and slid it back into his back pocket. 'I didn't know you had a daughter.'

Oh, dear God...

Lane blinked rapidly. 'I don't. She's my...goddaughter.'

She watched in terror as he walked around to the front of the pushchair and knelt down to engage with Tori. She watched him, heart in her mouth, waiting for the axe to fall. Waiting for any tell-tale sign of the horrifying realisation that he was looking at his own daughter.

But it didn't seem to happen. He just smiled at her and waved. 'She's gorgeous. What's her name?'

'Victoria. We call her Tori.'

'Have you given her parents a day off?'

'Something like that.'

This was dangerous territory, and she could almost feel her throat closing up with the fear. He was looking directly at his own daughter! Couldn't he see? Wasn't the magic of blood telling him, screaming at him that he was looking at his own child?

He stood up again, straightened, and she relaxed a little. Keen to get away, she began walking.

'Would you like to grab a coffee?' he asked.

She stopped, tense. 'Oh, I don't know if that's—'

'They do a mean caramel slice in the Jungle Café.'

She hadn't had a caramel slice in years. And if she refused him would it seem weird? They were meant to be trying to be kind to one another. If she backed off again, tried to avoid him, he'd *really* sense something was up and she wasn't ready for that conversation yet. And this way, if she pushed through her discomfort, perhaps she could find out a little more about him? Find out who he really was so she could judge him properly before she dropped her bombshell.

'All right.'

'Great! Let me help you.'

And he reached to take the pushchair handles and began pushing his own baby daughter down the path.

For a moment it was like a glimpse of a possible future. Cole taking Tori out and leaving her behind. She didn't like it. It left her feeling empty and her stomach hurt just at the thought of it.

So with an aching heart, she scurried to catch up, forcing a smile when she got alongside him and trying to get rid of the sense of dread within her heart.

He was right about the caramel slices. They had the perfect amount of rich, buttery pastry and a thick, creamy layer of salted caramel on top that was moreish and went perfectly with their cups of tea. And if it had been any other situation, and any other gorgeous man sitting across from her, she would have enjoyed it. Maybe even flirted a bit if Simon hadn't ruined things so terribly for her.

Instead, she sat opposite Cole, nervous and on edge. Wary of trusting anyone.

'So what made you become a HCA?' he asked her.

'My mum was a nurse and she loved what she did. I used to listen to her tell tales of what had happened at work each day and most of it sounded wonderful.'

He frowned. 'Most of it?'

'She didn't like the long hours. Or how sometimes she'd work past the end of her shift to make sure her patients were okay and then come home to find my dad was disgruntled. He didn't like playing second fiddle to her patients. He left,' she added, realising that she was oversharing. But she did that when she was nervous. She talked. Filled the silences.

'I'm sorry.'

'It's not your fault. And my mum never let the end of her marriage define her. She just does whatever she wants now—without having to ask anyone else's permission.'

She smiled at the memory of her mum doing a sponsored cycle ride to raise awareness of strokes. The day her mum had cooked just short of a hundred cupcakes to raise money for charity. How she still knitted and sewed.

'I grew up wanting to have patients, but without the stress or long hours of nursing. Being an HCA fitted that requirement perfectly.' She leaned forward over the table to turn the focus back on him. To take this opportunity to learn more about Tori's father. 'What about you? What made you become a doctor?'

'Something similar. My mum was a nurse, like yours, and my father was a GP and his father, before him. But it wasn't just because of them, or family tradition. I looked into other career paths, but nothing drew me the way medicine did. It was a calling and I loved every moment.'

Loved. Past tense. She frowned. Curious. 'Loved?' she repeated.

He laughed. 'I still love it. I do. But there have been times when I've felt dreadfully inadequate and useless and I've been angry that I couldn't do more when I needed to.'

He spoke vehemently, and she saw darkness in his eyes as he seemed to look back into his past. Lane knew the feeling well. She'd felt the same, watching Skye slowly die. There were medical advancements being made all the time! Why had none been made in time to help her? Skye had been so bright. So full of life! She'd deserved a long life, but it had been cruelly snatched away by a vicious disease that showed no mercy.

Cole looked sad himself, and she had to fight the urge

to reach out and lay her hand on his. She wanted to. But she still felt that this man was the enemy.

She looked at Tori, happily sitting in the highchair provided by the café, her face smeared with yoghurt.

'We all have those moments,' she said. 'When we wish we could do more.'

He met her gaze and she saw hurt there, and an understanding that she knew all too well. Had she misjudged him? Thinking his life was carefree? That he was a charming Lothario who bedded women left, right and centre, with the only thing to worry about was whether or not he had enough condoms in his wallet?

Ashamed, she broke the eye contact and looked down, grabbing her cup of tea to take a quick sip. It was still hot and burnt her tongue. But she took another sip anyway.

'I'm sorry. I didn't mean to bring up anything difficult.' She pushed the rest of her caramel slice away, having lost her appetite.

'You didn't. I just forget that you don't know.'

Don't know what? She wanted to know, but she also didn't want to push him. Not if it hurt him to bring up memories. He wasn't a charmer of women—he was *human*. He was real. Not the caricature she had made him in her mind before she'd met him. And why would he choose to tell *her* anything? He didn't know her. She was a stranger to him. A new colleague at work.

'My wife died.'

Oh.

'You were married? I didn't know that.'

He smiled and pulled his phone from his pocket, tapped at the screen a few times and brought up a picture of a him and a woman on a ski lift together, laughing and happy in what looked like a blizzard of snow.

'This is the last photo we had taken together before the accident.'

His wife was beautiful. And they looked happy. She quickly glanced at his face and saw love and wistfulness there. He still missed her.

'Where was it taken?'

They were the only words she could squeeze out. She wanted to say, *You look amazing together*, because they did. She wanted to say, *I'm so sorry for your loss*, but it just wouldn't come out, because if it did then she would speak of her own loss and that was too close to home.

'The Alps. We used to go every year, on our wedding anniversary. It was our fourth year there together and we took that ski lift up to the top of a mountain to come down on a Black Run.'

'What's that?'

'It's a ski run for advanced skiers. We'd done it before once or twice, but that day a storm was coming in and we thought we'd make it down one last time before it hit.' He sipped at his own drink, pausing for just a moment as if reliving it. 'We misjudged and the storm caused an avalanche.'

'Oh, my God!'

'We tried to outrun it. To get out of its way. And we were succeeding. Side by side, we raced down that *piste* as fast as we could. But Andrea must have hit something, because the next thing I knew she wasn't there, and I couldn't stop to look for her or I would have been buried alive.'

Lane's mouth felt dry. Her heart was pounding. 'What happened?'

'She was buried by snow. It took three days to find her and dig her out. The worst three days of my life.'

Lane heard raw pain in his voice.

'Her injuries were extensive. Even if we had found her in time she wouldn't have survived.'

'I'm so sorry, Dr Branagh.'

'Cole. Please.'

She gave a single nod in acknowledgement.

'At the autopsy they discovered that she'd been in the early stages of pregnancy. About six weeks. Neither of us had known.'

Lane closed her eyes and instinctively reached out to touch Tori's chubby little hand as she banged her toy down on her tray. To lose not just his wife, but his unborn child...

'I don't know what to say.'

He sighed. 'What *can* you say? These things happen? We should have been more careful?'

She shook her head. 'You weren't to know.'

'I often wonder about that. Whether we should have paid more attention to the weather report. Whether we even should have been up there. It goes around and around in my head all the time. The fact that we took that chance with our lives just so we could have the thrill of conquering a mountain. For the adrenaline rush of showing how good we were? How arrogant is that?'

She shook her head. 'No. You can't blame yourself.'

'Who *do* I blame?'

At that moment Tori began to get agitated, so Lane stood to undo the harness of the highchair and pulled Tori onto her lap, wiping her face with a paper napkin and passing her a beaker of water.

'We all do things we second-guess later.'

He nodded. 'Have you? Did it cost someone their life?'

She flushed and stood, swaying gently with Tori in

her arms. She couldn't tell him about the conversations she'd not had with Skye, because she'd been too afraid to tell her friend to abort the baby she'd so longed for. But should she have been braver? Should she have spoken her mind and told Skye that *her* life was more important?

No. She could never have done it. It had been impossible.

This conversation was becoming too uncomfortable!

Tori dropped her beaker just as a woman was passing by with her children.

She bent to pick it up and handed it to Cole. 'Bless her. She looks just like you. Got her daddy's eyes!' The woman smiled, gave Tori's fingers a little shake and then went on her merry way.

Lane stared at Cole in absolute horror, waiting for the realisation to appear in his eyes, but thankfully it didn't. He simply smiled at the woman as she left and then looked at Lane and laughed. 'They think we're a family. Well, I guess we look like one. A mum. A dad. A baby... What do you think to that Tori, hey?'

Lane wanted out of that café there and then! No hanging around—she needed to go! 'You must be needed back soon? To take photos?'

He glanced at his watch. 'You're right. Thanks for the tea and the chat. It was nice to catch up.'

Nice? It had been the most terrifying thing she'd experienced in months! 'Yes, it was...nice.'

'I'll see you at work on Monday.'

'You will.'

'Would you mind if I took a picture of the three of us? It's a new thing of mine. Trying to record good times. You never know when things could change. And when you're no longer with us, I'll have this memory to remind me.'

When you're no longer with us.

She knew he meant at work. The short contract she had to cover Shelby whilst she was away. But all she could think of was returning to her old life without Tori and that his *with us*, meant him and his daughter. But surely he couldn't do that? He couldn't take her. 'Sure.'

He activated the camera on his phone, came to stand alongside her, then draped his arm around her shoulder as she carried Tori and squeezed her in tight.

Lane looked up at the image on his phone. She could see the way they fitted together—her, Cole and Tori. Like a little family. Just as that woman had thought they were. Tori was smiling, as was he, so she forced a smile too, hoping it reached her eyes and looked genuine.

He pressed the button and saved the image. 'Give me your email address and I'll send you a copy.'

She wrote it on a napkin and handed it over. Then waved him goodbye as he left the café.

She sat there feeling sick and awful. Knowing she had to tell him about his daughter.

He wasn't a Lothario.

He was a widower. And he seemed compassionate and generous and authentic.

'Skye?' she muttered quietly. 'This is too hard.'

He'd not meant to say so much to Lane. She was a work colleague. New. Temporary. But she'd just been so easy to talk to, and it had been nice to sit there with someone—as if they were a little family. Even that woman had thought they were! It had been a long time since he'd been able to sit with someone and enjoy a cup of tea, just chat about life with someone who felt like a friend.

The memory made him smile and he brought up the

picture of them on his phone and looked at it again. He'd been looking at it a lot over the weekend. He knew that woman had only made an offhand comment, but if Andrea hadn't died then he might very well have been sitting there with his own wife and child. Maybe even a daughter, like Tori. The woman had said she'd got his eyes, and now he looked at her image he had to agree. They did look incredibly similar. How odd! Just one of life's strange coincidences…

His gaze went to Lane. She was smiling, but he remembered how tense she had been when he'd draped his arm around her shoulder. Had he overstepped the mark there? He had no idea of her past, he had no idea if she was in a relationship or not, but she certainly seemed uncomfortable with displays of affection.

Or maybe it was just *his* affection? Perhaps she'd felt awkward about it after he'd told her about his dead wife? Or maybe it was nothing to do with that. There could be all manner of reasons why a woman wouldn't want a man to drape his arm around her shoulders. There was so much you had to be aware of as a man, and rightfully so, as far as he was concerned. But he'd done it anyway—without thinking.

Cole, you really need to think about your actions! Isn't that what got you into trouble in the first place?

He put his phone away, then jumped when a red alert box buzzed onto his screen.

Help needed immediately in Reception!

Mary had pressed the alert button. All staff had it on their phone screen, in case they needed help, and it sent out an alarm to every screen in the practice.

He raced from his room and almost bumped into Lane on the way out of hers. He saw the issue immediately. Oscar Jameson was collapsed on the floor of the waiting room.

'Somebody fetch the Resus bag!'

'I'll get it!' Lane replied, turning back to the stock room, where the Resus bag was kept for emergencies such as this.

Mr Jameson was one of his patients. An elderly gent, in his eighties, who lived alone. If he remembered correctly, the medication he was taking included a statin, a blood pressure tablet and some glycerol trinitrate spray for angina.

Cole checked to make sure it was safe to approach the patient and asked the other people in the waiting room to stand back and give them space. He knelt by Mr Jameson and gave him a gentle shake of the shoulders.

'Mr Jameson! Can you open your eyes for me?'

Lane arrived then, with the Resus bag. 'What do you need me to do?'

He knelt to listen for breathing. To watch for the rise and fall of Mr Jameson's chest. Neither happened.

'Get the defibrillator ready. And the bag valve and mask.' He immediately began compressions of Mr Jameson's chest and shouted out an order to Mary. 'Phone for an ambulance!'

Within seconds Lane was cutting away Mr Jameson's clothing to expose his chest. It wasn't hairy, so she was able to place the pads in the correct place quickly. He had no pacemaker. No jewellery to move.

The machine spoke: *'Stop compressions. Analysing heart rhythm.'*

There was a moment of intense silence when Cole had

to fight the urge to *do* something, but he knew he had to wait for the machine to tell him what to do.

'*Shock required. Stand clear of the patient.*'

Cole made sure everyone was clear of Mr Jameson. 'Shocking.'

He pressed the button on the machine and the shock was delivered. He immediately continued with compressions as Lane smoothly hooked up the bag, valve and mask to the oxygen tank that was carried in the Resus bag. When thirty compressions were up, she performed a head-tilt, chin-lift, and sealed the mask around Mr Jameson's nose and mouth and delivered two breaths before Cole continued.

He was just thinking about which drug to administer when Mr Jameson made a moaning noise and his eyes began to open.

'We've got him. Keep the oxygen on high flow.' He leant down to speak to Mr Jameson. 'You're all right, Oscar. We've got you. You've had a bit of an episode. You're in the doctors' surgery.'

Oscar Jameson nodded and blinked, clearly exhausted by what had just happened.

Cole felt intense relief go through him at getting the man back, but he was very aware that things could still go the other way. He would need to monitor him until the paramedics got there, in case his heart stopped again. He looked at Lane, and her relief was palpable and they smiled at each other. They'd saved this man's life, hopefully.

'You okay?' he asked her, aware that situations like this could be frightening.

She nodded and smiled, her eyes bright with adrenaline. The way she was looking at him right there and then, he might almost have sensed that… No. He was being ridiculous. It was just the heat of the moment, that was all. They were colleagues. Nothing more.

When the paramedics arrived, he handed over the resus details, wishing he could go with them to see his patient all the way through, but knowing there were patients here who still needed him. Especially any that might have witnessed all this and be feeling a bit frightened.

'Maybe I should offer everyone here a drink or something?' asked Lane. 'We have juice in the kitchen.'

He liked it that she was thinking that way. He nodded. 'That would be a nice thing to do. Thanks.'

'And I'll bring you a strong tea. You deserve it.'

'So do you. Thanks, Lane. You were brilliant. I couldn't have asked for more.'

She looked into his eyes and he felt it again. A single moment of such pure attraction that it startled him to his very core. Along with the knowledge that they could be something more if he let it happen. That he could care for this woman if he were brave enough.

But he was afraid. He'd never been in a relationship with anyone since his wife had died. He'd gone out once and got drunk—had slept with a woman who'd run out on him in the morning—but…

Lane wasn't staying here long. She was a stand-in for Shelby who could be back any time. He had no idea how long he would have with her. Best to keep things on a friendship level.

The realisation was a let-down, after the euphoria of saving a man's life, but he had to be realistic. If life had taught him anything, it had taught him that.

When Lane brought him his tea, she set it down on his desk and then sat in the seat that his patients usually sat in.

He looked up at her. 'You okay?'

She nodded hurriedly. Then looked away. As if she felt awkward about something. 'I wonder if we could talk…?'

'Of course! But I have patients waiting right now—and so do you, probably.'

She smiled and nodded again. 'I do. But we need to talk. Sooner rather than later.'

He couldn't imagine what it was about, but clearly she was upset about something. Was it the resuscitation? Did she want to chat through it, make sure she'd done everything okay?

'Okay. Name the place and I'll be there.'

'The bandstand in the park? Say this Saturday, if you're not doing anything? Twelve-ish?'

He nodded. It was a strange place to go to talk, but okay… 'I'll be there.'

She stood up abruptly. Awkwardly. Clearly she was uncomfortable. What was going on that he didn't know about? Perhaps that was what wanted to tell him? He hoped so. He wanted to help.

'I'll see you later, then,' she said. And she went.

He sat there, staring at the door, wondering…

CHAPTER THREE

THE CLOUD COVER was thick as Lane walked towards the park on Saturday. She'd hoped for a better day. A day of sunshine and flowers in which she could drop the news she'd been holding so tightly against her chest and then make a quick getaway.

The last two weeks had proved to her that all her assumptions about Dr Cole Branagh had been wrong. He was a good man. A good doctor. Respected and kind and with a tragic past of his own. He could even have been a father already! But his wife had died and his baby with her. How did you get through something like that and still come out smiling?

Each night she'd gone home and cuddled Tori and played with her, sat with her, read to her at bedtime, and wondered just how much Cole would love to be doing this? How he ought to be doing this and how she was robbing him of precious moments with his child!

But wasn't Tori her child too? Legally anyway. For the last six months Lane had been there—for the first smile, the first laugh, the first tooth…

She was glad she'd made the decision to tell him, because not doing so had started to eat her alive and she couldn't continue that way. Hiding something so monumental. Hiding something that would change Cole's life. The more she kept Tori from him, the more time he lost with his daughter, and she didn't want him to blame her for that. She had always tried to do the right thing. Skye had asked her to decide if he would make a good daddy, and her brain was telling her that he would.

She knew Cole now. Or thought she knew him enough, anyway. He didn't seem the type of man who would take this news lightly and then walk away. He wasn't the Lothario or the charmer she'd imagined. He was just a man. A man she was starting to like. And it hurt to know that she was keeping this secret from him. But parents put their children first, and Tori deserved the right to know her father.

The bandstand was empty when she got there. Clearly the overcast weather was keeping people away from the park. She stood beneath its roof and looked out at the ducks on the pond, noting that on the far side there was a swan. A solitary swan, gliding across the dark surface. She thought about how swans mated for life and wondered where its mate was…

'Good morning.'

Her heart pounded as she heard his voice and she turned to look at him, glad that she'd left Tori with her mother. This conversation could go many ways, and she didn't want to have to worry about what Tori was doing as they talked. She wanted to be present. To explain everything to him.

Would he feel deceived? Would he feel she'd made a fool out of him because she'd arrived in his life under false pretences?

She turned, managed a weak smile. 'Hi…'

He looked good. But he always looked good. He had a

frame that made all clothes look good on him. He could have worn a potato sack and carried it off with panache and style. Was it too late to call this off and just pretend she didn't have to do it?

'How are you?'

'I'm good. A little puzzled as to why I'm here, though, if I'm honest.'

He stood away from her and waited. Unsure.

The bandstand had seats around its edge. She went to one and sat down, looking up at him and telling him with her eyes that he should sit next to her.

He did so, and then he reached out with his hand and covered her fidgeting fingers. 'Whatever it is you have to tell me, it's okay.'

He was comforting *her*. When it should have been the other way around. But she was grateful for his touch and she laid her other hand on top of his. It was trembling. Could he feel that?

'I hope so. I hope you'll understand.'

'Whatever it is, I'm here for you. I know we're colleagues, but I'd like to think we're friends too. We've saved a life, you and me, and that binds us together for ever.'

She smiled at the thought. Mr Jameson was still in hospital, but apparently he was doing very well and was expected to go home on Monday.

'What I have to tell you is…huge. Life-changing, in fact. And I want you to know that I didn't come here to deceive you. I came to…'

She couldn't think of the right words. The words that would be perfect and not hurt him. Because she cared about how he was feeling. He'd been through tough times, too. He'd loved and lost the way she had. And she'd seen how his face had changed, almost imperceptibly when she'd said *deceive*.

She tried to keep back the tears. 'I had to do it. I made a promise.'

'A promise? To whom?'

Soft rain was beginning to fall. She could hear it hitting the roof of the bandstand and she watched as droplets bounced off the leaves of the plants in the flowerbeds close by. She looked out at the park around them, as if it would give her strength to get through the next part. Saw the odd parent scurrying to put up an umbrella or get their kids off the play equipment so they could go home.

'To my best friend Skye. Tori's mother.'

He frowned, clearly not understanding what this was about, or why she felt the need to tell him about it.

She'd practised telling him. She'd stood in front of her bathroom mirror every day this week trying to have this conversation in different variations.

She'd blurt it out—*You're Tori's father!*

She'd say it gently. Angrily.

She'd tried saying it without blame, without expectation, and none of it had seemed right.

How did you tell a man he was the father of a child?

'We grew up together, Skye and I. We met at infants' school and instantly clicked. We had one of those friendships where we could finish each other's sentences, and many people thought that we could be twins.'

He smiled at her, encouraging her to keep going.

His hand was still holding hers. She liked that. His strong fingers were wrapped around her smaller hand. It felt right. Comforting. Supportive. But his being so close, looking at her so intently, was making her heart pound for many different reasons. Some of which she didn't want to examine right now, because nothing would come of her attraction to him. It couldn't possibly.

'She'd been feeling tired for a while. Listless. Lethargic. I'd been telling her to go to the doctor for ages, but she never went. She was scared of doctors. She was an orphan, you see. Had been raised in a care home where every time she saw a doctor he was sticking a needle in her. She said she'd felt like an animal being experimented on. I kept telling her they were only doing their job, but you know how it is… Some people just don't like doctors.'

He nodded. Just listening. Not urging her to hurry in her story. Patient. That was what made him a good doctor. He listened.

'She'd been thinking a lot about who her real parents were. Why they'd given her up. She kept saying the reason she felt ill was because she was a little stressed about tracking them down. Finding out the reason she'd been given away. Then she found her mother, who wanted absolutely nothing to do with her, so Skye went out and got drunk. She ended up going home with a guy but she never wanted to discuss it. Then her sickness got worse.'

'She was pregnant?'

Lane nodded. 'She was shocked at first—but then she was over the moon! She would have someone. A blood relation. Someone who would love her who she was related to. A baby girl or boy she could spoil. But when she went for her scan they discovered the real reason for her sickness.'

'What was it?' Cole's voice was gentle.

'Ovarian cancer.'

She remembered the moment Skye had told her. The way she had broken down into sobs and sunk to the floor.

How Lane had tried to hold her and comfort her, telling her not to worry, that there were things the doctors could do.

Her eyes burned with unshed tears. She looked at Cole through blurry eyes.

'The doctors told her they would try chemotherapy and surgery to treat her, but that her pregnancy complicated matters. The hormones created by the pregnancy were causing rapid growth in the tumour and they were worried that it would spread elsewhere. They told her that if she had a termination they would be able to try to save her life.'

She swallowed. Terrified of the part that came next. The part that angered her the most. She didn't want him to hear the anger in her voice in case he thought she was angry with *him*. This was her own frustration. Her own issue to deal with.

'She refused all treatment so that she could carry her baby to term. She'd never had a blood relative; she wanted her child so much. The doctors warned her not to wait. The cancer had been there for some time. They told her to abort the child. but she refused. I was angry with her for taking such a risk with her life. But I understood why she did it. She knew she wouldn't get to spend much time with her daughter, but she wanted her child to know how much she was loved from the very beginning. That she would never have given her up even for life itself.'

Her turbulent thoughts turned to what had happened afterwards. How much Skye had needed her and how that had torn apart her own relationship with Simon, who'd been so selfish that he hadn't been able to share his own girlfriend!

Cole squeezed her hand tight and brought her back to the present.

'By the time Tori was born, Skye's cancer had progressed so much there was only palliative treatment left. Skye didn't seem to mind. She'd said she'd done the right thing. Her only regret was that she'd never told Tori's father, but she hadn't wanted a stranger to watch her carrying his child while she was effectively dying and feel guilty about it.'

That was one of the things she had loved about her best friend. She had always thought of others first.

Cole's face had changed somewhat. Was he guessing at what she was about to say? Did he know? Did he suspect? Was he afraid of the next words that would come out of her mouth?

'So, Skye tasked me with finding Tori's father and letting him know about his daughter…'

She looked at him hesitantly. Her eyes confirmed what he had to be suspecting.

He let go of her hand and sat back.

Her hand became cool. Wet in the morning rain drifting in on an easterly breeze.

'It's you, Cole. *You're* the father.'

He sat there. Stunned. Lane's words whirling around his head like a storm.

A daughter? How could that be?

But already his brain was convincing him that it was true. There'd been that one night, what would have been his wife's birthday, just after she'd died. He'd not been able to sit alone in their house and he'd gone out to that bar for one drink—which had turned into two or three. Maybe four…

He'd been raging at the world. For its cruelty. Its unkindness. For taking away someone he had loved so much and with whom he'd had so little time. And in the midst of his despair there'd been a woman who had looked just as sad as he had. She'd sat at the bar, her hands wrapped around a whisky glass, staring into its depths, and she'd appeared to have the weight of the world upon her shoulders.

Her pain had drawn him towards her, and he'd asked her if she was okay. The doctor part of him had seen someone in pain and despite his own pain he'd still wanted to help. Her eyes had welled up and his heart had ached for her. And when she'd begun to cry he'd taken her outside for some fresh air. And when they'd got outside they'd begun to talk. And then he'd known the bar was not the safest place for her and had offered to take her home.

'She didn't want to go home,' he said quietly.

Lane looked at him.

'I told her I'd take her home, but she said she didn't want to go. That it wasn't a home—just a house. I didn't intend…' He rubbed at his face, disbelieving, then ran his hands through his hair. 'I took her to my place…got fresh pillows and blankets for the bed. I said I'd sleep downstairs. But somehow we got talking as we sat there, on the edge of the bed, and one thing led to another and…'

He felt his cheeks suffuse with colour as he remembered the guilt he had felt for sleeping with another woman.

'I thought we'd taken precautions, but clearly they didn't work. When I woke she'd gone. I never even knew her name. She left a note, thanking me for looking after her, for keeping her safe and making her feel she was worth something to someone, even if I was a stranger. She signed it with an "S". I guess now I know her name.'

Lane took her phone from her pocket and pulled up a picture of Skye. 'Is this her?'

He took the phone from her, stared at it for a moment. 'Yes. It is. You must think terribly of me. But I didn't take advantage of her, Lane. We were both grieving. I was feeling awful. My wife had been dead for only a few months, it was her birthday and…'

'It's okay. I understand that people deal with things in different ways.'

'I swear I never knew about Tori… I have a *daughter*?'

He suddenly got a flashback to that moment at the bird park, when the woman had said she thought Tori had his eyes, and now he understood the look on Lane's face when that had happened.

So she'd come here to find him? To decide what?

'You're her godmother?' he checked.

'And her legal guardian, as stated in Skye's will. It's all official.'

It was all so much! He was *a father*? To a little girl? 'So she's eight months old?'

Lane nodded, tears dripping down her face. And he knew how fearful she must have been to tell him the truth. He reached up to wipe away her tears and her hand caught at his, as if to stop him.

His breath seemed to catch in his throat. He realised how intimate an act it was and he dropped his hand away fearfully. Did he *really* want to stray into that territory? He'd just had some incredible news broken to him! Did he *really* want to stir the pot even further? He *couldn't* act on his attraction to Lane.

'I'd like to see her. Spend time with her, if I may?'

She nodded. 'Of course.'

'Could I see her today?'

Lane frowned and wiped her eyes. 'Right now?'

'I've already lost eight months. I don't think I want to lose any more.'

CHAPTER FOUR

LANE UNLOCKED HER mum's front door. 'I'm back!'

She could hear Tori chuckling and then there she was, the apple of her eye, being carried in Lane's mother's arms as she came into the hallway.

'This little munchkin has been… Oh, hello. You didn't say we had a guest.'

Cole stood on the doorstep behind her. Lane turned to him, invited him in and closed the door behind him.

'Mum? This is Cole. Tori's father.'

Her mother stared at him for a moment, then nodded. 'Big day for you.' She smiled. 'I best make us all a cup of tea! How do you take yours, Cole?'

'Er…white, please.'

'I'll bring it through. Lane, why don't you take Tori and Cole into the living room?' And she heaved Tori into Lane's arms.

Lane felt the reassuring weight of the little girl and happily nuzzled into her, inhaling her familiar scent and giving her a kiss on one cheek before turning her to face her father.

'Tori? This is your daddy—say hello.'

Tori blew a raspberry and then grabbed hold of Lane's collar and began pulling.

Lane entered the living room and put Tori down on the carpet, near to a box of toys. 'Take a seat,' she said.

Cole seemed to be in another world. As if he were far away and unable to hear. As if he was mesmerised by Tori, watching her.

Lane reached for his hand and squeezed it. 'You okay?'

He seemed to notice her then. Blinked rapidly. 'Yes, I'm fine. It's just...'

'Overwhelming?' She smiled at him to show him that she understood.

'You could say that. Is it okay if I...?' He pointed at the floor and she nodded, looking on as he got down on his hands and knees and sat on the floor next to his daughter. 'Hey, Tori. What's this?' He grabbed a pink brick with a cat painted onto it and tried to get Tori's attention.

Lane watched him for a moment. Had he had any idea when he got up that morning that his world was about to change? To expand? That he would be hit with news so great he would struggle to process his thoughts and understand how he was feeling? That by the end of the day he would have a child? A daughter?

She didn't envy him his turmoil. She knew how she'd felt when Skye had first asked her to be Tori's legal guardian.

She'd always wanted a child of her own, but she'd thought that dream had been put on hold when Simon left her. To be asked to look after Tori had been just what she'd needed to keep her smiling. To give her a reason to get up in the morning and carry on. Especially in the early days after Skye's death, when she had also still been reeling from Simon's desertion. This little girl meant *everything* to Lane.

Suddenly becoming a mother whilst going through the

grieving process had been a huge adjustment. She'd had to adapt quickly, with long days becoming long nights, often with no sleep. There'd been days when she'd just cried, but thankfully on those days, she had been able to turn to her mum for help, and she'd often taken Tori to give her a day to recover—to get her thoughts in order, come back stronger.

And she'd made it. And Tori had become her world. Someone she loved very much and didn't want to have to share. But she would have to if Cole decided to be the kind of father Skye had hoped he would be.

I've done the right thing. I've carried out Skye's last wish.

She watched Cole playing with his daughter. He was doing very well. After all, he was a stranger to Tori, and she could easily have cried and reached out to Lane for reassurance. But she hadn't. Tori seemed to like him, and he was being perfect with her. Letting his daughter decide the game, choose which toys she wanted to play with. Not forcing anything.

His face lit up every time Tori chuckled at him and that made her smile, too.

'Here's that tea, Cole. I'll put it up here on the mantelpiece, where it's safe.'

'Thank you, Mrs Carter.'

'Patricia. Call me Patricia. I'll leave you both to it.'

And then her mum disappeared again, back into the kitchen, understanding that they needed time together to process this.

'She looks like you,' said Lane.

Cole looked up at her and smiled. 'I think so, too.'

'I always thought she had her mummy's smile, but since meeting you I've realised that the rest of her is all her father.' She meant it, and she wanted him to see it. 'You must wish you'd known about her sooner?'

He looked bewildered. 'Well, of course... But life doesn't always work out the way we want it to. I wish Skye had told me. I wish she hadn't run out on me that morning without telling me who she was. I would have liked to make sure she was okay.'

Lane shook her head. 'I asked her about that night so many times. She tried to reassure me that the guy had been very nice. *You* had been very nice. A good listener. She'd been the one who had to listen when the social workers told her that her mother didn't want any contact and she just needed someone to sit and listen to what *she* wanted to say. You gave her that. I couldn't. I wasn't there for her the way I should have been. Perhaps if I had been then all this might never have happened.'

Tori yawned and began rubbing at her eyes.

Lane glanced at the clock. 'It's time for her nap. Let me put her down and then we can talk some more.' She scooped up the little girl, grabbing at her security blanket, about to take her upstairs.

'Wait!' Cole came forward, hesitated, and then planted a small kiss on his daughter's cheek. 'Okay. Sleep well, Tori. You be a good girl.'

Lane smiled and then took Tori upstairs, lying her in her cot, tucking her in and then gently closing the door. Normally she was very good at going to sleep by herself.

Back downstairs, she handed Cole his cup of tea. 'You don't want it to go cold. Mum makes a mean brew.'

He took the cup and sat down on one of the couches.

'How are you feeling?' she asked.

'I don't know! Bewildered, confused. Anxious.'

'I get it. I do. I felt that way, too, when I suddenly had to become a parent.'

'I don't *feel* like a parent.'

'I don't think anyone ever does. I'm assuming you'll want to do a DNA test?'

He smiled ruefully. 'I just need to process this. I think I'm still in shock.'

'You have time.'

Cole nodded. 'I guess we need to sort out what will happen in the future?'

She felt a chill. Already he was thinking about sharing her? How would that work? 'Yes, we do. But that can wait for a while. Get used to the idea, first.'

Cole tried to listen in to the baby's chest, but he kept grabbing at his stethoscope and chuckling. He smiled at the little one and asked his mum if she could hold his arms, but she didn't seem to be able to do it.

'I tell you what—I'll get in my bubble expert.'

He popped next door and rapped his knuckles against Lane's open door.

'Fancy blowing a few bubbles for me? I need to keep a patient occupied whilst I do an exam.'

Lane was wiping down the ECG machine. 'Sure— I'll be right in.'

'Thanks!'

He pulled open his bottom drawer and there was the bottle of bubbles he kept for occasions such as this. Bubbles never failed to entertain and delight, and they were much more interesting than a boring old doctor.

When Lane arrived he passed them to her. 'Little Sam, here, needs to see some of these.'

Lane smiled at him, and the genuine warmth of it,

stirred his insides. She seemed so different at work now. So much more relaxed. Looking back, he could understand how much strain she must have been under, keeping the secret about his daughter, knowing what she was withholding from him.

No wonder she'd seemed stressed and uncomfortable in his presence! And he'd thought it was first-day nerves!

As she blew bubbles, entertaining Sam, he got on with his examination, listening to the baby's chest and checking him over for rashes and high temperature. He seemed fine. He just had a cold, but his mum had been right to bring him in.

He told her it was a virus, and that she could give him infant paracetamol if she thought he needed it, and then said she must bring him straight back if she thought he was getting worse. Other than that, he reassured her, it should pass in a few days.

When Sam and his mother had left, Lane passed him back the bottle. 'Tori loves bubbles, too.'

'Does she?' His heart skipped a beat at learning something new about his daughter. *His daughter.* He had to keep repeating that to himself as it still didn't feel real.

'She does!'

'Then I'll have to buy her some. Could I come round tonight? After work? I'd like to spend some time with her before she goes to bed.'

'I've booked her in to a baby massage class at six, but you could come with us?'

Baby massage? He'd heard lots of good reports about that.

'I'll be there. Shall I pick you up from your house?'

She nodded. 'Know where it is?'

'No.'

She smiled and scribbled her address down on a piece of paper. 'Here you go.'

'I'll look forward to it.'

'Me too.'

She was quite nervous about Cole coming that evening. She wasn't sure why. Maybe because it was the first step, of many, by which he would slowly get to know his daughter more and more. That she had started a process she couldn't back away from now.

And she couldn't stop a small assembly of butterflies from beginning to perform aerial acrobatics in her belly.

Was it because some of the stress had gone? The stress of holding on to the secret that was now in the open? It had been so much easier to talk to each other at work today, and she'd found her thoughts straying to him often. Thoughts that maybe she shouldn't be having... She knew she was attracted to him—even though she'd tried not to be and kept telling herself she *shouldn't* be.

He and Skye had once been together, talking, finding in one another a wounded soul and finding comfort, and that it felt wrong to have the hots for one of Skye's exes.

They'd never gone out with each other's guys—it had been a firm rule, because they'd never wanted anything to jeopardise their friendship. But Skye was gone now, and she'd got to know Cole a bit, and she couldn't stop thinking about him.

But he was Tori's father! And that was all he could be interested in. His daughter. They had a friendship, yes, and it was one she was thankful for. It might easily have been ruined because of the secret, but it hadn't been. He'd not blamed her in any way. Not accused her of tricking him, or taking him for a fool, and she appreciated that.

He'd certainly not given her an ultimatum the way Simon had.

She liked Cole very much.

Maybe that was the problem?

Cole had been nothing but thoughtful, kind and caring. Not to mention handsome and totally unaware of how his looks affected all the women around him. Everyone at the surgery thought he was great. Even Mary the receptionist had a bit of a crush on him—she'd said so. His smile was infectious. And those blue eyes of his, even though they still held a shade of sorrow, could light up in the most beautiful way. They drew you in until you suddenly became aware that you were staring…

Lane liked spending time with him. Getting to know him. She suspected he would be a wonderful father, but she was still going to let him prove that. Because as soon as he did give her irrefutable proof, then what objections could she give?

What if they did get involved? Her and Cole? She wouldn't ever have to share Tori, then, would she? But that was the wrong reason to get involved. Cole had seen how well Tori was connected to Lane. She was Tori's godmother. She had been her mother since she was two months old.

At a quarter to six the doorbell rang and she rushed to answer it. Cole stood there, looking handsome in dark jeans and a white tee shirt that showed the muscles in his upper arms.

Don't look, Lane.

But it was too late. She'd noticed, and her eyes kept stealing glances at him without her even being conscious of it.

'Hi. You made it.'

'Of course. Nothing was going to stop me. Is she ready? Need help getting anything together?'

'No, we're all set. If you could just grab that bag over there? I'll go get the girl of the hour.'

'All right.'

He grabbed the baby bag that she'd filled with soft towels and a bottle of milk for after the session. She'd been told by the massage therapist that a lot of babies got sleepy after a massage, although some got hungry, so it was best to be ready for both eventualities.

She gave him directions and soon they were pulling up outside a house. Janet, the therapist, met them at the door and invited them in, and they were soon in a room full of babies and parents, all sitting on the floor in a circle.

'Right—welcome everyone! You might feel a bit warm! I've increased the heating in this room just a little because we're going to be stripping our babies down. But first, if you could lay the towel that you've brought on the floor for baby to lie on.'

Cole pulled a thick, fluffy towel from the bag, folded it in half and lay it on the floor, smiling across at Lane.

'And when you're ready, let's remove baby's clothes and nappy. Those of you with boy babies might want to have a second towel ready as they tend to like to pee when their bits are exposed to the air.'

There were some chuckles around the room.

'So, let's have the mums go first. Using the grape oil, warming it in your hands first, until they're fully covered, with slow, even strokes we're going to cover their shoulders and chests—like this.' Janet demonstrated on a doll.

Lane watched what she did and began stroking the oil onto Tori's shoulders. It was slippery and smooth but Tori seemed to like it, which was good. She'd never done this before, but she'd wanted to give it a try. Wanted to have as many memories as she could with Tori—they were so important. Like Cole said, you never knew when something might change.

Janet demonstrated how to massage the babies' arms, belly, legs and feet. Cole helped by squirting the grape oil into her hands each time she needed more. He was attentive and seemed to be enjoying himself.

'Okay, let's get the dads to have the babies. Turn them onto their stomachs now.'

Lane and Cole switched places and she watched as he tenderly took his daughter and turned her over onto her stomach. He talked to her all the time, gently whispering, telling her what a good girl she was, how well she was doing.

Janet gave more instructions on how to massage their backs, and again their arms and legs and feet.

Lane noticed that Tori was beginning to drift off. Her eyelids were getting heavy. Cole wrapped her in her towel and lifted her onto his lap, rocking gently as his daughter went to sleep. He looked up at Lane with such happiness in his eyes she couldn't help but smile at his success.

But she felt a little sad, too. And she hated herself for being so selfish.

This wasn't about her, was it? She'd come here to introduce a man to his daughter. To make sure they were good together, to see him be a good father. It had all seemed so simple months ago. But with every passing day the situation became more complicated.

She should be happy that Tori was letting him hold her. Felt comfortable enough to fall asleep in his arms. Lane had done her absolute best at raising Tori, but she had always felt like she was a stand-in and she couldn't help but feel a little left out.

They managed to get Tori in her car seat without her waking and Cole drove them home. He scooped her from the car with those powerful-looking arms of his and gently carried her upstairs and laid her in her crib. He looked down on her with pride.

'She needs Bunny Bee,' Lane whispered, pointing at a yellow bear.

Cole grabbed it and placed it beside his daughter.

'And Tootles.' She inclined her head towards the stuffed black cat that sat in the corner.

He didn't know everything yet, did he? But he would learn. How long would it take? Tori had survived. Lane had survived. So had Cole. They'd all lost someone precious. Now they were connected by that little girl who had got her through a difficult time and brought her immeasurable joy?

'We should let her sleep,' she whispered, and she turned to leave the room, pulling the bedroom door closed gently after Cole.

They both crept downstairs.

'That was amazing, Lane. Thank you for inviting me.'

'It was my pleasure. You need to spend time with each other. Get to know one another.'

He must have sensed the upset in her voice, because he tilted his head and lifted her chin with his finger. 'Hey, I'm not going to steal her away from you.'

She was looking into his eyes then. Those beautiful blue eyes of his. Did he know what kind of effect he was having on her lately? *Did* he? Because if he did then perhaps he wouldn't look at her like that. Or touch her face so delicately.

Those eyes made her want to sink into his arms and lay her head against his chest—have him squeeze her tight whilst he whispered sweet nothings into her ear. The yearning to be held was intense. The desire to feel comforted by him, by someone who would protect her and keep her safe, was something she could easily drown in.

Because for the last few months she'd had to be strong for others. For herself. For Tori. Surely it was someone else's turn to give *her* a soft place to fall?

But, no. She couldn't. Not with him. He was Tori's father and that would be complicated. She wanted to, but wasn't sure if she could.

'I know. It's just... I'm the one who's looked after her all this time. I love her like she's my own.'

'She's a very lucky little girl to have you.'

'She should have been luckier. She should have had her *real* mother.'

He nodded. 'Did Skye get to see her? Hold her? When exactly did she die?'

Lane sighed heavily. 'Tori was two months old when her mother passed away.'

'You've looked after her since then?'

'Since she was born, really. Skye was so sick towards the end and she needed me to care for Tori. The cancer had metastasised to her bones, her liver, her brain, her lymphatic system... She gave birth a month early. The doctors insisted upon it. They said the pregnancy was an added strain to her body.'

Cole nodded. 'I wish I'd known.'

His tone was so heartfelt she had no doubt that he was telling the truth. But this was getting awkward now. Standing at the bottom of the stairs, talking about Skye's death. It reminded her of Simon, too. His ultimatum. Him, or Skye and the baby? She wasn't used to a man being kind to her. She really needed him to go now, so she could clear her head.

'Do you want a coffee?' The words were out before she realised she'd said them.

'I'd love one. Thanks.'

He'd not expected the evening to go so well. He'd thought only Lane would get to do the massaging and he would watch as some weird spectator, feeling like a spare part when all he wanted to be was be *involved*. Doing something. Being part of this little girl's life now that he knew about her. He'd already missed so much! He didn't want to miss anything more.

Yes, it had been a shock. And he felt bad that Skye had not felt able to tell him the reason she'd been in that bar, staring into her glass with tears in her eyes. He'd always thought he was an approachable guy, someone people could talk to. It was part of why he felt he was such a good doctor—people felt able to confide in him.

But because he'd still been in the depths of a depression himself that night he hadn't pushed enough. Had just listened when she'd spoken about how alone she felt. How she had no one. He'd sensed depression in her. Had recognised a kindred spirit, currently suffering, and for a brief while they had given each other comfort in the only way they could.

It had never been about having crazy sex with a stranger. It hadn't even been about celebrating still being alive. It had been about two lonely people, needing to find comfort in the arms of each other. As simple as that. And it *had* given him comfort for a while—though afterwards he'd lain in bed and felt guilty that on his wife's birthday he'd taken another woman to bed. He'd hoped that Andrea would have understood. That she wouldn't have minded that he had sought solace from someone else who was hurting and that for a brief time they had made each other's world just a tiny bit brighter.

And yet somehow he now had this beautiful little girl in his life, and a second chance to do everything right.

Little Tori had let him massage her without crying. She had let him hold her until she went to sleep, and he had settled her into her crib for the night. He'd wanted to stoop down and press a kiss upon her cheek, but he'd been distracted by Lane telling him which cuddly toys his daughter liked to sleep with and suddenly absorbed in soaking that information in.

He would need to know this. He would need to know so much more! And he couldn't think of anyone better to learn from, than Lane.

Tori knew this woman as if she were her mother. And that was why he understood the look in her eyes when they'd stood at the bottom of the stairs and her face had looked a little sad.

It was clear the two of them had a great relationship. Not once had he heard Tori cry. She seemed a happy baby and that was thanks to the care and love that Lane had provided. There was no way he was going to just dismiss that.

Cole accepted the mug of coffee she pressed into his hands and waited for her to sit down on the couch opposite.

Her place was nice. Warm and comforting. He noticed a couple of pictures of Skye on the mantelpiece. Did she have others? And there was a huge bookcase, filled with fiction, that he longed to go to and look at to see what kind of books she liked to read.

'I want you to know I appreciate how difficult this must be for you,' he said.

Lane looked across at him. 'Do you?'

'I do. I know how I'd feel if I was in your position.'

She smiled. 'Well, I *was* in your position, once. Suddenly having a daughter after going through a great loss. It's a lot to take in.'

'It certainly is. And I want you to know... I guess what I really want to say is that you can count on me. I'm not going to walk away. I'm here. I can be depended upon. You can trust me.'

She looked down at the ground, then back up again. Clearly she was thinking about things that she didn't want to say. Was she afraid to say them?

'I'd like to stay involved in Tori's life—if you'd like me to, of course.'

He'd meant to show that he was open to how this relationship was going to go. That he didn't want to stand on Lane's toes, or demand anything.

This was so difficult. Of course he was going to make mistakes here! But he didn't want to upset Lane. Or Tori. Not at all. And the realisation of that made him realise just how much he cared for the both of them already.

'You're clearly the most important person in her life. You're her godmother. You'll never lose her. She will always know who you are and how important you are.'

He hoped that sounded better. Her face seemed to soften. It gave him hope that he hadn't offended her too much.

'She's my world, Cole. My reason to keep going. These last few months it's been hanging over my head, knowing I had to find you. In the early days I was still struggling to cope with my grief and raise a baby. I knew time was ticking away. Counting down. I never wanted to knock on your door and just tell you what had happened. I didn't think you'd believe me. I had no idea what kind of man you were. So, once I was properly on my feet, and knew what I was doing, I got the job at the surgery to see. Part of me hoped I could walk away without ever telling you, so I didn't have to share her. But now you know, and it *terrifies* me, because she has been all I've thought about for what seems like a lifetime. I could never let anyone hurt her.'

He understood that. 'Then we need to find a way to make this work for both of us. And for Tori.'

'Yes. We do.'

'A routine. A structure. So we don't confuse Tori, either.'

'All right. What do you suggest?'

He thought for a moment. 'Maybe to start with I could come round each evening? To play with her? Maybe take her for a walk? Get her ready for bed and put her down?'

'Okay. And what about weekends?'

'I can do whatever fits in with you.' He needed to show her that he wanted to work with her on this. He didn't want to seem like he thought he was the one who got to call the shots. She was the guardian, not him.

'I like to take her out at weekends. There's a Faery Fayre this Saturday. Everyone gets to dress as fairies. So you probably wouldn't want to do that.' She smiled.

He grinned. 'Are you kidding? I'd love it.'

'Really?' She looked surprised.

'Absolutely. Tell me when and where and I'll be there.'

Lane laughed out loud when she saw him at her door on Saturday morning. He wore his usual jeans and a shirt, but he also wore a large pair of fairy wings attached to his back and he had a swirl of green and pink glitter running along his cheekbone and curved around his left eye. He even held a silver wand.

'What do you think? Will I blend in?' He smiled at her.

Lane couldn't stop laughing. He looked like a *dad*. A dad trying to please his daughter. 'I think you might! Come on in. Come see my own little fairy.'

She led him through to the living room, where Tori sat on the floor, pink wings attached to her back by the elastic straps around her arms. She squealed and waved her arms when he appeared.

Cole stooped down to pick her up and settled her on one hip. 'You look beautiful! But, then again, you're beautiful anyway. Ready to rock the fairy world?'

Tori blew a raspberry and a bubble escaped her mouth.

'I'll take that as a yes,' he said. He turned to Lane. 'Anything I can help with? I've packed a small picnic basket in the car.'

'Oh! Right… That's great. Thank you. I just need to grab my wings and then we can go. Shall we go in my car? It means not having to keep moving the car seat.'

'Perfect. I'll grab the picnic from mine.'

They got Tori settled in her seat, after removing her wings, then Cole removed his so he could put on his seatbelt. When the engine started the usual music began. A woman's voice singing about the wheels on a bus.

Cole began joining in with the song and Lane smiled as she drove them to the fayre. How had she suspected he would be a terrible dad? He was giving this one hundred percent! Most men would shun the idea of dressing as a fairy, but not him! He'd gone for it—including make-up!

She reminded herself to take a photo of him when they got there.

Parking for the fayre was busy. She hadn't realised how busy it would be, and they had to park in a faraway field and put their wings back on before making their way back to the village high street, where the main fayre was being held.

There were flowerpot shies, instead of coconut shies. Stalls selling fairy outfits. A face painter. A bouncy castle. Lots of stalls selling food. There was even a dog show, with the dogs dressed as fairies! The cutest one Lane saw was a tiny little pug puppy, with purple wings and a small tiara on its head. And most people had made the effort too. Everyone was smiling—it really was perfect.

Cole bought them both some pink candy floss, and then he bought her a beautiful lei of pink and yellow flowers that he draped around her neck. She was having so much fun! She might almost believe they were a family.

She forced the thought out of her mind and pulled her phone from her pocket. 'Let's take a picture.'

Cole leaned in and she snapped the shot, showing it to him.

He grinned. 'Let's take one with Tori near all those balloons.'

He unclipped her from her pushchair and went over to a balloon seller, who had helium balloons of all designs— unicorns, rabbits, foxes, ladybirds. Just as she took the photo Tori turned to look at her father and laughed. It was a perfect moment. One that warmed her heart and made her want to be in the picture with the two of them.

'Excuse me,' she asked a woman passing by with her own children. 'Could you get a snap of us all together?'

The woman nodded, smiling, and Lane posed with Cole and Tori.

'What a great dad!' the woman said as she handed back the phone. 'My hubby refused to come!'

That made Lane feel good. Some men wouldn't feel comfortable coming to a fairy fair and dressing in wings and make-up, but Cole did. He was proving to her that he would go the extra mile to make memories they could look back on and smile. He was selfless and she was enjoying his company.

Why had she ever thought she was in love with Simon? The man had been the definition of selfish!

'Thank you.' She slipped her phone back into her pocket. 'Ooh, look—a fortune-teller! Shall we see what she says?'

Cole laughed. 'If you like. Do you believe in that sort of thing?'

'Not really, but I think it will be fun.'

Lane led them over to the small marquee where the fortune-teller sat. Her name was Melrose, and on her table she had a crystal ball, as well as a deck of tarot cards, and a sign told them she read palms, cards and minds!

Melrose invited her to sit down and Lane held out her hand for her palm to be read.

The fortune-teller gazed at her hand for a moment. 'You have a long, clear life line here.'

Lane smiled. 'Does that mean I'll live a long time?'

Melrose neither admitted it nor denied it. 'Your love line is straight, but then—do you see this curve here—it seems to take off? That's because you've found true love.'

'Okay…'

Found true love? Melrose was saying she'd already found it? Well, she had to be wrong, didn't she, because she was single right now. And she couldn't be referring to Simon, because there was no way *he* was her true love!

She glanced nervously at Cole, who held Tori in his arms. It couldn't be Cole. Yes, she liked him a lot—and, yes, she was attracted to him, but… No, fortune-telling was just a bit of fun, that was all. Nothing scientific about it. Nothing *real*.

'Your marriage line, here, is whole. Uninterrupted. Your relationship will last.' Melrose looked at both Lane and Cole.

The fortune-teller thought they were married!

'Oh, we're not together!' Lane explained, cheeks flushing furiously. 'We're colleagues, but nothing more!'

Melrose smiled and leaned back. 'You have some surprises coming your way.'

'What kind?'

'You'll travel overseas together.'

Overseas? Like…to a medical conference? Lane didn't think this fortune-teller was very good at all—but then again, what had she expected?

'And there will come a moment, quite soon, when you will have to make a leap of faith.'

'In regard to what?'

'That's all your palm shows. It's impossible to give exact details.'

Lane walked away from the fortune-teller feeling slightly aggrieved. She'd known it would just be a bit of a laugh, but for some reason she'd hoped—just a tiny bit—that the fortune-teller would tell her something that would ring true. In fact, she'd got almost everything wrong, and guessed at things in the future that were very vague.

She'd been the worst of cold readers and it was something that Lane would never try again. And what about the leap of faith. Had that already happened? When she'd chosen Skye and the baby over Simon? It had to be that.

It couldn't possibly be anything else.

Cole hadn't expected to feel hurt when he heard Lane explain that they were colleagues and nothing more. He'd thought they were more than that. More than people who just worked together. He'd hoped that they were at least friends.

She was the legal guardian of his daughter. He was the father. Yes, they worked together—temporarily—but he was making a real effort to make Lane feel that she belonged both at work and in this relationship they were forging. Yes, it was a work in progress, and perhaps it always would be, but to say they were nothing more than *colleagues*...? That suggested a distance between them. A distance that he'd hoped wasn't there.

Perhaps he was reading too much into what was happening here? Perhaps he ought to be focused on being the best father he could to baby Tori? Because *she* was the important one here and *she* was the one he didn't want to lose.

I don't want to lose Lane either.

It was perfect right now, wasn't it? The three of them. He was the father and she, technically, was the mother. They were a perfect little family.

Why would he want to change anything? But maybe he had to clarify his thinking? Be the best father Tori needed, be a good colleague to Lane and leave it at that? After all, did he really need to be involving another woman in his life? And his building feelings towards Lane were making him feel guilty. What if all this ended in a bad way? After all, it was what he was used to happening...

But even as he tried to convince himself that he needed to make a clear boundary with Lane a small voice in his head was shouting that it wasn't what he really wanted. That what he wanted was to be close to Lane. He looked at her now, pushing the buggy in her fairy wings, her dark brown hair swinging as she walked. He looked at the set of her jaw, the shape of her full mouth. The way she was biting that bottom lip as if she were thinking about something…

He had to look away. Concentrate on where he was going. There were so many people here!

Tori began rubbing at her eyes. Was she tired?

'Let's put this one in her buggy,' said Lane. 'I think she may go to sleep.'

He gently laid Tori in her seat and strapped her in safely, then gave her the cuddly toy she liked to hold when she slept.

Look at us. The three of us.

This could have been the family he'd once dreamed of doing stuff like this with. Here it was—his chance to enjoy it to the full—and all he could think of was that Lane had said they were colleagues and nothing more.

'You all right? You look…odd.'

She'd noticed. 'I'm fine,' he said.

'Maybe I should sprinkle some fairy dust on you? To make you look magical again, like you did this morning.'

He smiled at her attempt to cheer him up. She wanted them to be on good terms and so did he.

'Fairy dust?'

She pulled a small pouch from her pocket. It was filled with glitter. 'I bought some at a stall. You never know when it might come in handy.'

'It's glitter.'

'It's *magical* glitter. And it's environmentally friendly. Come on—hold out your hand and make a wish.'

He didn't want to. He felt silly. But, then again, he was standing there wearing fairy wings, and he had glitter on his face already, so what were a few more sparkles?

He held out his hand and she poured some glitter into it.

'Now, squeeze your hand tight, make a wish and then scatter it over your shoulder. Just make sure no one's walking behind you when you do—we don't want to blind anyone.' She laughed.

He liked the way her smile and her laughter lit up her face. It did something wonderful to her eyes. They *gleamed*. She was having a good time, and he didn't want to spoil that. So he squeezed his hand tight.

What to wish for?

To get to know Tori more? Or for a more formal arrangement with her? He looked into Lane's smiling face and the thought came unbidden.

I wish I could kiss Lane.

His gaze went to her smiling mouth. Her lips…

What? Where did *that* come from? He felt his cheeks colour and he scrambled to think of Tori instead as he threw the glitter over his shoulder.

'What did you wish for?' asked Lane.

'I can't tell you. Then it won't come true!'

She laughed and squeezed her own hand and her eyes tight shut.

He stared at her, welcoming this moment to just look at her and not have her observe him. Her childlike glee was mesmerising. What was *she* wishing for?

You could take this moment and kiss her.

He shook his head, trying to clear the thought. He couldn't kiss Lane. She was Tori's guardian. Her godmother. His *colleague*. If he did it would complicate all that was going on with them already—and they had enough between them to deal with without a romance, too.

What if they got together and the relationship didn't work out? How would that work with Tori? It could be a bitter split and she could take away his daughter. He didn't think she would—she seemed a nice person, and not the vindictive kind—but what if it happened? He couldn't lose Tori now and know it was his own fault. He'd lost his wife through a stupid mistake—he wasn't going to mess this up, too.

Lane opened her eyes and threw the glitter over her shoulder. 'Wish made. Let's hope they both come true.'

He smiled at her and nodded. 'Let's hope.'

CHAPTER FIVE

THEY WERE WALKING ALONG, thinking about where to have their picnic, when they noticed a small crowd of people up ahead. Lane looked at Cole, who frowned. It looked as if there was someone on the ground.

'I'll take a look.'

Cole dashed forward, gently pushing his way through the gathering.

Lane watched him get swallowed up by the crowd and thought she glimpsed blood on the person, but couldn't be sure.

Then she heard, 'Has anyone got any bandages?'

Her heart began to pound. Clearly someone was in trouble! She wanted to help too. Cole might need her.

She began to push her way through the crowd, using the buggy like a snow plough. 'Excuse me! I can help!'

The crowd parted and let her through and there, reminiscent of her first meeting with Cole, she saw an elderly lady lying on the ground. But this time she saw, beneath the woman's right leg, a lot of blood soaking into the grass.

'Cole?'

'Somebody call for an ambulance, please,' he said calmly. 'Let them know there's a doctor on scene, but

tell them they need to get here as soon as possible with a
pressure bandage.'

His hands clasped the lady's leg and they were slippery
with blood. An elderly gent—the woman's husband?—
passed Cole a white handkerchief, clean and pressed into
a square, from his pocket.

'It was an accident, Doctor. I didn't mean to do it!'

'What happened?'

'I was walking behind her with the trolley, in case she
needed to sit down. Her legs haven't been too good lately.
There was a bump in the grass and I pushed too hard to
get over it—the trolley went into the back of her leg.'

Lane could see that the lady had frail, friable skin. It
must have been ripped open by the metal of the trolley.

Cole had the handkerchief pressed tightly against the
wound, but blood was coming through. They would need
a pressure bandage quickly if she wasn't to lose too much.

'What's your name?' Cole asked the lady.

'Freda. Freda Mallard. Like the duck.'

Cole smiled. 'Well, you're bleeding, Freda, so I'm
going to keep my hand tight here to try and stop it—
okay? Are you on any blood thinners?'

'Warfarin.'

Lane's heart sank slightly. Warfarin meant her blood
wouldn't clot as fast as normal and she could potentially
lose more volume. If she fainted or went into shock…

This was hardly the best place for this sort of thing
to happen.

Lane knelt beside her, one hand clutching Tori's buggy,
the other reaching out for Freda's hand. 'I'm Lane. I work
with Dr Branagh, here, and we're going to look after
you—all right? Tell me about yourself and your husband.
When did you meet?'

It was important to try and make Freda focus on other matters than her leg. If she was right, this elderly lady would have a bit of the Blighty spirit and not panic.

'At a dance. He took my hand when Elvis came on and we jitterbugged to one of his songs.'

'A jitterbug? You must have had loads of energy.' Lane smiled.

'Well, in those days we did. Not so much now.'

Lane could hear sirens in the distance and began to relax slightly. Freda looked pale, but not too bad. And of course she had no way of knowing if this was Freda's natural colouring.

'Do you hear that, Freda?' Cole asked. 'Help is on its way.'

'Help is already *here*,' Freda insisted. 'I've got a fairy doctor, of all things! What do you think you've been doing?'

He smiled. 'I mean proper help. With the right equipment. The only thing I've got on me is fairy dust.'

'Well, a sprinkle of magic might help, Doctor—you never know!' Freda chuckled.

'Once we've got you in that ambulance I'll make a wish for you. To have a speedy recovery.'

'All right.' Freda smiled at him, clearly comforted by his good nature. 'Maybe just wash those hands of yours first, eh?'

Cole laughed. 'Definitely.'

'Will you come and visit me? It's been a long time since a young man held my leg so wonderfully, and I'm not sure I can let you go.' She chuckled as her husband clicked his tongue.

'She always was a flirt, Doctor. Watch your husband, young lady, before she makes off with him!'

Again people thought they were together! She made eye contact with Cole and smiled at him, but he looked away and her smile dropped. Had he not heard? Or did the thought of the two of them being together upset him that much? Yes, he was a recent widower, but she'd thought that they were getting along. Perhaps he still felt loyal to the memory of his wife? She couldn't possibly compete with the woman who'd once been the love of his life. Or perhaps he was just pretending to like her so he could get her onside? Men had always used her, or let her down, and right now Cole had it made—a daughter with a ready-made mother.

The thought chilled her, and she let go of Freda's hand so she could get out of the way as the paramedics arrived with their overstuffed green bags and began to get their equipment ready.

She stood holding Tori's buggy—thankfully she'd slept through the whole thing—and watched as Cole gave his analysis of what had happened to the paramedics.

He was good—she had to give him that. Calm. Collected. And he built a rapport with his patients immediately. Had even done so with her.

But to what end?

What was his endgame? To try and claim his rights as a father? To go to court? To fight her for custody? Was that possible? She didn't know. Had all she'd done—all the sacrifice, all the upset—been for nothing? What rights did she have?

I don't actually know. I should!

Would he give her an ultimatum one day? The way Simon had?

Give me my daughter or...

A bystander gave Cole a bottle of water to rinse his

hands with, and once the blood was gone he wiped them dry on his trousers.

'I'm just going to see Freda into the ambulance,' he told her.

She smiled and nodded, watching as he walked behind the paramedics, fairy wings glinting in the sunshine, with Freda in a chair and Freda's husband walking by his wife's side.

Look at him. So caring. So dedicated! I'm being awful, doubting him in this way.

What had he actually done to make her think so badly of him? Nothing! Absolutely nothing! He'd just given her a look that she might or might not have misread. That was all. If anything, this overreaction of hers was Simon's fault—for making her feel this way about anyone who seemed to want to get to know her. For always thinking that men were only out for themselves.

Lane had quiet words with herself as she waited with Tori for Cole to get out of the ambulance once he'd helped Freda's husband in and made sure he was seated safely in the back. He closed the door and waved through the blacked-out window, knowing that those inside could see him even if he couldn't see them.

He's a good man. He's given me no reason to doubt him.

Yes, he was a *very* good man, and his wife had been lucky to have him. He clearly cared deeply.

She wondered how long it would be before a guy like Cole cared about her the way she wanted to be cared for. She wanted to be loved intently. Genuinely? But how would she ever trust anyone to let them try?

The words of the fortune-teller came back to her— *'You've found true love.'*

Had she? Where? Perhaps she'd already lost it?

Or was it Cole?

Everyone they met seemed to think they were a family already—and maybe they were in their own little way. It was a different kind of family, but did it make them any less than any other? It was just a bit broken. In pieces. Maybe they were like a patchwork? Separate pieces being sewn together? And wouldn't that be perfect? The three of them together?

Perhaps Cole would take her overseas, like the fortune-teller had said. Maybe a trip somewhere with Tori—something like that.

Because surely it couldn't be anything else?

What was real?

And what was just fantasy and fake fairy glitter?

CHAPTER SIX

'YOU'VE BEEN QUIET the last few days. Are you all right?' Cole had noticed a change in Lane since the Faery Fayre. She was still her usual smiley self with patients and their colleagues at the surgery, but at other times, in quieter moments, he'd noticed that she seemed quite subdued.

'I'm fine,' she answered, nodding her head, before turning back to vacantly waft through the pages of a magazine during their lunch break.

He wasn't sure he believed her. But he didn't want to say so outright. 'Everything all right with Tori?'

Again the nod. 'Fine!'

Waft. Waft. Waft.

He tried to think of what this could be about. Not the fayre That had been a *good* day—medical emergency included! He'd checked up on Freda and discovered that she'd been bandaged up and returned home. He'd thought he and Tori had had a good day out—even if one or two people had thought they were a family!

It had been bittersweet each time that had happened. He'd wanted to be part of a family for so long! To be a good father. A good husband. He'd failed the last woman he'd promised his life to. He'd not kept her safe. He'd not immediately noticed when she'd fallen behind, and when he had it had been impossible for him to stop and go back. The first rule of attending any medical emergency was to check that it was safe to approach, and with the blizzard and the avalanche he would have died himself by going back.

Perhaps he ought to have gone? If he'd loved Andrea as much as he thought he had, then surely…

No. Stop it. You've been through this. It wasn't your fault. You did what you could.

He looked at Lane. She was telling him she was fine but clearly she wasn't, and perhaps this was the moment for him to make sure she was all right in every way? To go back and check? Because fate had taught him one thing so far: that a happy future was not guaranteed.

She'd been through a lot in the last year, hadn't she? Losing her best friend to cancer. Taking on a daughter. Fulfilling the wish of a dying woman to seek him out and share the baby she had come to love.

But sharing meant sharing with him. Perhaps she didn't want another man in her life. 'I understand this is difficult for you.'

She stopped wafting, looked straight ahead. 'What?'

'Tori. She knows you. You're her world. I appreciate that by being her mother you also have to put up with me. And you never asked for that.'

She glanced at him.

'Tori trusts you. Loves you. One day, I'd like her to feel the same way about me.'

Lane put down the magazine. 'Of course I want you to have that.'

He wanted to reach out. Lay his hand upon hers to emphasise that her friendship meant the world to him. But he couldn't. Because he knew that if he did, he'd want to do more. He'd want to move closer to her. To squeeze her hand tight and look deep into her eyes until she smiled at him. And then he would lose himself in that smile, and he wasn't sure if he was ready, if he was brave enough, to lose himself like that again.

Instead he managed a brisk smile, because that was safer, and because with the adrenaline rushing through his body he couldn't just sit there and—

'It's my birthday this weekend,' she said.

He turned. 'Is it? I didn't know that.'

'Skye and I would always go to the seaside on my birthday. We'd walk down the pier and play amusement arcade games, eat fish and chips and come home with armfuls of the cuddly toys we'd won on those silly grabby machines.'

She looked wistful, and he realised this would be the first birthday she'd spend without her best friend. That must be why she'd been so subdued lately. Birthdays and anniversaries after the death of a close loved one were always hard. He knew that.

'I'm sorry she's not here to do those things with you.'

'I knew it was coming, though. I've been trying not to think about it and telling myself it doesn't matter, but... It'll be strange not to go.'

'I'll take you,' he blurted out, and then he felt hot. Because he hadn't realised those words were going to come out of his mouth, and now that they were out, he couldn't go back on them.

Of course it would be fun to spend the day with Lane—he couldn't think of anything better—but the more time he spent with her, the more he wanted to touch her and hold her in a way that went far beyond them being just colleagues.

'You can say no,' he said.

But he'd seen her eyes light up at the idea, at the *hope* of going. 'You'd really take me?'

'I can't think of a better way to spend the weekend. We could take Tori.'

She grimaced. 'My mum's taking her for the day, to go and visit my aunt and uncle in Cirencester. She wanted to give me the day off. It was arranged ages ago.'

All that time alone. Just him and Lane. Without the distraction of Tori. The *chaperonage* of Tori.

'Oh, right…'

She looked disappointed. 'You only wanted to go if Tori was with us, didn't you? Of course. I should have realised—'

'I'd love to take you to the seaside.'

She stared at him as if trying to read him. To see if he was telling the truth. 'Are you sure?'

No, he wasn't sure. He'd never thought he'd feel attracted to another woman the way he'd felt attracted to Lane—not after his wife died—but here he was! Agreeing to a day-long date.

But how hard can it be? I've got self-control, and Lane doesn't see us as anything but colleagues, so…

'I'm absolutely sure.'

He smiled and nodded.

Just to prove it.

Lane had butterflies in her belly when she heard the doorbell, wondering how she was going to get through a whole day with Cole, without the distraction of Tori, and also how it might feel to be at the beach without Skye for the first time in years.

But when she answered the door she burst into laughter, because Cole stood there holding a massive bunch of helium balloons that he had to fight through, just to see her face.

'Good morning! Happy birthday!'

He thrust the balloons towards her, and she was smiling so much her cheeks hurt.

Just moments before she'd been crying, because her mother had given her a birthday card that Skye had written before she'd died. It had been unexpected, and it had reopened the door to all the grief she'd been stamping down on over the last few months.

'Let me put these somewhere.' She took them through into the living room and placed them in the corner by the window.

When she turned to face him her heart stuttered. He looked gorgeous today, dressed in dark jeans and a slim-fit black shirt that showed off his trim waist and broad shoulders perfectly. But that wasn't her main focus. Her main focus was his smile.

'And I got you this.' He passed over a small gift bag.

'Oh, you didn't have to get me anything.'

'Are you kidding me? Of course I did. We're…friends.'

Friends. She noted he hadn't said *family.* But then again, they weren't family, were they? She was Tori's guardian, her godmother, but the two of them weren't blood-related, like Tori and Cole were. They were father and daughter. Lane was an outsider to that. No matter what the paperwork said, he and Tori would be closer in some ways than she could ever be.

'Should I open it now?'

He nodded.

She opened the bag and reached in, pulling out a small square box. Jewellery? With shaking hands she slowly opened it, and gasped in surprise.

Inside was a beautiful silver bracelet with three charms on it. One charm was the letter S, the second, the letter T, and the third charm the letter L. *Skye. Tori. Lane.* Her beautiful goddaughter sandwiched between her and her real mother.

'This is beautiful!'

'You like it? I wasn't sure what to get you.'

'I love it.'

She went to put it on, but couldn't do it with one hand, so Cole came forward to do it for her. She stood there, heart pounding with Cole so close to her, breathing in his scent and his nearness, watching the way his fingers so deftly and easily fastened the bracelet around her wrist.

'Thank you. But where's your initial?'

He smiled. 'It seemed a bit presumptuous to put that on there.'

'You're Tori's father!'

'Yes, but the bracelet is about the special relationship the three of you had. What you forged together. I'm not a part of that.'

She looked up at him with awe and wonder at his thoughtfulness, and she just wanted to kiss him right there and then. Then she realised what she'd just thought of doing and felt her cheeks flush with heat.

'Well, I'm going to get the letter C put on as soon as I can.'

'Isn't it bad luck to buy charms for your own bracelet?'

She laughed. 'I don't believe in that nonsense. Besides, the worst things in life have already happened, haven't they? And we didn't buy any charms for our own bracelets before any of those happened.'

He laughed. 'I guess not. So, are you ready to get

going? We've got a long drive if we want to get to Weston before lunch.'

'Let me just grab my bag and we can go.'

She looked at him then. Truly looked at him. He was giving her everything. Reassuring her. Treating her right. He was so kind, and she doubted she would ever meet another man like him.

'Thank you, Cole. I mean it.' And she reached up on tiptoe to kiss him on the cheek.

Her lips brushed his skin, feather-light, but enough to feel the hint of bristles on his jaw and to feel her own skin against his. It was the briefest of moments but it would be etched into her memory for ever.

'It was my pleasure,' he said, his voice rough.

He was thankful to be driving. It gave him something to think about other than that kiss she'd given him.

Oh, who am I kidding? It's all I can think about!

He'd wanted to get her a gift she could treasure, but when he'd thought about what to get he'd realised he knew almost nothing about her! Apart from Tori, what else had they talked about? Skye, obviously. His wife, Andrea. But had they ever talked about Lane?

He didn't know her favourite anything. He didn't know what she'd been like when she was at school, if she'd ever had anyone special, what she'd wanted from life before cancer had taken Skye and given her Tori and changed the direction of her life for ever.

All he really knew was how special their relationship had been, so he'd got her something that would commemorate that for ever.

And she'd kissed him.

It had been a quick peck on the cheek, but when she'd

leaned in the way she had, on tiptoe, pressing one hand to his chest, he'd wondered if she'd felt his heartbeat quicken, if she'd noticed the longing in his eyes and the disappointment that he'd felt when she'd drawn away.

And then the guilt had set in. Of course it had! It was his constant companion.

It had plagued him for ages, keeping him solitary, keeping him alone. He'd not let any relationships happen. He'd had the occasional date when he'd felt lonely. But his one and only true diversion had been Skye, and after that he had battled with the voice inside him, telling him that he should never have done it.

He had been the perfect gentleman since then. Just wanting the pleasure of a woman's company, the conversation without the complications.

Friendship was all he had ever been after. And yet here he was in one of the most complicated situations he'd ever faced!

Lane affected him in a way he'd never thought would be possible again. And he didn't know how to feel about it. It would be so easy to let their relationship happen. He could have the family he'd dreamed of for years.

His body, his heart, wanted that.

But his logical mind screamed at him to stay away.

Which would win? He didn't know, and it was a delicious agony as he drove to Weston with Lane by his side, knowing she was close and that they had the whole day together.

He wanted to give her anything she wanted today. He didn't want the day to be bittersweet, though he supposed it would be, no matter how hard he tried. He wasn't Skye. He never would be. But he was determined to give her the best birthday she had ever had.

'What do you want to do first when we get there?'

She sighed. 'I want to see the sea. It was the first thing Skye and I would always do. We'd go to the promenade, kick off our shoes and run across the beach and paddle in the water.'

'Even today?' It was a little overcast. Not the perfect day for the beach, he had to admit.

She nodded. 'Even today.'

'Okay. And then what?'

She laughed. 'The funfair to play on the games and win cuddly toys.'

'We can do that. I used to be a dab hand at those grabby things.'

'Me too! We ought to have a competition. See who can win the most!'

He smiled. 'All right, you're on. First one to ten doesn't have to buy the fish and chips.'

'But they do get to buy the ice-cream.'

He grinned and nodded. 'Favourite flavour?'

'Mint choc-chip.'

'Mine too!' He laughed, enjoying how easy it was to talk to her even without Tori there.

He'd worried about that. Thought they would have nothing to say to one another. His daughter was the one thing they shared, but without her he and Lane were practically strangers to one another really.

'Have you ever been to Weston before?' she asked.

'Once—for a medical conference. But I was stuck inside a seafront hotel for the whole day, so I never really got to see it properly—though it was all lit up at night when I left.'

'I guess you're used to going overseas for holidays?'

He shook his head. 'Not always. We went to Scotland

once. Spent a weekend in Dublin—though I don't remember too much about that one!' He laughed again. 'What about you?'

'My mum always took me to the seaside each year. Skegness. Yarmouth. The Isle of Wight one year. I've never really travelled.'

'Why not?'

She shook her head. 'I've just never had the opportunity and…um…when I met *Simon* he was always working.'

He heard the way she said his name. The hesitation before. The emphasis. This Simon had meant something to her. 'A boyfriend?'

She glanced at him and nodded her head. 'Unfortunately.'

'Should I change the subject, or…?'

He didn't want to push, even though he was desperate to know more about her. What made her tick? And why had her relationship been unfortunate?

'No. We can talk about it.' She let out a sigh. 'It started as it always does. I thought he was my Prince Charming and in the end it turned out he was just a toad I should have thrown back into the scum-filled pond.'

'Ouch! How long were you together?'

'A year.'

'It was serious, then?'

'The first few months were bliss. Or my infatuation made me think it was bliss. He was handsome. Charming. Delightful to everyone. I asked him to move in with me, because I hated being apart from him, and he kept saying that we were inseparable. It was what I wanted to hear. That someone couldn't live without me. I wanted

to believe him, but I was already making too many excuses for his behaviour without realising I was doing it.'

He listened. Not just to the words, but to the tone in
which they were said. Her voice said so much that her
words didn't.

'I had a job in a nursing home at the time. It was
stressful…caring for elderly people with dementia. But
it wasn't them—it was the new management that came in
that really made it tough. Simon didn't like how much I
talked about it when I came home, but I was only trying
to blow off steam. I needed him to listen and he didn't
want to.'

'What happened?'

'Skye got sick. I'd been so wrapped up in Simon, so
engrossed by what I thought was love, that I hadn't been
seeing her as often, even though she was coping with
pregnancy by then. He didn't like me spending time with
her, but when she got diagnosed halfway through her
pregnancy I just knew I had to be there for her.'

Cole nodded. 'You were best friends.'

'Exactly. But Simon hated it that someone else had
my attention.'

'What happened?'

'I began going with Skye to her hospital appointments.
That often meant we were out for hours. I hardly saw
Simon, and when we did see each other we argued. He
kept telling me he needed me, too, but he wasn't sick, or
scared the way Skye was. And then she was told it was
inoperable, that the cancer had spread, and she told me
her plans about wanting me to be her baby's guardian.'

'What did Simon have to say about that?'

She laughed bitterly, shaking her head. 'He wasn't best
pleased. Looking after someone else's baby? He didn't

want to be a father. He could never be that selfless. When he discovered I'd already agreed we had a massive fight and he gave me an ultimatum. Him, or Skye and the baby.'

Cole was shocked. He didn't know what to say.

'She had no one but me she could turn to, and no one should ever have to die alone.'

He thought about Andrea. She had died alone.

'Why didn't Skye tell me? That she was pregnant?' he asked.

'She didn't think it was right to tell you. It had been a one-night stand—she couldn't imagine rocking up to your doorstep and telling you she was pregnant, and then telling you that she wouldn't live long enough to see her baby grow up. So she made a decision. Whether it was right or wrong, we can't change that now.'

'I would have liked to know her more.'

'You would?'

'Yes. She sounds like a very caring friend. A gentle soul.'

'She was.'

'I'm sorry this Simon hurt you. You deserve better than that.'

'Thanks.'

They were both quiet for a while. The signs to Weston promenade were now showing on the road as they got closer and closer.

It hurt him to know that Lane had been in such a terrible relationship. If he had been her friend back then, and he'd heard what this Simon had done, he would have gone round there and... What? Punched the guy?

Maybe... He wasn't a violent man, but he would have liked to defend her and let this Simon know in no uncertain terms just how low a life-form he was. He'd certainly sounded like a giant idiot. Selfish and unthinking. He could never treat a woman in such a way.

'Let's forget Simon. Forget ovarian cancer and death and celebrate life. *Your* life. Your birthday. What do you say?'

She smiled at him and gave a single nod. 'Let's do it!'

CHAPTER SEVEN

'READY?'

She beamed a smile at him. It was cold, and the wind was blowing hard now they stood on the exposed beach. It was even beginning to spit a little with rain. 'I am!'

She took her hand in his. 'Then let's go!'

They began running across the sand, the coarseness of it squelching softly between their toes. Some parts were firmer underfoot than others as they ran towards the sea that coursed towards them in low, frothy waves. As their toes hit the icy-cold water Lane squealed at the temperature, hopping over the low waves, water splashing up her legs, before they both stood there panting and staring out to sea.

She felt so amazing! So alive and...

As she stared out to sea, reminding herself that she did not have Skye by her side for the first time ever, she felt tears prick her eyes. Inhaling deeply, determined not to cry, she gazed out across the churning water and wondered if Skye was looking down at her, wishing she could be there, too.

She felt Cole squeeze her hand and she glanced at him in thanks. But he was gazing out at the water, too, as if he knew she needed this moment to remember her friend.

Needed this moment to shed a solitary tear because a new chapter in her life had begun. Without her best friend by her side.

Instead she had Cole by her side.

Who knew that he would be this great?

She remembered how she'd felt that morning a few weeks ago, sitting outside Liberty Point Surgery, not wanting to go in, because she'd felt sure she would find nothing but another greaseball. A charmer, like Simon, who used women for his own selfish needs.

Cole was nothing like that. And he'd proved time and time again that he was caring and kind.

The fact that he was handsome and attractive too...

She smiled. How could she hold that against him?

He was so easy to be with, and she liked it that he was holding her hand, supporting her, doing this with her. Making sure her birthday was still a day to remember. He'd not wanted her to be alone on her special day and that meant something.

'I'm glad you're here with me, Cole,' she said.

He turned to look at her, the wind ruffling the top of his hair. 'I'm glad, too.'

'It's cold, it's spitting with rain, and my feet feel like ice, but that doesn't matter.'

He smiled at her.

She loved his smile.

She went up on tiptoe again, to plant a kiss on his cheek as a thank-you. And there she paused, breathing in the scent of salt against his skin, the slight dampness of his hair, the way he held her against him. She pulled back slightly, looking into his eyes, not sure what she was doing or whether it was wise.

He looked back at her. Did he want her to kiss him?

She thought so. She hoped so. But what if it complicated matters? What they had between them was good at the moment—why confuse matters by kissing him? What if it all went wrong?

She smiled uncertainly and took a step back.

Did he seem relieved? Or upset? She couldn't tell.

'Let's go back,' she said.

He nodded. 'Sure.'

They didn't run back. They walked. Still hand in hand.

She relished the contact. The heat of his skin. The strength of his grip. It was almost as if he was saying, *Don't worry. I've got you. I won't let you go.* She felt safe. Protected by this tall man at her side. She almost didn't want to get back to the promenade, because then she would have to let go of his hand to put on her shoes again. She even slowed her walk so that it would take longer.

Reluctantly, she let go and sat on the wall, so she could brush the sand off her feet and put on her shoes.

He did the same, and then—*oh, yes!*—he held out his hand for hers and they walked towards the arcade.

They sat in the seated area of the fish and chip shop, eating their food, as outside the rain poured in a torrent.

Thankfully, inside it was warm, the air filled with the scent of food and salt and vinegar, and they both filled their bellies with perfectly cooked chips and the crispy thick batter around perfect pieces of meaty cod.

'Why is it that fish and chips always tastes better at the seaside?' Lane asked.

'I don't know. I'm sure there's a suitably confusing mathematical equation, researched by experts after years of study to explain it, but I'm just going to accept the fact that it does.' Cole smiled and dipped a chip into a small pot of ketchup.

Beside them sat a bag of sixteen cuddly toys that they had won from the arcades, and Lane was still quite pleased that she'd made it to ten before he had. They were cheap and tacky, but they'd been fun to get, and she was looking forward to taking them home and putting them in the hammock she had on the wall in Tori's room.

'I'm having a great birthday—thank you.'

'Hey, my pleasure—and it's not over yet.'

'No?'

'No! There's ice-creams to have, and then there's a ride that I think we should go on.'

She almost stopped eating. 'A ride?'

She'd never really liked rollercoasters. She'd ridden some quite tame ones...gone on a log flume once or twice...and she had hated the feeling in her stomach when they had dropped over the side and splashed her with cold water at the bottom.

'After all this food? Is that wise?'

'We'll be fine. Honest. I'll look after you.'

'You'd better.'

He smiled. 'Trust me.'

The rain had begun to clear as they walked towards the funfair. Lane bit her lip, wondering what ride Cole wanted to take her on and what excuse she could use to get out of it!

Part of her wanted to be brave and trust him, but another part of her told her she'd been on enough crazy rides in her lifetime and didn't really need to go on one more!

But she didn't want to be a spoilsport. And she didn't want to ruin the day the way she had once when she'd gone to a fair with Simon and he'd called her a Sulky Sue for not going on a giant rollercoaster.

So she walked beside Cole, her arm slipped inside his, and as they walked through the stalls where you could shoot at playing cards, or hook ducks, or throw darts at balloons she tried to lose herself in the traditional British seaside atmosphere—the noise, the aroma of candy floss and toffee apples and hot dogs with fried onions.

She saw a waltzer, a gentler teacup ride, a big wheel and a helter-skelter. Which ride was he taking her to? The Crazy Mouse? The Robo-Coaster?

'Here we go.'

She looked ahead in disbelief. 'The Ghost Train?'

He laughed at the look on her face. 'What did you *think* I was going to take you on? I can't even manage a carousel without wanting to throw up, and this is meant to be the scariest ghost train in the country!'

She shook her head and then rested it against his arm, feeling a world of relief. 'I can do a ghost train.'

'Let's sit at the front.'

And she laughed again as eagerly, like a child, he clambered into the front car and held out his hand to help her in. She sat beside him and he lowered the bar, securing them into place.

The ride attendant came by and took payment, checked their safety bar and then went to check on the others.

'You like scary rides, huh?' she asked.

'Gotta get that adrenaline rush somehow.'

She slipped her arm into his. 'I'll take care of you.'

'You'd better. I need to drive us home, and I won't be able to do that if I'm traumatised.'

The car slowly began to move forward.

Clack-clack.

From behind the dark doors that slowly opened in front of them they heard howls and ghost noises. Lane reached for Cole's hand and squeezed it as they passed into darkness.

The car twisted to the right, then to the left as skeletons and scary zombies suddenly screeched into the light, looming over them.

Lane gasped, and laughed, and then the car spun crazily to the left again, clattered through more dark doors, and there was an evil clown holding a bunch of burst balloons and reaching for them with spiky teeth. There was a crack of thunder and a flash of lightning and the car was yanked right and propelling them into a tunnel of cobwebs that brushed their faces and made them jump.

She leaned into Cole, laughing, and he leaned towards her. And then everything went dark and the car dipped down a metre or so, making their stomachs plummet, before lifting again as a ghost screeched right in their faces.

She turned to face Cole, to laugh with him, to enjoy this with him, and saw that he was gazing at her, his face full of joy. Suddenly the scary ride was forgotten. The flashes of light, the plunging into darkness, the pretend gore and blood—all gone.

All there was, was Cole. Beyond him the darkness flared with light, and there were figures, but she didn't know what. Didn't want or need to focus on them because of the way he was looking at her. His face flickered in the light, shade and shadow, and his eyes were intense as they gazed back at her...

And suddenly they were back in daylight and the ride had stopped.

His lips touched hers.

She deepened the kiss, welcoming the feel of his tongue in her mouth, allowing herself this moment that she had craved for so long, forgetting all the complicated issues that came with it, forgetting all the cruelty that had befallen them both and not caring whether this was sensible or not. Whether this was wise. All that mattered was him, and the feel of him in her arms, and the fact that right at that moment she didn't want anything else at all.

'Excuse me, can I get on?'

A child's voice broke the spell and they pulled apart. Her cheeks were flushed. She felt breathless and unsure of what to say. The adrenaline in her body wasn't from the ride at all, but from Cole.

The safety bar snapped back and he took her hand and helped her out of the car. They stood there for a moment, staring at each other, not knowing what to say…

Cole had not thought for one moment that he would end up kissing Lane that day. He'd intended to give her a fun day out, to take away some of the sadness that she would be feeling at not having her best friend to celebrate with as usual. The most he'd thought would happen was that he would get to know her a little more and deepen their friendship.

Had he ruined everything?

The crushing wave of guilt that flowed through him once again was familiar. He'd been out with women since his wife's death—just once or twice, when he'd felt he couldn't bear another night in alone—but he'd never done this. Kissed a woman as if he meant it. Kissed her as if he wouldn't be able to breathe unless he did so. Kissed her because he couldn't stop himself.

What they'd had between them would now be changed.

This desire…this yearning he had felt for Lane had slowly been building. He'd tried his best to ignore it, but sometimes you just couldn't fight something like that. It was primal. It was…*life*.

'I'm sorry. I didn't mean to…'

His words trailed off as he stared into her eyes. Her face. Her lips were still parted from their kiss and all he could think of right now was how perfect they had felt. How soft. How good it had felt to kiss her.

'No. It's all right. It was just…the heat of the moment.'

She didn't sound as if she believed herself one bit. Was she trying to let him off the hook?

'We need to keep things professional between us. It… er…' he swallowed hard, unable to stop thinking about that kiss '…won't happen again.'

She nodded. 'Right. No, you're right. It's complicated, isn't it?'

Complicated didn't adequately explain it.

'Yes, it is. So…what do you fancy doing next?' he asked.

He felt bad for trying to change the subject when something so monumental as he and Lane kissing passionately had just happened. It felt cowardly, and that caused even more guilt to come crushing down upon him. He couldn't bear it, so he randomly walked over to a stall and handed over a five-pound note to have a go on whatever that stall was.

It turned out to be a firing range, where little plastic guns were chained to the counter. He loaded the gun with tiny yellow plastic balls. Apparently he had to knock down a trio of dented cans. He aimed and got the first one off with a single shot, but missed all the others. He stared at the cans, at their dented exterior after a thousand hits, and wondered if his soul looked the same?

Happiness always ended in tragedy.

What had he been *doing* to let his feelings emerge like that? Lane was his daughter's godmother! Her legal guardian. If he screwed this up, she could walk away and he'd not be able to do a damned thing about it! Well...

He was meant to be getting to know his daughter—not falling for the woman who was her guardian. Not to mention the fact that they were work colleagues! In a tiny practice! If he ruined this the repercussions could be mighty—not just for him and his future with his daughter, but for his patients, too!

He'd messed with fire and this was the burn. Yes, he'd be lying if he said he hadn't thought about how convenient it would be if they *did* get together—but what if that was all this was and he was mistaking convenience and the promise of a ready-made family for real attraction?

Cole hadn't won anything at the stall, but he wasn't ready to turn away from it and see Lane's face.

What was she thinking? Did she feel rejected? She'd seemed to agree with him that the kiss had been a bad idea...but hadn't she kissed him back? She'd pressed herself against him. She'd run her fingers through his hair and it had felt so good! Were they the actions of a woman who didn't want to be kissed?

Or perhaps she'd been feeling like him? Had just got carried away in the moment and forgotten what really mattered just for a moment of madness? Or maybe she was the one playing him to get a ready-made family?

He turned from the stall and looked at her. Her hair was getting damp from the thin drizzle that was falling and she had no hood on her coat. 'Let's get you a brolly,' he said.

'It's fine.'

'No, it's not. I think I saw some in that gift shop.'

He bought her an umbrella, and because she was so much shorter than he was it gave him a good reason to walk apart from her, so that he didn't get poked in the shoulders by the spikes.

Whatever closeness they'd previously had, it now felt precarious. It was as if there was a wall between them. He knew that the wall was of his own making. But he needed it. That wall had kept him safe since Andrea's death, and right now he needed to reinforce it. To make it clear that Lane couldn't broach it. Look at what had happened the last time he had overstepped it.

Even if the memory of their kiss and how she had made him feel did make him want to rip that wall down brick by brick and cross the line once again...

'Have you two had a falling out?' asked Mary, the receptionist.

Lane had been standing at Reception, just passing the time whilst she waited for her next patient to arrive, when Cole had walked up, passed over some swabs to be sent to Pathology, and then walked away without saying a word.

She had been hyper-aware of him being there. Knew exactly that it had been *his* surgery door that had opened, *his* footsteps she'd heard approaching and had breathed in his cologne as he'd stood by her side to hand the swabs to Mary to put in the collection box.

She'd tensed when he'd stood next to her, even though she'd not meant to. But her birthday had ended so awkwardly, and he'd driven her home practically in silence, only making occasional comments on the rain or the traffic and then saying a hurried, 'Thank you for today,' when he'd dropped her off at her house.

She'd never before needed a hug from Tori so badly! Needed just to hold her and squeeze her tight and talk to her as if she were Skye.

'I made a huge mistake today. I kissed him. I kissed your father. And it was breathtaking and amazing and the whole world stopped turning for just a moment.'

She'd paused then, imagining Skye asking the question, *'And then what happened?'*

And then *nothing* had happened. She'd seen his shutters come down so quickly, and although it had been raining and cold all day, that had been the first time she'd felt a chill. The fun had gone out of the day and they'd both quickly agreed that maybe it was time to go home?

At the start of the day she'd imagined arriving home and thanking him with a big smile and a peck on the cheek, saying, *See you Monday!* as she skipped from the car. But nothing could have been further from the truth. And now she didn't know how to be around him.

'No. Not really,' she said now.

Mary smiled. 'Not *really*? That means you've at least had words of some kind. You can tell me; I won't tell anyone else.'

Lane smiled at Mary's persistence. 'He took me out for my birthday and it didn't go very well, that's all.'

'Oh…' Mary seemed thoughtful. 'How so?'

'It was raining and cold and just not the fun day we'd envisaged.'

'But surely then you'd be commiserating with each other? You froze faster than if you'd been dipped in liquid nitrogen when he came up beside you.' Mary tapped her finger against her bottom lip. 'Something else happened…'

'Nothing happened.'

'You sure of that?'

She smiled. 'Absolutely.' And then she felt a welling of relief as she saw her patient arrive for his free NHS Health Check. 'Mr Jammeh! Would you like to come down?'

As she escorted her patient down the corridor Mary leaned over the reception counter and called after her, 'I'll find out!'

Lane shook her head. She liked Mary. She was like the practice's mother hen, looking after all her chicks.

She opened her door and escorted her patient in.

At the end of the day Lane was just finishing off the last few things she had to do. She'd cleaned and wiped down her room, and now she needed to go into each doctor's room and make sure it had a good supply of blood and urine bottles, that the sharps bins weren't in need of being changed, and to check the bed curtain to see if it needed changing. Shelby, the practice HCA, had left her a check list, which was helpful, and she assumed that as it was late, the doctors all should have left by now to do home visits.

She switched off her computer and checked Dr Summer's room first. It was fine, and all she needed to do was make sure the examination bed had a fresh blue paper cover after wiping it down. After that she did Dr Green's room, knowing in her head that she was deliberately leaving Cole's room till last. Dr Green needed a new box of disposable tourniquets and some new needles.

She checked the nurse's room, to make sure the fridges were locked and secure and all the temperatures recorded in the file. Then she cleaned down the sluice, all the time listening for sounds from outside.

She couldn't hear anybody. No printer running off prescriptions, no typing, no doctor recording notes into a voice recorder.

He had to have gone, right?

With trepidation, she went to Cole's room. The door was shut and she pressed her ear to the wood for just a moment, resting her face against its cool, smooth surface, her eyes closed as she fought to remove the memory of that kiss.

Suddenly the door was pulled open and she almost fell straight into his arms.

'Whoa! You okay?' He dropped his briefcase to catch her, his hands holding tight onto her upper arms.

Blushing madly, she stepped back, freeing herself, straightening her tunic. 'Sorry! I was just about to come in, but I thought I heard you moving around inside and figured you were still working.'

She was babbling, because she didn't know what else to do. She couldn't make eye contact; she didn't feel brave enough for that just yet. They'd not really spoken to each other properly since that kiss, and now he was just standing there, staring at her as if in expectation, so she had to fill the silence.

'I didn't want to interrupt, so if you've still got stuff to do I'll just go—'

'Lane, it's fine. I'm just leaving.' He sounded disappointed.

Her cheeks felt like the surface of the sun. Did he think she'd been eavesdropping? Did he think she'd been afraid to come in?

'Oh, okay. I need to check your sharps bin and…um… anything else you might need…'

He nodded, picking up his briefcase. 'I think I'm out of green needles. Maybe some vacutainers.'

She nodded, heading over to his sharps bin to check it.

This way he can only see my back and not my face, because my face is hotter than it's ever been!

'Is it still okay for me to come over tonight to see Tori?'

The bin did need changing. She clamped down the opening so that it clicked into place. She'd forgotten they'd made a standing arrangement for Cole to come round each evening to see his daughter before bedtime...

Suddenly she had an image in her head of Cole tucking *her* into bed, leaning over to kiss her goodnight and...

Oh, dear God, think of something else!

'Yes.' She nodded rapidly. 'That's fine. As agreed.'

She turned to face him then, feeling that a smile was needed, but she couldn't meet his eyes. That would just be too much. Especially when she thought of how he'd rejected her after the ghost train.

She should have trusted her first instincts regarding Cole. He didn't want her! He was simply there for Tori! She had been a slight distraction for him—a blip—and she guessed he might be feeling guilty because of his wife, because how could she possibly compare with the love of his life?

Men never wanted her. Her dad had left her behind. Simon had wanted to control her.

Perhaps Cole had said the kiss was a mistake because he thought that if he got involved with Lane, it might somehow jeopardise his chances of spending time with Tori? That if he and she got together and then had a falling out...

Wow, I really know how to let my mind run away with itself.

Lane decided the quicker she acknowledged the fact that Cole was just there for Tori and not her, the better.

'I should be home about six,' she said.

'Seven okay? That gives me time to grab a bite to eat.'

'Seven is perfect.' She tried to smile again, but it faded rapidly as he walked away without saying another word.

What had she done? Ruining everything by kissing Cole? She must have been running a fever, or she must be a mad, mad fool, because this was just atrocious! He was never going to back away from his daughter and she'd better get used him spending time with Tori.

Oh, God! Lane was confused. *He* had kissed *her.* Passionately! They'd both been attracted to each other. She had felt the tension in the air, and she'd thought they'd both become lost in the moment, but...

She got Cole a new sharps bin from the storeroom and attached it to his wall, deciding there and then that when she saw Cole this evening she would put him straight as much as she could.

He had to know that anything emotional she showed was real. That she'd just got caught up in the moment of what had been a difficult day.

He had to know.

He *had* to.

CHAPTER EIGHT

TORI WOULDN'T EAT her dinner, much to Lane's dismay. She'd wanted her fed before Cole turned up, but today, it seemed, Tori thought that food was just for throwing onto the floor.

'Tori, no! Don't do that!' She scooped up some sweet potato mash from the floor and then washed her hands beneath the tap before returning to try and get a few spoonsful into her goddaughter. 'Open up—that's it… that's it… *No! Tori!*'

Tori kept turning away from the spoon, clamping her mouth shut, and Lane was beginning to get really frustrated. Why was she being like this? Normally Tori was brilliant at eating. She loved her food—couldn't get enough of it! But today…

'You don't want to eat today? Well, you do realise that you'll probably wake up in the night hungry?'

She used a wet wipe to mop up Tori's face and podgy little hands and wrists, then lifted her from the high chair and put her down on her play mat whilst she cleaned up a bit and wiped down the high chair.

She could feel her frustration building, already predicting a long night ahead when she'd get no sleep because Tori would cry endlessly. And she didn't want to start feeding her at night again, otherwise she'd think it was a new ritual and wake for milk every night.

'Just when I thought I'd got a handle on this mothering lark...' She leaned against the sink and closed her eyes. She'd worked so hard just lately. Trying to be the best mother Tori could have because she didn't have a real one...

A knock at the door broke her reverie.

Cole.

A sigh escaped her, and she dried her hands on a tea towel and went to answer the door. She pulled it open, expecting to see an uncertain, uncomfortable-looking Cole standing there, and that they would suffer a long couple of hours enduring each other's company, but she realised he was looking at her curiously.

'What? What is it *now*, Cole?' she asked angrily, already feeling close to tears. 'Because, quite simply, I've had a difficult couple of days and—'

He bit his bottom lip and managed an embarrassed smile. 'You have something on your cheek and your... erm...' he pointed at her chest '...shirt.'

She reached to her face and at the same time she looked down. Sweet potato. Heat flooded her cheeks in embarrassment and right there and then she felt she really would cry.

She bit her lip in a bid to stop the tears coming, but she couldn't stop the torrent that had clearly decided that now was the perfect time to humiliate her further. She burst into tears, and the fact that she'd been trying to hold them back so hard meant she gave a hiccupping sob and could do nothing but cover her face in shame.

He must have come in, closed the door, because suddenly he was holding her, comforting her, and she sobbed into his chest, wetting his shirt, trying to cry an apology. But he just shushed her gently and held her until her sobbing had subsided to just a few sniffs and hiccups of breath.

She didn't know how long they stood there like there like that, but what she did know was that she wished she could stay there for ever. But she couldn't, could she? Because he didn't want her.

She pushed away from him, wiping her eyes, hating to break the contact but knowing they ought to check on Tori. 'Sorry. I'm so sorry. I don't where that came from.'

'It's okay. Let me make you a cup of tea.'

She waved him away. 'No, it's all right—I can do it. I just need to check on Tori.'

'You check on Tori. I'll make us both a cup of tea.'

She nodded assent and led him into the kitchen, where he crouched down to say hello to Tori, then busied himself opening cupboards and the fridge to find everything he needed to make them both a drink.

With a steaming mug of peppermint tea beside her on the table, she glanced at Cole uncertainly and found him staring at her.

'Penny for them?' He raised an eyebrow and smiled gently. No judgement. Just friendship.

She hated the fact that she'd allowed a distance to build between them. He was a good man, no matter what had happened between them. Yes, he was here for Tori, but maybe he wanted to be her friend, too?

'It got a little too much for me tonight, that's all.'

He nodded. 'I get it. I mean, sweet potato is a tricky beast...'

She smiled at him. He was letting her off the hook.

'Tori wouldn't eat her dinner, and that was the final straw that brought my house of cards toppling down.'

'You're mixing metaphors, but I think I know what you're trying to say. Have you got a banana?'

A banana? What did that have to do with anything?

'Er...yes. Over there—above the fruit bowl.' She had a small hook there, that she could hang bananas from.

'My mum used to tell me that whenever I wouldn't eat my dinner I would get a banana instead, so that I didn't wake up hungry in the night.'

She smiled, imagining him as a small boy. 'But Tori doesn't want to eat anything.'

'Have you tried it?'

'Well, no, but—'

He peeled the banana, broke it in half and handed it to Tori, who grasped it with utter joy and mashed it straight into her mouth.

Lane shook her head in disbelief. 'You've got to be kidding me.'

'Sometimes babies pick up on stress, too. Perhaps she could sense your...unhappiness?'

He was broaching a subject she wasn't happy about him approaching. 'Maybe.'

'Want to talk about it? I'm a good listener.'

'I'm not sure you're the best person to tell.'

'Well, who would you normally talk to about this?'

She sighed. 'Skye.'

'But she's not here.'

No, and he didn't need to remind her about that. Just the thought made tears prick the backs of her eyes again. It had been such a difficult year. Skye's cancer, Simon's ulti-matum, all the *loss*, then taking on Tori and finding Cole.

Kissing him.

Being rejected by him.

Feeling used.

Should he be the one she spoke to about this?

'I've lost people, too,' he said. 'Lost what I never expected to lose. My heart. My wife. My unborn child. And then I learned that I'd lost the first few months of Tori's life. Lost the chance of getting to know her mother.'

She swallowed hard. 'You can't miss Skye?'

'I feel cheated of the chance to get to know who she truly was. She was the mother of my child and I feel I should have known her better. Should have supported her as she went through something so terrifying. As a doctor, I could have helped.'

'Her doctors couldn't do anything. It was too far progressed.'

'I know. But I would have liked the opportunity to meet Skye—to look into her eyes and let her know that I would help look after our daughter in the way she would have wanted. Help give her the best life.'

A tear slipped down her cheek and she hurriedly wiped it away. No more tears. Not tonight.

Could Cole give Tori a better life than what Lane could offer? 'Skye would have appreciated that.'

'I guess instead I can tell you.'

He was staring at her. Deep into her eyes. And she couldn't look away. It was intense. Intimate. Daring.

'I'm no fly-by-night, Lane. I'm dedicated. All my life I've wanted two things—to be a doctor and to be a father. This is my second chance; I'm not losing it.'

She stared back. 'But what if we ruin it?'

He frowned. 'What do you mean?'

'I love Tori and she's all I have left of Skye, and…' She couldn't finish the sentence. Couldn't say the words that had just formed properly for the first time in her mind. She was too busy analysing them herself. Thinking of what they meant.

'And...?' He leaned forward.

On the floor between them Tori had finished the banana—except for a few mashed bits around her fingers and thumb. These she ignored, so that she could play with her bricks.

'And... I love her. Like she's my own.' She couldn't voice her true fears.

He pressed his hand over hers on the table. 'We both do.'

She pulled her hand free and got up from the table. 'But you're her real father. Her real parent. Shouldn't she be with you? I'll never have the connection with her that you do.'

He stood. 'You will always be part of her life, Lane.'

She turned, feeling a fire in her belly. 'I've been her everything! I've been her mother these last few months, I was the one who stepped up, I was the one who sacrificed my life! And for what? To feel like this? Like I'm nothing, compared to you? If we shared her, how would that work?'

'We'll find a way.'

She raised a disbelieving eyebrow. 'Tori needs to have her bath now,' she said.

He sighed, clearly realising they weren't going to settle anything. 'Let me do it.'

'You don't know how she likes it.'

'Then I'll learn. Show me.'

So she did. She told him how deep the water needed to be. The right temperature and how to test it properly.

Which toys Tori liked best in the bath. Her favourite flannel with the clown faces on it. How much bubble bath to use.

And he did it. He bathed her. Played with her.

Lane looked on from the doorway, acknowledging to herself that this was what it was going to feel like as Cole took on more.

If she allowed it. It was an uncomfortable feeling.

'I'm just going to tidy up downstairs,' she said as Cole was drying Tori off and putting on her pyjamas. 'I'll get her last bottle ready.'

She went downstairs and picked up Tori's toys, her teddies, her blocks, putting them all away in a box behind the sofa. With everything away, she tried to tell herself that this was what her future would look like when Cole took on more responsibility. Empty and alone. Simon warned her not to do this. To take on a child that wasn't hers.

It was too much—too depressing to think about.

She turned and went back into the kitchen, making up Tori's bottle. It was time for her to go to bed. She guessed he'd want to do that, too. Learn her routines.

Stupidly, she'd never thought this would happen! She'd been so convinced that when she tracked him down she'd find some sleazeball who would dismiss Tori and walk away. But of course he'd not been like that, had he? He was kind and considerate and caring. He was a good doctor. A good friend. She had no doubt that he would be a good father, too.

As her legal guardian, she would always be a part of Tori's life, but what would she actually be? An outsider? A pretender? Someone who Tori came to view as a nuisance, because she wanted to spend time with her biological parent?

Slowly, with heavy feet, she climbed the stairs. At the top he waited for her, with Tori in his arms, babbling happily. A father with his daughter—as it should be. She should be happy for him. But she knew *his* happiness could cause *her* sorrow.

'Can I put her to bed?'

She passed him the bottle. 'Sure. I normally read to her as she drinks her milk.'

'Okay. Does she have a favourite story?'

'I'll show you.' She led him into Tori's room and passed over the book, watching as he lay Tori down with her bottle. Then she stood in the doorway and listened to him as he read the story, doing all the right funny voices and gently closing the book at the end when he realised that Tori was fast asleep.

They both crept out of her room and he half closed the door behind them. 'She must have been tired,' he said.

'She's very good at going to bed. I've never had any trouble with her.'

'It's because you look after her so well. She's a credit to you.'

She nodded, accepting the compliment. 'Thank you. I'm sure you'll find your way with her routines...'

There was a pause and she looked up at him, hopelessly. Closing her eyes in desperation and shaking her head at the unspeakable. Knowing he would understand that she simply had no more words for the pain in her heart and the fear she felt at the possibility of sharing Tori.

'I'm sorry I upset you on your birthday,' he said suddenly. 'At the fair. With the kiss. I didn't mean to imply it was a mistake. I just got scared, that's all.'

Her heart began to pound in her chest. 'I was scared, too.'

'So much has gone before and… I just didn't want to get into a situation where I let you down. Where I failed you. Us getting involved would be…'

She barely heard his words. Standing there so close, staring deeply into his eyes, she could feel herself edging closer and closer, her hands upon his chest…

And then they were kissing!

It was as if neither of them could help it. They were drawn together. Pulled together. Magnetic. Each needing the other. She could feel him beneath her hands, the strong beat of his heart, the solid muscles beneath his skin, the taste of him in her mouth—it was all she could do to remember how to breathe!

She wanted to absorb every ounce of him, feel every inch of him…

Her hands pulled at his shirt, tucked into his trousers, and searched beneath for his hot skin, the taut muscles of his belly, his chest, his back.

She needed his hands on *her*.

She broke the kiss. 'Come with me.'

She pulled him towards her bedroom, reaching for his shirt buttons the second they got inside.

He pulled her top over her head and his lips found her neck, her throat, and she gasped at the feel of his mouth upon her, the slick swipe of his tongue, the quick nip of his teeth. Pleasure and pain…each as intense as the sensation before it.

She could feel his arousal pressed against her and she revelled in it. Wanted it. *Needed* it. Forget everything else—that didn't matter right now. No matter what, she was drawn to him. As if she couldn't stay away. Even when she'd tried to create a barrier between them it had caused her pain and a depression like no other. It was as if she couldn't breathe without him.

They fell onto the bed with her reaching for the buckle of his belt. Did she have a condom anywhere? In her bedroom drawer? She thought there might be one. When she'd lived with Simon she'd always kept a supply in there.

She reached for the drawer. Yanked it open and blindly searched for something that felt like a condom packet. She pulled something out but it was a box of paracetamol. She threw it to the floor and reached in again. Cole was laughing, and this time she was successful.

Biting her lip with joy, she passed it to him and kissed him passionately. 'No surprise pregnancies this time,' she said.

He smiled and kissed her once again. 'Agreed.'

He woke to the sun peeping in through the curtains and a naked Lane spooning against him. She fitted perfectly, and he closed his eyes briefly as he relished the sensation of holding someone he—

Holding someone he *what*?

If it had been a mistake to kiss her, because it had made him scared, then what would *this* do to him?

But he was loath to break the contact. She felt so right in his arms, and last night had been...*wonderful*. He'd lost himself in this woman and it had felt so *good*. How could something that felt so right be a mistake? It couldn't, could it? Perhaps if they just took it slowly...?

Since he'd dropped her off after her birthday he'd felt awful about the way they'd parted. And then, at work, he'd not even been able to *talk* to her. To converse with her even about patients. It had been one of the hardest things he'd ever had to do—and he'd been through some tough things in his life, so that was saying something!

He'd never shut anyone out like that before. Not if he cared for them. If he had feelings for them. And why wouldn't he have feelings for Lane? She was a beautiful, intelligent woman and she was keeping his daughter safe and loved. If anything, she deserved his utmost respect, and he had treated her like a stranger.

At least they had moved past that now. But would she have doubts when she woke? Would she ask him to leave? Would she think he had slept with her to strengthen his connection to Tori?

He lifted his head to look at the clock. Nearly seven a.m. They'd have to get up for work soon. He'd like a shower if he could.

Lane moved slightly as she stirred against him and his thoughts instantly went to whether she'd want to share that shower with him. His hunger for her was not sated. He craved more.

He nuzzled into the back of her neck. 'Morning, sleepyhead.'

She stretched like a cat and then turned to kiss him. 'Good morning.'

'How long do we have?' he asked, thinking of the entirely different breakfast he could have this morning!

Lane glanced at the time. 'Not long enough. I bet she's already awake.'

'I'll go and get her.'

'She'll need a change of nappy.'

'Okay.' He kissed her on the tip of her nose and smiled at her. 'Are you okay? After last night?'

She nodded. 'More than okay. Are you?'

'I'm good.'

He gave her one last kiss and then threw back the covers and grabbed his boxers, pulling them on.

'Will you get her breakfast ready?'

'Yep. Do you want anything?'

'Whatever you're having is fine by me.'

She smiled. 'Jammy toast?'

'Sounds perfect.'

He went to get Tori and found Lane had been right. She was awake and gurgling away at her bunny in the corner of her cot.

Was this what it would be like to have a family? It felt right. But what if they were pushing things by making a giant leap like this? Yesterday they'd barely been talking and now… There was no going back now, was there?

But I feel happy right now. Why would I want to go back?

Because the last time you were happy it ended in tragedy.

He changed his daughter's nappy and carried her downstairs. His heart melted when she lay her head against his chest. She was such a loving little girl, with no idea yet of her sad history. Lane was doing a wonderful job, raising this little girl to be happy and bright despite how she must be feeling in dealing with the grief of her best friend's passing.

The smell of coffee and toast made his stomach rumble and he slid Tori into her highchair. Lane had already placed there some dry cereal, fruit and toasted soldiers, along with a bottle of milk.

'Can I help?'

She smiled at him and he loved the way she looked in the morning. Ruffled and sleepy and content.

'Everything's under control,' she said.

He poured some milk into his coffee and took a sip. Perfect! 'I have to leave soon.'

She turned at the counter, looking concerned. 'Oh? Why?'

'I can't turn up to work in the same clothes I left in. Mary would spot that a mile off.'

Lane relaxed a little. 'Okay.'

'I really enjoyed last night,' he told her.

'Me too.'

'Good. But we're going to have to be careful at work.'

She sat down at the table next to him, biting into a slice of toast. 'In case people notice that we're friends again?'

He reached for her hand. 'I think we might be more than that now.'

She smiled. 'Maybe…'

'And if Mary can spot that we're not talking to each other, she'll certainly spot that I'm looking at you in a different way.'

'In what way?'

'A way that says I've seen you naked and I'd like to see you that way again.' He grinned.

Lane covered Tori's ears and laughed. 'Shh… Not in front of the baby!'

CHAPTER NINE

LANE WAS IN a cheery mood when she dropped Tori off at her mother's house—so much so that her mum even commented on it. She tried to tell her that she'd just had a really good night's sleep, but she could tell her mum wasn't fooled. She would have to be much better at hiding her feelings when she got to work?

The sun was shining over Liberty Point Surgery when she arrived, and she spotted Cole's car already in the car park. She parked next to it and headed into work with a bright smile in place.

'Morning, everyone! Morning, Mary.' And there he was. 'Good morning, Dr Branagh!' she added as she passed him in the small kitchenette to get to the kettle.

'Good morning, Lane. How are you today?'

She smiled back. 'Very well, thank you. You?'

'I'm good!' he said, and headed off to his room.

And Lane smiled like the cat that had got the cream.

Mary came in, looking at her carefully. 'Okay, what's going on?'

She tried to look innocent. 'What do you mean?'

'You could barely look at each other yesterday and today you're all smiles like…' Mary paused as a thought struck her. 'Are you and he…*courting*?'

'Us?'

Mary grinned. 'I knew it! I knew it the second I saw you walking in here like everything's wonderful, sunshine and roses—and he hasn't shaved either!'

Lane tried to look puzzled and not to blush. 'I don't get you. What's him not shaving got to do with anything?'

'Well, clearly he had enough time to go home and get changed, but not enough time to have a shave. Dr Branagh has *never*—not once—turned up to work with anything less than a clean shave, *and* he has a twinkle in his eye and a spring in his step that I haven't seen since...' Her eyes darkened. 'Well, since Andrea...'

At the mention of Cole's dead wife the smile left Lane's face. 'You mustn't tell anyone, Mary. It's complicated.'

'Oh, lovey, it's *always* complicated. That's the nature of love.'

'Well, I don't know if we're *there* yet.'

Mary grabbed her mug from the kitchenette cupboard and grinned. 'I do.'

'You're hopeless! A hopeless romantic!'

'Well, in my day romance meant something. These days it's all sex and lust. Not that there's anything wrong with that—but in my experience it doesn't last. Love does.'

'Does it?'

Lane wasn't sure. She'd thought Simon had loved her the way she'd loved him and what had happened there? He hadn't been able to bear to share her at all. Had tried to isolate her. Given her cruel ultimatums and then blamed her when their relationship collapsed.

Was she being foolish, falling for Cole's charms? Naïve? Was she re-enacting history once again? Doomed to fail and never to measure up?

What if this relationship failed? If they even had a relationship! They'd spent one night together. Had that been lust? Or romance?

I don't know. Can't it be both?

'Love endures all things,' said Mary. 'What's that quote that says all couples who are meant to be are the ones who go through all the rubbish designed to tear them apart but come out so much stronger than anyone could ever imagine?'

Lane shrugged. 'I don't know. Is it in The Bible?'

Mary laughed. 'No, lovey—I think it was a meme on social media.'

She couldn't help but laugh, too. The idea of Mary being au fait with what was happening on the internet seemed odd. It didn't seem her thing.

But then Mary got serious. 'I like you, Lane, but I've known Dr Branagh for much longer and I know what he's been through. He doesn't need any more turmoil in his life. He doesn't need any more grief. Please don't cause him any. He's a good man.'

'I know he is. I won't hurt him, Mary. I promise.'

'Good. Now, then, let's get those doors open and let our patients in. We've got some work to do.'

Lane welcomed in her first patient—an elderly lady of seventy-two who was there for a hypertension review.

Lane greeted her and indicated that she should sit down. 'How have you been, Mrs Walker?'

'Just fine! As far as I know!'

'Been taking your medication regularly?'

Mrs Walker nodded.

'No headaches, nosebleeds?'

'None at all.'

'That's good. And have you been keeping track of your blood pressure at home? You have your own machine, don't you?'

'Sometimes I forget, but it's generally all right. Here's my last set of readings.'

She passed over an A4 sheet of paper with her blood pressure readings taken each morning and night. They were generally a little higher than Lane would like, but weren't sky-high.

'We'll do a blood test today—is that all right?'

'Of course. Anything you have to do.'

Lane began to gather the equipment she would need.

'I hear that you have a little one? A baby girl—is that right?'

'Er…yes…'

'Someone told me that her father is Dr Branagh?'

Lane froze. What had Mrs Walker heard? And who was talking about them?

'I'm sorry?'

'I don't mean to interfere, and it's really none of my business, but I do admire Dr Branagh so much. And when his wife died… Well, I'm sure you understand. To find out that he has a child after all is…' Mrs Walker searched for the right words.

Atrocious? A scandal? Gossip for the grapevine?

'Just wonderful for him. He so deserves happiness.'

Lane nodded. 'So does everyone else.'

Why was everyone so concerned about Cole's happiness? What about hers? *She* wanted to be happy, too!

'Could you roll up your sleeve for me, please?'

Lane performed the blood test and then used the patient's other arm to take a blood pressure reading. It was still a little high. One hundred and forty-two over one hundred and one. But perhaps Mrs Walker was excited about all the gossip? Or nervous about the blood test? Only she hadn't seemed nervous…

'We'll do another reading in a moment.' She tapped her assessment into the computer. 'What sort of exercise are you getting each week, Mrs Walker?'

'I do a bit of walking. To the shops and things.'

'Anything else?'

'Not really.'

'You don't smoke, do you?'

'Not any more. I used to, years ago.'

'And what about your diet? Do you use a lot of salt in your cooking?'

'A bit. And I do like to add some to my meal when it's on the plate.'

'Maybe you could consider cutting down? Even if you just start off by not putting it on your meals at weekends?'

Mrs Walker considered it. 'I could, I suppose…'

Lane took Mrs Walker's BP for a second time and saw that it had come down slightly—which was better, even if it wasn't great.

'We'll use this lower reading. So, I'll get your bloods sent off and if you don't hear from us assume everything's normal.'

'All right. Is that it? Am I done?'

'You're all done.'

She smiled and watched as Mrs Walker began to amble her way from the room. The burning question broke free before she could stop it.

'Can I ask…how did you hear about Tori being Dr Branagh's daughter?'

The woman stopped at the door. 'I heard it from my

friend Alice. But I think she heard it from *her* friend...
erm... Caroline, I think...'

So it seemed their little secret was definitely out, then?
Someone must have heard about Tori. Had Cole said anything? He might have told his parents? Did he even *have*
any? And if they'd told people...

'Right. Okay.'

'We all think it's wonderful. He deserves happiness
after all he's been through.'

So you said.

Lane smiled and nodded. 'See you next year, Mrs
Walker,' she said, even though she knew she wasn't going
to be here for very much longer. Shelby would soon be
back and Lane and Tori would be long gone.

Unless...

Did she dare think that she might have a chance at a
future with Cole? Was he even on the market for another
relationship? Could she measure up to what he'd had with
his wife? What would it mean, sticking around here? She'd
get to keep Tori in her life, that was for sure, and Cole?
She really did like the idea of keeping Cole in her life.
But that would only be if she could believe he was nothing like the other men in her life. Like *Simon.*

She crossed her fingers without even thinking about
it. Touched the wood of the chair opposite her.

Lane would take all the luck she could get.

Later she and Cole drove to the park, put Tori in her buggy
and began to walk, hoping to find a nice spot. It seemed
lots of other people had had the same idea, and the park
was filled with sunbathers and families enjoying an ice
cream.

In the centre of the park there was a small café, and

next to it a small aviary filled with beautifully coloured budgies and canaries up high and ground quails on the floor below. There were lots of toddlers gazing in and squealing at the birds, which fluttered and flew about at each noise.

'There's a space over there.'

Cole pointed to a space where they could lay their picnic blanket and they headed over the grass to claim the spot. Behind them was a small flowerbed, filled with roses and edged with lavender, thick with busy bumblebees.

Lane laid out the blanket and then set about unloading the picnic she'd packed. There were sandwiches and sausage rolls, grapes and fruit, yoghurt, rice cakes, pâté and crackers. Simple fare that would be easy to snack on.

'Did I tell you we've become quite the talking point?' she asked.

Cole raised an eyebrow. 'Us?'

'Well, more you. And Tori. People know she's your daughter.'

'And they think you're her mum?'

'No. They seem to know I'm not. God only knows what explanation they've come up with for that.'

Cole shrugged his shoulders as he helped put some food into a small bowl that had a suction cup on the bottom, so Tori couldn't throw it to the ground from her buggy tray.

'We know the truth. That's what matters.'

'It doesn't bother you that people are talking about you behind your back?'

He shook his head. 'No. Not really. They talked plenty when I lost Andrea. You can't stop gossip, can you?'

'But they could be saying the wrong thing! What if they assume you had an affair while you were married?'

'Then Tori would be much older than she is. I can only hope and pray that my patients' mathematical skills are as acute as I would like them to be.' He popped a grape into his mouth and made an appreciative sound. 'These are good.'

He stuck the bowl to Tori's tray and waited for the little girl to start eating, then sat back cross-legged on the blanket.

'Does it bother you?' he asked.

She looked down at the ground, loath to admit that it did. Simon had spread some awful rumours about her after she'd chosen Skye and Tori over him.

'It does, doesn't it? Why?'

'I once had a big group of friends. My own... Simon's. When we split we were the hot topic. It was hard to go anywhere afterwards because of it. People took his side. People I'd thought would have my back. I tried to tell them the truth, but Simon was a very effective storyteller.'

'They shut you out?'

'It was like I'd had an affair.'

'People act weirdly in situations they don't fully understand.'

Suddenly Tori let out a cry, and Lane whipped her head round to look and saw a bee fly away from Tori's face. Had she been stung?

'Oh, my God! Tori!'

She scrambled to her feet at the same time as Cole and tried to look at the baby's face, but it was hard because Tori was crying and her face was red and blotchy.

'Did it sting her? Where did it get you, sweetie? Tell

me…show me where it hurts.' She turned to Cole. 'What if we need ice?'

'She'll be okay. We don't know if it stung her. Besides, it flew away—don't bees die after they lose their sting?'

'I don't know. Why won't she stop crying?' Lane was jiggling her up and down, trying her best to soothe her.

'Here, let me try.'

Cole took Tori from her arms and began to gently sway her from side to side, but there was a look on his face that alarmed her.

'What is it?'

'Her face is beginning to swell.'

'That's the sting, right?'

'Could be… But there's also the flushing and… Are those hives?'

Lane tried to see, but it was hard. 'I don't know.'

'Let me listen to her breathing. Take her pulse.'

'Oh, come on—it can't be that bad.'

'Was Skye allergic to bee stings?'

Lane stopped, her blood chilling at a long-forgotten memory. 'There was a wasp sting once… The swelling lasted a few days, but she didn't get seriously ill or anything!'

Cole's face showed deep concern as he listened to Tori's laboured breathing.

'Call an ambulance. *Now!*'

CHAPTER TEN

HE'D THOUGHT THEY'D be having a lovely picnic in the park, enjoying being part of their new, weird family unit, but instead he was standing at the bedside of his daughter as a strange doctor injected her with epinephrine.

Her anaphylaxis had been rapid onset and had affected her breathing. The paramedics, when they'd arrived, had thankfully had a pen they could use to inject Tori with, and the doctors had given her another dose. Her pulse was getting stronger, but she was unconscious still and he felt awful. Helpless.

He couldn't lose Tori the way he'd lost Andrea and their baby. He hated feeling helpless, knowing that Mother Nature had struck his family yet again.

Why was this happening to them?

Was he doomed? Cursed? Destined to lose everyone the second he got close to them? The second he gave someone his heart, fate thought it was fair game to rip it out of his chest for a bit of fun?

'This is all my fault,' he said.

'No, No, it's not. It's mine. I should have remembered... considered... But it had never happened before, I...'

He looked at Lane on the opposite side of the bed. Both of them, despite their training, had gone into a panic with no EpiPen in sight, no medical equipment that could help them, no convenient doctor's surgery with its whole stock room in an emergency. They'd been ordinary people, with a just a phone and fear in their hearts at watching a loved one almost slip away.

'We could have lost her,' he said.

'We didn't.'

'But we could have. We should have been better prepared.'

Lane shook her head. 'How were we to know?'

He didn't want to say it, but... 'When Skye had her reaction, what happened?'

Lane looked blank. 'I don't know. I wasn't there. It happened when she was a lot younger.'

'But you'd been friends since you were small?'

'Yes. But it didn't happen when she was with me. It was on a day trip with the children's home, or something. I just remember her telling me about it once. An offhand comment about seeing the doctor because her leg had swelled up so badly she could hardly walk. I just assumed she'd had a bad reaction to the sting—I couldn't possibly have known that her daughter would be severely allergic!' She stared at him. 'You don't blame me, do you?'

He shook his head. 'Of course not! I'm just trying to get this straight in my head—there's nothing like this in my family medical history.'

The doctors with them issued an instruction to the nurses present to keep a watchful eye on Tori, then the lead doctor turned to Lane.

'She's had a bad shock, but she's getting better. We've stopped the main reaction and I'm very sure she'll wake up soon. We'll keep her on oxygen until she does, and the nurses will keep an eye out and make sure you go home with an EpiPen or two for future incidents.'

Cole raised an eyebrow. 'Future incidents? We're never letting her outside again!'

The doctor smiled. 'Everyone reacts like that, but she'll be okay. It just takes time to adjust to a new normal, that's all.'

'Thank you, Doctor. You're sure she'll wake up soon?' asked Lane.

'Absolutely. Her body shut down briefly, but all her vitals are coming back up to normal. You just sit and wait. I'll be around if you need a chat.' He patted Lane on the shoulder and then went on to his next patient.

Cole reached out for Tori's hand and grasped it in his own. It seemed so small and delicate. Like a rag doll's.

He brought it to his lips and kissed it. 'I'm never letting go again.'

Lane didn't want to leave Tori's bedside. She felt that if she took her eyes off her for even a second then something terrible would happen—like it had in the park.

If I'd been paying attention to Tori instead of worrying about gossip, for goodness' sake!

It was haunting to be back in a hospital. The last time she'd been in one it had been with Skye, hearing a doctor tell her that there wasn't any more they could do.

But Tori was breathing normally again. Her airway was clear, her skin was beginning to settle down from the bright red it had first become, and her observations on the monitor were practically normal.

Tori made a noise in her sleep, her eyelids flickering. 'She's dreaming.'

'I hope they're good dreams,' Cole said.

They could still see the indentation on Tori's neck where the bee sting had been, just under her chin. It was like a marker, pointing out their failure to protect her from harm. Lane still couldn't believe she hadn't considered the bee any danger. Wasn't she supposed to be Tori's guardian? Guardians *guarded*. They protected. And Lane hadn't done her job properly.

'Me, too.'

The nurse had brought them a cup of tea, but the drinks sat cooling on the side, both of them unwilling to take their eyes off Tori for a minute.

'At least we'll know going forward. And we'll have medication on hand in case of emergencies.'

Lane nodded. 'We'll have to make sure that when she starts nursery they have one in stock, too. Or should it be two?'

'It's two.'

'Right…'

'I guess one of us is going to have to stay overnight with her.'

Lane volunteered. 'I'll do it. You have work in the morning. I don't.'

'Will you be all right?'

She smiled. 'I have plenty of doctors at my beck and call, if needed.'

'Let's hope they're not. I feel awful at leaving her. What if she wakes and I'm not here?'

'She'll have me.'

She didn't see the look on his face. The one that said he wanted her to have *him*, too. 'You'll call me if anything changes?'

'Of course.'

He got up from his side of the bed and walked round

to her, taking her in his arms. For a moment they stood together, holding each other, taking comfort. It felt good to be in his protective arms again, and she couldn't imagine ever wanting to let go. But his patients needed him. He had a full clinic tomorrow.

She closed her eyes as he kissed the top of her head and squeezed her once more. 'I can be here at a moment's notice. Keep me updated, won't you?'

'Promise.'

They kissed goodbye and he kissed Tori on the cheek, whispering something she didn't catch in her ear. And then he grabbed his jacket and he was gone.

She watched him leave, knowing how hard it must be for him to do so.

Lane settled back beside the bed and lay her head on her elbows. She would watch Tori until she fell asleep herself.

'She's up, she's happy, and she's demolishing her breakfast.'

Cole listened to Lane's happy and very much relieved voice on the other end of the phone. He was so glad! He'd barely slept a wink the night before, only getting about an hour's worth after coming home from the hospital. He'd hated leaving Tori and Lane behind. He'd felt as if he was deserting them.

Today was the first day in his entire life that he really didn't want to be at work. Usually he was happy to go in, with a spring in his step, ready to see how he could help people that day. Even after losing Andrea and the baby he'd only had a few weeks off, and had returned to work feeling brighter and ready to work, welcoming the distraction.

But today he wasn't thinking about work. He was

thinking about how he'd nearly lost his little girl when he'd only just found her. How the doctors wouldn't have been able to tell him anything without Lane being there because he had no legal rights to Tori at all. No rights about her care…her welfare.

His time with Tori had been working out great. She wasn't afraid of him, she gave him cuddles, wrapping her little arms around his neck in a big squeeze that made his heart sing. She smiled when he came into the room and sat down beside her to play. She shared her toys with him, let him feed her, bathe her, put her to bed—all the things a real father would do.

He never wanted to lose that. *Ever.*

But she was in good hands. The hands of doctors. In a hospital. And Lane was by her side and she'd done a damned good job of keeping her safe and healthy so far— though he knew she felt guilty for not suspecting there might be an allergy to bee stings.

What was scary was how rapid onset the symptoms had been. How quickly Tori had gone from crying at the pain of the sting to almost losing her airway and passing out.

He never wanted to feel that scared again. That helpless. Never wanted to feel so lost. Surely it was time he looked into the possibility of making his relationship with Tori official? Make plans for the future? He knew he'd have to ask Lane, but he felt sure she'd be fine with it…

His first patient was Marcus Darby, who was in for a chat about his mental health. Marcus had been struggling of late, and Cole had upped his medication dosage and arranged counselling and cognitive behavioural therapy to get Marcus to cut down on some of his OCD rituals.

'How's it going today, Marcus?'

'Not bad, Doctor. Not bad. It only took me about twenty minutes to leave the house this time.'

'Twenty minutes? That's good. How long did it take you before?'

'A good hour, once I'd finished checking everything.'

'And what do you find yourself checking?'

'That the cooker is off. That the lights are off and the front door is locked properly.'

'How many repetitions are you doing?'

'Ten of each. I've cut down, though, so I'm happy with that.'

'So, do you think the counselling is helping?'

'A bit. She's made me see how my thinking is a vicious circle, feeding each behaviour, and she's given me some different ways to think about my rituals, so they cause me less panic.'

'That's good—good that you understand repeating the same behaviours over and over again may *seem* like a safety belt, but in fact what they're doing is tying you up more and more, trapping you in a cycle.'

'Exactly. I'm not trying to cut the behaviours out completely, but I'm getting them down to a manageable level first, before taking the next step.'

'And you've not replaced old behaviours with new ones?'

Marcus shook his head. 'No. I don't think so. I notice when new worries start up and I talk to myself out loud, with alternative opposite thoughts, until they seem less worrying.'

'So you're able to help yourself? That's good progress, Marcus. You should be proud.'

'Thanks, Doc.' He smiled.

'So you're happy to carry on as you are at the moment? You don't feel the need to change your dosage again?'

'I'm happy as it is. Maybe later, when I'm better, we can look at reducing.'

'One step at a time. Let's not rush this. It's easy to drop back into old habits if we move too fast.'

'All right. Well, thanks, Doc, it was good to see you again.' He reached out to shake Cole's hand.

Cole bade him goodbye and started writing up his notes into the system. When he was done, he checked his phone to make sure there weren't any messages from Lane.

He missed her. Missed having her close. Having her in the next room. For the last few weeks they'd been getting close, and though that had been a scary prospect at first, and he'd almost backed away at one point, now he could see just how much he'd needed her lately. Her being close by made him feel better. The touch of her hand. Her beautiful smile. The way she would try to cheer him when he was feeling blue.

It had been a long time since he'd had someone care for him like that. No one since Andrea, anyway.

It felt good to have that back. A partner. Someone with the same goals as him. A shared purpose.

His feelings for Lane had intensified of late, and although it scared him to think about what that might mean, he kept telling himself that it was okay. As long as they just took it one day at a time and didn't think too much about what the future held, then they could carry on as they were.

He didn't think she wanted anything more from him than that and that was good—because he wasn't sure just how much of himself he had to give. Because giving all his heart was too big an idea for him to contemplate right now.

She had some of it—he knew that. His feelings for her had got bigger and bigger with each night they'd spent together and each morning waking up in each other's arms, but...all of it?

That was too scary to contemplate.

That was too much.

He wouldn't admit anything more—not even to himself.

Day by day—that was all they needed to do.

And when he went to the hospital later he would take Tori a huge teddy bear.

He checked his phone again before admitting his next patient.

'She can go home.'

Cole froze, checked the doctor's face to make sure he wasn't joking. 'You're kidding? Already?'

'Her airway is clear; her observations are normal. She's eating and drinking well, passing urine and faeces—there's no reason to keep her here.'

'But...'

But it's unsafe out there.

The doctor seemed to understand. 'I know it's a scary prospect, but you're forewarned and therefore forearmed this time. You have her emergency kit—she'll be fine... let her live her life.'

'You mean don't keep her cooped up indoors?'

The doctor nodded. 'The temptation to do that—to wrap her in cotton wool—will be strong, but you must try to ignore it.'

Cole thought of his patient Marcus, and why he per-

formed all his safety behaviours to get rid of the worrying thoughts in his head, and began to understand him
even more. 'Okay…'

'You know where we are—and our doors are never
closed.'

'Well, let's hope we never have to walk through them
again.'

The doctor smiled, talked them both through the correct use of her emergency medication once again. and
then left them to pack up their belongings and leave. It
was amazing how much stuff they'd accumulated. Not to
mention the giant teddy bear, almost as big as Cole, that
he'd carried in just an hour ago.

Lane gave him a hug, then kissed him. It felt good to
get her reassurance. Her affection.

'We'll be okay. I'm sure of it,' she said. 'We'll tackle
this one day at a time.'

He was reassured that she was thinking the same way
as him. He nodded, and gathered all of Tori's bags and
her medication, and Lane sat the teddy bear on the back
of the buggy as she pushed Tori towards the exit and
home.

As they got to the front doors he felt a brief moment
of pure terror, imagining that every bee in the world
would somehow know that his daughter was vulnerable
and come buzzing down from the skies, but when they
emerged and nothing happened he relaxed a little. Not
much, but enough.

When Lane took his hand and squeezed it tightly he
knew that she'd felt the same thing, and he looked to her
with gratitude. They were in this together. He felt that

implicitly. They both had the same goal and that was to keep Tori safe, happy and loved.

One day at a time.

They'd promised not to wrap her in cotton wool and to live normally, but it was natural that they would be over-protective, and over the next couple of days they pretty much stayed in, popping out only to go to the supermarket.

Of course Cole was going to work every day, but he was rushing back to her house at night, to spend precious hours with Tori before bed.

Once, he didn't get to see her at all, as he had to go on a home visit one evening that turned into an emergency, meaning he'd gone with his patient to the hospital and waited until the patient's family arrived.

'You're a good man, Cole,' Lane had said, kissing him on the cheek when he'd finally come round late and passing him a longed-for cup of tea.

'I try… I know what it's like to be in hospital alone—and he was so nervous, waiting to see if he'd had a stroke or not. I couldn't walk away. It was my duty to stay.'

'And had he?'

Cole nodded unhappily. 'Afraid so. But he's in the best place now and he'll get great care there. The stroke team are excellent—I've had a few patients taken care of very expertly there.'

'Good. Now you're here, though, you can relax.' She reached for his tie and pulled it loose, unbuttoned the top button of his shirt and went on tiptoe to give him a kiss. 'Let me run you a shower.'

He groaned. 'Sounds wonderful. Thank you.'

'I could make it even better...' she said, with a cheeky smile.

'How so?' He raised an eyebrow.

'I could join you.'

'Well, forget the cup of tea—that sounds even more perfect.'

She started the shower and stood in front of him in the bathroom, slowly stripping him of his clothes, leaving only a smile.

As each piece of clothing was removed she allowed her hands to trace the musculature of his body as more and more of it was revealed. Then she began to take off her own clothes, and then she led him into the spray of water and steam.

She brushed his skin with soft, feather-light kisses, feeling his arousal grow and grow against her body. It was a potent feeling, knowing that *she* was doing that to him. That *she* had that power. That control. Could get that reaction from him.

He reached for her, pulling her closer, grinding her against him, and she smiled and sealed her lips against his in a deep, exploring kiss.

In the heat of the water and the heat of their bodies they allowed themselves to be consumed by the fire they felt within. These last few days they'd both been so stressed, with what had happened to Tori, and they'd been so confined by their fears. But now, with their daughter safely in bed, fast asleep, they could let out all the tension they'd been experiencing and enjoy the softer, more desirous side of life.

Lane moved against him, her soapy body pressed to his, feeling his hands upon her body, urgent and needful.

She groaned with pleasure and searched out his mouth, explored it with her tongue.

This man was all she needed right now.

And feeling this content. This happy…

When had she ever felt this way? She'd thought she had once, with Simon, but that had all been a lie. There'd been doubts with him even at the beginning, and she'd felt afraid for their future. She'd not been able to put her finger on it, and she'd put it down to it being her first ever long-term relationship. She'd been finding her feet… Learning… Not knowing if what she was doing was right, but hoping it was anyway.

But she'd got in too deep, too quickly. She'd had time to think since then. Now Lane was older, wiser, more cautious.

She had been terrified to take this step with Cole, knowing the complications of it, but it seemed to be working. He was a good man. Dedicated. Loving. Considerate of her and her feelings. He didn't seem to be with her just because it was good for his ego, nor did it seem that he was using her. She genuinely thought that Cole was with her because that was what he wanted. Not just because she came with Tori attached and to get access to one, he needed the other.

Yes, she was sure of it. As sure as her previously broken heart could be. And perhaps it was time for her to accept living in the present and forget about what the future held?

There came a time when you just had to make a leap of faith and trust in your instincts, and that was what she was doing now. She paused, remembering the fortune-teller's words, and smiled. Yes, she wanted to keep Cole in her life. He'd become so important to her and she couldn't imagine a future without him.

But right now was for having fun. Right now was for letting off steam and enjoying each other's bodies. No doubt they would dry each other off, go to bed and make love there, and in the morning she would wake in his arms again.

Life was almost perfect.

And she would do everything she could to make sure it stayed that way.

'Lane? If you're free could you pop into my room? I've a patient who might need a dressing—I thought you could give her a once-over.'

'Sure!'

She was just finishing another dressing, for a patient with a diabetic leg ulcer. She washed and dried her hands, entered the details of the wound assessment and the dressings used into the template on the computer, and went to see what she could do next door.

Cole's patient was an elderly lady with a bad cut to her leg.

'Oh, my goodness, how did you manage that?' Lane asked.

'In the garden. I had a fall and caught my leg on the chicken wire that sticks out from the chicken coop.'

'You have chickens?'

'Rescued ones. From those horrible farms they keep them in.'

'Oh, well… Well done, you. Right—let's have a little look at this, shall we? Are you prescribing any antibiotics?' Lane asked Cole.

She was worried about how dirty the chicken wire

might have been. She had no idea of what kind of germs and bugs dirty wire might be covered in.

'Not straight away. And tetanus status is up to date. So, let's dress it and see how it goes.'

'All right. I'll grab something to clean this first and then get some dressings on it. Wait here.'

She came back a moment later, and once they had the patient on the examination bed, raised to a suitable level for their backs, they began dressing the wound, with Lane doing the main work and Cole passing her tape and scissors and entering the details onto the practice system.

'There you go. All done. Tell Mary on the front desk we want to see you again in three days for a re-dressing. Twenty-minute appointment. But if it begins to feel odd before then, or you get hotness or pain, you call us straight away—okay?'

Lane pressed the button the bed that would lower it back down.

'Oh, thank you. You've both been so kind.'

'No problem at all. I'll leave you to it,' Lane said to Cole, and headed back to her own room to await her next patient, who was coming to have some staples removed after knee surgery.

As she sat at her own computer, to see if her patient had arrived yet—he had—she suddenly felt dizzy. It hit her like a wave. She gasped and had to hold her head to keep it steady, to try and fight what her inner ear told her was happening even though in reality it wasn't. She felt nauseous, and a cold, clammy sweat crawled over her. And then, as suddenly as it began, it disappeared.

She released her head carefully and blinked steadily, moving her head from side to side tentatively to see if it would come back. Nothing. Lane looked at the time on her computer. She hadn't eaten for hours. It had to be low blood sugar. She'd not had time to eat her breakfast that morning.

Dipping into her bag, she found a protein bar and ate that, and instantly felt better.

She called in her patient and examined his knee. It had healed very well. The wound was neat and dry, with no redness, no swelling, and no sign of residual infection, but stooping over him she could tell that her head still felt a little...*swimmy*.

Perhaps she was tired? Or maybe she had an ear infection? She'd been through a lot of stress lately with Tori, and perhaps she'd been working too hard? When had she last had a proper break?

It was hard, working almost full-time and looking after a baby, too. She'd been putting her own needs second to those of Tori, and to some degree Cole's too. And they'd been keeping each other awake at night—in the best possible way, of course!—but sometimes you just needed to sleep and get that full eight hours!

She decided to tell him that tonight they must just sleep. Maybe cuddle. But that was it. And that would be nice.

She smiled at the thought as she removed the staples in her patient's knee. 'This last one might pinch. It's very close to the edge of the wound.'

But her patient barely moved, and soon it was all done. She put a much smaller dressing over it as a temporary measure.

'Just leave this on for today, and then you can remove it. Take it easy over the next few weeks, and any problems, come straight back, okay?'

'Will do. Thanks.'

She waved him goodbye at the door and watched him

walk easily down the corridor towards the waiting room. Finally! Her morning clinic was done!

She covered the examination bed with fresh paper after wiping it down, and then settled down upon it—just to close her eyes for five minutes.

A cat nap… That was all she needed, and then she'd be back to normal working order for this afternoon.

CHAPTER ELEVEN

THE PASTA WAS bubbling away in the pot and she had garlic bread slowly going crispy in the oven. Cole was entertaining Tori whilst she prepped and cooked her own homemade tomato and basil sauce. Fresh tomatoes, garlic and basil, a splash of Worcester sauce, a couple of mushrooms and a chopped pepper. Simmering to perfection until it was ready. She served it with a grating of parmesan over each dish, yawning as she did so.

'Tired?' asked Cole.

'A little bit.'

'Maybe you should get an early night? I'll do the dishes and sort Tori out tonight. You go up. Read a book. Relax.'

'Oh, I couldn't do that.'

'Why not?'

She smiled. 'Well... Tori. She's my responsibility.'

'I'd like her to be mine, too. Let me take the reins. We've not spent much time on our own. When we've finished dinner go on up. Warm bath. Pyjamas. Sleep.'

She really did like the sound of that. It was so tempting... 'You wouldn't mind?'

'Course not! In fact, I'd love it. Not that I don't want to spend time with *you*, but me and my girl can have some one-to-one time.'

She crunched down on a piece of garlic bread. 'Okay. I accept your kind offer, good sir.'

'Great! And, if it's okay, I thought after dinner I could take Tori out in her buggy, for a walk.'

'As long as you're careful and take her medication with you.'

'Of course. That way the house will be quiet, and you'll get to relax in that bath.'

'Wow, keep spoiling me like this and I'll come to expect it every day.'

He smiled and twirled his fork in his pasta.

Had she said too much? Assuming there would be an *every day*…?

It was hard not to talk that way, with how well everything was going between them. In fact, she couldn't remember the last time she'd been so content and so happy. Was it wrong to talk about what was going to happen between them? Perhaps she should just enjoy each day as it came and not push for anything? No point in tipping over the apple cart. She reminded herself to just enjoy the present, even if she *was* worried about how absorbed they were in each other as a small unit.

But this had happened with Simon. Was it a tendency of hers?

'You know what would go great with this? Wine.' Cole got up and opened a bottle of red.

She smiled as he poured some into her glass. 'Cheers!'

She finished her meal, mopping up her plate with the rest of the garlic bread. She really had been dreadfully hungry, and even managed a small bowl of chocolate mousse for pudding. Then, after a cup of tea, Cole put Tori in her buggy, ready to go out for their walk.

'When I get back I want to find you either in the bath,

relaxing, or fast asleep in bed,' he said, kissing her on the lips.

'Message received and understood.'

She yawned again and he laughed, kissing the tip of her nose. 'Go on, get up those stairs.'

'Yes, sir.' She laughed too, and gave him one last sultry kiss—it was to be their last one that day. 'I'll see you in the morning.'

Cole closed the front door behind him and happily pushed Tori's buggy ahead of him as they began their walk. This was his very first time out with Tori on his own and he was determined to enjoy every moment of it.

Of course, he hoped to have many more moments alone with her in the future, but today was the first. A novelty. A gift, showing that Lane trusted him to be alone with her. And he fully appreciated her trust in *him*, knowing how hard it was for her to let go and allow someone else to look after Tori.

It blew his mind how anyone could have treated her the way that man had. That Simon she'd known. He sounded awful. She was well shot of him.

'Da-da-da-da-da!'

Cole smiled at Tori. She'd only recently started saying this and he was so proud that he'd been there to hear it. 'Yes, sweetheart. Daddy. Look! Can you see the big doggy coming?'

A man was walking towards them with a giant-looking dog. He wasn't sure of a lot of dog breeds, but he knew this one was a Newfoundland. It looked like a giant shaggy bear. He nodded at the man, who nodded back as they passed.

Cole had never been so happy in his entire life! Out

with his daughter. Doing *daddy* things. Wasn't this what he'd always wanted in life? To be a doctor and to be a father? And now he had both. Life couldn't give him any more surprises.

He was settled and they were happy.

Lane woke with what felt like a cold brewing. She propped herself up in bed on one elbow and was aware of a scratchiness in her throat and a blocked nose and silently cursed at the inconvenience. But it wasn't surprising. She often found that when she started a new job—whether in a new doctors' surgery or on a new ward in a hospital—she would come down with something as she adjusted to the new germs that populated that area.

She slipped her feet into her slippers, grabbed her bathrobe and went downstairs to make herself some hot water and lemon…maybe take a paracetamol or two.

Cole joined her a few moments later.

'Sorry, did I wake you?' she asked.

'No, I was awake anyway. Have you got a cold?'

She blew her nose on a tissue. 'Yes—unfortunately.' She could hear it in her own voice. All blocked up and nasally.

'Typical. The one day I've got that safeguarding training and I won't be at the surgery to look after you.'

She pecked him on the cheek. 'It's just a cold. I can fight this myself—don't worry.'

'Just make sure you take it easy.'

She laughed. 'With a full day of appointments? Sure!'

He pulled her into his arms. 'I prescribe a full course of hugs and perhaps a foot-rub when you get home tonight.'

'I'll take that medicine, Doctor, thank you. Now, off you go! Get ready. Haven't you got to be there by nine?'

He sighed and reluctantly allowed himself to be pushed away. 'Yes. All right. But call me if you need anything.'

'Will do. Now, *go!*'

He left the house, and literally five minutes afterwards Lane did the same, so she could get Tori to her mum's house, so she could get to work. She didn't kiss Tori goodbye, not wanting to give her the cold, but instead blew her a kiss from the doorway.

When she got to work she was feeling decidedly snottier than earlier, and her body was beginning to ache, so she took paracetamol, washed down with some juice, and used a nasal inhaler she'd bought from a pharmacy on the way in. It helped to some degree, opening up her nasal passages and allowing her to breathe better. She'd just soldier on.

She called her first patient down. 'Gemma Rush, please.'

'Hi, thanks for seeing me so promptly,' said the woman. 'I've got to go to work in the next few minutes.'

'All right... So, you're here for a BP check?'

'Yes. I've been on the pill for a while and the doctor asked me to get it done, so...'

'Let me just get the blood pressure machine.' Lane got the equipment from a cupboard and set it down. 'Okay... Keep your feet flat on the floor and try not to speak. That can raise the numbers somewhat.'

'Okay.'

Lane turned to activate the blood pressure template on the system, so she could enter the results, and realised her head felt a little weird again. It had to be the cold. It couldn't be because she was tired—she'd slept so well last night.

The machine's cuff deflated and Gemma's readings appeared on the screen. They were very good. One twenty over seventy-two, which was perfect.

She showed Gemma, who smiled and rolled her sleeve back down. 'So I can carry on taking the pill, then?'

Lane nodded—then wished she hadn't.

'Are you okay?' asked her patient. 'You look a little… off.'

Lane laughed awkwardly. 'I'm fine. I'm meant to be taking care of *you*, not the other way around! It's just a cold—I'll be fine. You'd better get off to work.'

Gemma smiled, reassured. 'Okay, well—thanks again for seeing me so early.'

'No problem. Take care.'

Gemma left and the smile dropped from Lane's face. She really was beginning to feel rough. Light-headed and shivery and…

She decided to close the door to her room, needing a moment to take a breather, but when she stood up the room began to spin, and before she knew what was happening the world faded to black.

She was completely out of it by the time she hit the floor.

She didn't know how much time had passed, but when she began to blink her eyes open she was lying on her side, on the floor of her consultation room, and Mary and the other doctors were looking at her with concern.

'Oh, thank goodness! I knew you didn't look right when you came in. How are you feeling?' Mary asked.

Dr Summer had his hand on her wrist, feeling for her pulse, and Dr Green was slipping the blood pressure cuff over her other arm.

'I'm fine! Just a cold. I'm okay now.'

'You fainted.'

'It's this head cold.'

'Seems more like flu. Your temperature is sky-high. I want you to go home for the rest of the day and take it easy,' said Dr Summer.

'But I've got patients!'

She couldn't go home! She had a full clinic, and she knew how awful it would be for Mary to ring all those people and cancel their appointments, make them for another day.

'They'll understand. Can you get home safely?'

'I drove here.'

Dr Summer thought for a moment. 'I'll drive you back. It won't take me long—people will understand. You can pick your car up another time.'

'Okay…' He helped her to her feet. She felt a little woozy still, but better than before. 'But no one tell Cole.'

Mary shrugged and smiled. 'I'm afraid we already have…'

Cole was listening to the safeguarding leader, making notes as he liked to do, when a text popped onto his phone.

Please call the surgery.

He frowned a little. What could that be about? He would only be here for a couple of hours. What had happened that needed his attention? The other doctors were more than capable of sorting out any problems. Unless it was something personal…

His first thought was to worry about Tori. Had she been stung again? But if that was the case then the text would have come from Lane, surely?

Unless the problem was with Lane? Was she hurt?

The thought of that disturbed him greatly, and he had a flashback to what had happened with Andrea.

Lane hadn't seemed very well that morning. She'd said it was only a cold, but what if it was something else? His mind raced a mile a minute. She'd been sniffing a lot...

As his thoughts naturally went to the tragic, he recalled a hospital story of how a patient had thought he had a bad cold, and was sniffing, and it had turned out he was leaking brain fluid through his nose.

It was a million to one chance—but so was being killed in an avalanche. Or by a bee sting!

His panic caused him to hurry out of the training room, and with trembling fingers he dialled the surgery.

Mary answered. 'Oh, Dr Branagh. Thank you for calling so quickly.'

'What is it, Mary?'

'It's Lane. She fainted.'

His heart began to pound. He *knew* it! It was all about to go terribly wrong for him—as it always did!

'How is she?'

'She's okay. Dr Summer gave her a thorough check-up and then drove her home.'

'Right... Okay...'

'He thinks she has the flu, and maybe an ear infection.'

Okay. Dr Summer was a good doctor. Thorough. He trusted him implicitly. If he said Lane had the flu, then that was probably it.

But it still didn't stop him from being scared out of his wits.

'Okay. I've got about another hour here, but I'll give her a quick call. Thanks, Mary.'

'No problem, Dr Branagh.'

He ended the call and let out a big sigh. Okay. She was fine. But to faint like that…?

Had she eaten breakfast this morning? He hadn't seen her eat anything. She'd had a hot water and lemon drink, but that was hardly filling, was it? He ought to have a word with her about looking after herself better…worrying him like this. But maybe later, when she was much better. She'd be feeling bad enough as it was.

He dialled her home number and she picked up after a couple of rings.

'Cole. Hi. They told you?'

'Yes. Are you all right?'

'I'm fine. Just… It was silly, really, I didn't eat anything this morning—I didn't feel like it—and then I took some paracetamol and a nasal inhaler, and my head was thick, and I got a little giddy…'

'A little giddy?'

'I passed out. But I've forced down some toast now, and I'm sat in front of morning television—which is really quite dire, I might add—with my feet up and I'm doing nothing.'

'Good.' She sounded okay, but that didn't stop him from worrying.

'I feel bad, though. All those patients that have got cancelled—'

'They will understand perfectly. Don't worry about them. An ear syringing can wait a day or two.'

'But Mr Cilliers has his big dressing today, and—'

'One of the nurses can squeeze him in. He won't miss out. You just concentrate on you. Will you be all right for a little while longer? I've got to complete this training, and then I've got an afternoon clinic, but I could pop home at lunchtime to check on you?'

It occurred to him that he'd called her place *home*. Was that wrong? It had felt right, saying it. He'd spent more time there than at his own place recently. But perhaps all this was moving too fast? They'd only just started to get to know one another and they were practically living together, like a family, and…

Was that it? Was he mistaking the convenience of their situation for something more? Calling her place home… It *wasn't* his home. He had one of those. And this scare with Lane's health…what if it had been something terrible?

'You don't have to do that,' she said.

'I know, but I will. You keep watching dreadful TV and I'll see you later.'

She chuckled. 'All right. And I might have a snooze.'

'You do that. Bye.'

'Bye.'

He stared at his phone for a moment and then put it into his pocket. He really ought to get back inside, but he couldn't help worrying. She'd sounded fine, and it certainly did seem as if she'd just not eaten breakfast and then done too much. And if this head cold had given her an ear infection too…

He'd feel better once he saw her for himself—that was all it was.

He would think about everything else later.

Lane was woken by the sound of the front door closing and she realised she must have forgotten to lock it, before falling asleep. She pulled herself up to a better seating position.

What time is it? I'm ravenous!

'Lane?'

She smiled, hearing his voice. He was so good to her! He hadn't needed to come, yet he had.

'I'm in the lounge!'

'Well, stay there. I'm just going to get you something from the kitchen.'

She pointed the remote at the television, muting it, and then found another big smile emerging onto her face when Cole came in, bearing a tray with a hot bowl of soup on it, with a crusty bread roll, and a small curl of butter on a plate.

'Oh, Cole! You didn't have to go to so much trouble!'

He simply smiled.

The soup smelled delicious! 'Is it chicken?'

'Yes.'

'Where did you get it from?'

'There's a stall on Bourton High Street that does home-made soups, filled jacket potatoes—that kind of thing. I've been there before to get lunch when I've been out on home visits. The woman makes her own bread rolls, you know. Try it. It's sourdough.'

Lane pulled off a small hunk and took a bite. It was gorgeous! She dipped another piece into the soup. 'Aren't you eating, too?'

'I got enough for two. I just wanted to make sure you got yours first.'

He disappeared into the kitchen and came back with his own serving. He sat on the floor by the coffee table and they ate companionably in silence, until their bowls were empty and their tummies were full.

'You look pale,' he said.

'Do I?' He seemed upset by something. Was he worrying about her having passed out at work?

'Yes. You should be in bed.'

'I don't want to give in to it.'

'It's not giving in. It's being sensible. Will you do as I suggest?'

She looked at his face and nodded. He wanted the best for her, and perhaps he was struggling with what was going on between them, too? It had to be a lot for him to take in. Things had been moving so fast between them and he knew about what had happened between her and Simon. Did he think she was being the same way with him?

Everything was so uncertain. This taking-things-day-by-day lark was difficult when there were no certainties in life. And there were still all the legalities to sort out.

'I've called your mum. She's going to keep Tori until I can pick her up after work, and then I'm coming home to make you dinner.'

'I can do it. I'm quite capable.'

'I know you are. But you've had a bit of a scare today. So have I. And neither of us need any more of those, thank you very much. Let me make sure you're rested—you can come back to work when you feel better. Mary was quite frightened to find you like that.'

Oh. She'd not thought about that. Poor Mary. She would have to apologise to her, and also thank her for taking care of her so well. 'Fine. I'll go to bed.'

'Good.'

He stared at her for a moment and then stooped down to give her a kiss, holding her face in his hands. He looked deep into her eyes, his face serious once again. 'Don't you ever scare me like that again—do you hear?'

She nodded. 'I promise.'

CHAPTER TWELVE

THE NEXT WEEK was rough. Lane had continued to fight the flu, but she'd slowly begun to feel stronger under Cole's watchful eye. And when she was able to get back to work she went straight over to Mary and gave her a big hug.

'What's that for?' she asked.

'For looking after me. I'm sorry if I scared you.'

'Nonsense. I did what I had to do. Thank goodness for all that first aid training we have to do, right?'

Lane laughed and nodded. 'Comes in handy at times.'

Mary slipped her arm into Lane's. 'Now, come and have a look at what I've put in the kitchen.'

'Have you been baking again?'

'Choc chip muffins and lemon drizzle.'

'You spoil us, Mary.'

Now she was dealing with a patient whose ear syringing had been put off due to her fainting episode. She quite liked doing it. It was satisfying to get all that gunk out. She knew that sounded strange. Some people couldn't bear to see congealed wax. But she always felt a sense of achievement at giving back her patients the ability to hear better.

'Nearly done, Mrs Watkins.'

She had to take care and make sure she didn't injure

the tympanic membrane that was the inner eardrum with the small water jet.

'Good. I can't tell you how long I've waited for this. I was meant to have it done the week before, but it got postponed then, as well.'

'Did it? I'm sorry about that.'

'Wasn't your fault. I was booked in with the nurse but I had to go see my granddaughter—she was having one of her episodes.'

'Episodes?'

'She's always getting emotional. Calls me whenever there's a problem. She never really had her mum around so she comes to me, you know?'

She smiled. She understood. Skye had come to Lane about a lot of things. They'd had such a close relationship, and she'd felt privileged that Skye had trusted her with things that she couldn't tell anyone else.

You see? You had an intense relationship with Skye, too. You lock on to people. You don't give them space. That's why Cole has been odd with you these last few days.

Cole had been the perfect doctor to Lane whilst she'd had the flu, but since then she'd sensed a distance between them—a gap that was beginning to widen—and it frightened her. She felt a little hurt, too…

But she'd had a lot of time to think whilst she'd been ill in bed, and she'd realised that she'd contributed a lot to all the problems in her relationships by not saying how she truly felt. If things with Cole were to be different then perhaps she ought to tell him how she felt? That way he'd know where she was coming from.

'She thought she might be pregnant, but of course she wasn't.'

'How old is she?'

'Just eighteen—but we've kind of helped raise her, so we're very close. Her mum was useless, to be honest.'

Lane continued to squirt water—she was practically done. 'What made her think she was pregnant?'

'She felt sick. Tired. Apparently her monthly was late, but when we sat down with her she'd just counted wrong, that was all. Anyway, she's not—so the panic is over and I can get my ears done.'

'Well, it's good, that she wasn't. Unless she wanted to be, of course?'

'No, no. Her and her boyfriend have only been seeing each other a few months. It all got a bit too intense a bit too soon, that's all.'

Been there, done that.

She passed her patient a tissue and discarded the cardboard cup into the clinical waste bin. Then she went to put the machine in the sluice so she could clean it in a minute. She removed her gloves, washed her hands, and tapped the details of the procedure into the system.

'There we are, Mrs Watkins. All done until next time.'

She tried to smile. But she was still thinking about Cole. About Tori. About where they all stood.

Mrs Watkins gave her thanks and left, and Lane felt her shoulders sag when she was alone in the room again. She looked at the wall that separated her from Cole's room. They'd only known each other a few weeks and they were practically living together. They hadn't even spoken yet about arrangements for the future. Perhaps they should?

She loved him. But could she tell him? *Should* she?

Maybe it was all too soon and she was moving too fast. *Again.* Telling him how she felt would change everything, and if he didn't feel the same way then what?

She knew he cared for her. He'd looked after her so well whilst she'd been sick. But...

But she'd seen the doubt in his eyes.

Perhaps he was scared about what the future held, too? What if announcing her feelings would help *him*?

She kept trying to dismiss her doubts, but the more she fell in love with him the louder those voices were becoming.

If he rejected her it would break her heart in two. But wasn't it best to be honest? If he didn't reject her, if he felt the same way, then everything would be alright. It would be wonderful!

Lane looked at the purple fob watch that was pinned to her tunic. Ten minutes past ten. Six hours or so before work ended.

She had another patient waiting. A young girl of nineteen, who was there for spirometry with reversal to check and see if her breathing could be helped by using inhalers. Perfect. She could concentrate on that for a while.

Lane fetched the equipment and connected it to her computer. Then she called her patient in.

Cole had one last home visit to do before he could go home and put his feet up for the night. He was looking forward to that. He was exhausted! And he wanted a shower to wash away the cares of the day. It had been a long one. And it hadn't ended yet.

This patient didn't need treatment specifically. But she'd recently been diagnosed with a brain tumour and he wanted to pop in and see how she was. It seemed the right thing to do. He'd been looking after this patient for over five years, and remembered when she'd first come to him with chronic headaches, nausea and dizziness.

Deborah let him in and he wiped his feet. 'Hey, Debs, how are you doing?'

'I'm all right, Dr Branagh. You didn't need to come and see me at home—I could have come to you.'

'Oh, it's no problem at all. Kelvin home?' Kelvin was Deborah's husband.

She nodded. 'He's in the kitchen. Can I get you a cup of tea?'

'That'd be lovely. Thanks.'

She escorted him through to the kitchen and he shook Kelvin's hand and sat down, on their invitation, at the kitchen table.

'So what's the plan? Have you seen your consultant lately?'

She nodded. 'Chemotherapy will start in two weeks. It's going to be quite aggressive treatment, he said, and I should prepare myself for some bad side effects.'

'They can give you some meds to help alleviate those.'

'Yes, he mentioned I could have some steroids and some anti-nausea medication if I need it. I'm a little more worried about losing my hair.'

She ran her fingers through it, stroking it, smiling, and he could see she was trying to be brave.

'After that, if they can get the tumour to shrink a little, they said it'll be easier to remove with surgery.'

She was so young to have cancer. But then he guessed Skye had faced the same thing at a similar young age. Deborah had a little girl, too. Sienna. But she was older than Tori. About two years old, if he remembered correctly.

'You could try cold capping.'

'He mentioned that. I'll probably give it a go.'

'How's everyone taken the news?'

'Family's been good. We can't tell Sienna, though, she won't understand. But I wonder if…if you think I should make a will…just in case?'

A will. In case she died.

Another young woman whose life could be cut short.

What was the universe trying to tell him?

'It's a sensible thing to do, but you must try and remain positive.'

'Oh, I will! But I just need to know that Sienna will be taken care of.'

He found it strange that he should be seated here, discussing her arrangements, when he hadn't been able to help Skye. It really began to sink in what she must have felt. What she must have feared losing.

He understood that fear. He couldn't imagine having to make that kind of decision himself, knowing he was to be a parent. Could he have done it? He'd given life a lot of thought whilst Lane had been ill, and his fears had been fed by the past.

Was he *meant* to be with Lane? He had very strong feelings for her—of course he did—but was it too much, too soon? He thought about her relationship with Simon, how she'd said it had been all-consuming. Well, didn't *they* have the very same thing going on right now? Was she feeling smothered? Because he thought that he might be. Not by her. But by the intensity of his feelings for her and what that meant.

He couldn't breathe sometimes because he worried so much.

He'd already lost everything once. Did he dare risk losing all he cared about again? Legally, he had no rights at all if he screwed this up between them.

Plus, he really wanted to spend more time alone with

Tori. Just the two of them. Could he apply to the court for parental responsibility? Discuss gaining formal access to Tori? He didn't think Lane would mind—after all, he was Tori's father.

It was great to be with Lane, working together to make Tori feel secure with him. But they were always together with her, and if Tori cried Lane comforted her, because she was used to being the one who responded. He needed the opportunity to learn what to do when Tori needed something.

He resolved to speak to Lane about that tonight. He had no idea what the future held for him and Lane, but he did know that he wanted a future for him and Tori.

She was his daughter and he would do anything for her. He would give his life, if need be.

Lane would understand that. She had recently been letting him take Tori out on his own, but that had just been for the occasional walk. He wanted to have a whole day on his own. A weekend, maybe? Lane might appreciate the rest! She'd been Tori's main carer for nearly a year, without a break and that had to be part of the reason she'd been so ill lately.

'It's good to plan,' he said now. 'You need to make sure your family will be okay.'

Deborah smiled at his approval.

He sipped his tea and watched as Sienna came running into the kitchen, trailing her blanket behind her. Deborah scooped her up into her arms and kissed her daughter's cheek.

His mind was made up. He would speak to Lane tonight.

Tori was splashing about, enjoying her bath, when Lane heard the front door open downstairs. She'd given him a key, trying not to make a big deal out of it.

'We're upstairs!' she called down, feeling her stomach churn and her heart pound even faster.

What was the best way to tell him? She was scared. Terrified. This was such a big step. But it was one she thought was the right thing to do. Tell Cole how invested she was in their relationship. He needed to know where he stood.

'Great. I'll be right up.'

She heard him put down his bag, drape his coat on a hook, and then his footsteps as he trotted up the stairs.

She gave him a big smile when he appeared in the bathroom doorway. 'Hey.'

'Hey, yourself. Anything for dinner?'

'We've had some chicken, veggies and rice. I put a plate for you in the microwave.'

'Thanks.'

She smiled at him, wondering how best and when the right time would be to start this conversation. The man had just come back from work. He'd had a long day, plus home visits to make. He was probably shattered. Probably best to leave the heavy relationship talk until after he'd had something to eat and a chance to clean himself up. It wasn't something that could just be blurted out.

'I've got this,' she said. 'You get something to eat.'

'You're sure?'

She nodded.

He smiled and headed back downstairs, and soon she heard him pottering about in the kitchen and the microwave being switched on.

She let out a pent-up breath and gazed at Tori. 'What do you think, Tori, hmm…? What will Daddy say?'

More than anything she realised she needed Cole! She loved him. But the last man she'd loved had left her. She could be about to ruin everything they had. Their friendship. How well they got on. How good a little family unit they were. She might mess all of that up by pressing her own selfish issues!

But she needed to show him how serious she was about what they had, and by affirming that, she hoped it would show him that they could *do* this, live this life that they were building and do it together.

She felt sure he felt the same way too. Didn't he act like they were in a relationship? A serious one?

She scooped Tori from the bath, wrapping her in a big fluffy towel and laying her on the floor to dry her properly.

She could feel herself trembling. Her heart racing.

Tori giggled and Lane pulled her towards her, wrapping her not only in the towel but in a massive bear hug. She closed her eyes. Soaking in this moment. This moment of near serenity.

Because she had to tell him. Had to let him know. She couldn't live in limbo. She needed certainties.

And she hoped and prayed that he would say those three words she longed to hear more than anything.

With Tori bathed and in her pyjamas, playing in her playpen, Lane straightened things in the kitchen and cleared up in there. There wasn't much to do. Cole was very good at tidying up after himself.

Looking around, she realised just how little of him there was here. None of his things. No possessions. Did he feel he didn't belong? Perhaps soon, when she'd spoken to him, he would feel better about everything? Bring some more of his stuff over?

When there was absolutely nothing left for her to do

she went into the living room and sat down on the couch beside him.

He smiled at her and she reached out to take his hand. She squeezed it tight, taking a moment to just marvel at his strong hand entwined with hers, at the shape of his forearm, the chunky watch on his wrist. All the little details she loved about him.

'You okay?' he asked.

'Yep. I'm fine. Good. You?'

She thought he looked a little distracted—as if he had something on his mind.

'Yeah…'

'I…er…wonder if we could talk for a minute? If you're not too tired?' she said.

Now he looked at her. 'Sure.'

So this was it. Her big moment. And now it was here she found herself feeling nervous and wanting to giggle.

He locked eyes with her, still holding her hand. Still smiling. She hoped he would still be smiling when she told him how she felt.

'But can I tell you about what I've been wanting to say first?' he asked.

She nodded. 'Of course!'

'You and I have been getting on really well…' he began.

She beamed. *Yes*. They *had*. That was why this was such a perfect moment to tell him the truth about her feelings.

'And Tori and I have really got to know one another…'

'You have. And it's been beautiful to see.' She smiled.

'And you've let me take Tori out for a walk…that kind of thing. But… I want more, Lane. I need more than that.'

This was it. She could feel it! He was going to tell her

he loved her too, and then there would be kisses and hugs and laughter as they fell into each other's arms…

'When she was in hospital, it made me realise how—legally—I had no right to any of the information the doctor was giving us. If you hadn't been there I'd have known nothing. It made me feel…apart from you. Like an outsider.'

He wasn't, though. She'd been trying to show him that. That she could give him everything he wanted.

'So, I've been thinking really hard about this, and…'

She squeezed his hand tight, a big smile on her face, waiting to hear those three little words.

'I'd like to take Tori home with me for a while. For it to be just the two of us. I feel I really need to build that father-daughter relationship.'

Lane sucked in a breath, trying not to let her smile falter. But this *wasn't* what she'd been expecting!

He wanted to spend time alone with Tori?

'Just the two of you?' she said slowly.

He nodded. 'Yes. With your permission, obviously.'

She nodded hurriedly, still smiling, trying her best not to look as if she'd just been punched in the gut. Of *course* he would want some precious alone-time with Tori! Why *wouldn't* he? She was a wonderful little girl. He was her father. Of course she didn't mind! But it was hardly the declaration of love she'd hoped to hear. In fact, he seemed to be thinking about making plans that only included himself and his daughter.

I knew it! I knew I felt a distance growing between us!

But she didn't want to lose face in that moment. And in her heart she knew, he had a right to see more of Tori—no matter the legalities. He was her father. What was she?

'Of course, you can,' she said at last.

'I thought about taking her tonight. Getting her used to sleeping over at my place.'

His place. Of course. He wasn't thinking of uniting the three of them at all, was he?

'And I've thought about contacting a solicitor.'

Her face froze.

'To see if I can officially be named as her father. If I can be put on the birth certificate and apply for parental responsibility. Although I'm not sure on the legalities, to be honest.'

'You're thinking about applying for joint custody?' She stood there awkwardly, trying not to feel hurt, trying to seem as if she was open to his suggestions.

Cole frowned, shaking his head. 'I don't know... Maybe?'

'It sounds a great idea. Although it might take a while.'

'So you don't mind if I take her? It'll give you a rest for a while...after your illness.'

Lane couldn't bear to stand there a moment longer, her heart breaking in two, as Cole showed her very clearly that he was only thinking of a future with his daughter—not with her.

'I don't mind at all. In fact, now that you mention it, I *do* feel quite tired. Do you mind if I go to bed early? You know where her things are...'

'Are you okay?'

'Mmm-hmm.'

She turned tail and ran up the stairs, into her bedroom, and slammed the door. She flopped onto the bed and began to cry. She had known a distance had started growing between them...but for him to so cruelly state that all he wanted was to spend more time alone with his daughter! He wasn't thinking of *her* at all!

All that time she'd been sick with the flu she'd known something was wrong! Had he been too afraid to say it whilst she'd been sick? Had he been waiting for her to feel better so he could sideswipe her with his plans?

She froze, hearing his footsteps coming up the stairs. They stopped outside her bedroom door. She stared at it, awaiting the knock, but then she heard his footsteps once again, going back down. Him gathering things together. His voice, speaking soothingly to Tori. The front door, opening and closing.

They'd gone.

Both of them. She knew Tori would be fine. She was with her Dad! It was something, she knew that, eventually, she may have to come to get used to.

Cole sat in the soft play centre, watching Tori play in a ball pit for babies. She seemed fascinated by all the brightly coloured spheres around her, and was taking great joy in picking them up and trying to throw them.

He'd gone ahead and taken Tori from Lane's last night, but he felt terrible. Lane had *said* she was fine with him taking Tori on his own, but clearly she was upset. Was she feeling threatened by how close he was becoming to Tori?

She'd seemed her usual self lately, despite the flu. If anything, *he'd* been the one to try and create a distance. Had she picked up on that and thought he was looking to make a split? Simon had given her an ultimatum. Had she thought he was going to give her one, too?

He'd been up all night thinking about it, and his head felt thick with lack of sleep.

She really had seemed upset about him taking Tori. But surely she wasn't cross about his wanting to be an important figure in Tori's life? It was only right. He was her *father*!

He'd been happy to play their relationship Lane's way because he hadn't wanted to talk legalities right from the get-go. He hadn't wanted to upset his daughter, who clearly had a fabulous relationship with Lane. Lane was all Tori had ever known! But putting things on a legal footing had been more and more on his mind ever since Tori had got stung and ended up in hospital.

But now he was here, alone, and he wasn't going anywhere, and he didn't think there was anything wrong in wanting to know that Tori would reach up her arms for *him* when she wanted picking up. That when she cried, she would know she could go to *him* for comfort. That when she wanted to snuggle she could do so with *him*. That was what fathers did. They were there for their little girls. He didn't feel in the wrong for having asked for this part. He refused to feel guilty for it.

But…

But he and Lane had been getting so close, sleeping together, and he cared for her very much indeed. Of course he did!

But was it love?

He felt fear even *thinking* about it.

He'd loved a woman deeply before, and his loss of her had changed him as a person. Those early days and weeks after losing Andrea had been the worst days of his life.

Did he have the capacity to feel that way again? To risk his heart and put it out there?

Perhaps Lane had done him a favour? Life had given him a taste of what he could have and he'd been enjoying it, revelling in coming home to Tori and Lane, but had they been moving too fast? Perhaps involving a solicitor *was* a good idea, before it all got too complicated?

Cole knelt beside the ball pit and began to play catch with his daughter. She looked up at him with her beautiful blue eyes and laughed, and he knew he had Lane to thank for such a happy, contented daughter.

Was it his responsibility to make Lane happy and contented in return?

Had he been with her because of Tori?

Or had he been with her because he'd wanted to be? *Needed* to be?

The house was very empty without Tori or Cole. Lane had never actually been in her new home alone and it seemed very quiet. She had a whole weekend ahead of her before she expected Cole would be back. She knew she ought to use the time constructively, to get things done rather than moping around, but she couldn't because all she could think of was Tori and Cole.

The downstairs bathroom needs a deep clean.

That would take her mind off them, wouldn't it? If she made herself focus on inconsequential stuff like that?

Or she could go through her wardrobe and chuck out the stuff that no longer fitted, sort out the things she wanted to donate to the charity shop. Out with the old, in with the new. She had to accept the new …

She stood in front of her wardrobe and opened the door. Inside was a full-length mirror and she stared at her reflection.

She looked paler than usual, her face a little puffy, her eyes red with dark circles beneath. She wore an old tee shirt and a pair of jeans with a hole in the left knee.

How had she been so blind as to think that he might be falling in love with her, too?

Her talk with Cole had not gone the way she'd expected. And now he was out, alone with his daughter, which was apparently what he'd always truly wanted. Maybe he had cared for her a little, but it had not been love—and Lane knew she deserved to be loved. She would accept nothing less; she was worth more than a casual friendship with benefits.

The knowledge of that didn't stop her heart from aching, though. She loved Cole. Had allowed him into her broken heart and thought he was repairing it for her.

I always jump the gun. I always expect more from people than they're willing to give.

It was a fault of hers. A bad habit she would have to learn to break.

But there was no point in just standing here and staring at her reflection! She would do something useful!

So she reached into the wardrobe and grabbed a pile of clothes. If she was going to do this, then she was going to do it right!

'Dr Branagh!'

Cole was taking Tori for a walk through the park and who should be calling out to him but Mary, the receptionist from the surgery. She had a young dog on a leash. A golden retriever puppy.

'Mary! Hi, how are you?' He leant forward to give her a kiss on her cheek. 'And who's this little guy?'

'This little guy is a girl! Her name's Skylar and I'm out with her trying to get my ten thousand steps. I've got one of these thingamajigs…' she showed him the black strap around her wrist '…and it's been showing me that

I've only been doing around two thousand a day! Pathetic, isn't it? So, me and Bill got ourselves a puppy, to make ourselves get out and about more.'

He smiled and ruffled the dog's head. 'Good idea. Hello, Skylar.'

'Just you two out today? Where's Lane? At home with her feet up?'

He gave an unconvincing smile. 'Something like that…'

Tori squealed at the puppy excitedly, reaching forward to try and grab the dog's tail.

'Careful,' said Cole.

'Oh, Skylar's good with youngsters. She puts up with all my grand-kiddies chasing her about all day. Poor dog is pooped after their visits!' She looked at him, head tilted to one side. 'You okay? You look like death.'

'Thanks. I didn't sleep very well.'

'Tori keeping you up?'

No. Lane.

'Just couldn't sleep.'

'Well, that's to be expected, isn't it, with a baby? Lovely day, though! Get some fresh air into you—no doubt you'll sleep better tonight.'

'I hope so. I was just thinking about families and making memories. I'm thinking about taking more pictures.'

'That's a good idea! I could take some now for you, if you like! I'm a dab hand with a phone camera.'

'Would you mind?'

'Course not! Where shall we take them?'

'The flowers are in bloom by the bandstand—it'd be nice to get one done there, I think.'

Cole had wanted a photo of him and Tori for ages. He'd got some casual shots of Tori on his phone—ones that he'd snapped when he could—and of course there was the one of him, Lane and Tori dressed as faeries at the Faery Fayre.

He tried not to think back to that day. It had been so early in the relationship for all of them, but he'd thought they were happy. He'd thought he was doing the right thing, going at Lane's pace in his relationship with Tori, but he'd felt so much like an outsider at the hospital that time she'd got stung, and he'd just known he wanted to take further steps. Steps he'd hoped Lane would be happy for him to take. Hadn't she come here to find him?

He'd expected this to be a happy day. Just him and Tori in the park. But his heart just didn't feel in it.

Tori was in a pretty pink dress with a white cardigan, and Cole was wearing a blue shirt and jeans. He hefted her onto his hip and went and stood in front of the bandstand among all the roses. There didn't appear to be any bees today.

'What about here?'

'Okay.'

Mary stood in front of them and took shot after shot—some close-up, some panned back—and managed to take an absolute stunner when Tori randomly reached out to try and catch a butterfly that flew past.

'They're great.'

Cole smiled as Mary swiped through them afterwards, to show him. But though he smiled outwardly, inwardly he felt sad. It would have been nice to have got Lane in these photos, too… He was missing her terribly—something he hadn't expected to feel so keenly after just a few hours.

He looked at the pictures again. Did he really want pictures of just the two of them? Him and Tori? They were great. Absolutely they were. But someone was missing.

Had he hurt her feelings, asking for time alone with Tori? She'd seemed pretty shocked, even though she'd tried to hide it. But he loved his daughter, and he also loved…

His breath caught in his throat.

Love was what mattered.

And he knew he loved Lane!

Would she want to hear that?

I should have knocked on her bedroom door. I should have gone in. Explained.

He missed Lane like crazy.

He missed not having her with him. Her smile. Her laughter. The way she made him feel.

He wished more than anything in the world that he could tell her that he loved her…but he was too scared. If he announced it to the world—if he made it official—then…what? What did he fear would happen?

He'd opened his heart completely to Tori—why couldn't he do the same for Lane?

He thanked Mary for taking the pictures.

'Oh, no problem at all! Well, I'll let you get on. I've still got…' she looked at her gadget '…five thousand two hundred and seventy-one steps to do.'

'Mary?'

'Yes, love?'

'You and Bill… You've been together a long time?'

She nodded. 'Forty years next month. Never thought we'd get this far, to be honest. I could easily have killed him a few times!' She laughed.

'Was it ever scary?'

She looked at him carefully. Smiled. 'Of course! I'm often scared. Of loving him too much. Of losing him. You know he had that stroke a few years ago?'

Cole nodded.

'But I'm there because I love him. Because life without him is a horrible prospect. Because I want us to be together for as long as we can be.'

'But eventually something will happen, won't it? Life does that to us. Takes away those we love.' He thought of losing Lane and Tori, the way he'd lost Andrea and the baby. Could he face such losses again?

Mary fed Skylar a small treat from her pocket. 'Yes. But why deprive ourselves of the time we *do* have together? Of the one person who makes us happier than we could ever be alone? One year with Bill is better than no years with Bill. Now, I know what you're thinking, Dr Branagh...'

'Mary, I've told you before, call me Cole.'

She smiled. 'You loved Andrea, right?'

'Of course. But I lost her.'

'But you still have all those happy memories of her, don't you? Of the love you shared?'

He nodded.

'Imagine if you didn't even have that.' Mary raised an eyebrow. 'I'll leave you be now. Say hello to Lane for me. It's her last week next week, isn't it?'

Of course. He'd forgotten that. 'Yes.' Her last week. She would be leaving soon. If he told her he loved her, would she think he was only doing so to get her to stay? To not take his daughter away?

Mary smiled. 'It would be a damn shame to lose her.'

He nodded. 'Yes. It would....'

Lane had taken three bin bags full of clothes to the local charity shop and cleaned her house from top to bottom.

But all she could conclude from her efforts was that it sucked to be alone. More than sucked.

Her heart ached. She missed Tori so much, but she also missed Cole. He had become a part of her as much as her goddaughter had.

She hadn't realised just how much she had come to depend upon them being together. On having them in her life. It had only been one morning with them gone and already she felt their absence keenly.

All her life she had kept quiet when things got tough, and last night she had done the same thing again. She'd wanted to tell Cole how she felt, but she had silenced herself after his revelation about wanting more time alone with Tori. Yet again she had let other people steer her life for her, and she felt cowardly and angry at herself.

She'd never told Skye how she had truly felt about losing her. She'd never told Simon what a selfish man he was and how he ought to have more capacity for thinking about other people's feelings than his own.

She'd never got to tell her father how hurt she'd been that he'd left when she was little.

And so, when Cole had said how he'd like to take Tori home with him alone, she'd automatically caved and said that it was okay—zipped her lips about her own wants and needs.

Lane had had enough of other people making the decisions in her life. And as she stood there, looking at her clean and empty home, she resolved to tell Cole exactly how she felt. She was going to tell him off for messing with her heart. For making her fall in love with him and then breaking her heart in two. She didn't care if she made a fool of herself, because she was fed up with being silent and fed up with never telling people how she truly felt.

It might just be the most embarrassing thing she'd ever do—but to hell with it! She *would* be heard!

A light knock at her front door interrupted her thoughts. She really didn't feel like answering, and almost didn't. But then she thought it might be a delivery, and she was awaiting a parcel, so...

With heavy feet she traipsed downstairs and opened the front door—and instantly felt her heart begin to pound and her pulse start to race.

It was Cole.

And he stood there with Tori on one hip.

Tori squealed at seeing her and reached out. Lane couldn't help but smile at her baby girl as she took her in her arms. Couldn't Cole cope alone? Was that why he was back early?

'Is there a problem?' she asked.

'Yes. A huge problem.' Cole stared at her uncertainly.

'What is it?'

'You love her,' he said.

What was he going on about? 'Of *course* I do.'

'I know you do—and yet you just let me take her, like it was nothing. Something isn't right, and it's been bugging me, and it finally came to me. You gave her up as if it was simply something you'd have to get used to.'

'Well, that's what you want, isn't it? You and Tori to spend time alone?'

'Not in the way you believe. Yes, I want to spend time alone with her—I still think that's a good thing to do—but... But I'm getting side-tracked. I'm here to tell you that...'

She looked at him heart pounding. 'What?'

'Can I come in? I don't think I should say this on the doorstep.'

Against her better judgement she stepped back and let
him in. It felt good to have Tori back home. It felt good to
see him, too. She'd missed him, even though she hated to
admit it, and it was difficult keeping up this front when all
she wanted to do was tell him that she loved him, throw
herself into his arms and feel safe again. The fact that she
couldn't do that was making her sound curt.

In the living room, she put Tori down. She instantly
crawled over to her box of toys and began dragging things
out.

'So?' She stood opposite him, a coffee table between
them.

'I *do* want alone time with Tori. It will be good for me,
but I don't want to do it without knowing we can come
home *to you*.'

She continued to stand there, arms folded, staring at
him. She knew what she wanted to say. But clearly he still
had plenty of talking to do, so she decided to stay silent
and hear him out. Then she would say her piece.

'I'm her father, but you're her mother! We were a family the first day we met. I didn't know it, but we were. I
tried to fight against it. I'm sure you did, too. But it happened anyway. I wasn't sure I could fall in love again. I
wasn't sure I could be that brave. But you make me feel
that way, Lane. You make me feel that anything is possible. That us being together is possible.'

Had she heard right? Had he said those words? Was
he telling her that he loved her? This wasn't about Tori?

The thought made her heart race.

'What are you saying, exactly?'

She needed him to clarify. Because she had a bad history of getting these things wrong. Because right now she
wanted to grab onto him and never let go—but if there

was some small chance that this was still a rejection, then she didn't want to embarrass herself any further.

He smiled then, his eyes brightening. 'I'm saying I love you. I'm saying I have loved you for a long time and I want to go on loving you for the rest of my life. I'd like us to be the true family we are. I'd like you to marry me.'

Her heart was soaring. He loved her? He truly loved her?

'You love me?'

'Yes! I do.'

He came over to her, took her hands in his, lifted them to his mouth, kissed the insides of her wrists before holding them against his heart.

'I can't be without you. *We* can't be without you.'

'I thought that you...' She shook her head and sank against him, holding him tight. 'I thought I might lose you.'

'You'll never lose me. *Or* Tori.'

She sank into him, squeezed him tight. Grateful that she'd been so terribly, terribly wrong about him.

He pulled back to look into her eyes. 'Well? What do you say?'

She laughed. 'I'm saying... I love you, too. I'm saying yes to being a family.' She blushed. 'I'm saying yes to being your wife—if you'll have me, of course.'

He pulled her into his arms and kissed her like she'd never been kissed before.

She sank into his embrace, knowing that no matter what was to come she and Cole would be together for ever...

EPILOGUE

WHEN LANE WOKE she instantly turned to check on her baby. Lorelei had been born late last night, at three minutes to eleven, and had emerged into the world with a loud cry to announce her arrival.

Lane had looked into Cole's eyes and seen his tears, then she had pulled him close and they had hugged one another, crying, as the midwives cleaned up their newborn daughter before passing her over.

Lorelei was a beauty. But what baby wasn't?

Lane had been unable to stop looking at her all evening.

'You need to get some sleep. Both of you,' the midwife had said eventually.

So Cole had reluctantly gone home to catch a few winks and Lane had lain in the hospital bed, one eye on Lorelei's crib, as if she dared not look away in case her baby disappeared.

It had been a whirlwind of a pregnancy, but so much easier than she had thought. She'd had the usual uncomfortable symptoms, and she'd secretly worried that something might go wrong, but that fear had been lifted the moment she'd safely delivered Lorelei and held her baby girl in her arms. She was perfect. Ten tiny fingers and ten tiny toes.

Now Lane scooped her up and just sat there in the bed, holding her and looking down at her. Was it possible to love a human being so fiercely?

Yes, it was. She already knew it was.

She'd worried about that. She loved Tori so much, she had wondered if she would be able to love another to the same degree—but she realised now that the heart had an infinite capacity to love.

Loving another never took the love away from someone else. It just got more. It got bigger. Better than ever before.

Lorelei had Lane's nose and mouth, but her father's eyes, and she could already see the similarity between Tori and her new daughter. She liked that. Liked that there was a familiar trait. They were a family. Bigger than before, but so much better!

There was a gentle knock at the door and Cole peered around it. 'Ready for visitors?'

She smiled and nodded. 'You couldn't stay away?'

'How could I?'

He crept in, holding Tori's hand, and then scooped up his eldest daughter and put her on the bed, so she could see the baby.

'What do you think, Tori? This is your baby sister.'

Tori leaned in for a closer look, smiling. She hesitantly reached out and touched Lorelei's face, then leaned in further and kissed her on the cheek.

'Baby sister!' she said.

'Yes. Baby sister. This is Lorelei.'

'Lorry-bye!' Tori laughed and they all laughed with her. That was cute!

Cole draped his arm around Lane's shoulders. 'How are you feeling today?'

She let her head fall against his chest, then looked up at him and beamed a happy, contented smile his way. 'I feel as I always do when I'm with you. Like the luckiest person in the whole world.'

He kissed her, then kissed both his daughters. 'Not possible.' He smiled. 'That honour is all mine.'

* * * * *

BEST FRIEND
TO DOCTOR RIGHT

ANN McINTOSH

MILLS & BOON

For my amazing and wonderful niece, Victoria,
and my grand-uncle, Dr. William "Billy" Aird,
both of whom have been inspirations to me.

CHAPTER ONE

ALTHOUGH UNEXPECTED, THE sound of the buzzer heralding a visitor hardly registered.

Dr. Mina Haraldson lifted her head briefly off the couch cushion to stare blankly at the television, where a show she didn't recall putting on flickered in the gloom of her living room. Thick mental fog blanketed her more securely than the heavy quilt she was huddled beneath, giving her respite from the world. There was a vague recognition of something unusual having happened, but she had no idea of what it was until the buzzer went off again.

No need to answer, or even see who it was. She hadn't ordered food or anything else. Her parents, having been convinced their immediate presence was no longer necessary, had gone off to Florida for their usual winter break. Her brother was at home in BC. She knew that because she'd been forced to put on a happy tone the night before, for their weekly Friday night telephone conversation.

If she'd failed to convince Braden of her well-being, he'd have said something.

Somehow she must have done a good job. He'd rung off without trying to interrogate her, taking her word that all was well.

Perhaps now that her medical career was over she

should take up acting. After all, a one-handed actor was far more feasible than a one-handed surgeon. She'd put that on her "future prospects" list, if she ever got up enough energy to start one.

Tears clouded her vision, and she closed her eyes. Leaning her head back against the cushions and pulling the quilt back up under her chin, she drowned anew in her reality.

Her uselessness.

When the buzzer went a third time, her jaw clenched. "Go away!"

The shouted words drowned out the TV and echoed in the apartment, but the person down in the lobby couldn't hear them, and the buzzer rang again.

Then her phone beeped, as well.

"Oh, for…"

Untangling her arm from the quilt, she fumbled around on the ground for her phone. Unlocking the screen, she squinted at the message, her heart turning over as she read it.

Answer the door, girl. Calypso Kiah is here and ready to party!

"Kiah?"

Shock dispelled the rage as swiftly as it had risen and was then overwhelmed by a rush of delight so intense Mina's head swam.

What was he doing here, now? He'd said he was going to Calgary for his cousin's wedding, then coming to Toronto to visit, but that wasn't until the twenty-fifth. Or was it the twenty-first?

Good grief, what date was it today anyway? What day?

She couldn't remember. Funny how, when you had nothing to do or to concentrate on, the days ran one into the other.

Obviously, she'd totally lost track of time.

Mina tried to sit up, was caught in the folds of the quilt and, in her eagerness to rise, put both hands down on the cushion beneath her and heaved.

Pain shot like jagged shards of glass up her arm from the nerve endings in her stump, making her fall, cursing, back onto the couch, dropping the phone as she went.

It was over a year since the accident, but she still forgot. Still tried to use her hand.

Still, somewhere deep inside, apparently hadn't accepted her left hand was gone.

And each reminder made her heart stop for an instant, denial washing through her, as strong as it had been the day she woke up in the hospital and learned about the amputation.

She couldn't find the phone, was still gasping from the pain, cradling her left arm against her chest with her right hand.

But it was Kiah, and she couldn't let him leave.

He was her oldest and very best friend in the world.

She hadn't seen him in person for five years.

Frantically kicking her feet, she freed herself from the quilt. Her cell phone was set up to unlock the downstairs door, but she'd never mastered the art of using it efficiently with one hand. So she tumbled off the couch and ran to the panel beside the front door to hit the intercom button.

"Kiah. Kiah, are you still there?"

There was a pause and, for a sickening moment, she thought he'd gone. Then his voice, deep and melodic, its island rhythm hardly distorted by the intercom, came through.

"Of course I'm still here, girl. You can't get rid of me so easy."

Knees weak, she leaned against the wall, a smile breaking over her face, silly tears once more filling her eyes.

"Thank goodness. Come on up."

As she buzzed him in, she was suddenly aware of the state of her apartment. The unwashed cups, an old pizza box and wadded-up tissues littering the coffee table. The crumpled quilt, half on, half off the couch.

It was a mess, and she wasn't in any better shape, now that she thought about it.

When last had she even bathed, much less washed her hair? She'd been wearing the same shapeless sweatpants and sweatshirt for at least two days. For a brief instant shame racked her, but it wasn't strong enough to do more than mute her overwhelming joy and excitement.

After all, it was *Kiah*.

Pulling open her front door, she stepped halfway out into the corridor, her heart pounding as she stared down the hallway toward the elevators. Finding herself jigging from one foot to the other like an overexuberant child brought a bubble of laughter, but it stuck in her throat, burning, instead of breaking free. Emotions too numerous to recognize swamped her, rushing through her system in first hot and then cold waves.

When the ping of the elevator sounded from around the corner, Mina's world seemed to stop for an instant, and then resume in agonizing slow motion. It felt like a year before a shadow fell on the carpet; another eon passed before Kiah stepped around the corner and came toward her.

Bundled up to the hilt, as was only to be expected for someone who'd come from a tropical island into the Canadian winter, he was unzipping his parka as he walked. Through the haze of delight misting her eyes, Mina took note of the changes in him since the last time they'd been together. He looked older. New lines at the corners of his eyes, some gray salting the hair at his temples. But his smile as beautiful as ever: white teeth gleaming against his dark skin, the little dimple on his left cheek winking.

Just seeing him made something deep inside her shift, loosen, unravel. Where before she'd been lost in a fog, suddenly everything was in sharp, clear focus. Illuminated brighter than she'd expected. Dazzlingly so.

"Oh, Kiah!" she cried, as he got close enough to envelop her in a huge bear hug. "I've missed you so much!"

And, to her surprise and consternation, she burst into tears.

Kiah picked Mina up and carried her into the apartment, glad she had her face buried in his shoulder so she couldn't see the shock on his face, in his eyes.

This wasn't his Mina. More like a shadow of his friend.

The old Mina was always neatly put together, no matter the occasion. Even at the beach, or wearing jeans and a T-shirt, she gave off an air of tidy confidence. Not now, though. Wearing shapeless clothes, with stringy hair and a face sallower than it should be, even allowing for winter pallor, she'd been almost unrecognizable when he came around the corner. And when he hugged her, he realized she'd lost so much weight it felt as though she'd snap in two should his arms tighten too much.

Then there was the fact she was sobbing pitifully. In the more than twenty years since they'd met, he could count on one hand the number of times he'd seen her cry, and even on those occasions, it was nothing like this. She hated to cry, and always exerted Herculean effort to curtail the tears, indulging for a brief moment before getting herself back under control. Right now, she seemingly had lost every ounce of control she possessed, and it was kind of freaking him out.

Yet, growing up surrounded by women, Kiah knew what *not* to say to a sobbing female. So he sat down on the sofa and, pulling Mina's frail form close, repeated over and over, "I got you, sweet girl. Kiah's got you."

His heart ached to see her this way, but he was fiercely glad he was the one there with her, supporting and comforting, just as she'd been there for him all through the years, since the very beginning. Grade seven, to be exact. Mrs. Nowac's class.

He'd still been traumatized by and grieving over the loss of his father, terrified of this new school, the new life he'd found himself living. From the first moment he'd set foot in Moraine Academy, he'd known he didn't belong, and was sure he never would. The only way he and his little sister Karlene got into the prestigious private school was because his mother's employer, Mrs. Burton, had pulled strings and gotten them scholarships. And the only reason she'd done it was because it was the closest school to her mansion, and she wanted her housekeeper available in the mornings, not driving her kids to school.

They'd had to walk the four miles to school, since there were no buses going there. All the other kids got dropped off or, if they were old enough, drove themselves. As he and Karlene trudged onto the school property, he'd seen the scornful looks the other kids gave them, checking out their cheap, bargain-basement clothes and no-name shoes.

Karlene had noticed, too.

"I hate it here already," she'd said, loud enough to prove she didn't care who heard. Kiah hadn't replied. Normally he'd have tried to give it a positive spin, but just then he was overwhelmingly sad, really low on optimism, and couldn't in good faith disagree. He, too, was wishing he were back in their old school in Scarborough, surrounded by the friends they'd made the year before.

He'd walked Karlene to her class then made his way to the room he was assigned to, getting there just as the bell rang. Knowing the other kids would have seats picked out already, he waited by the door until the rest of the students had settled into their chairs, then looked up and found the last empty seat in the room.

On his way there he kept his head down, not making eye contact with anyone, yet aware of how everyone in the room was staring at him. The other kids' whispers surrounded him like the buzz of bees. Even all these years later he still remembered it, clear as day.

"We have a new student," Mrs. Nowac said, once he was seated. "Hezekiah Langdon. Please make him welcome."

"Hezekiah?" The derision in the boy's voice was accompanied by a kick to the back of Kiah's chair. "What kind of stupid name is that?"

The wave of laughter rippling through the class hardly mattered. Kiah already knew he had no business there. All he could do was wish things could go back to how they'd been—before his father died, and his mother had totally lost control. He'd thought coming to Canada would be exciting but it had all gone to hell. His father had been the one who held everything together and gave his children the love and support they needed, while keeping his wife's anger and bitterness in check.

Now that he was gone, the world was a bleak, frightening place.

If Kiah had had a magic wand, he'd have waved it and been back on St. Eustace. Probably running on the beach, or playing cricket with his friends.

"It's Biblical. Hezekiah was a king of Judea. You should know that, Justin. Isn't your grandpa a pastor?"

Kiah had been half-aware of the girl in front of him turning in her chair but thought she'd just been staring and giggling like all the others. When he heard her defending his name, he'd looked up and, for the first time, his gaze met Mina's.

She was so cute his heart stumbled over itself. Her hair swung around her fine-boned oval face like a curtain of amber, and her wide-set chocolate brown eyes, tilted slightly at the corners, twinkled. Later on, he learned she'd gotten her eye coloring and shape from her Korean mother, while the lighter hair had come from a trip to the beauty salon. Not that her hair was as dark as her mom's. Mr. Haraldson, her father, was almost white-blond, and in Kiah's estimation Mina was a perfect combination of her Korean and Scandinavian heritages.

"That's enough now, class." Mrs. Nowac had shushed them, causing Mina to turn back around and face front. Then the teacher started talking about the first lesson of the day.

"Smart-ass. I'll deal with you later, Mina Haraldson." Justin obviously didn't like being upstaged, and whispered the threat just loud enough for Mina to hear.

"Just try it," she replied, without turning around.

And despite his mother's firm injunction to keep his head down and not make any trouble, on pain of a thorough thrashing, Kiah turned and gave Justin a scowl.

"Yeah, *Justin*." He made no effort to temper the swing and tempo of his accent the way he'd learned to do since moving to Canada, and the name rolled out like a dirty word. "Just try it."

When Mina glanced back at him and grinned, he'd suddenly felt better, as though life just might be worth living after all.

She hadn't had to befriend him. She was from a well-respected family and popular in school, not a misfit like he was, yet she'd gone out of her way to make him feel welcome and, after a little while, her friends had accepted him, too.

His mother hadn't been pleased about their friendship. Not that there was anything that made his mother happy.

"You have no business making time with that girl," she'd said, shaking her finger in his face. "You an' she no have nothing in common, and if she father find out 'bout you, he not goin' be happy."

"We're just friends," he'd protested, knowing how truly upset his mother was, from the way her English deteriorated into St. Eustace patois.

"Make sure you keep it that way," she'd said, turning back to the stove and rescuing the ripe plantains frying in the pan before they burned. "We don't need no trouble 'round here."

He knew what she meant, of course. The Haraldsons were rich, like Mrs. Burton, and he was a little black boy from nowhere—son of one of their neighbors' hired help. Kiah had believed his mother when she said Mr. Haraldson would be angry if he found out but, to his surprise, it had been the complete opposite.

Without Mina and her family, who'd treated him as though he were one of their own, he'd have been lost, and who knew where he'd have ended up? They'd been there for him during all the worst moments in his life, in a way his mother never had.

Witnessing his father's fatal heart attack, barely a month before meeting Mina, had devastated him, left him floundering, unmoored. Mina's friendship had helped him get through it, just as it had helped him deal with his mother's increasingly violent rage. And when his sister had died, she was the first person he'd called.

She was the best friend he'd ever had, and now she needed him to repay all the care she'd given him.

As Mina's sobs abated, Kiah leaned forward, holding her with one arm, and snagged the box of tissues off the coffee table. Clearly, this wasn't the first crying jag she'd had, if the used tissues strewn around were any indication. Pulling out a couple, he thrust them into her hand, noticing for the first time how she'd crossed her left arm over her body and tucked her stump out of sight.

His heart broke all over again.

"I'm sorry," she mumbled, mopping at her face.

"For what?"

"For crying all over you, of course," she replied, burying her face back into his neck. "For being such a soggy mess."

He chuckled, as she no doubt meant him to, with the reference to one of the classifications they'd come up with for different types of people they'd met. "Soggy mess" was reserved for the whiny, weepy, complaining type. Not her at all.

And in his estimation, not what she should be apologizing to him for. She should be sorry for not telling him how deeply she'd sunk into depression, and for not asking for help. He was trying to formulate the right thing to say, but before he could figure it out, she sighed, and from the way she suddenly relaxed, he realized she was falling asleep. Then Mina conked right out, so abruptly he wondered how much rest she'd been getting.

Sliding down slightly in the couch, he made himself comfortable, cradling her across his lap. Eventually he'd transfer her to her bed, but not yet. If this was what she needed, he had no problem staying exactly where he was.

Reaching down, he gently took her left arm in his hand and lifted it. Mina didn't stir as her sleeve dropped down, revealing the site of her transradial amputation. He was surprised that she wasn't wearing a compression garment—a shrinker—since he'd read about the efficacy of its use for controlling edema, and how important it was for pre-prosthetic fitting.

There were so many questions he wanted to ask about how she was managing with the loss of her hand. Some of them he'd tried to ask her before, on the phone, and she'd brushed him off, wanting only to talk about her then-ongoing divorce from Warren the Worm. Just thinking about her ex-husband had his temper simmering, but Kiah pushed his antipathy aside. Now wasn't the time to indulge.

Just as it wasn't a good time for the dampness making him blink, as he looked at where Mina's small but eminently capable hand used to be. The last thing she'd want, or probably needed, was his sympathy.

She'd always been driven, in control, and fearless. Whatever needed to be done, she'd been there with a plan.

Seeing her like this, drifting and seemingly broken, was almost too much to bear.

Lifting her arm a little higher, he pressed a gentle kiss just above the surgical site and then laid it back across her stomach, making sure not to jostle it. He pulled the sleeve back across to cover the stump.

"I got you, sweet girl," he whispered, before also kissing the top of her head. "Kiah's got you."

CHAPTER TWO

MINA DRIFTED UP from a dreamless sleep, the first she'd had in she couldn't tell how long. Despite her eyes being gritty, she actually felt rested. When had that become such an anomaly that she had to lie still in bed for a few minutes savoring it?

Then she remembered.

"Kiah!"

Dammit, she must have fallen asleep after crying all over him the evening before. Had he left?

Then she noticed the faint sounds of reggae music coming from her living room, and what could only be kitchen noises. And...

"Mmm," she muttered, tossing back the sheets. "Bacon."

When she opened her bedroom door, it was to indeed find him in front of the stove, his head and shoulders moving in time to the music, and she leaned on the doorjamb to watch him, a smile spreading across her face.

As though sensing her regard, he turned to look over his shoulder, and his answering grin warmed her better than any blanket ever could.

"So you're finally up, eh?" He did a little shimmy to the music and waved the spatula at her. "Sleepyhead."

"Yeah," she replied, suddenly aware of her grungy

state and bed head. "Do I have time for a shower before breakfast?"

"Sure," he said easily, turning back to the stove. "But don't take too long, or everything will get cold."

"I won't," she called, already heading back into her room, her stomach growling in protest of the wait. She could also smell ripe plantain frying, and it had been far too long since she'd had any of the island delicacy. He must have gone to the grocery while she was sleeping, since she knew there definitely hadn't been any food in the house.

Rushing through a shower, but taking the time to wash her hair, she tried not to think about the grilling Kiah was bound to give her after he fed her, if he even waited that long. They'd talked on the phone at least twice a month, often more, since the accident, and he'd tried so many times to find out what was happening with her arm. He'd couched the questions both as a friend and as a doctor, but there'd been a barrier inside her, a wall around everything to do with the loss of her hand, and she'd evaded answering.

It had been easier to tell him about how Warren had left her—although she was too embarrassed to repeat all the horrible things her ex had said. Like how she was no longer someone he was proud to be seen with. That her stump disgusted him, and she wouldn't be an asset to their relationship anymore. Only afterwards did she find out he'd actually been cheating on her from before the accident, and had planned to leave her anyway. The fact that he'd use the loss of her hand as an excuse just showed what a waste of skin he was.

So it had been better to talk to Kiah about her determined fight to ensure Warren didn't take advantage of the situation and con her out of more than his share.

Oh, and he'd tried. His underhanded double-dealing had completely opened her eyes to facets of his character she'd ignored all the years they were together. Warren had become, in her and Kiah's old parlance, a snake oil guy. It was totally in keeping with some of the things he had boasted of doing in his law practice, but like a fool, Mina had never thought he'd turn on her that way. Especially since he was the one who'd wanted to end the marriage.

Thankfully, his cruelty had spurred her out of the depression that had settled over her after she'd lost her hand, even if only temporarily. She'd hired a lawyer known in the Toronto legal circles as the Rottweiler, and the one female attorney Warren had admitted he hated going up against in family court. Jalissa Chang had made sure Mina got everything she was due, and a bit more, too.

Mina had been angry—mostly at herself—and that anger had sustained her. While she had known for a long time things weren't going well between her and Warren, she'd ignored the problems, putting them down to how busy they both were. In truth, now that everything had come out, and in light of the way he'd treated her, she wondered if she could ever trust her judgment of others again.

They'd been together since they were sixteen. How could she not have realized a long time ago how truly selfish and immoral he was? She'd also let him steer her away from motherhood by saying he wasn't ready, or didn't want a pregnancy to derail her career. He'd couched it in terms of delaying it, but now she saw it as a denial, and that was something she was having a hard time getting over. She's always wanted children, but at her age, single, unemployed, and with only one hand, that particular dream seemed unattainable.

As did most of the plans she'd once had.

During her darkest times, she'd known Warren was right to leave her, as useless as she'd become, but she couldn't condone his meanness. So she'd concentrated on the divorce and everything that went into getting the separation agreement finalized. It had taken almost a full year, by which time she only had a month or so before the divorce, too, was done.

That was when everything truly fell apart.

She was always at her worst when she had nothing to do. Nothing to plan for or look forward to.

"Well," she said aloud as she rinsed her hair. "Now you have breakfast with your best friend to look forward to, so no feeling sorry for yourself today."

By the time she came out of the bedroom, all squeaky clean and dressed in something other than shapeless sweats, she felt better than she had in ages. Even noticing that Kiah had cleaned up the place brought only a small pang of guilt.

Something about being around this man always made her life better, and she was going to enjoy it for the short time he'd be in town.

"Come on, lazybones," he said, putting two plates laden with bacon, eggs, toast and plantain on the dining table. "I'm starving."

"I can't believe you'd call me that, Mr. I'll-Sleep-'til-Noon-If-I-Want-To."

"Ha," he said as he pulled out her chair. "Those days are long gone, now that I have Charm to take care of." The face he pulled was a mixture of fond amusement and a grimace. "I miss those days sometimes."

Glad of a conversational topic that didn't involve her arm or her divorce, Mina asked, "How is Charm doing? And Miss Pearl?"

"Charm is growing like a weed. It's hard to fathom that she's almost twelve already, and Granny is doing well, considering her age and the health problems she's had."

Kiah's grandmother had had a stroke just after he'd qualified as a general surgeon, and he'd been his niece's guardian for five years, ever since his sister Karlene's untimely and tragic death. Miss Pearl's ill health had initially drawn him back to St. Eustace, and although the stroke had been minor and Miss Pearl had fully recovered, he'd stayed. While Mina understood the appeal of home and family, she often silently lamented the fact he'd never come back to Canada.

She'd missed him so.

"Twelve, already?" Her mind boggled at the thought. Mina had been at the hospital when the little girl was born. It really didn't seem that long ago. "That's crazy."

Tucking into his food, Kiah just nodded, but she was all too aware of his gaze on her, at least until she picked up her fork and started to eat. Then he relaxed and concentrated on his plate, rather than her.

While they ate, he kept the conversation light, telling her some more about Charm—her dance lessons and determination to be a singer when she grew up—and his cousin's wedding in Calgary the weekend just gone.

"Was your mother there?"

Kiah shook his head and swallowed before answering. "I was worried that she'd turn up, even though she wasn't invited, but thank goodness she didn't. Apparently, I'm not the only person she's alienated and cut out of her life."

"No doubt," she agreed, knowing better than to ask if he'd be looking her up while he was in Toronto.

Kiah's relationship with his mother had been fraught for as long as Mina had known him, and he'd often said he thought she had an undiagnosed mental disease. Mina wasn't so sure. To her it seemed more like a personality problem. Mrs. Langdon could put on a nice face to outsiders, but to her children she was mean, selfish and controlling. The kind of person who, because they weren't happy, felt everyone else around her should be unhappy, as well.

Her assessment seemed to be confirmed when, after Karlene's death and Kiah's last big run-in with his mother, Miss Pearl had said, "I've known your mother since she was a child, and her parents spoiled her by making her feel she was the most important person in the world. Your father, God rest him, was such an easygoing man he continued that when they married. She never could stand it when she didn't get her own way, and has to take it out on everyone else when it happens."

That strained and often frightening relationship with his mother had scarred Kiah in so many ways.

Obviously not wanting to talk about his mother anymore, Kiah said, "I asked Roydon who in their right mind has their wedding in Calgary in January, and you know what he said?"

"What?" she asked, already chuckling. His cousin was a jokester.

"'Man, what better time to do it? I get to go off on my honeymoon to somewhere warm, while everyone else is here, freezing.' They're going to Mexico for two weeks."

"Hey, you can't fault his logic," she said, laughter making her lighter in a way she hadn't been in a long time. "Lucky them, heading for the sunny south."

Yet, even with the amusing conversation as he described the wedding and reception, she was on edge, knowing it was only a matter of time before he got on her case about her life.

He finished eating before she did, and leaned back in his chair, his coffee in hand. Mina immediately tensed. She knew that overly casual stance.

"I want to talk to you about something."

Here it comes.

Trying to be as nonchalant as he pretended to be, she made herself pick up a slice of bacon and wave it in his direction.

"What?"

Had she kept the defensiveness out of her voice? Mina wasn't one hundred percent sure.

"I want you to come to St. Eustace with me and register as an orthopedic specialist."

Dumbfounded, she stared at him, the strip of bacon suspended about two inches away from her lips, and like a ninny could only once more say, "What?"

Kiah must have heard the shock in her voice, because he held up his hand and leaned forward, all pretense of casualness gone.

"Hear me out," he said as she gaped at him. "There's a new Caribbean Clinicians' Union formed, and St. Eustace has joined. It gives new doctors a chance to go to various islands and learn from a variety of doctors and specialists. You can help us prepare, in the eventuality we're accepted into the program."

Mina just stared at him, still at sea, and Kiah made an impatient sound.

"Don't you see? We have great doctors, but this is a whole new world to us. We're not a teaching hospital, so there is some confusion about how to put together a comprehensive training program. This is an area you're extremely knowledgeable in, and it's a great way to put some of that knowledge to use. And while you're there, you can upgrade some of our surgical abilities, too. It would only be for a month or two, or as long as it takes you to put the program together."

The pain that flashed through her was primal, the anger instinctual and blazing.

"Are you crazy?" Mina realized she was shouting but couldn't stop herself, and she got up so fast her chair toppled over behind her. "I can't expose myself like that, in a hospital. What use is a one-handed surgeon? Am I really even a doctor, still?"

She turned away so Kiah couldn't see how close she was to crying, and the rage left her as swiftly as it had arisen. Her shoulders slumped under the weight of the truth she was about to articulate out loud for the first time.

"Don't you see? I'm of no use anymore."

"Nah," came the stern reply, Kiah's voice hard, almost cold. "I don't see that. But what I do see is that you've become a coward."

Mia spun around so fast she almost lost her footing, and Kiah had to stop himself from jumping up to catch her if she fell. There was a sheen of tears in her eyes, but, as he suspected, she was once more furious, rather than sad.

He much preferred her that way.

"What did you say?"

She wasn't shouting now but speaking softly, slowly, and that was even more dangerous. But he was committed.

"You're a coward. Here you are, hiding away, letting all the knowledge you have in your head go to waste, and when I offer you a way back to life, you call me crazy.

When you don't have a feasible argument, turn to insults, huh? Is that how things are going to be?"

Her jaw worked, as though she was trying to get words out, but they were stuck in her throat.

Probably choked by the rage he clearly saw in her eyes.

"What the hell is wrong with you, Kiah? Didn't you get the memo? I lost my hand. I can't operate anymore—"

"But you can teach and supervise, help us figure out how best to train the doctors that'll come to us," he blatantly interrupted her, which he knew she hated almost more than anything else. "Your skills have attracted everyone from sports stars to politicians to have you work on them. Why let that knowledge and experience, that reputation, go to waste? What else do you have going on? Oh, sitting around, crying and looking out onto the gray winter skies? Sounds lovely."

His sarcasm almost pushed her over the edge. She went so far as to take a step toward him, as though ready to physically lay into him.

"What the hell do you know about it?" she snarled. Literally snarled, with her lips curled back, teeth exposed. "How I choose to spend my time is my business, not yours."

Nodding, as though in agreement, would make her even angrier, so he did it.

"True, but when have I ever stayed out of your business? I'm offering you a chance to continue to do something with your medical career, and you're acting as though I'm asking you to single-handedly do spinal surgery on the Pope, with the Swiss Guard watching over your shoulder."

She froze. Went completely and utterly still, staring at him with an expression of something like bewilderment on her face.

"What did you just say?" she asked, almost whispering.

"I said, I'm offering you the chance—"

"No. No. After that."

He thought back, wondering what she was getting at, then slowly said, "You're acting like I'm asking you to single—"

Horrified with himself, he stopped. How could he have been so thoughtless, so careless? There were a million other expressions he could have used. Why the hell had he picked that one?

Her lips twitched.

Tears filled her eyes.

Kiah got up, ready to apologize, once he got his voice back from wherever the heck it had gone.

Then Mina burst out laughing, the sound so unexpected, so sweet, it rocked him back on his heels.

"Oh, God," she howled. "Single-handedly…"

Relief washed through him like a heated wave, and Kiah couldn't help but laugh with her, even though his legs felt shaky.

Then they were in each other's arms, holding themselves up by the combined effort, laughing until Kiah got a stitch in his side.

Once they regained some kind of composure, he leaned back and looked at her.

"So I take it this is a yes?"

She wiped her eyes on her sleeve and snorted.

"Of course not." His stomach sank, until she gave him a grin and continued, "But I'll think about it."

And he knew, right then and there, that he had her.

So he grinned back and said, "All right, think all you want, but we leave next Thursday."

CHAPTER THREE

MINA WAS SURE Kiah's plan was one of the stupidest she'd heard in a long time, but despite her misgivings, less than a week later she was heading to the small Caribbean island of St. Eustace.

Every time she voiced an objection to the trip, Kiah had an answer.

"We need your help."

"No use wasting that expensive medical degree."

"You hate winter, anyway."

That one brought her up short, and she gave him a narrow-eyed glare.

"I do not hate winter. I taught you how to ski, remember?"

He'd snorted, a derisive sound he'd mastered by the age of thirteen and always knew just how to use to best effect.

"Actually, it was your dad who taught me how to ski. And I remember you grumbled the entire time about the cold. Après ski is more your style. Admit it, you're a bit of a disgrace to your Swedish heritage."

That led to a heated argument she knew she couldn't win but also couldn't resist engaging in.

Kiah had that effect on her, and she had to admit she loved it.

He'd also done something no one else had been able to do for over a month: he'd got her out of the apartment, and back into life. Between taking her out to eat and forcing her to go and get her hair done, Kiah wouldn't let her languish at home the way she wanted to.

Yet, through the laughter and teasing, the rehashing of times past and the inevitable questions of "Whatever happened to…?" there remained a painful, raw spot in her chest. There was no way to avoid the awkward moments that arose, like when the salon owner asked if she wanted a manicure, or people stared when they realized she was an amputee. Grief welled inside her every time, reinforcing the little voice whispering, *You're no longer whole. You're deficient.*

The only person who didn't look at her differently was Kiah. Being around him somehow took her beyond the place of pain she was living in.

Now, looking out the window of the plane as it banked to come in for a landing, the sight of the verdant land ringed by aquamarine water along the beaches and rocks made her heart sing. She'd always loved the island and its people, and it felt amazing to have something to anticipate with joy rather than trepidation. After all, if she didn't feel up to the task of working at the hospital, she just wouldn't complete the paperwork Kiah told her the administration had prepared.

Despite his bullying her into the trip, filling out her paperwork was one thing Kiah couldn't do for her, and she considered it her ace in the hole. Her plan was just to stay a few weeks to catch her breath and, if she decided not to take up the offer of work, head back home. She still wasn't sure she'd be doing anyone any favors by pretending her amputation hadn't made a massive difference in her abilities.

When they landed and disembarked, she paused to take a deep breath of warm air, her spirits rising even more.

St. Eustace lay southwest of Grenada, just a little more than halfway to Trinidad, and was a little-known tropical paradise. Being back on the island, seeing the backdrop of lush, rolling hills in the distance, standing under the bluest sky imaginable, caused a bubble of happiness to rise into her chest.

Okay, so she had to admit the trip was a great idea. Not that she was inclined to share that information with Kiah.

But when she looked at him, caught him grinning at her, she realized he knew already.

Suddenly feeling like a two-year-old, she stuck out her tongue at him, and his smile turned to laughter.

They would have gotten through customs and immigration a lot quicker if every other person hadn't stopped, wanting to greet Kiah, or Dr. K, as he was known. And every one of them gave Mina the once-over too, many outright asking who she was.

"This is my best friend, Mina," he told one elderly lady, slinging his arm over Mina's shoulder.

"Best friend? So when you getting married?"

Kiah laughed, and Mina smiled, too, but when he replied they really were just friends, the lady flapped her hands at them.

"If you find a best friend of the opposite sex, and you love them, you need to marry them. You think is so easy to find that?"

Then she stomped off, grumbling under her breath about the younger generation not having any sense.

Kiah and Mina chuckled together, and she couldn't

help teasing him. "You've been saying that 'She's really just a friend' thing for more than twenty years. Aren't you tired of having to repeat it?"

Kiah squeezed her shoulders. "Ha ha. But yes. Sometimes. Especially when people give me that look, as though there's something wrong with me for having you as a friend."

He was navigating through the crowds as he spoke, steering Mina along with his hand, which was now on her back.

"I used to get that at university, too." She sent him a mischievous, sideways look. "But you must have realized that, since the other women on my dorm were always all over you when you came by."

Kiah pushed his lips out and twisted them to the side in impish derision. "I used to tell them I planned to steal you from Warren, just to get them off my back. Besides, at this point, I don't dare get married to anyone else. No woman would stand for me having not only a female for a best friend, but a beautiful one to boot."

Her heart clenched, and for an instant she was overcome with the ridiculous wish that he'd meant it, and they could go back in time so he could save her from marrying Warren.

But he was just joking, so she replied, "That's the most sexist thing I've heard you say in a long time. You should be ashamed of characterizing all women that way. Besides," she added, giving him another sidelong look, "that's just an excuse. You darn well know that's not the reason you don't have a girlfriend."

"Oh?" he said, letting her go to fish out the car keys from his pocket. "So what's the real reason, Miss Smarty-Pants?"

"It's because any woman you're interested in would

have to be intelligent, and if she is, she'd be too smart to be with you!"

"Damn," he said, staggering away from her, clutching his chest. "Straight through the heart."

And they were still laughing together as they got the luggage and then themselves into the car.

When they reached the house, Kiah's grandmother, Miss Pearl, greeted Mina like a long-lost child, hugging her so tight she squeezed the air out of Mina's lungs. Then she beckoned to the young girl standing in the doorway, and said, "Charmaine, come and say hello to Auntie Mina. You remember her, don't you?"

Charm came forward slowly, not out of shyness, Mina thought, but more cautiously than anything else. The resemblance to Karlene, her mother, was so strong Mina had to fight to keep smiling, suddenly wanting to cry instead.

"Yes," Charm said, her solemn expression not changing a mite. "I remember her."

"Well, give her a hug, then," Miss Pearl insisted.

Mina held up her hand. "You don't have to hug me if you don't want to. Why don't we shake hands instead?"

She saw Charm's gaze dart to her left sleeve and then back up to meet Mina's.

"Okay," she replied, holding out her hand to shake.

"Nice to see you again," Mina said, glad to note Charm had a nice, firm grip.

"You, too," the young girl mumbled, before turning away to grab one of the bags and head back inside.

Was she remembering that the last time she'd seen Mina was right after her parents' deaths? She'd been in shock, frightened and traumatized, but sometimes those were the memories that stuck with you. The aftermath of tragedy. The people who witnessed the worst days of your life.

"Hey," Kiah said. "Aren't you going to say hello to your favorite uncle?"

Charm paused and gave him a stare blander than dust. "You're my only uncle," she rebutted but stopped to give him a kiss and accept a hug as she went past.

They spent the afternoon settling in, and then it was time for dinner. Mina kept glancing at Charm, often finding the young girl looking back at her. But once their eyes met, Charm looked away.

She wasn't completely surprised when, as the meal was winding down, Miss Pearl got down to brass tacks.

"So why aren't you wearing your prosthetic?"

Even though she'd been expecting the hard questions, she still balked when having them fired so head-on. But there was no escape. When she sent Kiah a pleading glance, it was to find him looking down at his plate.

Zero help there.

And she didn't want to tell Miss Pearl what she'd told Kiah: until there was a prosthetic available that could help her perform surgery, she wasn't interested.

So, trying to sound upbeat and matter-of-fact, she replied, "I don't have one yet. I'm still trying to figure out which one will be best for me."

That was when she found out where Charm got that drier-than-dust look from. Miss Pearl had it locked down.

"Humph," the older lady said. "You should have had one long ago. The longer you wait, the harder it will be to get used to it. And it's not as though you can't afford a really good, useful one, too."

"Granny," Kiah murmured. "Could you let Mina have a couple of days before you start lecturing her?"

"Humph," Miss Pearl replied again, as she got to her feet. "Charm, come help me clean up."

"I'll do it," Kiah said, pushing back from the table. "Your turn tomorrow, Charm and Mina."

And with a wink Mina's way, he gathered up the dishes and followed Miss Pearl to the kitchen.

Mina glanced over at Charm and found the young girl looking at her in return. This time Charm didn't turn away but tilted her chin up in the air.

"Why are you looking at me like that?" she asked, the defensiveness in her voice clear.

"Because I can't get over how much you remind me of your mom. I'm sorry I'm staring," Mina added, realizing how rude it must seem.

"In what way am I like her?" Charm shot back, looking as though she didn't really expect an answer that would suit, and Mina couldn't help chuckling.

"Well, not just how you look—and you do look a lot like her—but even just then, how you spoke reminded me of her. Do you know what her favorite saying was, when we were young?"

Charm shook her head, still looking skeptical.

"She'd always say, 'Prove it,' any time someone said something she didn't agree with or didn't know for a fact to be true." Mina felt a wave of sadness but tried not to let it show. "She didn't take any nonsense from anyone."

Charm considered that for a moment and then asked, "Were you good friends with her? Like you are with Uncle Kiah?"

Mina shook her head. "Not as good friends. She was a little younger than us, and…" She hesitated for a moment, and then decided honesty would always be the best policy with Charm. "Well, your grandmother didn't approve of her hanging out with us. She'd let us take her to the movies or the fair sometimes, but mostly your mom had her own friends."

She was expecting Charm to ask why, but the youngster just gave a little frown and said, "Did you like her?"

"Your mom?"

Please don't be asking about your grandmother.

Charm nodded, her gaze intent on Mina's face.

Heaving a silent sigh of relief, Mina nodded back. "I did. She was the kind of person who was honest with how she felt. You never had to guess what she thought. And she had a great sense of humor. One of those dry, slightly sarcastic ones, you know? But she was never mean. She didn't say things to hurt anyone, just told the truth, as she saw it."

A little smile touched the edges of Charm's lips. Then she glanced toward the kitchen before looking back at Mina once more, the smile fading.

"Granny Pearl and Uncle Kiah don't talk about her much."

Mina's heart ached, and it took everything she had to keep eye contact with Charm and not tear up.

"Sometimes, when something hurts so much, it's hard to talk about."

It was the best she could offer, but it seemed to satisfy Charm, who nodded slowly again.

Then, as if she'd had enough of that topic, she tipped her chin toward where Mina's left arm lay on her lap, and said, "So what happened to your hand?"

Taken aback, Mina didn't answer right away, and Charm frowned, her eyes narrowing. "Oh, I get it," she said. "You get to know every little thing about me, but I don't get to ask about you."

Mina couldn't help chuckling, although it came out of a throat that felt too tight for comfort.

"There you go again. You sounded just like your mom." Then, still being subjected to Charm's glare, she continued, "My hand got crushed in a boating accident."

Just saying it out loud again brought a rush of emotions—rage, pain and grief all wrapped up together. Charm's frown softened, although not totally going away.

"Couldn't the doctors do anything to fix it?"

Mina shook her head, the irony of it still bitter. "It was too badly damaged, and couldn't be saved. That's what I used to do, you know—fix broken, crushed and shattered bones. When I saw the X-rays of my hand, I knew even I couldn't have done anything other than what the surgeon who worked on me did."

There were footsteps in the hallway leading from the kitchen, and when Kiah came into the dining room, both Mina and Charm turned to look at him.

"What are you two up to in here?" he asked, giving them an exaggeratedly suspicious glance.

Totally deadpan, Charm responded, "Plotting to take over the world."

"Well," he shot back as Mina sputtered into laughter. "I'm sorry to interrupt the planning session, but it's time for you to start getting ready for bed. All your homework done?"

"Yes," Charm said. "I didn't have a lot. Just some math problems, and they were easy-peasy."

"Lemon-squeezy?" Kiah tacked on, making it a question.

"You know it," she replied, pushing back her chair and getting up. "Mrs. Hastings is talking about letting me do some advanced work for the rest of the year. I brought home a note about it but told her she'd have to wait for you to get back before she got an answer."

"I'll take a look at it tomorrow," Kiah said, snagging Charm as she was going by and pulling her in for a hug.

Even though Charm said, "Uncle," in a disgusted tone, Mina saw how she rested her head against Kiah's chest and smiled when he planted a kiss on the top of her head.

"Have your shower, and then you can read for half an hour before it's lights out, okay?"

"It's still early," Charm said, ducking out of the hug and heading for her room. "If I hurry up and bathe, can I read for an hour?"

"Bathe properly, and then forty-five minutes."

"Deal," came her answer from down the hall.

Kiah gazed after her for a moment, and then turned his smile on Mina. Something about the tender set of his lips melted her heart, and she smiled back.

"If I don't keep an eye on her, she'd stay up all night reading," he said, holding out his hand to Mina. "Let's go sit outside for a while. There's a nice breeze tonight."

Instinctively she took that outstretched hand, and then everything froze, just for an instant.

Something shifted inside as an indescribable sensation crashed through her, causing a jolt of adrenaline, sharpening her consciousness so that she saw Kiah as though for the first time. Became aware of his beauty anew, just as she had so long ago when she'd watched him walk past her desk on the first day he'd come to school.

And as though to emphasize the strangeness of it all, she caught a hint of his scent, warm and woodsy, as familiar to her as her own, and yet suddenly different, too. Not that it had changed, but it was somehow interpreted in a new way, so that her pulse began to pound and warmth flooded her belly.

"Mina?" Kiah's gaze sharpened, became probing. "You all right?"

The words shocked her out of whatever the heck she'd been going through, and she blinked, as though awaking from a dream.

"What? Yes, I'm fine," she replied, getting to her feet, firmly shaking off the last vestiges of her strange mental hiatus, although they wanted to cling, like cobwebs. "Just woolgathering for a second. Lead the way."

Kiah didn't move immediately, just held her hand, his fingers firm and strong around hers. "You sure?"

"Of course I'm sure. Come on. I could use a little cool breeze just about now."

And that was no word of a lie. In fact, she'd go so far as to say she could use a cold shower. The lingering effects of whatever she'd just gone through felt suspiciously like arousal.

But that was impossible.

Wasn't it?

"You Canadians and your inability to enjoy whatever the weather is. You constantly complain about it being too hot, or too cold, or too wet, or whatever."

His teasing words were exactly what she needed and led to a spirited argument about his expecting her to not feel the heat when coming out of the winter's cold. But even while they were going back and forth with each other, she felt his gaze on her and knew something had irrevocably changed.

Now she needed to figure out what it was.

CHAPTER FOUR

SINCE HE WASN'T back on call until the Sunday night after their arrival on St. Eustace, Kiah's plan had been to take Mina around and reacquaint her with the island. That went out the window when, the day after they got there, he was called in for an emergency meeting at the hospital, in his capacity as a member of the medical board. In addition to being a surgeon, he wore many hats at the hospital, since the island was small and the number of doctors to call on wasn't large, either.

"There've been reports of possible cases of the chikungunya viral disease in Trinidad, and because we have a lot of people going back and forth between the islands, the minister of health wants to make sure our action plan is solid. Miss Pearl is going, too, since she's the head of the district nurse program, so you might as well come along with us. You can nose around the hospital while we're in the meeting. Maybe even sign the rest of the paperwork so they can finalize your work permit."

Mina was still sitting at the dining table, finishing the last of her coffee, and when she looked up, Kiah saw the refusal in her eyes without her saying a word. He had a battery of answers to combat her excuses, but before they got to that point, his grandmother came into the room.

Miss Pearl gave Mina a visual once-over and then said, "That's too casual for the hospital. Hurry up and change into something else, or we'll be late."

To his surprise, after a short pause, Mina got up.

"Okay," she replied, shocking Kiah with her meek acquiescence. "Give me a few minutes."

Kiah watched her retreating back for a moment, before turning and finding his grandmother's steely gaze resting on him.

Before she could say anything else, he forestalled her with an upraised hand. "And no, although I'm still nominally on vacation, I don't plan to wear these flip-flops to the hospital."

But Miss Pearl didn't seem interested in his casual footwear. Instead, she said, "We should include Mina in the meeting with the minister."

"Why, Granny? She's an orthopedic specialist, not an epidemiologist."

His grandmother gave him a scathing glare, then moved closer, lowering her voice to say, "Use your head, Hezekiah. How long do you think she'll be satisfied by writing manuals and formulating procedures? She's in transition, but eventually she's going to have to figure out what she wants to do next."

"And how will this benefit her?" he asked, trying not to let his irritation show in his tone. If anyone was going to help Mina, it should be him, not his grandmother.

Miss Pearl narrowed her eyes. "She has to be reminded she was a doctor first, before a surgeon. There are a lot of options open to her, but until she realizes that, she'll make no progress. I've already told a number of people about her, and I think she'll be a lot busier than she expects. Besides, there's nothing wrong with her recognizing all the potential here."

Why did it sound as though there were layers of meaning in that statement he was missing?

Before he could question his grandmother further, she turned away, adding, "Now go change into proper shoes, or you'll make us late."

When Miss Pearl used that tone, no one in their right mind disobeyed, especially not her family, so Kiah headed back to his room, still contemplating her words.

She was on the wrong track, he knew. His sole intent on getting Mina to come to St. Eustace was to bring her back to life, give her something to do other than sit around, depressed and wallowing. Once she got back on her feet and was ready to go on with her life, there was no way she was staying here.

There was nothing on their quiet island that would hold her, once she got her head straight. Mina was a creature of the city, used to the bustle and noise, not to mention the frenetic activity of a large, major teaching hospital. She'd had an active social life, too, mostly thanks to Warren the Worm's determination to make a name for himself in Toronto's legal circles. The slower pace of St. Eustace wouldn't hold her interest for long.

Kiah was sure of that.

What was important now was helping Mina come to some kind of peace with the loss of her hand. Kiah had watched her, listened to her, and wasn't fooled by the happy face she was showing the world. Even without her breakdown when he'd arrived at her apartment, he'd have known. Sometimes, when she didn't realize he was watching, he saw her agony of spirit in the downturned lips and shadowed eyes, and he wanted to grab her, hold her, tell it would all work out.

But he knew better than to shatter the illusion she tried so hard to keep up, since doing so would make her retreat, probably all the way back to Canada. Mina always had to feel in control—of herself, her world. Losing her hand, and that sorry excuse for a husband, had shaken her confidence, and he wanted to help her get it back.

He'd also done a lot of research since her accident, wanting to be able to offer all the support and assistance she could possibly need. In his estimation, she hadn't gone through a proper mourning period. Instead, she'd used the excuse of Warren and his crap to push her feelings about the loss of her hand and her job aside, bottling it up inside.

Unless and until she could reconcile herself to her new reality, she'd be stuck. And while getting her back into the hospital setting would be good, he wasn't sure how sitting in on the upcoming meeting would help. It would no doubt be dry and somewhat boring.

At least, he thought, as he heard her leave her room and walk down the corridor toward the front door and rose to follow, it would get her out of the house for a while.

Getting her out of her funk would probably be a lot harder.

Having hoped to put off any talk of going to the hospital to sign papers, at least for a few days, Mina had jumped at the chance of being included in the meeting. She'd ignored Kiah's narrow-eyed look in her direction when she agreed to Miss Pearl's suggestion, and now made sure to walk with the older lady, avoiding whatever comments he was planning to make.

Just being in the hospital had brought a rush of longing

to prickle the backs of her eyes. Once upon a time, this would have been her milieu, a place she'd feel completely comfortable in. Now the bustle and scents of the hospital were somehow alien. Like wearing a piece of clothing you used to love, which had shrunk in the dryer and just didn't fit properly anymore.

The minister of health's eyebrows rose when Mina was introduced to her.

"Nice to meet you, Dr. Haraldson," she said, giving Mina's hand a firm shake. "I've heard a lot about you, and I'm happy you've decided to lend your expertise to our efforts regarding the Clinicians' Union over the next month."

Mina had to resist turning to glare at Kiah. Obviously, he'd made her participation out to be a done deal and, since she prided herself on her reliability, she was now well and truly trapped for at least a month. It could be longer, depending on what exactly they needed her to do. She wasn't one to leave a job half done.

But there was nothing for it but to smile at the minister and say, "It's my pleasure, Minister Barrows." But as soon as the minister turned to go to her chair at the head of the table, Mina sent Kiah a look that promised retribution.

He responded with the sweetest of smiles, which just annoyed her even more.

"As you all know, there have been several cases of chikungunya reported on Trinidad," Minister Barrows said. "And we need to make sure we're doing everything possible to try to protect St. Eustace from a similar outbreak."

"We haven't had a major outbreak of a vector-borne disease on the island since the early 1990s," Miss Pearl said, obviously for Mina's sake. "Although there has been an increase in cases, year over year, for the past five years."

The representative from the Public Health division nodded, adding, "We have an ongoing program of public service announcements aimed at reminding citizens how to minimize the mosquito population, and be mindful of being bitten. So far, they seem to be effective."

As the meeting went on, Mina was surprised at how interested she became. The minister spoke about their reluctance to restart a fogging program, since it was hard on wildlife and people who had any weakness of the lungs. Then she grilled everyone on how they could beef up the existing mosquito eradication program. When all that was suggested was an increase in the frequency of the public service announcements on the television and radio, Mina found herself interjecting.

"How old are the announcements?"

Minister Barrows wrinkled her brow and turned her gaze to the public health officer, who shrugged slightly and replied, "I believe they were developed either during or just after the 1992 dengue fever outbreak."

"Why do you ask?" The minister looked back at Mina, that slight frown still in place.

"Well, you might want to consider doing a new set of PSAs, if the ones you're using are almost thirty years old."

The scowl intensified. "Why?"

"If you think about it, you have an entire generation—those younger than thirty—who don't know what a major outbreak entails, and probably aren't as cautious as they should be. Couple that with announcements so old that people probably don't even listen to them anymore, and you have a recipe for the type of apathy that could derail your efforts."

There were a few moments of silence while everyone considered her words, and Mina felt heat gathering at the back of her neck. Did they think she was talking nonsense?

Then the minister shook her head, still scowling, although slightly less ferociously.

"I see your point, Dr. Haraldson, but unfortunately our yearly budget won't stretch to new announcements."

Kiah leaned forward and said, "Now that I think about it, that thirty-and-under demographic might not even be watching local television or listening to the radio very much. Even if you don't have the funds for new TV and radio announcements, you should, at the very least, put something out on the social media platforms they *are* tuned into."

"It would be much less expensive," Mina said, backing him up. "And how about the schools? What kind of outreach are you doing there?"

"None that I know of," Miss Pearl replied. "But the district nurses go into the schools regularly, so it wouldn't be difficult to come up with a plan to add to the usual talks we give."

"Getting the young people involved could have a huge impact," Kiah said with a wry smile. "As a parent, I know how much children love to be able to take their parents to task over things."

They all chuckled, even Minister Barrows, who said, "I concur. My sons are in their teens now, and convinced I know nothing worthwhile."

"How about some kind of contest in the schools, to tie in with the district nurses' lectures?" Mina suggested. "Something to get them talking, debating the possibilities?"

That led to a spirited discussion, and a number of

ideas were floated, none of which seemed to strike the right chord.

Then Mina had a brainstorm.

"Are the kids here like the ones in Canada, where most of them have cellular phones?"

Once more everyone focused on her, and Miss Pearl replied, "Almost all of them. It's the bane of us older people's existence. You can hardly get them to hear you, much less listen half the time."

"Then, let's kill two birds with one stone," Mina said, excited by her idea.

Kiah started laughing, and she knew he understood exactly what she was thinking, even before he said, "A video competition?"

"Yes." She couldn't help beaming at him. "Let them produce the PSAs. All the phones nowadays have pretty good video capabilities, and I think we'll be surprised at the ingenuity the children will display."

"And any quality issues could probably be cleaned up by the graphics folks," Kiah added. "It will make people sit up and take notice, as well as get the kids fired up."

The air of sudden excitement in the room was exhilarating as she and Kiah batted ideas back and forth, with comments and questions from the other meeting members. By the time they wrapped up, the proposal seemed set to go forward.

"I think we have something worthwhile here," the minister said, with no small measure of satisfaction. "Thank you all for your input, and I'll keep you all informed as we initiate these new ideas."

The meeting was adjourned, and Mina got up and stretched.

The minister paused on her way to the door and said,

"Thank you for participating, Dr. Haraldson. This may not be your area of expertise, but I can already see you'll be a valuable resource going forward. Sometimes a fresh perspective is more useful than empirical knowledge."

"Thank you, too, Minister, for letting me sit in on the meeting. It was very interesting."

"You're welcome." Then she looked from Mina to Kiah, and back again. "You two make a good team."

"Don't they?"

Miss Pearl's tone was brisk, as usual, but for some reason Mina felt a little wave of heat rise into her face.

Kiah just laughed.

"That's what comes when you've known a person for an unconscionable length of time. You start reading their mind."

"Whatever the reason, I'm grateful for it," said Minister Barrows, heading for the exit, her little entourage trailing behind her, shedding farewells as they went.

"Don't just stand there," Miss Pearl said when it was just the three of them left in the room. "Take Mina and show her around the hospital."

Kiah held up his hand, stopping the elderly lady before she could say anything more.

"Granny, that can wait. I'm still on vacation, and fully intend to make the most of it before I'm back on call Sunday night. I'm taking Mina to the beach. Do you want a drive home?"

Miss Pearl surrendered far easier than Mina expected. Only with the tightening of her lips did she show any signs of displeasure.

"No," she replied, giving Kiah one of her dry looks. "I'll take a cab when I'm ready."

Mina kept pace with Kiah, but tension tightened her

shoulders and she was clenching her teeth as they left the building and approached the car. Finally, unable to bear the thought anymore, she stopped. Kiah took another step before he realized she was no longer walking, and turned a questioning expression her way.

"I don't want to go to the beach." Even being shown around the hospital, although also stress-inducing, was preferable to the thought of putting on a bathing suit or sitting in the heat with a long-sleeved shirt on.

Kiah's eyebrows rose.

"Why not? You love the sea."

The anger that stormed through her system was stronger than she could control, and she glared at him. He knew exactly why she didn't want to go but seemed determined to make her say it.

She stepped closer, almost got into his face, and said, "I don't want people staring at me. I don't want to have to answer when some nosy person asks what happened to my hand. And, most of all, I don't want anyone's pity."

Kiah's expression turned stony, his lips momentarily firming into a hard line before he replied, "The only person pitying you is yourself."

Anger turned to rage in a flash, sending a blaze of fire into her veins, and she clenched her hand into a fist, raising it, ready to throw a punch for the first time in her life. Kiah grabbed her wrist, firm fingers even hotter than her fury-heated skin.

"Dr. K!" A breathless female voice came from behind her, breaking them apart. "Dr. K. Wait."

Mina was gasping, trying to regain her composure. She rubbed her wrist, which almost burned with the sensation of his fingers lingering there, and kept her back turned as someone ran up to where they were standing. Kiah, damn him, looked as cool and unruffled as a bucolic stream, making Mina even angrier.

"Yes, Nurse? What can I do for you?"

"Dr. Golding is asking you not to leave." The nurse must have run all the way, her words coming out in little rushes of air. "We have a patient coming in, and he's asking Dr. Haraldson to assist in his care."

And just like that, Mina's fury morphed to cold, nausea-inducing fear.

CHAPTER FIVE

SHE FROZE.

Heart pounding so hard it made her light-headed, she was barely able to make out what the nurse was saying.

"Scuba diver... Accident... Speargun spear through the thigh... Coming in by ambulance from Barefoot Bay."

That much she gathered. The rest was lost, drowned out by the buzzing in her ears.

What did the doctor think she could do to help? Since the accident, she hadn't seen a patient, hadn't treated or even diagnosed an injury. Without her left hand, she was useless. Why couldn't everyone come to terms with that, the way she had?

"Mina." She came to when strong hands closed on her shoulders, and Kiah's gentle voice broke through the stinging noise in her head. "Mina, the ambulance will be here any minute. We need to go get ready."

"I... I can't, Kiah." The words croaked out, just making it past the jagged ball of terror in her throat. "I can't help."

He gave her a little shake, and his voice took on that stubborn, take-no-guff tone she knew all too well. "Of course you can help. You're a doctor. That's what we do. And John Golding is young, inexperienced. If he needs help, how can you turn your back on him and the patient?"

"But without my hand…"

He gave her another gentle shake.

"Mina, you lost a hand, not your brain. Don't you know how valuable the experience, the knowledge you have in your head is?"

The question drew her up, made her think, forced her to focus on Kiah's eyes, the strength and confidence in his gaze.

And she drew on what she saw there, knowing he was right, even in the midst of her fear.

"Okay," she said, although her voice still wavered, and she trembled. "Okay. Let's see what we can do."

"Good girl." Kiah smiled, then bent and lightly kissed her lips. "We can be your hands; you just guide us in what we have to do."

Then he was leading her back into the hospital at a quick walk, as she was trying to forget how wonderful his lips felt against hers, how it was that, not her fears, which was making her heart pound.

She must be losing her mind to even notice such a thing. After all, this was Kiah, and they'd been exchanging platonic kisses like that since they were just kids. Or maybe it was her brain's way of distracting her from what she considered a scary situation.

If that was the case, it was effective, her fear dissipating as soon as she went back through the hospital doors.

The nurse was waiting there and immediately said, "If you'll come with me, Dr. Haraldson, I'll get you some scrubs."

"Thank you," she replied, hurrying after the other woman.

Once she'd changed, the nurse led her back to the emergency room and into a cubicle, just as a siren could be heard in the distance.

The man who approached her looked as though he could still be in high school, although his voice was deep and confident as he said, "Dr. Haraldson, thank you for assisting. I'm John Golding."

She nodded, giving him a slight smile as she went past him to a shelf where the gloves were. "Nice to meet you, Dr. Golding. What can you tell me about the patient?"

"From the ambulance report, the twenty-five-year-old patient, Donovan Exeter, was scuba diving when he was shot through the thigh with a speargun."

"A through-and-through?" she asked.

"No, the spear is still in situ. It entered through the anterolateral aspect, with the tip and about two inches of the shaft exiting the inner thigh. The paramedics wrapped the leg to keep the projectile as stable as possible."

"Any signs of distal ischemia, pulse deficit or hypotension?"

"No. The limb is warm, both the dorsalis pedis and posterior tibial pulses are strong, and his blood pressure is high, not low. He is also able to move his toes."

While they spoke, Mina had pulled a pair of gloves from the dispenser, and it was only now that she realized she had no way to put them on. Not to mention, no left hand to wear one on. Up until then, she hadn't given a thought to the fact her truncated limb was on display in the scrubs, but now embarrassment threatened to make her walk out. Yet, she could hear the clatter of the gurney and knew the patient was almost there.

Gathering all the poise she could manage, she turned to the nearby nurse and said, "Please assist me in putting on these gloves."

To her surprise, the nurse didn't even blink, but said, "Of course, Doctor."

The nurse held a glove, and Mina slipped her right hand into it. But when it came to the left…

"I doubt it will stay on," the nurse whispered quietly.

The gurney came through the door, Kiah accompanying the paramedics from the bay, and there was no more time to dither.

"Thank you," she said to the nurse, then moved forward to evaluate the patient, sticking her left arm into the pocket of her scrub top. Hopefully, she'd remember to keep it there.

Then it was an exercise in frustration as she was relegated to watching everyone else do the hands-on stuff, while she could only advise.

It quickly became apparent the only way to know how much damage was done to Donovan Exeter's leg was via X-ray.

Mina moved to the head of the bed, to explain to him what was going to happen next.

"Mr. Exeter, we're going to have to do some scans to see how much damage was done to your leg internally, before we attempt to remove the spear."

With the patient's consent in place, he was taken to radiology.

"Do you think he'll need to have an angiogram?" Kiah asked as the three doctors followed the patient. "If so, I'll have to call in the chief radiologist, who's off today."

Mina shook her head. "I'm reasonably sure any vascular damage will be slight, just from the position of the spear, and his ankle/brachial index is well above danger level. There's also no signs the femur was damaged, but we'll find out for sure after the X-rays."

And to her satisfaction, she was correct, although there

was no way to know absolutely what they'd find when the spear was removed. In cases like this one, the embedded projectile put pressure on the wound from the inside, often staunching bleeding from damaged veins and arteries. It was only when that pressure was released that they'd know for sure what needed to be repaired.

At the last minute, she balked at going into the operating room.

"The wound tract looks clear," she whispered to Kiah. "Some moderate hematomas to be evacuated. There's nothing special I can add to the surgery, and I'll just be taking up space."

"I'm letting John do the surgery," he replied. "We'll both supervise. But if anything unusual does come up, I want you there to make sure we do the best we can for the patient."

When she started to object, Kiah held up his hand, stopping her midsentence.

"Donovan Exeter is twenty-five, Mina. Still a young man, hopefully with a lot of years ahead of him. The least we can do is ensure he has full use of his leg, not take the chance he's maimed because of a silly accident like this one."

Mina turned away so he couldn't see the gleam of tears in her eyes. What he said was right, and hit home with a blow straight to her heart. No one should have their life, or livelihood, curtailed because of an accident.

"Okay," she said, proud when her voice came out normal, not strained or trembling. "I'll go scrub in. And I have to figure out what to do with this damn stump. I can't wear a glove on it, and the sock isn't sterile."

The last part came out fierce and strong, annoyance

sweeping the last of her uncertainty away, and giving her a new, albeit strange, problem to focus on.

"Hey," he said, putting a hand on her shoulder. "We'll work it out, okay?"

"Sure. Sure," she muttered, stalking off toward the surgical ward, feeling his hand fall away, although the sensation of the pressure and comfort it afforded lingered.

Kiah watched for Mina to come into the scrubbing area, and when she stepped through the doors, already capped, masked and wearing disposable booties, her body language spoke volumes. Here was a woman who wished herself anywhere but where she was.

He was about to go to offer her help with scrubbing in, when a nurse stepped to Mina's side and said, "Can I assist you, Dr. Haraldson?"

"Please," Mina replied, her tone cool and controlled. "And thank you."

The nurse put on her nonsterile apron and then did a thorough job of scrubbing her hand and arm.

Kiah paused on his way into the gowning area and said, "I'll gown up, then help you with yours."

"Thank you."

Anyone who didn't know her would think her response merely polite, but Kiah wasn't fooled. Mina was hating every moment of the situation. She was one of the most self-sufficient and capable people he knew, and having to let someone else help her do something that had become second nature for her must sting.

It was all he could do not to send her a sympathetic glance, but he restrained himself. One hint of kindly concern would just make her even more annoyed and self-conscious.

Yet, for all his worry, she handled the gowning and gloving better than he'd expected, telling the nurse to let her try opening the gown and putting it on herself.

"After all, I'm going to have to get used to doing this, aren't I? In an emergency, no one has time to be fiddling around, helping me."

With an expert flick of her hand, she got the gown partially open and stuck her left arm in. Then Kiah held his breath, watching from the corner of his eye as she used that arm to shake the fabric, trying to get the right armhole open.

"There," she said as she pushed her right arm in, and she might as well have danced a jig, too, she sounded so elated. "That worked better than I expected."

"Me, too," he admitted, sending her a grin, which, although hidden behind his mask, was probably unmistakable. Once the nurse had tied the gown, he said, "Now for the gloves. Have you decided how to handle them?"

"As usual," she said, the challenge in her voice unmistakable. "I'm not operating, so the floppy fingers won't matter, and my forearm and gown should keep it on."

"Aye, aye, Captain," he replied, and was rewarded with a distinct glare from her already flashing brown eyes.

Then they were joined by John Golding, and once he had scrubbed in, they entered the operating room.

Mina had been right about the extent of the injuries, and when the spear was removed, there was little work to be done, except for the evacuation of the clots.

"Watch his blood pressure," Mina told the anesthesiologist. "That would be one of the first signs that we missed vascular damage."

Kiah was enchanted, watching her in theater for the first time. As soon as she'd stepped through the door, all signs of self-consciousness or annoyance disappeared, and she was all business. Yet, in spite of being the specialist, she let John set the pace, only answering his questions, not telling him what to do unless he asked.

And despite Kiah's best intentions, his determination not to cut her any slack because he felt sorry for her, his heart ached, knowing that from now on, hers would be only a supporting role.

It made him want to rage, to bargain with God, to cry. He'd give his own hand if she could have hers back.

"Great job, Dr. Golding," Mina said as the young doctor was applying the negative pressure bandage. "You've got good hands."

John looked up, his eyes gleaming. "And thank you, Dr. Haraldson, for guiding me so expertly."

By the time they met up again, once more in street clothes, Mina looked a totally different person. Euphoric. Grinning.

"That went well," she said as they headed for the car. "There were a couple of times I wanted to grab the instruments and do it myself, but it wasn't as horrible as I thought it would be."

"Is this where I get to say I told you so? Because you know I'll be all over that," Kiah responded, earning himself a swat on his arm.

"Don't you dare."

"You're a natural-born teacher," he said. "I didn't realize how good until I saw you in action."

Mina shrugged. "I've never had a problem instructing others. I guess that's why Toronto South asked if I'd consider staying on as a lecturer. I said no, because I couldn't fathom not having my own practice, or being unable to operate anymore."

Shock brought Kiah to a halt. "They offered to have you stay on, and you refused?"

Mina kept walking, not even looking back as she replied, "Yep. Couldn't see it happening."

But she probably could now, Kiah realized, his heart sinking at the thought of her leaving even sooner than he expected she would.

CHAPTER SIX

THAT EVENING, AFTER DINNER, Miss Pearl said, "The two of you should go out, since you didn't get to go to the beach this afternoon."

"I was planning to help Charm with her homework," Kiah said.

Mina knew he'd felt a little guilty, being away and leaving all the parenting chores to Miss Pearl, but the old lady just flapped her hand at him.

"She did it at Mrs. Gordon's house this afternoon, and I checked it when she got home. Besides, it's Friday night. She deserves a little rest from schoolwork."

"And Granny said she and I could watch a movie tonight," Charm added.

Kiah wrinkled his nose. "One of those sappy romances the two of you love so much?"

Charm turned to Mina and said, "I don't know why you hang out with him, Auntie. He doesn't know the first thing about romance."

"Oh, really?" Kiah narrowed his eyes at his niece in mock anger. "I'll have you know I'm very romantic."

"I'll ask your girlfriend," came the pert reply. "If you ever get one."

Mina almost choked with mirth, and even Miss Pearl

seemed hard-pressed to stop herself from laughing. Though the old lady had the wherewithal to reprimand her great-granddaughter for sassing her uncle, she also had to press her lips tight to stop from joining in with Mina's laughter.

Kiah pounced, tackling Charm on the couch, tickling her and saying, "Apologize to your favorite uncle!"

"My only uncle!" she shrieked while laughing, trying to avoid his fingers, which had unerringly found her ribs.

Eventually, Miss Pearl said, "That's enough, Hezekiah. You'll make the child throw up."

"Ah, sah," he said, flopping back against the couch cushions and tugging a still-giggling Charm against his side. "You see what I have to put up with?"

Charm laid her head on his chest and snuggled in close. "Uncle, how come you didn't pick me up at school today? I thought you would."

"Auntie Mina and I had to help with an operation at the hospital."

"Oh. That's cool, but I didn't think you'd be back at work so soon."

Mina could hear the disappointment in the young girl's voice, but there was no reproach in her tone. The two of them there, together, looked perfect, and Mina felt a warm, sweet glow watching the interplay. Kiah may have fallen into parenthood through tragedy, but it was obvious he was doing a good job of it.

"I didn't plan to be, but I got called in unexpectedly. How was school?"

"Good. We have a new boy in class. His name is Ramesh, and he just moved here from India. The other kids laughed when they heard his name, but I told them not to. Told them that our names probably sound weird to him, too."

The correlation between what Charm described and Mina's first meeting with Kiah was unmistakable, and the wave of nostalgia sweeping through her made Mina smile.

Then Kiah looked up, his gaze colliding with hers, and in his gleaming eyes she saw something she'd never seen before. Something powerful and raw that stole her breath and turned the previous warm glow to heat, which raced out from her belly into her bloodstream.

Time slowed, stopped. Everything faded away, leaving just her and Kiah, caught in a moment for which there were no words, no explanation easily found.

Still holding Mina's gaze, Kiah dipped his head and kissed Charm's hair.

"My sweetheart," he murmured. "That's the most beautiful thing you could do."

Mina looked away first, unable to hold that intense gaze a moment more.

Shaken, she got up, saying, "If we're going out, I should shower and change."

As Mina got to the passageway leading to the bedrooms, she heard Charm ask, "Are you really going out, Uncle Kiah?"

It made her pause, waiting to hear what was said. While she got no sense that Charm resented her, Mina could understand why she might not want her uncle to go back out. After all, not only had he not picked her up from school that day, but he'd also just got back from his trip to Canada.

"Don't you want me to?" Kiah asked in return.

"Yes, I do want you to. If you stay here, you'll just make rude comments and ruin the good parts of the movie."

Chuckling quietly to herself, Mina continued on her way, as Kiah appealed to Miss Pearl for help.

"Granny, are you going to let her talk to me that way?"

"Huh. I'd chastise her, but we all know is the truth she's talking."

But by the time Mina got to her bedroom and closed the door behind her, her amusement had faded, and anxiety took over.

Going out was the last thing she wanted to do. Sure, she been elated earlier at being back in the operating room. Remembering, on a visceral, soul-deep level, why she'd become a doctor, and knowing for the first time since the accident she'd find a way to be true to her calling.

It was a little like awakening from a deep, restless sleep, with the sense of time lost, she thought, as she climbed into the shower.

But that was the hospital. A place where no one working there would be inclined to be curious about a one-handed person. Anywhere else, she was sure to get those strange looks and stares, the inquisitive questions.

Yet, hiding from it wasn't going to change anything, and that reality was something she'd steadfastly refused to accept.

Caring for the patient today had brought it into focus. She was in a state of transition from the life she used to have, to a new way of being. Looking back, she wondered where things had gone wrong, and why she'd made some of the decisions she'd made. But in truth, no amount of navel-gazing was going to change a moment of her past and, in order to go forward, she had to find acceptance.

Lifting her left arm, she looked at her stump, turning it back and forth under the water. Seeing and examining it fully for the first time. She'd been trying to ignore it, to pretend that at some point she'd look down and her hand would, magically, be there.

So much denial, and anger, and sadness, over something no one—nothing—could undo.

Tears threatened, but she held them back, despite the fact she felt only a lingering sense of sorrow, not the racking pain she associated with thoughts of the accident and memories of her loss.

"It's time you got your head on straight, Mina Haraldson." The words echoed in the shower stall, weightier for being spoken aloud. "No more feeling sorry for yourself or pretending that losing your hand means everything is finished. Time to make a new plan and get on with life."

Then she stuck her head under the spray, letting the water wash away the tears she swore would be the last she shed for Warren, for the accident, for the loss of her hand. For a life that had, if she were honest, grown stale and gray despite her love for her work.

Onward and upward.

By the time she'd dressed and looked at herself in the mirror, Mina felt she'd successfully covered any evidence of her tears. A little eyeshadow and mascara did wonders, she reflected, and her linen pirate-inspired blouse, with its flouncy cuffs, hopefully would camouflage her stump.

Even her new determination and just-finished pep talk couldn't totally reduce her tension, but seeing Kiah in a bright orange shirt somehow made the outing far less stressful.

"Going for the Bird of Paradise look?" she asked, earning a giggle from Charm and a glare from Kiah.

"Don't you like it?" he asked, striking a pose, one hand behind his head, the other on an outthrust hip. "Will it embarrass you to be seen with me like this?"

"Would you change it, if I said yes?"

"Nope," he said, striding across the room, then doing a dramatic turn. "I'd run downtown and see if I could find a pair of matching pants."

"You see how bad he is, Auntie?" Charm said, shaking her head.

"Oh, you'd be surprised at how many ladies love a man in a blinding shirt," Mina replied, making even Miss Pearl chuckle.

In truth, the shirt emphasized Kiah's handsomeness, showing off his dark, smooth complexion and sparkling eyes. As he kissed first Miss Pearl then Charm goodnight, Mina found herself hard-pressed to take her gaze off him. The effect of the look he'd given her earlier lingered beneath her skin, heightening her awareness of him. No matter how often she told herself it was just a sweet, nostalgic moment, her body refused to listen. Instead, she was extremely conscious of their closeness within the confines of the car as they got underway.

But she made sure to keep the conversation light, hoping these new sensations would fade.

They better.

Kiah found himself watching Mina carefully as they left the house.

He wasn't sure what had passed between them earlier, when he'd reacted to Charm's story. His niece's words had taken him back to the first time they'd met, and his gaze was drawn straight to Mina's.

The memory had been there in her eyes, too, but it had been soft, fond, while he...

Hell, he didn't even know what he'd been projecting, only knew the raw emotion in his blood wasn't soft. Or fond. No, it had been fierce, almost desperate. And God only knew what Mina thought his expression meant.

He half expected her to bring it up, but she didn't. Instead, she chatted about Miss Pearl and Charm's movie date, as though that was the only thing of importance occurring that evening.

It was a relief.

When they pulled up to the little club on the beach, she gave a cry of delight.

"I remember this place," she said as she opened her car door. "It wasn't called the Sweet Spot then, though, was it?"

"No," he replied, smiling at her enthusiasm. "It was called Yellow Bird the last time you were here."

"We had a blast that night, although that young woman who took a shine to American Jimmy got so drunk and became obnoxious when he wouldn't take her home with him. Whatever happened to Jimmy?" she asked as they approached the door. "Is he still around? He's a fun guy."

"He is still around," Kiah said, of the man who'd come to work on St. Eustace fifteen years before and never left. "He's been seeing a really nice woman, and I heard he's gone to Barbados to meet her family."

"Sounds serious," she said as she looked around the small club. In true Caribbean style, it was still almost empty, since most people came out later. It was a nice night, warm, with a hint of sea breeze, so they wound their way through the tables to the other door, which led to the patio.

There they found a table near the railing, within eyeshot of the sea lapping on the nearby rocks. Once they sat down, Kiah continued the conversation.

"Apparently he's asked her to marry him."

"I'm a little surprised. Wasn't he the local Romeo?"

Kiah chuckled. "Once Jimmy met Sharon, that was it. You can tell from just seeing them together how in love with her he is."

Mina turned her gaze toward the water, a pensive expression flitting over her face for an instant, making him wonder what she was thinking. But before he could ask, she faced him again and said, "Charm was asking me about Karlene last night, after dinner."

His heart rate kicked up in reaction to her words, and he scrubbed his palm along his cheek, getting his emotions under control, before asking, "What did she say?"

"Just asked me what I meant when I said she reminded me of her mother. Wanted to know if I liked Karlene. Things like that. She said neither you nor Miss Pearl like to talk about her, and I think she needs you to."

The weight in his heart increased, grew almost unbearable for a moment. Then he took a deep breath, trying to regain his equilibrium. When Mina reached across the table to take his hand in hers, Kiah hung on to it, as though it were a lifeline.

"We used to, when she first came to us, but every time we mentioned Karlene's name or said something about her, Charm shut down. Granny and I agreed to stop, figuring when Charm was ready to talk about her mother, she'd let us know. Ask questions. I think, somewhere along the line, not talking about her turned into a habit."

She squeezed his fingers a little tighter.

"Well, discuss it with Miss Pearl, and the two of you come up with a plan. It's been five years since Karlene and Roy died. Maybe Charm has questions she needs answered. Not just about her mom, but about what happened."

He shook his head, unable to help it. The last thing he

wanted was to have to discuss her parents' murder-suicide with Charm, but in his gut he knew he'd have to.

"She needs to know why it happened, Kiah. Charm probably hates her father, which is only natural under the circumstances. No doubt you do, too, in some ways. But the difference is, half of her comes from Roy. She needs to understand what happened."

"I still don't fully understand it, Mina." His throat felt raw, just as it had the night after the phone had rung, and a police constable had called from Canada to inform him Karlene and Roy were dead. Then, though, it was because he'd roared in anguish, unable to restrain himself, mindless with grief. Now it was because he knew he'd have to relive it, sometime soon, for Charm's sake.

Mina stroked the back of his hand with her thumb, as though trying to soothe him as best she could. It helped, but not enough to make the conversation palatable.

"Roy was suffering from PTSD. You know that."

"But how do you explain that to a twelve-year-old?"

"Charm is more than mature enough to hear the truth. That her father went off to war one man and came back another. That he tried to get help, but it wasn't enough."

Now anger edged the fear and sadness aside, and he welcomed it. "Do I tell her that her grandmother, who's a bitter, controlling woman, couldn't stop stirring up trouble? Tell her that her poor father, already fighting the demons in his head, couldn't take any more of his mother-in-law's nagging and bickering? Does she get to hear that part, too? Because I can't even say it without feeling ill."

"No," Mina said softly, her eyes full of gentle wisdom and care. "She doesn't need to know that part. That's more than is necessary right now. But she does need to know her father wasn't a monster, which means she's not half monster too, if you see what I mean?"

"I do see what you mean," he said, the reluctance clear in his tone. He, better than anyone else, recognized the effect knowing you had a monstrous parent could have on a child. Then he shook his head, his lips twisting to the side for an instant. "But why is everything so difficult, Mina? Why can't life be simple?"

"I wish I knew, Kiah. I really do."

Just then the waiter approached and Mina let go of his hand, leaving him suddenly hollow and bereft.

CHAPTER SEVEN

SHE'D WANTED A change of subject, away from American Jimmy and his new girlfriend, but going from that to Karlene and Roy, and Kiah having to talk to Charm about them, left her raw. Both were subjects that made her heartache all the harder to bear, albeit in different ways.

Not that she was bitter, really; she wished nothing but the best for Jimmy and his lady. But hearing about them falling in love was a reminder of how unlikely it was that she'd ever be in a similar situation. Warren and his ugly truths had put paid to that.

Then talking about Karlene and Roy... *Ouch.*

She'd been the one Kiah called, after hearing from the cops, and it was Mina who'd gone to the police station to be with Charm. The memory was one that haunted her still, and she could only imagine how Kiah felt about having to relive that time with his niece.

So, having the waiter come to take their drink orders was something of a relief.

"Rum punch?" Kiah questioned, after the waiter left. "You remember how strong those are, right?"

Mina gave him a grin and nodded. "Yep, but I feel like celebrating, and I know you'll take care of me if I get a little tipsy."

The club started filling up, and people gravitated to their table. A couple of men, whom Kiah introduced to her as Slim and Henkel—she never did get their real names—were the ones who stuck around, while others came and went. They were fun, trading jokes and stories with Kiah while flirting outrageously with Mina, who laughed it all off.

"Hey, why you so nosy, Henkel?" Kiah broke in to the conversation, as his friend started questioning Mina about her life.

"Cho, man. Just trying to get to know this lovely lady a little better," came the easy reply, accompanied by a sly grin. "I think your *friend* is old enough to take care of herself. You mind your own business."

"On that note," Mina said, laughing as she got up, "I'm going to the ladies' room."

There was no way she was hanging around for the part when he asked her what happened to her hand.

She'd seen the men glancing at her empty sleeve whenever she raised her arm above the level of the table, and knew it was coming. If she could forestall it until after she'd had another rum punch, maybe she could come up with a witty, pithy reply.

There was a bit of a line for the bathroom, and by the time she came back outside it was to find the dance floor crowded with people, all jumping and dancing to a popular calypso song. And there, in the midst of it all, was Kiah.

Mina kept walking, even though her first impulse was to stop and stare. The woman dancing with him was gorgeous, with long, professionally streaked hair, impeccable makeup and an hourglass figure on full display in a tight, skimpy jumpsuit.

And if she danced any closer to Kiah, they'd be wearing the same pants.

Why that annoyed Mina as much as it did, she didn't want to contemplate, but it took everything she had to keep a slight smile on her face and not look back at the gyrating couple.

Slim and Henkel got up as she approached, and Henkel held out his hand. Then he did a little sideways shimmy toward the dance floor.

"Come dance with me, Mina," he said.

She laughed and shook her head, already lowering herself into her chair. Thankfully it was facing away from the dance floor, so she could avoid the display going on there.

With an elaborate sigh, Henkel sat down beside her and, resting his elbow on the table, put his chin in his palm so he was looking right into her face.

"So, Miss Mina, how long are you staying here with me?"

He made it sound as though she came specifically to see him, and would be moving into his house any minute, and she couldn't help chuckling.

"I'm not sure yet. Probably about a month. Just until I get the new systems I'll be working on for the hospital squared away."

How a man of his age could still achieve puppy-dog eyes was a mystery to Mina, but somehow he managed it.

"If you need someone to show you around and take you to nicer places than this, just let me know, you hear?"

Slim kissed his teeth and rolled his eyes, then leaned forward so he was almost right between Mina and his friend.

"Don't go anywhere with him. You don't need an old reprobate like him hanging around."

"Who you calling a reprobate?" Henkel abandoned his attempt at flirtation and rounded on his friend.

"You, same one," was the reply.

"Huh. If I'm so much of a reprobate, how come you're always hanging out with me?"

"Because I'm one, too," was the response. "But I'm just honest about it."

Mina couldn't help laughing at the banter, even though her thoughts remained fixed on the dance floor. The song had changed, but Kiah hadn't come back.

As though reading her mind, Slim looked that way and shook his head, before taking a sip of his drink.

"Aii, sah. That Trini girl goin' wine off Kiah's pants front, if he's not careful."

"We used to call him 'Calypso Kiah' back at university," Mina said, trying to sound nonchalant, and steadfastly resisting the urge to turn around to gawk, too.

"Not surprised," Henkel replied, his eyes narrowing, so that Mina wondered exactly what was happening. "You knock two tin cans together on the other side of the island, and that man is there to dance. *Whew*, that woman getting on bad."

"Getting on bad" was one of those all-purpose expressions Mina had learned over years of knowing Kiah. It could mean anything, from praise of the woman's dancing skills to her being about to start a fight, but somehow she didn't think Henkel meant the latter. His eyes were wide, and he raised a hand to fan at his face.

Slim chuckled. "Niesha's been trying to reel Kiah in for the last six months, not realizing she hasn't set the hook yet."

Henkel shook his head. "Lost cause, that man. She

could hook me, reel me in and sink me, all in that time, and I wouldn't even mind."

"Ha, that's what you say now, but Niesha would chew you up and spit you out without blinking, and if she ever looks at you the way she looking at Kiah now, you'd run *so* fast."

Okay, now Mina had to glance over her shoulder to see what it was the men were looking at, and when she did, she wished she hadn't.

With her body pressed flush to Kiah's and one arm draped over his shoulder, Niesha was staring up into his face with an expression of blatant hunger. And that swivel thing she was doing with her hips…

With heat rising at her nape, Mina forced herself to turn back around and reached for her glass, trying to push away the emotions bubbling in her chest. It wasn't as though she wasn't used to seeing women throw themselves at Kiah. That had been happening since they hit puberty and the girls started noticing how handsome he was. Yet, somehow, tonight was different.

It actually *hurt*.

She took a long swallow of her drink and tried to focus on what the other men were saying. And by the time Kiah made his way back to the table, Niesha in tow, Mina thought she'd got her inexplicable jealousy under control.

"Whew, that was something, boy." Niesha sank into a chair and flipped her hair back over one shoulder, giving Kiah a sultry glance as he sat next to her. "You know how to move, man."

Kiah just laughed, glancing at Mina, who quirked her eyebrows at him, trying not to show him her teeth, the way she wanted to.

"Niesha, this is my friend Mina. Mina, this is Niesha."

"Hi," Niesha said with a grin, but Mina thought her eyes were watchful. "You're Kiah's friend from Canada, right?"

"Yes," Mina said, smiling in return, although it was the last thing she felt like doing.

"I don't know how you stand the cold up there. I like things *hot*."

The look she gave Kiah made it obvious she considered him one of those hot things she liked.

"It's not so bad when you get used to it," Kiah said, sending Mina a mischievous grin. "Although Mina always complained all through winter, and she was born there."

Mina made a blah-blah-blah motion with her hand back at him, which made him laugh, then Niesha leaned toward him, pressing her ample bosom against his arm.

"While I remember, I'm putting together a team for the bank's fund-raising 5K run. Join me?"

And after that Niesha dominated the conversation, leaving Mina mostly to her own thoughts, since they were talking about places and people she didn't know. And when Kiah tried to draw her into the conversation, she resisted, albeit with a smile, unaccountably annoyed with him, although he'd really done nothing wrong.

Kiah glanced at his watch and decided to call it a night. He'd had more than enough of Niesha, who was loud, brassy and handsy, too. She'd dragged him onto the dance floor while he was on his way to the bar, and, as hard as he tried to keep a decent distance between them, she'd been all over him like polyester on a humid day.

Normally he didn't think twice about dancing that way. But since Niesha had made it clear on several occasions that she was willing to have an intimate relationship with him, and Kiah wasn't interested, it didn't feel right to encourage her.

Worse, once back at the table, she'd totally taken over, hardly giving anyone else a chance to get a word in edgewise. He'd been unable to resist making the comparison between her and Mina, who didn't need to slather on makeup or wear a barely-there outfit to be beautiful. And although she'd consumed a number of rum punches, Mina hadn't gotten loud or boisterous, nor demanded the attention of everyone at the table be focused on her.

Even though he thought Mina was still too slender, he preferred her more subtle curves—her delicacy—to Niesha's buxom figure.

But he was going to have to have some sharp words with Henkel, who was hanging all over Mina as if he was about to smother her. Not that Mina seemed to particularly mind, since she just laughed and had a joking reply to most of his advances.

Kiah didn't know why seeing the other man whispering in Mina's ear made him so annoyed, but it definitely had to stop.

As soon as he said they were leaving, both Niesha and Henkel objected, but Kiah didn't bother arguing with them. Instead he put his arm around Mina's shoulders and, with a last round of goodbyes, led her out of the club.

"You can stay, if you want," she said, once they were outside. "No need to leave on my account."

Kiah paused. "Did you want to stay?"

"No, but I can grab a cab home, if you wanted to go back in. Niesha seemed very disappointed that you were leaving so soon."

Kiah started walking again, tugging Mina along with him, his arm still over her shoulders. She was walking steadily, but he'd seen how many rum punches she'd drunk, and wasn't taking any chances. The unpaved, gravel-covered parking lot was uneven. "I can't help that. Besides, I'm really not interested in her."

"She's very beautiful."

Kiah snorted. "Not my type."

They'd gotten to the car but before he could open her door, Mina turned her back to it, blocking the handle. "Kiah, when was the last time you had a relationship?"

She knew the answer, he was sure, but he replied anyway. "Not since Valerie and I broke up. Why?"

She didn't reply to his question, just tilted her head to one side, her shadowed gaze searching his. In the faint light from the street, which cast her cheekbones and tender lips into sharp relief and made her eyes look wide and alluring, her face was mysterious.

"You never told me what happened between you. You'd sounded happy with her."

Kiah rubbed at his cheek. This was the last thing he wanted to talk about, especially on the heels of their earlier conversation about Karlene and Roy.

"We had a parting of the ways, Mina."

She huffed out a little breath, her lips curving, although she didn't really look amused.

"What caused it, this parting of the ways?"

"We…disagreed on the advisability of my taking custody of Charm. Valerie was very up-front about not wanting to raise another person's child."

"Wow." Mina sounded genuinely shocked. "So what did she think should happen to Charm, then, if you didn't take custody?"

"I don't think she much cared."

Mina scowled. "That's the worst thing I've heard in... in forever. I hope you told her where to get off."

He couldn't help the bitter, rueful bark of pseudo laughter he gave. "I'm afraid I did, and I'm not proud of it. I hadn't lost my temper like that in years."

Mina shook her head, her lips firming for an instant. "You'd just gone through the tragedy of Karlene's death, and were under the stress of your mother and her nonsense. No one could blame you for losing it. Charm's future was at stake."

He blamed himself, though, for the loss of control, for expecting Valerie to be more supportive than she was. "I should have expected her reaction. She'd already told me she wasn't interested in having children at all."

"And you agreed with that? Before this...disagreement?"

Kiah nodded, watching Mina's expression, wondering where she was going with this entire conversation.

"It didn't really matter to me, whether we had kids or not. I actually would have preferred not to. You know I've always said that between my father dying so young and my mom's emotional instability, it's probably better these genes don't get passed on. My thoughts on that haven't changed."

"Even though you've been tested for the congenital condition your father had?"

He noticed she didn't mention his mother and was glad. He didn't want to discuss her if he could help it, nor talk about how much of her he sometimes saw in himself. Like the night he and Valerie got into it, and he'd said some truly hurtful things before walking away, knowing he desperately needed to cool off.

"It's not worth the risk," he said. "I didn't plan on it, but I have Charm to take care of, and that's enough for me."

"Is it really?" She held up her hand, as though knowing his answer already. "Forget I said anything. It's the rum talking. I worry about you, want you to be happy."

"I am." Even as he said it, he realized it was true, and a lot of his present happiness came from being there just then, with her. "And I want the same for you."

Something changed in her expression. If he didn't know her as well as he did, he'd have missed it, but even so, he couldn't interpret the emotion that suddenly shadowed her eyes and fractionally tightened her lips.

When she reached out and trailed her fingers along his cheek, so lightly they could have been butterfly wings, he froze, startled by the surge of emotion engendered by her tender caress.

"Let me tell you a secret," she said, leaning in so her face was close enough that he could have kissed her, if he dared. "Sometimes it's far easier to accept your limitations than it is to fight against them and get your heart broken."

Before he realized her intention, Mina closed the gap between them and placed her lips on his. Soft and sweet and warm, they teased his mouth, moving ever so slightly, and now he recognized what he was feeling.

Desire.

Need.

But this was Mina.

Mina!

And although he wanted to pull her closer, deepen the kiss into something carnal and fierce, he held himself as still as possible, hardly daring to breathe, lest she figure out what he was feeling.

She pulled back, her gaze searching his, then she turned away, fumbling with the handle of the car door, saying, "Dammit, Kiah. You got me drunk again, and now you won't take me home to bed."

"Lawd," he groaned, hoping she would think he was just grousing and not wishing he could do just that—take her home to his bed, and make love to her all night long.

And he knew she'd interpreted it the way he hoped when she laughed, and would have tumbled headfirst into the car if he hadn't had a firm hold on her arm.

CHAPTER EIGHT

MINA AWOKE ON the morning after Kiah had taken her to the club by the beach, and lay staring at the ceiling, trying to sort through what had happened the night before. It was a complete departure from her usual self, almost beyond comprehension.

Why'd she been jealous of Niesha monopolizing Kiah's time and dancing so erotically with him? It wasn't as though she'd never seen Kiah flirting and dancing with women before. Hell, she'd teased him about his amorous adventures since they were fourteen or fifteen.

But last night had been different. She'd seethed, wanting his attention for herself, not on the beautiful, bountiful Niesha.

And then, if that weren't bad enough, when they were standing in the parking lot, she'd had the overwhelming urge to kiss him, and she had. The jolt of awareness and desire rocketing through her body when their lips touched had made her sudden physical attraction toward him abundantly clear.

Rolling over onto her side, she stared sightlessly at the window.

She wished she could put it down to the rum, but she

knew that while she'd been a little tipsy, she was nowhere near drunk enough to use the alcohol as an excuse.

And there'd been no reaction from him to the kiss. Not that she'd expected him to grab her and ravage her on the spot. That would have been ludicrous and hysterical. But wouldn't he have at least tried to kiss her back, if the thought had even fractionally crossed his mind? And when she'd seen his expression afterward, it had been blank, with perhaps a hint of a question in his eyes.

No interest or passion.

Not even a touch.

The entire situation was embarrassing. And confusing.

Where had these feelings even come from?

Sighing, she sat up, since she could clearly hear the rest of the household stirring. Hopefully, Kiah would think nothing of what had happened between them, and look at the kiss as one of their usual friendly salutes. If he brought it up with her, she had no idea how to react, or what to tell him.

Thankfully, he didn't mention it, and everything seemed normal, except for her heightened awareness of his every move.

Kiah came into the kitchen, where she was helping Miss Pearl fix breakfast, and asked, "Hey, you want to go for a drive after breakfast?"

"Sure," she replied, although wondering if it was a way to get her alone to talk about the night before. Then she turned to Charm. "You coming with us, kiddo?"

Besides the fact that she enjoyed Charm's company, the little girl would be a good buffer between Kiah and herself, until Mina could figure out what was going on inside her own head.

"Yes," was the reply, laced with more eagerness than

she'd expected. Then she understood why. "It'll be much better than staying here and reading my history book. I have to do an essay, but it's so boring."

"Wasn't my favorite subject, either," Mina confessed. "But it's important to understand why things in the past happened the way they did. You know the famous quote about forgetting the past, don't you?"

"The one about having to repeat it?" she asked. When Mina nodded, Charm sighed. "Granny says it all the time. Usually when I make the same mistake twice."

"If you're tired of hearing it, then don't make silly mistakes over and over again," was Miss Pearl's tart remark from over at the stove.

Charm wrinkled her nose, and Mina swallowed her chuckle. No sense in letting the old lady know her great-granddaughter was silently sassing her!

"When is your essay due?" Kiah asked.

"Not for two weeks," Charm replied, turning her best begging face to her uncle. "I have lots of time."

"Okay, you can come," he said, continuing over her cry of jubilation, "but I want to see a first draft by the end of next week."

"Can we stop at Salty's and get roast corn?"

"Sure," he said, earning another whoop from Charm.

The day was gorgeous, with just a few puffy clouds drifting overhead in the azure sky and a nice breeze coming off the coast. Port Michael, the capital of St. Eustace, was situated on the southeast side of the island, and Kiah turned the car east, following the road that hugged the coast.

Charm was in high spirits and carried on a running, largely one-sided commentary of the music she liked, TV shows she'd watched, and the latest drama going on at school. Kiah put in an observation or answered when necessary, leaving Mina to follow her own muddled thoughts.

But despite doing her best to appear as if nothing at all had changed, she found herself noticing little things about Kiah that she hadn't really paid attention to for a long time.

The deep, warm timbre of his voice; the rumbling laughter that flowed from him so easily.

How broad his shoulders were, and how the muscles in his arms and legs flexed and relaxed beneath his clothes.

Those sensual hands, with their long fingers and broad palms.

The absolute, breathtaking beauty of his smile, and the way the corners of his eyes crinkled when he was amused.

In a strange way, it was like seeing him anew, all her favorite things about him enhanced and more appealing than ever.

Yet, she was sure she couldn't, shouldn't trust what she was feeling right now, as it could be just a by-product of the upheaval in her life. Coming to terms with the losses she'd sustained didn't automatically inure her to the pain, and the fear of losing more. Maybe Kiah represented stability, and she was grasping at the safest straw she had, because she'd been adrift so long?

Thinking about it that way made her a little sad, and she sighed.

"Everything okay over there?"

Kiah's question shook her out of her reverie, making her realize the conversation between him and Charm seemed to have stopped. She half turned to send him a smile.

"Fine, just wondering what they'll have me doing at the hospital on Monday. What time do we leave to get there?"

His eyebrows quirked up slightly as he threw her a quick glance. "I'm on call tomorrow night, but if there's no emergency and I'm not called in, I'll leave home at about seven, drop Charm off to school and head into the hospital then."

"And what happens if you're called in and already at the hospital?"

"There's a taxi driver who'll come for Charm. He can drop you off then, too, or come back for you afterward, if you don't want to be up so early."

"My friends at school like it when Uncle Kiah drops me off." Charm's comment, dripping with scorn, came from the back seat. "They think he's cute."

"I think he's cute, too," Mina couldn't help saying, casting Kiah a mischievous grin. "Don't you?"

"He's all right," Charm said grudgingly. "But my friends get all silly over him and that's gross. He's so *old*."

They'd turned off the coast road and were going up into the hills. Kiah took his foot off the accelerator.

"Okay, that's it," he said, shaking a fist in the air. "I'm letting you out here. You can walk home, missy."

"How far are we from Salty's? I'll just stay there," came the irrepressible reply, and Mina couldn't hold back her laughter.

As it turned out, it wasn't that far from the roadside shack. As they pulled up, Mina was surprised at the number of cars filling the small parking area and overflowing onto the road.

"Ah, the parking gods are with me today," Kiah said, when a car backed out of the lot just as they pulled up.

After he'd slotted his car into the space, they all got out, and Charm ran off right away to join the line, leaving them to follow at a slower pace. Kiah slung his arm over her shoulders, the way he often did, but today it felt heavier, his muscles more solid, and a shiver of awareness traveled down Mina's spine.

"So you think I'm cute, huh?"

"Don't be fishing for compliments, Hezekiah." She tried to channel Miss Pearl, making her voice stern, but he just chuckled, tightening his grip on her.

"I don't find it complimentary that a bunch of twelve-year-olds are standing around ogling me. It fills me with self-doubt. Are they the only ones who think I'm cute? Is that why I can't get a date?"

They'd paused under a shady tree, where they could see Charm's slow progress toward the head of the line without having to join her in the hot sun.

"You can't get a date because you're not looking for one," Mina reminded him.

"True," he replied easily. "But speaking of dates, Henkel looked like he was putting some serious moves on you last night. Did he ask you out?"

She glanced up at him. There was something almost too casual about the way he'd spoken, but with his dark glasses firmly in place, she couldn't read the expression in his eyes.

"No offence to your friend, but I think he'd make moves on any woman who crossed his path. I didn't take him seriously at all."

"He's not a bad guy, and usually is more talk than action, but I got the impression he really was into you."

"I'm not interested in anything like that, right now."

"Like what? Going out? Having a little fun?"

She found herself tucking her left arm up under her right, where it was safely out of sight.

"Not interested in being gawked at, like a freak."

Kiah dropped his arm and, putting his hands on her shoulders, turned her to face him. His expression was solemn, with a hint of temper tightening his lips.

"First off, you're not a freak, by any means. You're the same gorgeous, wonderful woman you've always been. And secondly, I was not suggesting that you put yourself in a position where Henkel would be *gawking* at you."

Even with him saying those lovely things about her, the tone of his delivery sparked her temper in return, and she gave him a narrow-eyed glare.

"What kind of position is that?"

He put his face down close to hers, so his breath brushed across her skin when he spoke.

"Like sleeping with him."

Although that was what she was expecting, Mina couldn't find an answer, her brain short-circuiting. It was on the tip of her tongue to say, *I don't want to sleep with anyone, except you.* Thankfully, her tongue had cleaved to the roof of her mouth, making uttering even a single word impossible.

Heat trickled out from her core, and her knees suddenly weakened.

What would it be like to make love with Kiah, feel those strong, wonderful hands on her skin? Just the thought had a sheen of perspiration breaking out on her brow.

Mortified at the turn her thoughts had taken, she ducked out from under his hands and away from his too-intent stare.

"Just because I'm recently divorced doesn't mean I'm desperate," she said, as much to herself as to Kiah. "You don't have to worry that I'll *get on bad* while I'm here and embarrass you."

And before he could reply, she changed the subject, asking about the hospital protocols, and if he had any idea of what she'd be facing.

Already she knew she was really just a figurehead, a paper tiger being used to make the hospital look good to the Clinicians' Union, but that no longer stung the way it had before. She was trying to see it as a foot in the door, and a way to figure out what else might be possible for her in the future.

"I was told you'll have a staff of administrators to help you get the systems in place," Kiah said. He knew she hadn't really paid much attention to the reams of information they'd sent her in Canada, and he hadn't pushed her to look at it, seeming just content to get her agreement to come back to the island with him. "But I also think you'll be asked to see patients, like you did for John. Hopefully, that works for you."

"That should be fine," was what she said out loud, but inside she was thinking it would be doubtful she'd be seeing many patients. After all, the scuba accident was an anomaly, and surely the hospital had other competent orthopedists?

"Charm's almost at the counter," Kiah said, touching her arm. "Let's go."

Once they got their food, they found a spot at one of the picnic tables set up among the trees, and tucked in to their chicken, roasted yam, and, of course, roasted corn.

"I remember having this when I came on vacation from med school that year, and it tastes just as good now," Mina remarked, between licking delicious barbecue sauce off her fingers.

"Clearly we're going to need more napkins," Kiah said and got up to head back to the counter for some.

As he passed another table, one of the men sitting there called out to him, and Kiah stopped to chat.

Charm sighed. "Everywhere we go, people know him."

"Well, St. Eustace isn't very big, and he's well known because of his work, so it isn't too surprising."

Charm didn't seem terribly impressed with that explanation and shrugged. "Yeah, but it would be nice to have him all to myself sometimes."

Ouch. Was that aimed at Mina, too? It seemed to be, when Charm went on to ask, "Auntie, are you going to live with us forever?"

Hoping to reassure the young girl, Mina shook her head.

"No, I won't be," she said, giving Charm a smile. "I'll probably be with you all for a month and then I'll go back to Toronto."

Charm gave her one of those level looks that seemed too adult for such a young face.

"I think you should just stay with us," she said, surprising Mina no end. "Everyone's happier when you're around. Especially Uncle."

Not knowing what to say to that, Mina took a bite of roasted yam, hoping Charm would find something else to talk about. But when the next conversational salvo came, Mina realized the first one would probably have been a better bet.

"Auntie, do you think I'm too young to have a boyfriend?"

Good Lord! Why was she the recipient of this particular question? Then she realized Miss Pearl would probably go ballistic if Charm brought it up with her, and Kiah... well, Kiah, out of sheer terror, would probably tell her to stop her foolishness.

"Do you want a boyfriend?" she asked, trying to buy a little time to gather her thoughts.

Charm twisted her lips to one side, looking so much like Kiah it was almost comical. "I don't know. Some of my friends keep saying they have boyfriends, but I think most boys are gross and silly."

"Well, just because your friends say they have boyfriends doesn't mean you have to, as well, if you don't want one. Besides, boys don't grow a brain until they're a lot older than you all are now, so you'll probably keep thinking they're gross and silly for a few years yet. Give it a bit more time before you get into the whole boyfriend thing, is my advice."

Charm giggled. "You're joking, about boys not having any brains, right?"

Mina nodded, chuckling, too. "That's what my mother always said, and it made sense to me. I have a brother, and I thought he was a mess for a long time. It wasn't until he was in his twenties that I thought he was actually growing up."

Charm's eyes widened. "Will I have to wait that long before I start liking boys?"

Mina shook her head, smiling, suddenly happy, and proud to have been chosen for this girls' chat.

"No. It'll probably happen sooner than that."

"Oh, *whew*," was the response. "I don't want to be that old before I start dating."

"Wait, what's this about dating?"

Neither of them had noticed Kiah coming back, and both looked up at him as he stood beside the table. The look of horror on his face made Mina want to laugh, and she couldn't resist giving him a little smirk.

With a shrug, Charm turned back to her roasted corn

and said, "Nothing, Uncle. Auntie and I were just talking, and she said boys don't grow a brain until they're older. When did yours grow?"

The dirty look she got from Kiah made holding back her laughter impossible. And it got worse when he replied, "I'm not sure I ever grew one. Or if I did, sometimes I think I've lost it all over again."

Even still laughing, as she watched him slide onto the bench and felt another wave of desire rush through her body, Mina understood exactly what he meant.

CHAPTER NINE

ALTHOUGH HEARTENED BY what he saw as Mina's improved outlook on life, Kiah couldn't help worrying about how she'd fit in at the hospital. Not that she was difficult, or hard to work with, but small Port Michael Public Hospital was a far cry from the huge Toronto South.

Which was why he didn't interrupt when he heard Miss Pearl telling Mina, "It's going to be different from what you're used to, because all our doctors play as many roles as necessary. You're here in an advisory capacity as an orthopedic surgeon and trained instructor, but that doesn't mean you can't help out in other situations."

Mina had just nodded and murmured her agreement, but Kiah had seen the skepticism in her expression, and knew she was probably wondering what that entailed.

And if she could be of help with only one hand.

By the end of her first week, though, Kiah felt more relaxed about the way things were going.

"It really is different," she told him as they were driving home together. "A lot more paperwork than I'm used to, and a slower pace, until there's an emergency. And they'll call me in to consult as soon as there's even a hint that I might be useful. I oversaw a student nurse wrapping a sprained ankle today."

"Not something you'd usually be bothered about, is it?"

"Nope. But I kind of like it. It's like going back to the beginning. Getting a reset."

"Like residency all over again, huh?"

That made her chuckle. "But at least I get lots of sleep this time around."

The household, too, settled into a routine that Kiah found all too easy to appreciate. Leaving home in the morning with Mina and Charm, and Miss Pearl on the days she was going to the hospital early, too, made him happy. It felt way too much like the way family life should, and he had to keep reminding himself it was only temporary.

And he couldn't help noticing how Charm gravitated to Mina, asking her opinion or getting her to help with homework. At first he worried that Miss Pearl would be upset, or think her role was being usurped. But the old woman didn't say anything, and Kiah often saw her smiling over at the pair, as though happy to see them together.

Then he worried about how Charm would react when Mina left.

She'd lost so much in her young life already. Would Mina's return to Canada distress her?

He already felt as though it would break his heart to see Mina go, and didn't want his niece going through the same thing.

But it was too late to wonder if he'd done the wrong thing by inviting Mina to St. Eustace. She was here, and he'd just have to live with the fallout of his decision.

To add to his concerns, there was a difference in the dynamic between him and Mina, and he was at a loss to pinpoint it, or figure out why. All he knew was that although they talked and laughed and teased as usual, he sensed a reticence about her, as though she was withholding something from him.

Part of him wanted to find out what was going on in her head, but his ego wouldn't let him ask. For most of their relationship, he'd prided himself on being able to read her every mood, and it irked him when he couldn't.

Just as the surging desire he felt for her shocked and annoyed him, although perhaps it shouldn't. If he'd had his way, she'd have been his first girlfriend, but that definitely hadn't been in the cards for them. For all these years, that young boy's crush had been pushed to the furthest recesses of his mind, never to be thought about.

Having her around all the time now, though, brought all the old awareness and emotions swirling to the surface.

He caught himself watching her when she was oblivious, noticing again the graceful, bouncy way she walked, hips and hair swinging; the way light and shadows played across her face. The sweet curve of her lips when she smiled, the siren's call of her laughter.

But he couldn't avoid also hearing his mother's voice in the back of his head.

"Hezekiah Langdon, don't you dare touch that little girl, or I swear on your father's grave I'll beat you within an inch of your life and send you back to your granny. You don't deserve someone like that."

It didn't matter that she'd said it twenty years ago, or that the threat shouldn't mean anything to him now. Back then it had been the worst punishment she could come up with, and she knew it. By then he'd decided he wanted to study medicine, and if he was exiled back to St. Eustace, that probably wouldn't be possible.

He'd also come to rely on Mina and her family to keep him sane and help him learn how to survive, and thrive, in

Canada. They'd opened their home to him, let him know he was always welcome. He'd gotten Mina to admit she'd told them about the abuse he suffered at home and, for a while, he'd felt as though Mr. and Mrs. Haraldson were only kind to him out of pity. Eventually, though, he'd realized they treated him like one of their own kids and had grown to depend on their emotional support. There was no way he was risking losing that because he fooled around with their daughter.

So, although Mina was the only girl he'd really wanted back then, he'd decided their friendship and his future were more important, and had put thoughts of being with her aside.

And of course, there was Warren the Worm, who'd swooped in when Mina was just barely sixteen, and never left.

He's gone now.

No. He couldn't afford to think that way. Nothing had changed, really. He still couldn't afford to lose her friendship, albeit for much different reasons. He also couldn't offer her anything she couldn't find, get, or have on her own.

If it were anyone else, he'd be sending out feelers, trying to see if they were interested in an affair. But this wasn't some random woman he could sleep with and then walk away from without it leaving scars.

In fact, even having these thoughts was shocking. He'd invited her to the island to help break her out of her funk, not to complicate her life, or his, further.

Putting it to himself that way helped, if only minimally.

Partway through her second week at the hospital, she sought him out for some advice.

"I got a call from a coach in Trinidad, asking me to

examine one of his players—a youngster named Yanique Smith—who's been having issues with his shoulder. I told him I'd call him back, but I wanted to check to see what the protocol is."

Kiah whistled. "Smith plays on the Trinidadian under-sixteen national cricket team and is being touted as the next Andy Roberts."

Mina's blank stare made him chuckle. Canada may also be an ex-British colony, but they didn't share the rest of the Commonwealth's obsession with cricket, as her befuddlement made clear. "Who on earth is Andy Roberts?"

"He was a top fast bowler for the West Indies, and this young man is said to be on his way to being as good, if not better."

"Be that as it may, I don't know how to handle this. I don't even know how his coach heard I was here, or whether it's against hospital protocol to have patients fly in from outside for private consultations. Besides, I don't want to step on any toes. I'm sure they have perfectly capable orthopedic specialists in Trinidad."

"I'm guessing it's one of two things," Kiah said, turning her toward the executive offices. "Either word has got out that you're here, through the Clinicians' Union, and the coach wants to have Smith looked at by the best doctor he can, or he doesn't want it to get out that Smith is injured. Taking him out of Trinidad to get treatment could make it less likely that the public finds out."

"Okay," she said slowly. "So what do I do?"

"Check with Dr. Hamilton. As the hospital director, he can advise you better than I can."

It was the first of several calls from other islands, and even South America, with patients wanting to be seen by Mina—some for diagnosis, others for second opinions.

Passing Dr. Hamilton a couple days later in the hall-way, Kiah found his arm grasped, and himself the recipient of a huge grin.

"Kiah, this idea of yours to have Dr. Haraldson come here was brilliant. She's already increasing our profile, and revenue." The older gentleman gave Kiah's arm a shake and continued, "Please start working on her to get her to stay on permanently. At this rate, we would be devastated to lose her after only a short time."

Kiah could only smile weakly and say he would, although he had no intention of doing any such thing. He couldn't even think about her staying permanently with any equanimity, much less broach the topic with her.

Worse, he was starting to think she was staying too long as it was.

No matter how he argued with himself that physical attraction had no place in their relationship, he couldn't stop wanting her.

How was he going to resist her much longer?

Mina found herself far busier than she'd ever expected.

She'd thought they'd stick her in an office and mire her down with paperwork, only trotting her out when they needed to show her off to the Clinicians' Union, but it wasn't like that at all.

Instead, she found herself doing all kinds of things she hadn't done in years, not all of which included anything to do with the musculoskeletal system. And it was always a joy when she was called on to work with Kiah.

Somewhere along the line, she'd forgotten just how good his technique and bedside manner were. Watching him put patients at ease or comforting someone in pain just made her heart ache a little. Yet, hadn't she been the recipient of his tender care all these years? Funny how she'd taken it all for granted.

Trying to put a little distance between them hurt, but seemed completely necessary. Her longing for him, which she'd tried repeatedly to put into perspective and set aside, wasn't abating. Achieving that distance was, however, more difficult than ever, since they were both working and living together.

That was, until a slew of requests for consultations came into the hospital, and it was rare she and Kiah actually shared patients.

"It's not surprising, Dr. Haraldson," Dr. Hamilton told her. "Your reputation is wonderful, and, even though you no longer operate, having you diagnose and suggest treatment options is a huge boon for our patients. And the hospital."

He'd asked her to come to his office, and now he gave her a winning smile. "As it is, I'll like to offer for you the opportunity to join the staff permanently at full salary. We're offering a two-year contract, with the option to extend whenever you want."

Stunned, she just stared at him for a moment, trying to think it through. It was completely unexpected. Hell, she'd been at the hospital less than the month she'd initially thought she'd be.

Getting her thoughts together, she smiled as best she could back at him. "Thank you, but let me give it some thought before I say anything. I really wasn't expecting this, at all."

Even though he looked a little crestfallen, Dr. Hamilton agreed, but asked that she get back to him within the next couple of weeks, and she agreed she would.

Why she kept that information to herself and didn't

discuss it with Kiah, she wasn't sure. Maybe because she wasn't sure how he'd respond. Or perhaps she just wanted to make that decision on her own.

After all, she'd come here because he'd suggested it, and she'd been at too low an ebb to make a plan for herself. It was about time she got back to organizing and running her own life again.

Deciding not to do anything about her physical attraction toward Kiah wasn't an easy choice, but one she thought best. The worst-case scenario, which was him telling her she was being ridiculous, and then not wanting to be around her out of disgust or embarrassment, wasn't viable, in her estimation.

The stress of it all was wearying, though, and of course Kiah noticed.

"You okay?" he asked quietly one night while they were sitting on the veranda, and she'd fallen silent, caught up in the questions circling in her mind.

"Sure." She infused as much jocularity into her voice as she could, but he wasn't fooled.

"Don't lie to me, Mina. I know you too well. You've been a little off for the last few days. Are you in pain?"

He was referring to her arm, and she knew that, so replied, "No, my arm is fine."

"So what is it? Are you bored?"

That brought a little huff of laughter. "Are you kidding? I've been running up and down the hospital, trying to learn all the systems and develop new ones, plus getting called to consult. I've had a rising cricket star with bursitis, a Belizean marine biologist with chronic leg weakness after a fall, and a Grenadian soccer player with a broken coccyx. How on earth could I be bored?"

"I didn't mean at the hospital, Mina. I meant here. It's a far quieter life than you're used to."

Didn't he know she'd been happier since being here than she could remember being before? Couldn't he recognize how having him, and his family, had filled her to overflowing.

With her dreams of motherhood shattered, being on St. Eustace, interacting with Charm, was fulfilling a deep-seated need in her heart. The knowledge that Kiah doubted her ability to fit in with them and be happy was enraging.

She turned to glare at him.

Cognizant of Miss Pearl and Charm just inside, she kept her voice soft but infused it with enough ice to make winter in Toronto seem hot in comparison.

"I'm not two, Kiah. Or even twelve. I don't need to be entertained by you or anyone. And, for your information, everything is fine, so stop bugging me, okay?"

He didn't even give her the satisfaction of getting angry with her in turn; he just sat there, nodding slowly, his far-too-knowing gaze searching her face.

"Sure," he said, as if she'd asked him to take her to the supermarket or something trite like that. "Whatever you say."

"Ugh," she said, ready to let loose another salvo.

"Auntie?" Charm's voice floated out from the living room, forestalling Mina's next spate of words. "Can you take a look at this project I'm doing?"

"Sure. Be right there," she replied, still glowering at Kiah.

"Saved in the nick of time," he murmured, having the nerve to smile as she stood up.

Mina paused just in front of him and said, "Sometimes, Kiah Langdon, I don't like you very much."

"But I'll always love you, sweet girl, so that makes up for it."

"Ugh," she said again, turning away so he couldn't see she'd teared up as his words struck home, and made her feel even worse.

That night, after she'd gotten ready for bed, the phantom pains, which had plagued her for the first few months after the accident and then abated, returned with a vengeance.

CHAPTER TEN

As was Mina's way, she didn't stay angry for long, and was back to her usual self the day after their argument.

But not really her usual self, in Kiah's estimation. Despite her denials, he knew something was going on with her, but she wasn't confiding in him the way she normally would. It hurt him, but he'd learned his lesson and didn't push. Hopefully, when she was ready, she'd let him in on whatever was bothering her.

"I haven't had a chance to finish putting the training plans together, with all the consultations I've been doing," she said to him and Miss Pearl that evening. "I hope you don't mind if I stay on with you a little longer. Maybe just a couple more weeks?"

"Of course we don't mind," Miss Pearl replied, before Kiah even had a chance to open his mouth. "Stay as long as you like."

"Like forever," Charm said as she came into the room on silent, bare feet.

Miss Pearl narrowed her eyes. "I hope you weren't eavesdropping on big people's conversation, Charmaine."

"No, Granny. I was coming down the hallway and heard you, that's all."

But Kiah thought she looked a little sheepish and decided he should talk to her about it later.

More important, he'd noticed shadows growing under Mina's eyes, and especially with him, she was quieter even than before. Miss Pearl noticed, too, and asked if Kiah knew what was going on, but he had nothing to tell her.

Charm was on half-term holidays, almost wild with excitement about a camping trip she was going on with a group from school the next day. Miss Pearl was going, too, as a chaperone.

"You're going to camp, Miss Pearl?" Mina asked, obviously surprised.

"No, child," was the stout reply. "The youngsters will sleep in tents, and a couple of the mothers will, too, but there's a nice little cottage, with a bed for me to sleep on. I think they only invite me because of my cooking."

"That's not true, Granny." Charm sounded genuinely outraged at the suggestion. "You're a lot of fun, too."

Both Kiah and Mina were off for the day, and when Mina suggested they take Charm to the beach, he jumped at the chance. He knew how much Mina loved the ocean, and she'd resisted going since she'd been on St. Eustace.

It gave him further hope that she truly was on the mend, notwithstanding whatever was troubling her.

"Will your arm be okay in the sea, Auntie?" Charm asked with a little frown.

"In the hospital we use salt water to clean wounds," Mina replied. "And although that's sterile, not seawater, my arm will be fine. Mind you, I wasn't planning on swimming anyway."

With preteen logic and no hint of discretion, Charm asked, "So what's the use of going to the beach, then?"

"To get some sun?"

That earned her one of Charm's dry-as-dust looks, and Kiah stayed out of it, squelching both the urge to laugh and to suggest they do something else instead.

Mina had to make up her own mind, at her own pace.

When she came back out, dressed for their excursion, she was once more wearing a long-sleeved shirt, but it was light and gauzy, clearly showing the bikini top beneath.

Miss Pearl was fussing that she hadn't known they were going to the beach that day.

"I would have fried up some chicken for you to take."

"Don't worry, Granny," Kiah told her, stopping to give her a kiss as he went by. "We'll grab something on the way."

"Some foolishness, like fast food. It's not good for you, you know."

Probably trying to distract her, Mina asked, "Aren't you coming with us, Miss Pearl?"

That earned her another dry look for the morning.

"Child, my last swimsuit rotted away to nothing about twenty years ago, and I have no intention of replacing it. Kiah, make sure you take an umbrella, and Charm, did you put on sunscreen?"

"Yes, Granny."

Miss Pearl gave Mina the same searching look. "Have you?"

"Yes, ma'am," was the meek reply, and Kiah had to turn away so neither of them saw his grin.

The beach at Rickard's Cove was packed with both locals and tourists, but they found a spot not too far from the water to put down their beach mats and hoist their umbrella. As Mina settled in under the shade, Charm was already shucking her sundress in preparation for running down to the water.

Kiah sat next to Mina, watching as Charm was diverted from her dip by some school friends calling her name. In an instant, she went from eager child to jaded preteen, joining the little gaggle of girls on the sand. The little cadre chatted and giggled, eyeing some boys who were also huddled together a little way away.

Not too long ago, she'd have been nagging him to come into the water with her, or to play with her in the sand.

He sighed. "She's growing up so fast."

"Mmm-hmm," Mina agreed. "I still have a hard time believing she's almost a teenager. Time has flown."

"She's so smart. I keep hoping she'll give up on the idea of going into show business and become a doctor."

Mina laughed softly. "Medicine is a calling, and you know it. Remember some of the people we went to school with, who were studying to be doctors only because their parents wanted them to? They were mostly miserable and lost. You don't want that for Charm."

"No."

But there was a melancholy weight on his heart. Nothing to do with thoughts of Charm's future, which he was sure would be bright, no matter what she decided to do.

As so often happened, Mina seemed able to read his mind.

"Karlene would be so proud of her and of the job you're doing, Kiah."

"I like to think so," he replied. "But I wish she were here to raise Charm herself."

Mina's hand was cool against his shoulder, her fingers squeezing gently.

"I know you do."

When he laid his cheek against her hand, she sighed and squeezed again.

Mina was quiet for a moment, and Kiah turned to watch Charm and her friends. The boys were setting up to play cricket on the grassy stretch between the sand and the parking lot, and the girls were watching them, all giggles and sassy smiles.

Lord, it was too soon for that particular can of worms to be opened, in Kiah's opinion. Just the thought made his stomach curdle. When it came to his niece, he definitely wasn't ready to deal with the boyfriend-girlfriend thing just yet.

Yet, said a little voice in the back of his head, *at that age weren't you secretly pining for the very woman sitting next to you?*

That may be true, but he really didn't want to think about it right now. Not with the sensation of her hand on his shoulder, the gentle sound of her breathing reaching his ear, even over all the ambient noise.

A group of four young women strolled by, and Kiah, still lost in his thoughts, hardly noticed, until Mina sighed and said, "Wouldn't it be nice to be that age again, but with all the knowledge we have now? Before all the failures of life piled up on us, and everything seems so much harder?"

She sounded so pensive he sat up straighter and turned so he could see her face.

"What failures, Mina?"

"Oh, like my marriage, my career, my life." She smiled slightly and lifted one shoulder in an abbreviated shrug. "Stuff like that."

His rush of emotion was visceral, almost too much to handle. Tenderness, anger, worry, all tangled up together and froze his vocal cords for a moment. When he could finally find his voice, he asked, "How can you classify your life as a failure?"

She waved her hand, as though trying to brush his words away, but still replied, "I know I've done some good, professionally, but in my personal life, I've failed. I let my dreams fade away instead of fighting for them, and let Warren dictate what I could and couldn't have. I fell into the trap of trying to be the perfect doctor and the perfect wife and didn't really spend the time to think about where I'd end up."

"What did you want and didn't get?"

He was almost afraid to hear her answer. Somehow already knew what she'd say.

"I wanted a more balanced life, with time to spend doing things other than working and networking. More time outdoors or traveling. And…"

She looked away, out over the ocean, as though no longer willing to face him.

"And what, sweet girl?"

"I wanted a family."

Mina spoke so softly he shouldn't have been able to hear her, but he did anyway, and the words ripped through him. Strange to think it was something they'd never talked about over all the years of exchanging confidences, something she'd never mentioned and he'd never asked.

With hindsight, Kiah realized he'd probably been dreading hearing she was pregnant with Warren's child, hence his reticence.

Was it horrible to be glad it had never happened, even if only because Mina could make a clean break from the worm without the constant tie of being the mother to his children?

But that wasn't what she needed to hear right now, and he knew it.

"You can still have a family, Mina. You're still young."

It shouldn't hurt so much to say it, but his chest literally ached as the words left his mouth.

She shook her head, trying to smile although her lips trembled a little. "It feels as though it *is* too late. I don't know if I ever want to marry again, and I'm still trying to come to terms with getting along without my hand, and figuring out what the future holds, career-wise. By the time I sort those things out…"

He wished he could tell her it would all work out, that he would make it work out for her, but that would be a lie. Instead, he said, "You're getting there, I can see the changes already. Take it one day at a time. See where things go. But if you want a family, I know you'll make it happen. That's always been your biggest strength—your determination, and the drive to get whatever it is you set your mind to."

Her lips quirked. "According to Warren, no man in his right mind would want a washed-up surgeon with a disgusting stump and no prospects."

Kiah couldn't stop the curse that rolled from his lips, and the anger that overtook him too swiftly to be fully contained. Reining it in took every ounce of his control, and it was still vibrating under his skin when he replied.

"I don't want to hear anything that jackass had to say, and you need to put it out of your mind, too. You're the most beautiful human being I know, inside and out. Any man with a lick of sense would grovel at your feet if he thought it would give him a chance with you."

Even me.

Her lips parted, as though she would reply, but instead,

she looked around and said, "I think I want to go for a swim after all. Come with me?"

Surprised by the sudden end to their conversation, and knowing how self-conscious she was about her missing hand, he immediately agreed. And pride, along with another emotion he couldn't—or wouldn't—name overwhelmed him, as he watched her unbutton and take off her blouse, and then walk, head up, back straight, down to the water.

"Auntie!" Charm came loping over, a huge grin on her face. "You're going into the sea?"

"Yep," Mina answered. "You coming?"

"Last one in is a rotten egg," Kiah shouted, running past them, too full of joy at Mina taking this huge step not to let some of it out.

And he roared with laughter at their twin cries of "Not fair!"

Once she'd made up her mind to stop hiding her arm, it felt as though a weight had lifted off her chest.

She'd told herself, over and over, that she was fine.

Healed.

Back to the way she'd been before the accident.

But it had been a lie.

Now she knew she'd never be that person again. Accepted that reality. Working again had helped to show her how much she still had to offer. And Kiah's words, said in a way that brooked no argument, made her really think about how much she'd allowed Warren's hateful words to affect her self-esteem. With the light of truth and anger in his eyes, Kiah had illuminated the self-serving lies her ex had spewed so as to make what he was doing seem logical.

The confidence Kiah always had in her, his assertion

of faith that she'd get her life back on track, meant more to her than he could ever know. He always knew exactly what she needed to bolster her self-confidence, and let her know she could be, and do, whatever she put her mind to.

Revealing herself fully had taken that assurance to another level.

Sure, there were some people who stared, and Charm had no problem telling them her friends had asked about Mina's lack of a hand, and even wondered how she could still be a doctor.

"I told them that you use your head, and your other hand, to make people well again," she said, not even realizing the profundity of her comment. "You don't have to be perfect to do whatever it is you want to, right, Auntie?"

"You got it, kiddo."

Charm's surety in her abilities warmed her heart, and seeing the pride on Kiah's face made it all the sweeter.

And she couldn't avoid thinking about Kiah's avowal that there was still time, and a chance, to have the family she wanted. He'd sounded so certain she could make it work, if that was what she decided to do.

She wished she could help him get past his own antipathy toward parenthood. From seeing him with Charm, she knew he was already a wonderful father, and although she knew how much he feared being the type of parent his mother was, she knew he never would be.

It wasn't that she felt everyone had the same urge or desire to procreate that she did, but she couldn't help wondering if old fears, rather than logic and true desires, might be the source of his decision.

That night, exhausted from the sun and the soporific effects of the seawater, was the first in many she slept deeply, unaffected by her arm.

But the next day the pains were back, and it took every ounce of concentration she had, to get through the workday without incident.

The missing hand alternatively burned and itched, driving her to distraction.

Part of the problem, she knew, was that her stress levels were through the roof. The physical therapist had warned her that might happen, but she hadn't paid much attention, especially when the pains hadn't come back during her depression.

She still hadn't given Dr. Hamilton an answer, and the timeframe he'd set was running out. And her unerring desire for Kiah had resisted every effort she made to lock it away.

Until she sorted those things out, she'd have to find some other way of handling the pain.

That evening the household was in uproar as Charm whirred around, trying to pack everything, including the kitchen sink, it seemed, to take camping.

"Charmaine, stop." Miss Pearl's sternest voice only moderately slowed the little girl down. "Pick one of those toys to take with you and put the rest back in your room."

By the time Miss Pearl and Charm were being picked up, Mina had a headache to go with the phantom pains, but she kissed them both goodbye, and stood at the gate to wave until the SUV had turned the corner.

"Wow," Kiah said, slinging his arm over her shoulders and turning her back toward the house. "Let's not do that again anytime soon."

Mina chuckled weakly, just wanting to sit down and enjoy some peace and quiet, although she didn't know how much enjoyment she'd get out of anything tonight.

"Charm's just excited to go on her first camping trip,"

she said, and even she could hear the weariness in her own voice.

Kiah led her over to the sofa and gently pushed at her shoulders, so she sat.

"You want a cup of tea? Something to drink?"

Concern was patent on his face, those dark watchful eyes trying to divine what was happening with her, and, before she could stop them, tears filled her eyes and overflowed onto her cheeks.

Kiah knelt down in front of her to cup her cheeks.

"Sweet girl. Tell me what's wrong. Please. Let me help you, if I can."

That made her laugh through her tears, but there was a hysterical edge to her mirth.

Kiah used his thumbs to rub at her cheeks, then got up and sat on the couch beside her. When he reached out and pulled her onto his lap, she didn't resist, wanting the closeness, even if it wasn't as close as she wanted to get. Burying her face in his neck, she let his warmth seep into her, fill her.

"What is it, Mina?"

"Phantom pains." It came out as a low moan. Somehow being here like this with him made the sensation increase. "It burns and itches."

"Why didn't you tell me before?" The anguish in his tone was clear. "What can I do to make it better?"

"Get me my hand back?"

She was trying to joke, to lighten the mood, but his arms tightened around her, and his chest shuddered when he inhaled.

"If I could, I would, sweet girl. You must know that?"

It sounded like he was about to cry, too, and she couldn't bear it.

"I'll be okay, Kiah. It'll pass."

"I know an acupuncturist, but I doubt she's still open at this hour. Damn it, Mina, why didn't you say something earlier?"

Even though he sounded angry, it was the caring she heard in his voice.

"I was trying to handle it myself," she said.

His chest rose and fell on a sigh. "You know that as long as I'm around, you never have to face anything alone, don't you?"

"I do." She sighed in turn. "But sometimes I need to do things for myself. I can't lean on you for everything."

He didn't reply, but there was something about his stillness that made her raise her head to search his face. His expression was intent, and somehow the way he was gazing at her made her heart rate pick up, and the ever-present need flower bigger, and hotter, in her core.

"You can, you know," he said quietly. "Any- and everything. No matter how little, or big, or off the wall. I've always got you, sweet girl."

It took everything she had inside not to let her gaze drop to his mouth, not to tell him how much she wanted him to kiss her and make love to her. Something inside her whispered that would make everything right, but she knew better than to trust that voice. Besides, Kiah didn't think of her that way, and the thought of his rejection was too much to bear.

So, instead, she snuggled her face back into his neck, inhaling the warm, sexy scent of him, even as she tried to ignore the desire flowing like liquid fire through her veins. There was no place she'd rather be than in his arms, so she shifted a little closer on his lap, craving additional contact.

Then it sank into her brain what she was feeling

snugged up against her thigh and, for a brief, glorious moment, she thought his erection was a sign he wanted her, too. Her heart rate soared, and she tightened her grip on his waist. But even as she felt him pull her in a bit more, sanity returned.

The right thing to do would be to ignore it, leave it alone, but Mina felt compelled to comment anyway. After all, they'd been calling each other out over stupid or embarrassing stuff for years. Why buck the trend now? Besides, laughing about it hopefully would get her back on an even keel.

"You really have been going through a drought, haven't you?" she murmured, bumping his crotch gently with her thigh, so there was no mistaking her meaning.

She expected a chuckle, or a witty riposte, not the silence that followed her comment, or the restless movement of his hands on her back, which felt suspiciously like a caress.

Eventually, Kiah inhaled deeply, then replied, "My sexual drought has nothing to do with it, sweet girl. That's all for you."

CHAPTER ELEVEN

HE'D HOPED SHE wouldn't notice or, even if she did, wouldn't comment, but once she had Kiah knew he couldn't let her go on believing it was just an automatic reaction on his part. That if it were anyone else, his body would respond the same way. Not after the conversation they'd had on the beach, when she'd told him the disgusting things her ex had said.

No. Mina needed to know she was still as desirable as she'd ever been.

To him even more so than ever before.

Seeing her every day over these past weeks, in all her various moods—vulnerable and confident, laughing, crying, and everything in between—had been an emotional revelation. For so long he'd pushed his attraction to her down deep, refusing to let it grow beyond the treasured friendship. Distance had made that easier, but now there was, literally, no hiding from the truth.

He wanted her, badly.

Mina hadn't responded verbally to his words, but he could feel her rib cage rising and falling rapidly beneath his hands, and her stillness was, in itself, telling. Kiah could almost hear the wheels turning in her head, and it worried him.

Had he frightened or repulsed her? Was their relationship, so carefully nurtured and vastly important to him, in jeopardy, now that she realized his lust for her?

Then she shook her head, just once, against his neck and said, "I know you don't really mean that."

He snorted, wishing he could find the situation more amusing than he actually did. "I mean every word. I'm not fifteen, and I don't get aroused as though I were. Ask Niesha, and she'll tell you she got no reaction from me, although she tried her level best."

Reaching down, he tipped her chin up so he could meet her gaze.

"You think I was kidding when I told you how beautiful you are? I wasn't. And I could have added the fact you're incredibly sexy. I've always thought so, and having you around has reminded me just how much."

Color tinged her cheeks, and that made him chuckle.

"You're blushing," he said, reaching up to run his index finger over her overheated skin. "I haven't seen that in a while."

"I haven't been called sexy in a while," she retorted. "Actually, in forever."

Kiah kissed his teeth, once more annoyed at the thought of how poorly she'd been treated by her scumbag ex.

"You should know it, though. Don't you notice how men look at you? At the club, the hospital, on the beach yesterday? There's an air about you, Mina—sultry and sassy and sexy, all combined to make you irresistible."

It was her turn to make an incredulous noise. "You've never had a problem resisting me."

"Our friendship has always been too important to gunk up with sex," he said, trying to be honest without giving too much away. "Losing you because we slept together and it didn't end well wasn't a chance I was willing to take."

Her gaze searched his, and although her lips quirked into a ghost of a smile, her eyes were solemn. "Is that what sex does? Gunk things up?"

"It definitely can," he said, his heart thumping, wondering where the conversation would end up leading, although he was trying to stay realistic. "If the people involved let it."

"And if they don't let it?"

His heart stopped for an instant, and then set off galloping again. Already aroused, his body tightened, almost to the point of pain, and his lungs seized, making replying impossible in that moment.

The logical part of his brain was telling him not to take this any further, to walk away before things went sideways, but his body... Oh, his body was screaming for him to see where this would lead.

Trying desperately to take the path of reason, he finally found the wherewithal to say, "It would be risky, Mina. Just agreeing not to let it change things doesn't mean things wouldn't change anyway."

She nodded slowly, never breaking eye contact. "But what we share can never really be broken, can it? Dented, or bent, maybe, but I'll always be your friend, and you'll always be mine. My best friend. I..."

She paused, looked down, and once more his breath caught in his chest at the sheer beauty of her, the fact they were even having this conversation slamming home again.

"You what?"

She looked back up, meeting his gaze again. "I don't have a lot of experience, Kiah. You talked about men being interested in me, but it scares me—the thought of being with someone new. These feelings I have for you, those *don't* frighten me. Somehow, wanting you feels right."

She shrugged, as though not sure she'd found the right words, and although there was no lessening of his desire, his heart sank just a little. He was to be an experiment, then. A gateway to finding out what it felt like to be with someone other than the worm.

Hearing that should have lessened the desire, but it didn't. Instead, strangely, it added another layer to his need, making it even harder to resist the temptation on offer. Trying to figure out why was impossible with her gleaming eyes on him, her hand cupping the back of his neck, as though to pull his lips down to hers.

"God, Mina. You're making it really hard for me to say no."

"Then don't," she replied, then gave a little grin. "I like that I'm making it hard."

She bumped his erection with her thigh again, and Kiah choked on the chuckle rising in his throat. Trust Mina to make him laugh at a time like this.

"You wretch," he said, his arms tightening around her waist against his best intentions. "You're leading me astray."

Her laughter was soft, sultry. "I'm trying my best, but you're stubborn. It's like leading a mule."

His amusement faded, and he lifted his hand to stroke her cheek. "If we do sleep together tonight, and want to again, it can only be for these couple of days while Granny and Charm are gone."

She was still smiling, enticing him closer, as she nodded. "Yes. The last thing I need is disapproving looks from Miss Pearl, or having to explain to Charm why I'm coming out of your room."

Besides, for her it was just for the experience, not the potentially life-altering event Kiah suspected it would be for him.

His brain tried once more to tell him not to risk it, that making love to Mina wasn't safe, or even sane. But her fingers were moving on his nape, making goose bumps fire down his back. And she shifted on his lap, her scent rising to fill his head, driving out all thought of anything other than her and this once-in-a-lifetime opportunity.

"Are you sure?" he asked, even as his head was dipping, the words coming out when their lips were almost touching.

And she replied by closing that gap, and his brain short-circuited with that first, glorious kiss.

There was no time for contemplation, for further worry about whether what they were doing was right or wrong. All Mina could feel was Kiah's kiss.

The vibration into her lips, as he growled low in his throat.

The movement of mouth on mouth, and the sweep of his tongue, seeking entrance.

She didn't just invite the deepening of the kiss, she demanded it, welcoming it with the kind of ferocity she didn't know herself capable of.

This was no tender seduction. Not on either side.

Instead, it had all the explosive power of a lightning storm. The inexorable flood of a tsunami.

He pulled her closer so she felt the pounding of his heart against her breasts, the thrust of his erection now beneath her thighs. Twining her arms around his neck, she strained against him, ravenous for his touch.

His lips left hers and found her throat. The sound that broke from her was one she'd never heard before: rife with need and delight, a symphony of desire.

"Last chance, Mina. Stop me now if you're not sure."

She tried to laugh, but it stuck in her chest, held there by the immensity of her arousal.

"I want you." She finally got the words out, but they were choppy, born on her labored breathing. "I need you, Kiah."

"Ah, sweet girl. My sweet girl. Come to my bed."

"Yes. Oh, yes."

Now things settled, became almost calm. Not her racing heart or skyrocketing need, but the admission of mutual desire gave them reprieve from the rush of desperation.

He rose and set her gently on her feet, standing for a moment in front of her, his dark eyes mysterious and probing. Then he turned and led her down the corridor, and into his bedroom.

She reached for him, but he held her arms, his gaze traveling along her body, sparking reactions wherever it settled. Her breasts tingled, nipples tightening further into aching points. Goose bumps rose across her belly, and her legs trembled.

Slowly, oh-so slowly he undressed her, his hands skimming her flesh, his breath harsh and growing faster with each piece of clothing that fell away. Under his rapt focus, she blossomed, felt beautiful in a way she'd never experienced before. There was no need for words between them. Not now. Not when he looked at her as though she were the most precious woman in the world.

And she didn't feel self-conscious when she was naked and he was still clothed. Rather, she felt eager, bold and powerful.

It was her turn, then. And she took her time, both from necessity and desire. Unbuttoning his shirt single-handed, sweeping across his chest and then one shoulder at a time to ease it away, unreasonably pleased when he shivered and his eyes drifted closed.

She got his pants undone, too, and reached into his briefs to grip the hard length of him in her hand, making him groan and, this time, shudder.

"You'll have to help me with the rest," she whispered, not letting go or ceasing the motion of her hand, fascinated by the feel of him, his obvious pleasure.

He grasped her wrist, and she looked up, only to be snared by the heat in his eyes.

"You need to stop, Mina. You're making me crazy."

"I want to."

"You're bad. But I want to return the favor."

He tugged her in close, kissed her until her head swam and her legs were like jelly. How they ended up on the bed, she wasn't sure; she only knew he was touching and kissing her in ways that blew her mind and sent her body soaring.

Making love with Kiah was everything she'd imagined it would be, and so much more.

More intense.

More arousing.

More satisfying.

He set her aflame, then made that fire into an inferno only he could douse.

She found herself arching, pleading, opening herself to his fingers and lips in the most wanton, beautiful of ways.

When she lost control, it was with joyous abandon, welcoming the ceding of power to his touch, without even a hint of shame or fear.

Now the desperation was back, and she pulled him close, wrapping her legs around him, urging him to fill her, to take her back to that place of ecstasy.

"Mina, wait," he said. "We need to use protection."

With a little growl, she loosened her grip on him, and said, "Hurry."

She lay there, watching him sheath himself, even that mundane action an aphrodisiac. When he came back to her, she welcomed him, and as he slid into her body, stretching her, she mewled with pleasure.

"I want you," she panted, tightening her strong thighs so he couldn't escape. "I need you, Kiah."

He groaned, gave in, pushing forward to give her his entire length, and she cried out.

"Yes. There. Oh, yes."

He shifted, went even deeper, then began to move, each thrust and retreat causing little spasms deep within her, until they all started running together, and she found herself once more on the edge of completion.

"Mina. Mina. Mina."

It was a chant, a benediction, and her body responded, as though the sound of her name in his hoarse, desire-struck voice was the final touch she needed.

Her orgasm came with the force of a runaway train, barreling through her, causing every muscle and sinew to stiffen, shutting down her nervous system, making lights flash behind her tightly closed eyes.

And hearing, feeling Kiah join her, took the sensations straight to sublime.

CHAPTER TWELVE

KIAH LAY IN the dark, wondering if he was dreaming.

It all felt too good to be reality, and he wished he could, like Mina had, fall asleep, so as to hold on to the perfection.

But although his body was sated, his brain wouldn't shut off, his thoughts confusedly swinging from euphoria to fear, and back again.

They'd made love. Him and Mina. She'd shared her body with him in the most wonderful, meaningful night of his life.

Their kisses, the love they'd made, had been sheer perfection.

He'd been right to worry making love would change their relationship, and use that instinctive knowledge to try to stop it from happening. He already felt a shift inside, the emotional bond he'd always had with Mina transforming in a way he didn't want to contemplate.

It scared him, the way she'd made him feel, the rightness of touching and kissing her, the joy he'd gotten from hearing her cry out in pleasure. The utter ecstasy he'd experienced in her arms.

Down this road lay the type of madness he'd tried so hard to avoid all his life.

The insanity of love.

His mind whirled, bringing up ghosts of the past, as though to emphasize the severity of the danger he was courting.

His father collapsing, dying in front of him.

Mom, losing the only stabilizing force in her life, and morphing from a relatively normal person into something close to a monster, turning on her children, blaming them for everything.

Kiah had had the Haraldsons to run to when things got bad at home. Karlene hadn't been so lucky.

"Those damn people done steal one of my children." He heard his mother's voice, as clear as it had been that night, when he'd tried to take Karlene with him, just to get her away from his mother's poisonous tongue. Remembered her crazed stare as she held on to Karlene, silently daring Kiah to tear her daughter from her arms. "They not getting the other one."

He'd had to turn away from the plea in Karlene's eyes, and make his escape.

Roy, battered and broken in spirit after a bomb had killed four of his friends, tearing through the troop transport he was on. Unable to function, despite his love for his wife and daughter, harangued by his mother-in-law at every turn.

Kiah had seen it firsthand while visiting Canada, and he'd tried to tell Karlene what their mother was doing wasn't healthy.

She'd shrugged. "She's trying to help me out, Kiah. Taking care of Charm when I have to work. I don't listen to her when she's bad-mouthing Roy. He's a good man."

"Tell her not to come over anymore," Kiah had said. "She just upsets Roy, and he doesn't need that right now."

"How can I tell her she can't see her granddaughter, when she's helped me out all this time?"

And no matter what he said, Karlene made excuses for Mom and, in Kiah's estimation, her devotion to their mother had cost Karlene her life. Cost Roy his, too.

Funny how, until Mina had mentioned it, he hadn't thought about what Charm might think of her father. Kiah had been too busy hating him to even consider talking about him, although they'd had a good relationship in the beginning, and Kiah had thought him perfect for Karlene.

And Roy had loved Charm. Somewhere there were pictures he'd retrieved from Karlene's house after the horrific tragedy. Pictures that showed Roy holding his daughter at various stages of her life. That showed his absolute love and devotion.

How could that love not have stopped him from doing what he did?

Those were the questions that made Kiah afraid.

He'd examined his own character and knew there were situations he absolutely needed to avoid. He was as faithful and caring as his father, who'd put up with his wife's moodiness and meanness without complaint, but he also had his mother's temper. He'd discovered that young, when he'd finally had enough, and had gone toe-to-toe with Mom, unable to stop himself from shouting right back at her. Having to walk away when he realized he was about to completely lose control, fearful of what might happen if he did.

The more you cared about people the easier it was to hurt them, or be hurt in return. He'd had enough of that to last him a lifetime.

He and Mina had crossed a treacherous line tonight, and now he'd have to deal with the fallout. Unfortunately, the only way he'd be able to know what came next would be to see how Mina reacted in the morning.

But he wanted her again.

Desperately.

If this was to be the only night they spent together intimately, he wanted it to be as intense and memorable as possible.

Enough to last him the rest of his life.

So he woke her slowly, bringing her up from sleep with gentle caresses.

She stretched in his arms, her hand finding the back of his neck, pulling him down for a kiss.

If he could die then, in her arms, kissing her sweet mouth, he'd go a happy man.

"Kiah," she said, his name infused with such longing his heart dipped and raced to hear it. "You make me feel so good."

"That's my aim, sweet girl," he replied, touching her softly, trying to retain the memory of her silky flesh, the heat and need of her, in his fingertips.

"You've exceeded your goal."

Then words were unnecessary as their bodies took over, desire rising like flames to lick at their skin, demanding they touch more, kiss harder, wrap around each other, as though never to let go.

Need, sharp and undeniable, brought them back together, Kiah sinking into her, losing himself in the rhythm of love. Tumbling, as though down a mountain, when she cried out, clenching around him, and threw him into orgasm.

Mina awoke with bliss still echoing through her body, and lay still for a moment, savoring it. Beyond the window, birds were chirping and doves were cooing, enhancing her sense of well-being.

A small part of her was still disbelieving, a little shocked at what had happened the night before, but the rest of her practically purred, sated and love-drunk.

Wanting more.

A smile curved her lips, and, even to her, it felt sly.

"Hey, sleepyhead." Kiah's deep voice sent a thrill of desire down her spine. "You're finally awake."

Opening her eyes, she blinked over at him. He was smiling, too, but his gaze was shadowed. Watchful.

Mina's stomach rolled.

"Hey yourself," she replied, hitching herself up on the pillows so they were eye to eye.

"How're you feeling?"

Did he mean her arm, the rest of her body, or emotionally? Mina tried to figure it out but failed. Kiah was holding his own feelings close to his chest. Best to just jump in with both feet, since that had always been their way.

"My arm feels fine, and the rest of my body is humming, it's so happy."

So maybe not both feet, since she hadn't mentioned anything about her head space. She'd held back, waiting to see where he was at, before she said the wrong thing.

His eyes sparked with a hint of the fire she'd seen in them the night before, and her nipples tingled as goose bumps broke out across her shoulders.

Then the light faded, and he rubbed his hand across his chin, his morning stubble rasping beneath his palm.

"I need to know that what happened hasn't changed anything between us," he said, giving her a level, guarded look.

"We agreed it wouldn't."

"I know, but I—"

"You what?"

She wasn't letting Kiah off the hook. Whatever he had going through that head of his needed to be let out. Expressed clearly, so there was no miscommunication.

"Dammit, Mina. You know you mean more to me than anyone outside of my family. I need to know you're okay with what happened last night. That we're okay."

Tilting her head, she took in his expression. There was a hint of anguish in his eyes, and his lips were tight, almost angry. No matter what she felt, she knew he needed her reassurance.

"Kiah, nothing, and no one, could ever change what I feel for you. Last night was amazing. Magical. I've never been so thoroughly satiated in my life, and I'm glad I found that with you, because I trust you more than anyone."

His expression lightened, and, for the first time that morning, his smile touched his eyes, as well as his lips.

"Okay. Good." His eyelids dipped, and his smile changed, becoming sensual. "It was amazing for me, too…"

She smiled, and although she knew she should just take what she'd already been given, and not get in any deeper, said, "Want to see if it's as good in the cold light of day as it was last night?"

"Oh, yeah," he said, his lips already just a breath away from hers.

And it was even more glorious than it had been before, Mina thought later as she stood under the shower, after Kiah had left to go to work.

Thank goodness she was off that day, because there

was a lot she needed to work through, and it would definitely have distracted her from her job.

Why did it feel as though her entire life had led up to last night? That the experience of making love with Kiah was the most perfect moment she'd lived?

He didn't see it the same way, she realized. It seemed that, to him, what had happened was a one-off. Or a three-off in this case. Maybe even a more-off, since Miss Pearl and Charm weren't back until tomorrow, and they had the place to themselves tonight. Apparently, he was okay with letting this new, sexual component of their relationship fall away thereafter.

She wasn't sure she was.

If she'd rediscovered her confidence in St. Eustace, it felt as though her deepest, most sensual and loving self had come to light in Kiah's arms. Giving that up, just as she'd found it, was a nonstarter.

Not that she thought it could continue on indefinitely. Even without him stating it was only for these few glorious days, eventually, and more likely sooner rather than later, she'd be going back to Canada. Why couldn't they enjoy this new aspect of their relationship for as long as they could?

How to convince him of that was another question, but one she vowed to tackle with vigor and focus. She'd need to be gentle with him, give him space to work it all out in his own way, but that didn't mean she had to be passive. It wasn't her style, anyway. Never had been, except for those months when she'd floundered, lost and unable to see a way out of her nightmare.

Kiah had been the only one who'd known what to do, and if it weren't for him, who knows how she'd have ended up?

That gave her pause as she stepped out of the shower and started drying off.

Was she avoiding all her unresolved feelings and issues, and using Kiah's lovemaking as a way to not face them? He'd warned her that sex muddied the emotional waters, even when both parties knew it wasn't going any further.

Was this sexual adventure with Kiah even healthy?

Maybe, she thought, rubbing the towel over her hair, she needed to sort herself out before deciding whether the change in her relationship with Kiah was advisable and should continue?

But deep in her heart, she already knew: a fundamental change had taken place, whether they liked it or not. All she could do was prepare as best she could, and see where it ultimately led.

Then her already chaotic world was further disarrayed by an email from Toronto South formally offering her a full-time teaching position, as the deputy chief of orthopedics.

She sat back, looking at the screen, her heart racing. It seemed like something of a miracle, the culmination of all her career dreams. While they'd originally asked her to stay on as a lecturer, and she'd refused, the position of deputy chief hadn't come up before.

It couldn't have happened at a worse time.

Yet, the choices she faced career-wise seemed nowhere as important as deciding what to do about her feelings for Kiah.

She still hadn't told him about the job offer from Dr. Hamilton, and didn't really plan to tell him about the Toronto offer, either, until she figured out what she wanted to do. Hopefully, the director would be discreet and not spread the word about wanting her to stay.

Part of her rebelled at the thought of leaving St. Eustace; yet, she also had to be practical. Letting her emotions over the change in her relationship with Kiah muddle her thinking wouldn't help her make good decisions.

She spent most of the day going over the tutorial plans she was working on for the hospital, trying to lose herself in work rather than let her mind obsess over the night before. Yet, more than once she found herself staring off into space, smiling, her body tingling at the memories bombarding her.

By the time Kiah got home, she was glad to set her laptop aside, as she looked up to smile at him. His gaze seemed watchful, making her wonder what he was expecting. So she went out of her way to sound casual, almost breezy, as she greeted him.

"Hey," she said. "Long day, huh?"

"Emergency cesarean," he replied, flopping down beside her. "Her OB was on the other side of the island, and couldn't make it back in time to operate. Mom and baby doing well. Father's a blithering mess, though. It's their first."

Mina chuckled. "So many of them are, when delivery time comes. I don't think the fact they're about to be a father truly sinks in until they actually see the baby."

Kiah smiled, resting his head back on the couch and closing his eyes. "And I don't think any of them have a clue what to expect during the actual birth. Intellectually, they have an idea, but the reality still comes as a shock."

There, that was normal, she thought, except for having to battle the urge to grab him, kiss him, take him back to bed. He didn't want that new twist in their relationship to become a regular part of it, so she had to honor his wishes.

Let him make the first move, if he wanted to.

"Miss Pearl left food in the fridge, but I wasn't sure what you'd want. It looks as though she thought we'd be inviting an entire army over while she was gone."

He chuckled, rolling his head to look at her. "That's how it always is, when she leaves even for a couple of days. And when she comes back, she'll want to know why it looks as though nothing was eaten."

"Well," Mina said, stretching, and swinging her feet down to the ground. "In that case I guess I should go and pull something out so she doesn't get mad at us."

"Mmm-hmm," Kiah agreed, even as he was reaching to pull her onto his lap. "Don't want Granny vexed." With a hand on her nape, he tugged her unresisting form close. "She's scary when she's vexed."

"That she is," Mina agreed against his lips, her heart singing, her pulse going haywire.

It wouldn't last forever, she knew, but she'd take whatever he wanted to give.

CHAPTER THIRTEEN

CHARM AND MISS PEARL came back the following day, both exhausted, and with the older lady limping.

"It's just a sprain," she said, when Kiah asked her what had happened.

"We were going down to the river this morning, and Granny slipped," Charm said. "She scratched her hand, too," she added.

"Let me take a look, Miss Pearl." Mina tried to guide the older woman to a chair, gently insistent when it looked like her patient was going to balk. "It won't take a moment."

While she grumbled, Miss Pearl allowed Mina to remove the bandage she'd wrapped around her ankle, so Mina could see the affected joint. Kiah went and retrieved the first aid kit, and, on his return, took a look at his grandmother's hand.

After a thorough examination of the ankle, Mina looked up at the older woman.

"There's a fair amount of bruising and swelling, so you know I'm going to prescribe the RICE treatment, don't you?"

Miss Pearl looked as though she wanted to argue, but

Kiah looked up from dressing the cut on her hand to say, "Listen to Mina, Granny, and don't be difficult."

"RICE? What's the RICE treatment?" Charm asked. She'd been leaning over Mina's shoulder, watching what was going on.

"It stands for rest, ice, compression and elevation. Granny needs to stay off her foot for a couple of days, put ice on her ankle and keep it wrapped up. And she should keep her foot elevated, too."

Charm straightened and gave her great-grandmother a long look. "Okay, Granny, you're under chair arrest for the next couple of days, and Sheriff Charm is going to keep an eye on you, so make sure you behave."

Miss Pearl scowled, but no one paid her ill temper any mind, as they all pitched in to make her comfortable.

Once she was settled, with her leg up on a low table and ice pack in place, Kiah said, "Charm, go have a shower, while I get dinner heated up."

"Okay," she replied around a huge yawn. "But somebody's going to have to help me comb out and plait my hair when I'm finished."

"I can help with the combing," Mina said. "But not the plaiting."

"It's my ankle that's hurt," Miss Pearl interjected, sounding put out. "I'll plait it for you when you're ready."

When Charm had gone to shower and Kiah was in the kitchen, Mina fiddled with the remote, trying to find the older woman something to watch on TV.

"Leave that, Mina," Miss Pearl said, the timber of her voice commanding. "I want to ask you something."

"Okay," she said, giving the other woman her undivided attention.

"One of the mothers on the trip is a nurse at the hospital, and she says there's talk that Dr. Hamilton has offered to bring you on staff."

"I heard the same thing."

Kiah's voice was unruffled, and unexpected, since she hadn't heard him enter the room. When she glanced at him, his expression was neutral, but his gaze was watchful.

She felt put on the spot, especially when looking from one to the other she encountered equally questioning gazes.

"It's true," she said, trying not to sound defensive. Then she held up her hand. "But before you start cross-questioning me as to why I didn't mention it, I wanted to think the offer through, before either giving him an answer or telling you both about it. And I also got an email, just yesterday, offering me a position at Toronto South. So I have to take that into consideration, too."

There was a clatter, as Kiah dropped something and it fell to the floor. When Mina finally looked his way, it was no use, since he was bending down to pick the utensil up off the floor, and she couldn't see his face.

"So have you made a decision?" That came from Miss Pearl, while Kiah went back to laying out the cutlery on the dining table.

Mina took a deep breath and kept her gaze fixed on the older woman. She didn't know how Kiah would react to what she was going to say next, and wasn't at all sure she wanted to see.

"I haven't. I spoke to Dr. Hamilton today, asking for more time to decide."

"Well, I hope you make the right choice," the old lady said, more than a touch of asperity in her tone. "I'm not surprised at either of those offers, but I know which one I think is the best fit for you."

"Well, they both came as a surprise to me," Mina

confessed. "I wasn't sure I'd even be able to continue practicing medicine, despite all the encouragement I was given after the accident. And I have to say, it's nice to have options again."

Even if both those options left her in an untenable situation.

"We'll have to prepare Charmaine, in any event," Miss Pearl said. "If you decide to go back to Canada right away, she'll be sorely disappointed."

That caused a hard pang of guilt and pain, but Mina acknowledged the truth of the statement. Charm had stolen a big piece of her heart.

"But—"

"Leave it now, Granny."

Kiah's tone brooked no argument, and even though the older woman pressed her lips together, she didn't say anything more. Mina turned in time to see his back disappearing down the corridor to the kitchen, and even just the way he was walking told her he was angry. Miss Pearl looked toward him, too, and then back at Mina.

"You better go talk to him, child. He's upset."

Mina had to squelch the urge to put her fingers in her ears like a child, and insist she didn't want to, but, with a sigh, she stood.

"I guess I should," she said.

Miss Pearl held out her hand for the remote and Mina handed it over, before heading for the kitchen, trying not to drag her feet as she went.

Kiah was at the stove, stirring a pot of what smelled like beef stew, the microwave humming in the corner. He didn't look up when she came in, although she knew, without a doubt, he was aware of her entrance.

"Hey," she said, pausing at the end of the counter, where she could see his profile. "Are you angry?"

His eyebrows raised fractionally, then fell back into place. "Why would I be angry?"

"Oh, I don't know," she said, unable to keep the sarcasm out of her voice. "Because I didn't tell you about Dr. Hamilton's offer, or the one from Toronto South? Something like that?"

He grunted but didn't say anything, and Mina felt her annoyance level rising. This was Kiah at his uncommunicative best, and it never failed to rile her up. But this time she was determined not to get sucked in.

"I didn't tell you when the offers came in, because I really needed to think it through. To my mind, it didn't make sense getting everyone, especially Charm, wrought up over something I hadn't figured out yet. I've been drifting along, letting things happen to me, rather than taking the initiative. That needs to stop."

Kiah's lips firmed, but he still didn't reply, and Mina sighed.

"Okay, listen," she said, letting some of her irritation bleed into her tone. "Whatever it is you're thinking, let me know when you're ready to share. Because I'm not standing here and letting you make me feel as though I've done something wrong, when I haven't. I'm trying to do the best I can, and if you can't figure that out, tough cookies."

Then she turned and left, hugging her exasperation close, so as not to let any other emotion take over.

Damn Mina.

Kiah tossed the spoon into the pot and just barely missed getting splashed with hot stew.

Of course, he was angry.

Even more so now, after her pseudo explanation.

Was sleeping with him one of those things she'd *drifted* into? From Kiah's perspective, it seemed as though that was something she'd wanted, nearly as much as he had.

And drifting into the job here had done her a world of good, helping to put to rest her worries regarding her abilities since losing her hand.

To make it sound as though all of that was just happenstance riled him up.

Yeah, he could admit the offers she'd received deserved the deepest thought before being accepted or rejected, but it didn't mean she couldn't talk to him about them, warn him. It had been bad enough hearing about Dr. Hamilton's offer through the rumor mill at work, but to also find out she had another offer from Toronto had made his stomach roil.

He pulled out one of the kitchen chairs and lowered himself into it, scrubbing his hands over his face.

Neither her leaving nor staying permanently were things he wanted to contemplate. Both eventualities came with consequences he couldn't even begin to calculate.

It would be better if she left. He'd gotten way too used to having her around as it was, and now that they'd slept together, being near her all the time was doing crazy things to his body.

And his head.

If she went back to Canada, things could go back to normal.

Right?

But he knew he was lying to himself, thinking that they would. She'd made an indelible mark on his entire family. Plus, back home, Mina would have the freedom to date, and sleep with, whomever she wanted, which could lead her to the life she dreamt of.

As her friend, he should be happy with that thought, but it just made him angrier.

Kiah would have probably marched back into the living room and caused a scene if it weren't for the scent of scorching meat.

Jumping up with a curse, he moved the pot off the burner and turned off the fire. Grabbing the spoon made him swear again, and drop the red-hot implement.

He had to get a grip on his anger, if only for Charm's sake. He couldn't let his niece see how upset he was and start asking questions.

Sighing, he went to get a pot holder, and then used it to hold the spoon and gently stir the stew, being careful not to pull any of the burned stuff off the bottom.

The reality was that Mina had already become an integral part of their lives. The sense of rightness of having her here, the joy he got seeing her each morning, riding back home with her in the evening, just seeing her around the place, was unmistakable. Since they'd slept together, that sense of belonging had just grown.

It really was better that she go sooner rather than later.

But he didn't want her to.

He wanted to keep her right where she was.

It was the most selfish impulse ever, and he knew it. Having no intention of initiating any further changes in their relationship and, in fact, being determined to back away from making love with her again, he had no right to make any demands.

If ever it was time to put his money where his mouth was, this was it, and he did his best to stuff all his anger and confusion down, as he dished out the food.

"Charm, come help me carry these in, please," he called.

The youngster came into the kitchen, scuffing her feet, looking so dejected Kiah's heart ached for her. Yet, he knew neither Miss Pearl nor Mina would have said anything to her about what was happening.

"Hey, what's the matter?" he asked, knowing full well what the problem was.

"Nothing."

It was barely more than a mumble, but her eyes glistened with tears.

Putting down the dish in his hand, Kiah pulled out a chair and pointed to it. "Sit."

With obvious reluctance, his niece did as bid.

"Were you listening to the conversation between Granny, Auntie and me?"

"Yes, but it was an accident."

He shook his head. "I don't think it was, Charm. That's a bad habit to have, and you need to stop eavesdropping. If you want to know something, ask, but don't sneak around trying to hear things that don't concern you."

Her lower lip trembled. "I'm sorry. I won't do it anymore, but is Auntie really going back to Canada soon?"

"She might be. But even if she goes back, I'm sure you can go visit her, if you wanted to." Just the thought of Charm going to Canada made his stomach churn, and added another layer of pain to the whole situation.

"She always said I could, but suppose she changes her mind?"

Kiah chuckled, although the last thing he felt was amusement. "Listen, I've known Auntie Mina since I was the same age you are now, and she never, *ever* says anything she doesn't mean, okay?" Tugging her out of the chair, he hugged her and gave her a kiss on the top of her damp head, adding, "Everything will work out, Charm. Just wait and see."

"Okay," she said.

But although Charm seemed to take heart, Kiah couldn't help wondering if he believed his own optimistic words.

CHAPTER FOURTEEN

DINNER WAS TENSE. Although the adults tried to keep up a facade of normalcy, Charm was unusually quiet and a little surly. So much so that, after she'd helped to clear the table, she declared she was going to go to bed, without anyone reminding her it was time.

Mina found it telling that she wasn't asked to come and tuck Charm in, as she often had been in the past. Instead, it was Kiah who went to make sure she had turned out her light.

When he came back into the living room, he said to Miss Pearl, "Do you think you can manage by yourself for a little?"

"Of course." She sniffed, as though annoyed. "I got back up the hill from the stream after I twisted my ankle, so I'm sure I'll be able to get myself to bed without any problems."

He turned to Mina. "Do you want to go get a drink somewhere?"

"Sure," she said, not bothering to disguise the frost in her voice. "Just let me go change."

She was spoiling for a fight, and she knew it. Whatever he had to say, she was ready to give it all right back to him.

Wasn't he the one, back in Canada, who told her she

needed to get on with her life? What right did he have to be upset because she was doing exactly that?

With that in mind, as they were driving toward the Sweet Spot, she said, "If you want to talk about what I told you earlier, I don't think we should do it in public."

He slanted her a glance and said, "Yes, I want to discuss it. So, if that's how you feel, what do you suggest?"

"Let's just go to the beach. We can walk and *discuss*."

But if he thought he was going to berate her for keeping the news to herself, he'd better have a damn good argument, because she was loaded for bear.

The moon was waxing, almost full. The scene at Rickard's Cove, with its backdrop of coconut trees, would have been romantic if Mina wasn't simmering with annoyance.

Kiah waited while she took off her sandals, and then they walked silently together down toward the water. It occurred to her that, before they'd slept together, they'd probably have been holding hands, or Kiah would have put his arm around her shoulders, and the memory made her suddenly sad.

"You think I'm upset because you didn't tell me what was going on, but that isn't true."

She'd been so lost in melancholy reminiscences his voice startled her, but it also brought her back to the moment, and her anger.

"Really?" Injecting skepticism into her tone wasn't difficult at all. "So what is your problem then? Because it sure seems like you're sulking for having been left out of the loop."

"That's not it, Mina." There was a note of frustration in his voice. "Sure, I was annoyed that I had to hear about Hamilton's offer at the hospital, instead of from you, but I have bigger concerns than that."

"Like what?"

"Like Charm's well-being. Yes, I want what's best for you, and I know deciding what that is, is your job. It's just not going to be easy, no matter what you choose. Especially for Charm. She heard us talking earlier, and is upset just at the idea of you leaving."

Of course, he was thinking about the effect on Charm. What had happened between them didn't come into the picture, at all.

Not for him, anyway.

"Kiah, no matter where I am, Charm is always welcome. In fact, I'd love to take her to Canada. I can't think of anything more fun than the thought of showing her around Toronto, or taking her to Niagara Falls."

"That's another thought that fills me with dread," he said, and she could actually hear it in his voice. "Charm in Canada."

"Why? Don't you trust me to take care of her?"

"Of course I do. I wouldn't trust her with anyone else. It's just…"

He stopped and stood facing the water, rubbing his hand across his cheek, the way he always did when upset.

"Just what?" She spoke gently, realizing they'd gotten far from the topic of her job prospects, but not minding. There was something deeper at play here, and she wanted to know what it was.

"I don't want her seeing Mom, and don't know that I can stop it happening, if either of them wants to see the other."

His words rocked her back on her heels, and before she could formulate a reply, he went on.

"Mom's toxic, Mina. You know that. She drove Roy to do what he did, and then had the gall to want to fight me for custody when it turned out Karlene and Roy had made me her guardian. You remember?"

"Of course I do," she said gently, unable to stop herself putting her hand on his arm, out of sympathy, and a shared sense of remembered grief.

It had been one of the worst things she'd experienced. They'd all been shocked and horrified by the tragedy. All except Kiah's mother, who'd told anyone who'd listen she'd known it was going to happen. That Roy was evil, and a wastrel who'd stolen her daughter from her.

Not trusting Warren, even then, to do it properly, Mina had found Kiah a lawyer who'd petitioned the court on his behalf. Somehow, he'd convinced Mrs. Langdon, or her attorney, not to pursue her own claim, and Kiah had gotten full custody.

Outside the courtroom door, Kiah's mother had told him, flat out, she never wanted to have anything more to do with him, within earshot of Charm, Mina and everyone else.

It had been horrid and uncomfortable, and one more blow to him in an already tragic situation.

"I can't let her poison Charm, Mina. Not when she's just getting to the stage that she's wanting to hear about Karlene and Roy. Mom won't have anything good to say about either of them."

He paused, his throat working.

"And she won't have anything good to say about me, either. She never did."

Now she was angry again, but not at him. At his mother, and the soul-sapping hold she'd always had on Kiah.

Mina tightened her fingers and shook his arm, hard.

"Hezekiah Langdon, you listen to me. You're a wonderful man, an amazing doctor and a fantastic father to Charm. Nothing your mother can do, or say, can change any of that, you hear me?"

He chuckled, but it was edged in pain.

"You have to say that. You're my best friend."

"No," she said honestly. "I don't have to say that, and wouldn't if it weren't true. For instance, if you were a crappy doctor, I'd leave that bit out. Or if you were a mediocre father, I'd be nice enough not to mention it. But I don't recall our friend contract stating anywhere that I had to lie to stroke your ego, so I'm not going to do it."

His laughter was more natural by the time she was finished, just as she'd hoped, but she wasn't prepared for him to turn to her, and say, "So you think I'm a wonderful man, eh?"

Caught in a trap of her own making, all she could do was shake her head and send him a scowl.

"Why're you always fishing for compliments? It's one of your least attractive traits."

Which just made him laugh harder, and when he pulled her in for a hug, it felt so natural to go into his arms, the way she had so many times before.

However, this wasn't old times, and in the new reality she was living, Kiah Langdon wasn't just her friend, but had also been her lover. The man who'd shown her more pleasure than she'd ever dreamed possible.

So being hugged didn't feel safe, or comfy-cozy the way it used to. Instead, her body reacted, heating and softening, her heart rate kicking into high gear, her nipples tightening until they ached.

She wanted him, so very badly, but couldn't have him, and she searched for something to say to distract her from the need weakening her resolve.

"Do you remember the night by the lake, up at my parents' cottage?"

There had been several, but he hummed assent, the sound rumbling into her cheek, as though the shared memory had drifted from her brain into his. "Just before we went off to residency. How could I forget? You asked me to run away with you."

"Yes. I was terrified I wouldn't be able to hack the program. That they'd figure out I was a fraud and kick me out."

"Plus, your mom had that breast cancer scare, and your grandfather had just been diagnosed with Parkinson's. It was a bad time for you."

"But you talked me down off the ledge. Plus turning me down for the freedom flight."

"I didn't know it was a flight to freedom," he said with a soft chuckle. "All I could picture was your dad and Warren hunting me down like a dog, thinking I'd kidnapped you."

She snorted. "I doubt either of them would have minded much."

He was quiet for a while, and that was when she realized his heart was pounding, too. He shifted his body slightly away from her and, guided by an impulse she couldn't control, she shifted, too, bringing his erection flush against her stomach.

Kiah inhaled, his chest expanding, muscles rippling, and Mina caught back a moan of desire.

How could she want him so much, even knowing it would never lead anywhere? Where was her pride? Her sense of self-preservation?

"Why do I want you the way I do, Mina?" Kiah's voice was quiet, almost contemplative, but rough. "When I close my eyes at night, all I can see is you. When I hear your voice, I remember you crying out my name. It's like you've gotten into my blood, and now I can't get you out."

She was trembling, but made one last-ditch effort to lighten the mood, to break the spell of moonlight and lust that had settled over them.

"Are you calling me a virus?"

"If you are, I'm afraid it's incurable." Now his voice was anguished, the pain unmistakable to her Kiah-sensitive ears.

It made her realize how much he didn't want to feel that way, how much the change in their relationship hurt him, although she didn't know why. And knowing he was hurting made her hurt, too.

She took a step back, easing out of his arms so as to look up into his beautiful, moonlit and shadowed face, wishing she could see whatever it was in his eyes.

"We don't have to go on with this, Kiah. We can just be friends, no matter how hard that might be. We've come too far to lose what we do have, and we can move forward from this."

When he pulled her back in against his chest and buried his face in the space between her neck and shoulder she thought he was going to acquiesce.

But instead, he murmured, "One more night, Mina. Please. Give me one more night with you."

And it didn't even cross her mind to refuse.

Kissing on the beach, in the moonlight, was enough to drive him to lunacy with the sheer, urgent intimacy of his mouth on hers, the interplay of their tongues.

He knew it wasn't right, that he was flirting with de-struction, but Kiah couldn't resist Mina's lure, the need that drove through him each time she spoke, or laughed, or simply breathed.

His hands roamed her body, slipping beneath her shirt to slide across the skin of her back, and he felt the goose bumps rising in their wake when he reversed course. And he shivered at the sensation of her hand on his nape, pulling him closer, and her soft breasts against his chest.

Wanting was like fire in his veins, or lava, making him hard, reducing him to a column of desire, ready and willing to be incinerated by the woman in his arms.

Something about Mina spoke to his soul, called to him, so he raced to her like a sailor to a siren.

She'd joked about being a virus, but at times it felt exactly like that. A virus without treatment or cure, that never left the system but flared up at will.

This, he promised himself, would be the last time he made love with her. If this madness wasn't corralled, contained, it would devour him whole, leaving nothing behind.

"Let's go home," he said, coming up for air. "Before I try to make love to you here."

"We can't, not yet." Her voice was raw, as desire-rough as his own. "Miss Pearl will still be up."

He cursed, dropping his chin down to his chest, her giggles lightening his heart, although they did nothing to tamp down his libido. It was on the tip of his tongue to say he didn't care, but that wasn't strictly true. Granny not only had very traditional views on how men and women should behave, but she also harbored hope he and Mina would get together as a couple.

She hadn't been reticent about saying so to him either, over the years, although surprisingly she hadn't mentioned it recently.

There was no way he was giving her any false hope by letting it be known he and Mina had slept together.

Resting his forehead against Mina's, he said, "The joys of being a thirty-five-year-old man who lives with his grandmother. Why do I feel so much like a teenager right now?"

Her giggles increased, but her hand swept lightly across his cheek.

"Because we're in the kind of predicament teenagers find themselves in all the time. All revved up, and nowhere to go." She kissed the tip of his nose. "Let's go have that drink and regroup. Then we can see how we feel after that."

But he recognized a reprieve when he saw one, and shook his head.

"Let's just go home. This was a bad idea anyway. We both know this isn't healthy." It almost killed him to say it, but he knew it was true. "We can't be together, as a couple, so we probably should stop torturing ourselves this way."

Her amusement fell away, and she tried to search his gaze. With the moon behind him, he hoped she couldn't read the anguish he knew was reflecting in his eyes. Then one corner of her mouth tipped up, and she nodded.

"Okay. Probably a wise plan."

And she bent to pick up her sandals from where they'd dropped onto the sand, and they headed back to the car.

She'd been on the island for only a short time, but it had been enough to tear his life, his heart, apart. The years stretched ahead, threatening his sanity with the knowledge of what his options were—either seeing her all the time but not touching her anymore, or not seeing her at all.

He couldn't decide which would be worse.

CHAPTER FIFTEEN

THE TENSION IN the house hadn't abated the next day, and Mina was glad to be working, although speculative glances at the hospital upped her stress. Knowing the entire staff had heard about the offer from the director and was wondering what she planned to do added to the pressure.

While Mina was in the small staff cafeteria having lunch, there was an all-hands emergency, after a bus carrying dozens of people overturned on one of the country roads. The call went out for all available doctors and nurses to go to the emergency department, stat. Quickly tossing the rest of her sandwich, she took off at a gallop, deciding to take a shortcut through an older part of the building, which would get her to emerge quicker.

Once inside, she was surprised at how quiet it was but then realized they'd probably pulled staff from here, as well. There was only one baby visible in the NICU, with a nurse tending to him or her, and through an open door she glimpsed a mother nursing her child. Obviously, unlike the emergency room, it was a quiet day in the maternity and labor ward.

As she got to the doors leading back outside, they swung open, and a hugely pregnant woman pushed through, almost falling into the corridor. Mina grabbed her, lending her support.

"The baby coming." The woman was panting, holding her belly, and her face was covered in perspiration. "The baby coming."

"Come with me," Mina said, hastily leading her around the corner, toward the labor ward.

But the woman stopped and bent double, moaning.

Obviously, they wouldn't make it to labor without some help.

"Nurse!" Mina called. "Nurse!"

But no help was forthcoming, so, as soon as the mother-to-be seemed able to walk again, Mina hurried her into the first room they came to.

"I'm a doctor," Mina told the woman, trying to be reassuring, although her own heart rate was going wild. It had been years since she'd delivered a baby, and back then she'd had two hands. "Let's get you on the bed and take a look."

"It's coming," the woman moaned, after Mina got her partially undressed and lying down, and went to the end of the bed to examine her.

One peek told Mina the woman knew exactly what she was talking about. Right there, in plain sight, was a little patch of hair.

"Nurse!" Mina bellowed, just as the cell phone in her pocket buzzed. Did she even have time to answer?

A quick glance showed Kiah's name, so she jammed it on speaker and threw it onto a handy chair, on her way to the sink to wash her hand as best she could.

Gloves? What the hell was she going to do about gloves?

"Mina? You there?"

"Yes, but I can't speak for long."

"Did you get the call out for the bus crash?"

"Yes," she shouted in the general direction of the phone, while looking in vain for a sterile towel to dry up. "But I'm delivering a baby."

"You're what?"

"It's coming! I want to push!" yelled her patient.

"Hold on, Mama," Mina said in response, trying not to yell, too, as she grabbed a handful of gloves she couldn't even put on. "Wait until I tell you to push, okay?"

"No. No. I want to push now!"

"Mina, where the hell are you?"

"Maternity!"

Another peek showed it was almost time for the baby to make its appearance, with the mother's cervix almost perfectly dilated. Looking around, Mina spotted a package of disposable bed pads, and, sticking it between her knees, held it with a corner of a glove and tore it open. At least now the baby would have something clean to land on, she thought, as she spread it between the mother's legs.

Having put a glove over it, she laid her stump on the mother's belly, hoping it wouldn't freak her out, and rubbed soothingly, saying, "It's okay, Mama, you're doing real good. Give it a couple more seconds, then you can push all you want, okay?"

"Argh!" was the reply, as the mother arched with the pain of her contractions, but she waited until Mina told her, before she pushed in earnest.

The baby crowned before retreating slightly, and then, as Mina chanted, "Push, push, push," at the mother, the little head emerged.

"Good job, Mama," Mina said. "Now don't push again, until I tell you."

She hadn't been able to put a glove on her hand, so now she used the sterile latex like a pot holder, while turning the shoulders.

Then they were off to the races again, and in a trice, the baby slid out, already crying.

"It's a boy, Mama." Mina felt tears prickle her eyes as she looked down at the wrinkled, slippery little bundle lying on the bed. "You have a baby boy."

"Woo-ee," was the weary reply. "Another one?"

Then, suddenly, there was what seemed like a dozen people rushing into the room, and Mina was able to abdicate her position, although she felt strangely aggrieved about it. She'd delivered the baby, all by herself, but they weren't going to let her cut the cord? It didn't seem right.

But her part in it was over, so, as the obstetrician took her place, she dodged a nurse pushing a cart and turned toward the door.

And there was Kiah, shaking his head, amusement tipping his lips, although his eyes looked solemn, maybe even a little sad.

Haunted.

Why that touched her so deeply, she didn't know, but she stepped close to him, wishing they weren't in the hospital, so she could hug him tight, the way she wanted to.

"Delivering babies now? What's next? Juggling?"

So they were going with the jokes. That suited Mina just fine, and she wrinkled her nose at him.

"Yep," she answered, swinging by him and tossing her gloves into the bin by the door. "With knives."

The triage situation at the hospital lasted most of the day, and Mina found herself back in theater that afternoon, supervising a delicate spinal operation on the driver of the bus.

"In the past, we'd have airlifted him to Port of Spain, but if you think you can guide Dr. Golding through it here, we'll get him prepped for surgery," Director Hamilton said.

Mina looked at the MRI and CT scans, and talked the operation through with John Golding. Then, reassured the young doctor seemed up to the task, she agreed to oversee the surgery.

Kiah, who'd also been in theater most of the day, came in to observe the operation.

"You missed the best part already," Mina told him, sending John Golding a wink when he glanced up from the endoscope. "John's just about finished, and ready to close."

Since they hadn't been in the operating room more than fifteen minutes at that point, Kiah knew she was just talking smack.

"Why are you even here?" he asked her. "I thought you'd be down in the mat ward again."

Mina sent him a dirty look, before concentrating once more on what was happening on the table. With her guidance, John performed the bilateral thoracic laminotomy, to relieve pressure on the patient's spinal cord, and then spinal fusion on two lumbar vertebrae, all without a hitch.

But, although pleased with the outcome of the surgery, it was the delivery of the baby that stayed with her afterward.

In that moment, when she'd seen the newborn lying there, she'd realized she really was ready for a family. She'd probably never have a baby of her own, but adoption was definitely an option, in her books.

The decision was bittersweet, since with the realization came the knowledge that the only man she wanted to father her child wasn't interested in doing so. Kiah Langdon, although ideal father material, didn't want children. And even if he did, it was doubtful he'd choose her as the mother anyway. Theirs was a relationship that had taken a turn neither of them expected, but the physically intimate part of it wasn't destined to continue. He'd made that plain despite his obvious desire for her, which, although he'd said it wasn't, actually probably *was* just a by-product of his self-imposed sexual drought.

Yet, however despondent that thought made her feel, Mina knew she'd make it through, no matter what. She'd come to comprehend that, prior to the accident and the end of her marriage, she'd lived a pretty charmed life. There'd been little struggle—if she didn't count medical school—and things had come far too easily for her. Who was she to rail at fate, rather than try to steer her own destiny?

She'd always love Kiah, as a friend and more, but she wasn't going to stop living, just because he didn't love her as a woman.

As exhausted as he was that evening, Kiah felt restless, and jumpy, too.

When he'd gotten to the door of the maternity ward and seen Mina kneeling at the foot of the bed, looking at the newborn, he'd thought his heart would explode. The expression on her face, one of mingled wonder, joy and elation, was so beautiful he could only stare, enraptured.

Wishing for a moment like that for her.

Wishing he could be the one to share it with her wasn't something he could contemplate and still retain his sanity, so he pushed that particular thought aside.

The barrier he'd built up over the years about fatherhood was too strong to overcome. Seeing his father die, knowing the pain that loss caused both him and Karlene, had made him leery. Recognizing his anger issues, inherited from his mother, had cemented the decision not to have kids of his own. Who knew what kind of parent he'd turn out to be? One who devastated his family by dying early, or one who did it by staying alive and bitter?

Sure, he was nominally Charm's father now, but that in itself only made his choice seem even more sound. There were times when he barely controlled the impulse to holler at her, and he couldn't help thinking sometimes that she was at the age now that he'd been when his father died. She'd already been through so much. He could only pray she would be a little older, on steadier ground, before she had to suffer any more losses.

Like losing Miss Pearl.

After all, she was already in a tailspin over hearing Mina was going back to Canada. Hopefully, she'd weather the parting with a minimum of trauma.

Yes, having a family was something Mina wanted. He could only hope she would one day get it, and he'd have the strength to be happy for her.

Then, as they were all in the living room watching TV, there was a news report about a baby who'd been born weighing a whopping seventeen pounds.

"What is it with babies today?" he muttered, earning a sideways glance from Mina.

"Lawks," Miss Pearl commented. "His poor mother, carrying that much weight around."

"How much did I weigh when I was born?" Charm asked, obviously intrigued.

"Seven pounds, three ounces," Mina said, before Kiah could even think back that far.

"How do you know that, Auntie?"

Mina smiled, and the fondness in the way she looked at Charm was almost his undoing.

"I was there," she said. "It was me who coached your mom, and I got to cut your umbilical cord, too."

"Really?"

"Really."

Kiah thought that would be the end of the conversation. Even though Mina had warned him that Charm was asking about her mother, he expected her to retreat from any further discussion.

But instead, she asked, "How come?"

"Well, your daddy was in the army, and your mom was alone when you decided you were ready to be born, so I went to the hospital and was there when you popped out."

"Where were you, Uncle Kiah?"

Taking a deep breath, and trying to sound as though talking about it didn't hurt almost more than he could bear, he replied, "I was here, with Granny. You weren't supposed to come for another two weeks, so I didn't get there in time."

"Huh," she said and, thankfully, turned her attention back to the TV.

But later that night, when he went to tuck her into bed, he realized it really had been just the beginning.

"Uncle, do you have any pictures of me with Mommy and Daddy?"

"I do," he said, his heart aching all over again. "Do you want me to find them for you?"

"Yes, please. And…and can you tell me more about them? Not tonight," she added quickly. "But sometime soon?"

"I can, and I will, sweetheart. Whatever you want to know."

Making his way back to the living room, Kiah felt as

though the world, which just a few weeks ago had felt so stable, now wobbled like quicksand under his feet.

"Charm was asking about her parents," he said without preamble, waiting to hear Mina say she'd warned him, and he was amazed when she remained uncharacteristically quiet.

"It's not surprising," Granny said, with a sigh tacked on. "I was wondering when she would."

"Do you remember where we put the pictures, after I came back with her from Canada?"

"Yes. They're in a box on top of my wardrobe. We can get them down tomorrow."

"And I have some I can send back from Canada," Mina added. "I think Charm would get a kick out of some pictures of you in high school and college, Kiah, as well as the ones I have of her parents."

"Lawks," he said, unable to stop himself smiling across at her, even as he shuddered to think how Charm would react to his past fashion sense and hair styles. "You'd do that to me?"

"I sure would. And with pleasure," she added for good measure.

Those were the moments he would miss most when she was gone, he thought. The easy banter. The shared history that came out in stories and jokes.

He was already sure which job she'd take. St. Eustace couldn't hold her, not when compared to the prestige and excitement of the job on offer in Toronto.

He'd miss his best friend, just like he missed having her as his lover, but her going back was for the best. For all of them.

When everyone else had gone to bed, Kiah stretched out on the couch and turned on a documentary, with the volume down low. He knew from past experience he was too keyed up to sleep, and could only hope the murmur of the commentator and the flicking screen would have a soporific effect.

The sound of a door opening down the corridor had him lifting his head, and when he saw Mina come into the room, his heart hammered in reaction.

"Hey," he said. "Everything okay?"

"Fine," she replied as she went by into the kitchen.

After a couple of minutes, she came back with a glass of water in her hand, and paused at the entrance to the hallway back to her room.

"Kiah, can you give me the name of the acupuncturist you mentioned a while back, please?"

He swung his feet down off the couch, instantly concerned.

"The pains have come back?"

She nodded, and he couldn't help remembering how their lovemaking had seemingly stopped them the last time. He knew she wasn't angling for more of the same. That was one choice that had already been settled, although he wished it hadn't. Then he could scoop her up, carry her to his room, and love on her until her missing hand was the last thing on her mind.

But that wasn't feasible, or advisable, so he thought back to all the research he'd done after she'd had the accident, and patted the couch beside him.

"I'll give it to you in the morning," he said. "In the meantime, come here. I want to try something."

She shifted from one foot to the other, as though torn. "I'm just going to take a pain pill and try to get some sleep."

"Come on," he said, giving the cushion another couple

of pats. "I read about a technique that's supposed to work kind of like a mirror box. There's no harm in trying it, and you might get some relief. At least enough to fall asleep."

Seemingly still reluctant, she slowly made her way over and sat beside him on the couch. At his direction, she turned sideways, with her knee up on the cushions, so she was facing him.

"Okay. Now close your eyes and give me your hands."

"You mean hand, don't you?" she asked, cracking an eye open just as he shook his head.

"No. Keep your eyes closed and give me both hands."

Hopefully, she understood what he was trying to achieve, and could trick her brain into thinking he was holding both her hands in his.

As she closed her eyes again, he started a gentle massage on her right hand.

When he felt her fingers tense up, as though she was going to pull her hand away, he asked, "When last did you speak to your parents?"

"Day before yesterday," she replied, and he felt her hand relax with the distraction. "I talk to them at least twice a week."

"How're they doing? Are they still in Florida?"

She chuckled. "It isn't spring in Ontario yet. They're not going back there unless they're sure there'll be no more snow. Dad says he's too old for that nonsense anymore."

"I don't blame him." Kiah hoped his voice was soothing, but having her this close, touching her, even just her hand, had awakened his libido. "That, and the ice storms, make me glad I don't live there anymore."

He adjusted the pressure of his hand, making it a little softer, and she sighed.

Heartened, he continued to speak softly. "And how about Braden? What's he up to?"

"Oh, the usual. He's talking about expanding the acreage, putting in more trees. And I think he's actually getting serious with the woman he's been seeing. He talks about her all the time."

"Have you met her yet?"

"No, I haven't been to BC since they started dating, but I've invited them to come visit here. He's the only one of the family who's never visited St. Eustace."

"That's true," he said, and his voice sounded a little rougher, even to his ears.

He saw her swallow, the movement obvious in her delicate throat, and knew he wasn't the only one who felt the rising erotic tension.

"He...he asks about you all the time." Her voice was breathy, the sound making him want to groan with need. "Says he can't remember when last he saw you."

Kiah couldn't answer. It was all he could do just to keep up the gentle caresses, and not tug her onto his lap, so as to ravish that luscious mouth.

Then there was the sound of a door opening, and she opened her eyes, catching him staring. He had no doubt the desire in his eyes was unmistakable, as was the current flowing through their one, seemingly innocent, point of contact.

"Hezekiah, is that you?"

They were still staring at each other, their gazes locked, the electric flow holding them bound together, as he answered Miss Pearl.

"Yes, Granny. Me and Mina."

"You two should be in bed."

"Yes, Granny, you're right. We should."

"Go on, then," came the unknowingly fraught reply. "Don't be staying up this late."

As Miss Pearl closed her door again, the tension between them was thick enough to drink, and in the dim glow of the television he saw the rush of color staining Mina's cheeks.

Keeping his voice calm took everything inside. "How does it feel now?"

"Good," she said, the corner of her lips tipping up for an instant, as though she tried to smile but was unable to find the wherewithal. "Thank you."

For a long moment, neither of them moved, and Kiah felt heat billowing out into his veins.

"Go to bed, Mina," he whispered, his gaze dropping to her lips, lingering there for an instant, as he released her hand. "If you don't, I'm going to try to follow Granny's advice."

She nodded, before pushing to her feet. Picking up the glass of water, she took a step away, thankfully before he lost his head completely.

"Night," she said. "And thanks."

"Anytime, sweet girl. Anytime."

Then she was gone, leaving him even more edgy than when she found him, even though he'd thought earlier it couldn't get any worse.

CHAPTER SIXTEEN

ALTHOUGH BOTH MINA and Kiah tried to keep the atmosphere the same as it had been, Charm was still mopey, and Miss Pearl's temper definitely wasn't improved by her enforced immobility.

By day two of the RICE treatment, she was downright testy.

"I don't care what any of you say," she told them all the next evening. "I'm due to run a clinic up at Red Ground tomorrow, and I'm going."

"You should be fit enough," Mina told her cautiously. "But it would be best if you don't stand on your foot all day."

That earned her a sniff and an upturned nose from the older lady.

"I'm supposed to be at Morningside tomorrow, too, Granny, and the hospital is providing me with transport. We could ride together, since I'm passing Red Ground on the way."

He'd mentioned having to go to the smaller hospital to see some patients, and potentially do a couple of elective surgeries so the patients didn't have to traverse the length of the island to have them done. Although Mina was off that day, he hadn't suggested she go with him, and she'd tried not to be hurt by the omission.

After all, it was better to put some distance between them, especially in light of her reaction to his proximity. Just those simple touches last night had fired her libido, leaving her weak-kneed and shaky on her walk back to bed. And once there, she'd tossed and turned, her desire for him keeping her awake half the night. The only good thing was that he'd once more banished the phantom pains, so they hadn't added to her frustration.

"That would be better than driving with Nurse Maxwell," Miss Pearl said. "Her driving is horrible."

"Goes too fast?" Kiah asked.

"No. She doesn't go over twenty miles per hour, and slows down if she sees anything coming toward her. Gives me a headache just thinking about it."

Mina laughed, but the sense of walking on eggshells was hard on her, as was being around Kiah all the time, without being able to touch him. Although it had been normal for them to touch casually, and nothing had been said between them, they both seemed to have come to the conclusion it was better not to, and avoided it altogether.

Then, that night, the strain in the house came to a head with Miss Pearl barking at Charm, who'd been particularly snippy that evening. Having been ordered to her room by her great-grandmother, the young girl stomped off down the hallway and closed her room door with enough force to almost be called a slam.

Miss Pearl seemed set to shout after her, but Kiah intervened.

"Leave it alone, now, Granny. She's already upset, and if you go after her any more, she'll have a meltdown."

"The child is sulking, Hezekiah. And then she has

the nerve to bang the door? In my day, that would earn a good spanking."

"Good thing today is a different day," he replied mildly. "Besides, you haven't been an easy roommate over the last couple of days. Of all of us, you should be willing to cut her some slack."

The elderly lady's lips tightened, but she also looked a little ashamed, and it wasn't too long after that she declared herself tired and went to bed.

"Should I go check on Charm?" Mina asked, wanting to help.

Kiah hesitated for an instant, and then nodded. "Maybe she'll talk to you. I've gotten nothing but grunts and monosyllabic answers from her today."

Was he trying to make her feel guilty?

Whether he was or wasn't didn't really matter, Mina knew, because she felt that way all on her own, without outside prompting.

She'd never thought her choices would have the kind of impact on the others they seemed to have had. Charm in particular was tugging at her heartstrings, even while being a bit of a pain. No amount of reassurance that they would stay in contact, no matter what Mina decided to do, made any difference. Charm seemed to feel Mina was set to desert her, and no one could convince her otherwise.

Mina tapped on her door but received no answer. A slightly harder knock got no response, either, so Mina took a chance and opened the door a crack to peep into the room. What she saw moved her, and made her sigh.

Charm was curled up on her bed, still fully clothed, fast asleep. But there were tear tracks clearly visible on her cheeks, and even in repose her lips were set in an unhappy frown.

Going in, she found the little girl's nightie under her pillow and gently roused her, so that she could change into it.

Still half-asleep, Charm said, "I haven't cleaned my teeth."

"Come on, then," Mina said, getting up and leading her into the bathroom.

When Charm was finished with her ablutions, it was back to bed, but Mina was a little concerned, as the youngster felt a bit warm to the touch.

"Are you feeling okay, Charm?"

"Yes, Auntie," came the sleepy reply, but she was almost back to sleep before Mina could pull the covers up to her chin.

Bending, Mina kissed the warm, smooth cheek, and slicked her hand over Charms braids.

"Sleep well, baby," she whispered.

When she straightened and turned to the door, it was to see Kiah there, watching.

She put her finger to her lips and he nodded, his tender gaze melting her deep inside.

Walking toward him felt as though it took forever, each step causing the desire that constantly simmered beneath her skin to get hotter, until she tingled with need.

And it was there in his gaze, too, which morphed from gentle to fierce as she neared. When he turned sideways for her to pass him on the way out the door, she could almost feel his arousal coming off him, like static electricity, raising goose bumps on her arm and back. Bringing her nipples to yearning attention.

He took her hand and led her down the corridor past her room, which was next to Charm's, and into his.

They shouldn't be together like this, with his niece

asleep just down the hallway, and his grandmother on the other side of the house, probably still awake. But nothing could stop the explosive desire that swirled and snapped between them, urging them to touch, to taste, to give and to take.

It was an erotic revelation to Mina, made somehow more intense by the necessity for silence, and the knowledge that they had to hurry.

Not that it took Kiah long to make her come the first time. Already he'd learned what aroused her, and how to take her over the edge. He caught her low sound of abject pleasure with his mouth, kissing her until the final shudders eased, and she lay limp in his arms.

Then he kissed her some more, his hands bringing her body back to yearning life, until she was twisting against him, silently, desperately begging for more. The way he caressed her, his hands gentle, adoring, awoke within her a sense of wonder. She became beautiful, because he looked at her as though she were. Became powerful, because of how he reacted to her touch.

Pushing away from him, she tugged at his hand, positioning him on the edge of the bed. When she straddled his thighs to take him deep into her body, it was her turn to muffle the sound of his appreciation with her lips.

It was a wild, ecstatic ride, which culminated with her biting his shoulder, while he shuddered and whispered words of ecstasy into her neck.

He held her close for several long, sweet moments, as their breathing and heart rates slowly returned to normal. And it felt almost surreal to get up and silently get their clothes back in order, before going back out into the living room.

Mina thanked the heavens when the room was empty.

At the last moment she'd had the horrible thought that they'd come out and find Miss Pearl sitting there, waiting for them.

Still without talking, they wandered out onto the back veranda, and Mina sank into her chair with a satisfied sigh. Her legs felt wonderfully wobbly, and the surge of endorphins had relaxed her almost to the point of sleep.

And it was strangely easy to just sit and chat, even laugh a little with him, considering how fraught the last days had been, and how thoroughly they'd broken their agreement. They could go back to staying away from each other the next morning.

At least, that was what Mina told herself.

"I should turn in," he finally said, looking at his watch. "It'll be a long day tomorrow, with everything Morningside wants me to do."

She heard and understood his reluctance but did nothing to waylay him, merely got to her feet and waited for him to do the same, making sure to take leave of him with just a wave. Nothing more.

That way she wouldn't be even more tempted to drag him off to her room and make love to him again.

The next morning Charm said she wasn't feeling well, and went back to bed without eating breakfast. Miss Pearl was unimpressed, even when Mina said she'd thought Charm might have a fever, though the thermometer said her temperature was only very slightly elevated.

"We'll keep her home today, but it's back to school for her tomorrow. Half-term holidays always make it difficult to get children back into the school schedule."

Kiah rolled his eyes but made sure to do it where only

Mina could, and his grandmother couldn't, see him. Mina held in her chuckles and somehow kept a straight face.

"I'll keep an eye on her today," she said as they heard the beep of a horn outside, heralding the arrival of their transportation. "I'm sure she'll be okay."

But Charm showed signs of getting worse as the day progressed, complaining of a headache, and with a spike in her temperature that worried Mina. Since it was flu season, even in the tropics, she gave her a dose of acetaminophen and kept an even sharper eye on her than before.

She called Kiah early in the afternoon and left a message asking him to call her back, but before he could, she knew she had to make a decision. Charm was excessively sleepy, and now complaining of joint pain to go along with her blinding headache.

All kinds of horrible thoughts were going through Mina's head, especially with the memory of the not long past camping trip. Encephalitis, meningitis, the dreaded chikungunya—none of them were off the table, in her mind, and she made the decision to take Charm to the hospital.

It was only as she was getting Charm dressed that she realized she also had to figure out how to get her there. Should she call an ambulance? The taxi driver the family used on almost a daily basis?

"Auntie," Charm said with an air of urgency. "I'm going to be sick."

And Mina got her into the bathroom just in time for her to lose what little she'd eaten that day.

That made the decision for Mina.

Without thinking too much about it, she finished helping Charm put on her clothes. Then she fetched a basin from the washroom, and, grabbing the car keys and her handbag on the way out, led the youngster to Kiah's car.

Just as she had finished strapping Charm into the front seat, and placed the basin on her lap in case of need, her phone rang. She answered it as she closed the passenger door and started around the car to the driver's side. The relief swamping her, as she heard Kiah's voice, was visceral.

"Hey, I got your message. What's up?"

"I don't like how Charm looks. She's lethargic, with joint pain and a blinding headache so bad it made her throw up. It may just be flu, but I'm taking her to the hospital."

"Did you call an ambulance, or Mr. Brown?" he asked, referring to the taxi driver.

"No," Mina replied, already sliding into the driver's seat. "I'm driving her myself."

"Jesus, Mina." The stress quotient in his voice rose a number of levels. "How bad is she?"

He knew she hadn't driven since the accident, and wasn't used to the St. Eustace streets, or driving on the left-hand side of the road. Hearing she was worried enough to even attempt it was making him panic.

"I'm sure she'll be all right," she replied, trying to calm him, even though her own anxiety was through the roof. "I'm just playing it safe."

"I'm on my way back, as soon as I find the driver," he said. "And I'll pick up Granny, too."

"Good," she said, glad it was a right-hand drive vehicle, so she could adjust the seat without too much trouble. "I'll call you from the hospital."

Thank goodness the car was automatic, as well, so once she'd got it in gear it was just a matter of steering, and remembering to stay on the proper side of the road.

Charm moaned softly from the seat beside her, wringing Mina's heart.

"What hurts, baby?" she asked as she drove through an intersection perhaps a little faster than was wise.

"My head. The light hurts, even with my eyes closed."

"We're almost at the hospital, okay? We're going to get you all fixed up."

God, she hoped she was wrong, and it was nothing more than a bad case of the flu, but her intuition warned her it was something more serious. Better to be safe, and look like an overly concerned mother, than sorry later on.

When she pulled up outside of emergency, it was to find that Kiah had called ahead to warn them she was bringing Charm in, and there was an orderly and nurse waiting with a wheelchair. As they eased the girl out of the car Charm vomited again, and the nurse and Mina exchanged worried looks.

"Don't leave me, Auntie," Charm said, holding on to Mina's arm.

"I'll be right here, baby, but I have to move the car, in case an ambulance or another emergency comes in. Go with Nurse Schofield and I'll be with you in a minute."

But it wrung her heart to see the fear in Charm's damp eyes, and when she'd found a spot to park and was running back to the building, she had to dash away a few tears of her own.

"Dr. Jonas is in with her," the head nurse told Mina, once she was back inside. "Go on in."

"Dr. Langdon is coming in from Morningside—"

"I know," the nurse said, walking briskly and leading Mina to a cubicle. "He told us what was happening, and said he was giving you the power to make any decisions necessary regarding Charmaine's care until he arrived."

Behind the curtain, she found Neil Jonas examining Charm, with a nurse in attendance.

Mina put her hand on Charm's shoulder and said, "I'm back, baby."

The little hand came up, and Mina grasped Charm's fingers, watching but not interfering, as the examination continued.

After Dr. Jonas was finished, he said, "Charmaine, I'm going to step outside with Dr. Haraldson for a few moments, and then she'll come back in and stay with you, okay?"

Charm's fingers tightened almost painfully. "You're coming back, Auntie?"

"Of course I am." Mina leaned down and kissed Charm's feverish brow. "I won't be gone long."

Seeing Charm like that rattled Mina. She'd become so used to the sassy, irrepressible young woman who seemed older than her years in many respects. Now the child she really was had come to the surface, awakening a deep vein of protective instincts in Mina.

"It could just be a bad case of the flu," Dr. Jonas was saying, and Mina forced herself to concentrate. "But are there additional risk factors I should know about?"

"She went camping over the half-term holidays, up at Justice Peak," Mina said. "It made me worry about insect-borne viruses, perhaps even causing encephalitis, or meningitis."

Neil Jonas nodded, his gaze darting back to the cubicle, before coming to rest on Mina. "I don't want to play around with this. We've had one case of viral encephalitis in the northern side of the island, near to where she was camping, in the last week, so there's a precedent we have to take into consideration."

He took a breath, and Mina's heart dropped, knowing what he was going to say, even before he said, "I'd like to do a lumbar puncture, to be certain, before I start treating her with drugs she might not actually need."

That was when Mina realized it didn't matter whether you were a doctor, or not. When it was a child you loved, there was no easy way to make a decision that would seem like a no-brainer to the attending physician.

She turned away, tears filling her eyes, and she pinched the bridge of her nose to hold them back. There was the urge to call Kiah, let him decide, but she knew he'd have the very same reaction she was having right now. He also might not be able to bear the thought of Charm going through such a painful, and potentially dangerous, procedure.

Yet, Mina also knew Dr. Jonas suspected, as she herself did, that Charm's illness was serious enough to need medical intervention beyond anti-inflammatory drugs.

Both encephalitis and meningitis could be fatal, or have long-term effects, if not diagnosed and promptly treated. Mina knew she couldn't take the chance with Charm's life and future.

"Okay," she said, turning back to face Dr. Jonas. "Do the spinal tap. Will I be allowed to stay with her while you do it?"

Normally parents were advised not to remain in the room, but she'd promised to stay with Charm, and she wanted to keep that promise. Besides, she wasn't a parent, and she was a doctor to boot. Surely those things would count for something?

"You can, if you want to." Dr. Jonas gave her a knowing look. "You know better than most what's involved, so if you think you can handle it, then yes."

"Of course I can," she said, with far more confidence than she was actually feeling, and a sinking sensation in her belly, which told her she was a stone-cold liar.

CHAPTER SEVENTEEN

St. Eustace was a small island. The kind that it doesn't take more than four or five hours to circumnavigate, depending on the time of day, and how fast you drive. But to Kiah it suddenly appeared to have grown to the width of Canada, since it seemed to take forever to get back to Port Michael.

Mina had called a couple of times, updating them, and Kiah had almost lost his mind when she told him that Neil Jonas had performed a lumbar puncture on Charm.

He hadn't said anything untoward, he didn't think, but even with the knowledge that it had been successfully done, and Charm had been admitted pending the results, he was enraged.

"Hezekiah, you know Mina would never agree to anything she didn't think was necessary," Granny said, but her voice wobbled, showing how badly all of this was affecting her, too.

"They shouldn't have done it without my permission. They could have called—"

"You told them Mina would make the decisions until you got there, and she did as you asked. Do you think it would have been an easy one to make? Would it have been easy for you?"

But Kiah was in a head space where logic couldn't touch him, where rage sustained his sanity, keeping all other emotions and impulses at bay.

When they finally arrived at the hospital in Port Michael, he was a ball of fury, ready to let fly at anyone who got in his way.

Neil Jonas was at the nurses' station when he got up to the wards, and Kiah found himself wanting to punch him in the face. When the other man saw him approaching and gave him a solemn nod, the urge only increased.

"It's definitely viral encephalitis," Neil said after a brief greeting. "The lab results just came back, and I've ordered treatment. I want to keep her in for a couple of days under observation, but although it's a bad case, it was caught early enough, and she'll make a full recovery."

"Thank the Father," was Miss Pearl's response, but although the news was good, it did nothing to lessen the churning ball of anger in Kiah's belly.

When he entered the hospital room and found Mina sitting beside Charm's bed, not even the sight of her worn, tired face could touch him.

Only Charm's wan smile somehow cut through his rage, and he moved to her side, leaning down to kiss her forehead.

"How are you feeling, sweetheart?"

"A bit better," she said. "They said the headache should go away soon, but Auntie's made them turn the lights down for me. And I have to lie still, because of the thing they did to my back." She looked past him to say, "Hello, Granny."

"Why you want to scare an old lady like me, Charmaine?" Miss Pearl took one of Charm's hands and bent down for a kiss. "My heart can't take the stress."

"I didn't mean to, Granny. You know I didn't." Charm sounded genuinely contrite, and Miss Pearl chuckled in response.

"I do know you didn't mean to. I'm just teasing you."

"Sit here, Miss Pearl," Mina said, having already got up from the lone chair in the room. "I'll see if I can find another chair from somewhere."

Kiah hadn't looked at her, after that first glance, but now he knew he needed to vent some of the ire still filling his chest, and the one who seemed to deserve it most had just walked away.

"I'll be right back, Charm," he said. "Granny, stay with her for me, please?"

"Uncle, wait." Charm caught hold of his hand, making Kiah pause. "Can you bring me something to eat? I'm hungry."

"Okay, love." He bent to kiss her forehead again, and then strode out of the room, looking for Mina.

When there was no sight of her, he went over to the nurses' desk.

"Did you see which way Dr. Haraldson went?"

The nurse on duty pointed toward the door leading to the stairs, and Kiah made a beeline for it.

When he opened the door, he didn't hear footsteps, but there was a soft, almost imperceptible sound echoing in the stairwell. It seemed to be coming from above him and so, although the rising staircase led only to the roof access, which was always locked, he went up, instead of down. Turning the corner on the landing, he could see her, sitting on the top step, her hand to her face, rocking back and forth.

She must have heard his footsteps, because she looked

up, but her tear-stained face and reddened eyes couldn't melt the icy fury in his heart.

It must have shown in his eyes, or expression, because she got up, the tears still rolling down her cheeks.

"Kiah, please don't be angry with me right now. I don't think I could stand it."

She sounded so defeated, so sad, and it was then he realized: he wasn't angry with her.

All the fury inside was aimed squarely at himself.

He was the one who'd put her in a position to make the heart-wrenching decision about the lumbar puncture, who'd caused her the pain so clearly etched on her face.

"I did what I thought was right, for Charm." The words came out in little bursts, in between her sobs. "You know I'd never do anything to hurt her, if I could h-help it."

He wanted to tell her he knew, and understood, but all the old terror and agony he'd carried through the years clogged his throat.

All the fear came back, beating at him, as though to break him. Swamping him, until he thought he might drown.

Suddenly he was twelve again, watching his father die, impotent to help. Having his mother blame him, although he'd done the only thing he'd known how, which was call for an ambulance. And then he was thirty, getting the call about Karlene and Roy, learning he'd failed to give them the help and support they'd needed to get through the toughest of times.

And now, he'd put the responsibility of Charm's care on Mina's shoulders, instead of taking it on his own, the way he should. Making Mina cry, in a way he'd only seen her break down once before, at the loss of her hand.

Then, to make it worse, he'd gotten angry, when it was all his fault.

How could he do that? Cause so much pain, and translate that into the kind of rage that made him want to punch the walls, shout at the top of his lungs? It was all he could do to close his eyes, stand motionless, lock his knees, so as not to kick and scream.

"Kiah—"

Mina's voice broke through the bombardment of his thoughts, and he realized she was holding him, her arm around his waist, her hand cupping his cheek, her worried gaze searching his.

She was holding *him*, as if he was the one in need of sympathy, of reassurance.

Once more he'd failed at doing the right thing.

Unable to speak, to articulate everything swirling and snapping in his chest, he bent and kissed Mina's forehead, his heart breaking all over again, as tears filled her eyes once more.

"Kiah, she's going to be okay. That's what's important."

But he couldn't hear that right now, not with any kind of equanimity. All he could do was ease out of Mina's embrace and walk away, hoping to get some kind of control over himself, before he did any more harm.

Mina made it as far as the ladies' room before she lost it again, hiding in a stall to shed some more tears, although they made her feel worse than before.

Damn Kiah. Damn him straight to hell and back, for making her feel as though she hadn't done her best. As though she had somehow failed him and Charm.

She couldn't find it in her heart to forgive him. Not yet. Maybe never.

All the years of friendship and understanding, the connection they'd shared, had been shattered, because he apparently didn't trust her to do right by a little girl she loved, probably almost as much as he did.

How else could she interpret his actions, the anger she'd seen in his expression?

While staying with Charm as she had the lumbar puncture, hearing her cry and trying to soothe her, she'd hardly been able to stand it. The love she had for Charm was so strong it almost rivaled that which she had for Kiah himself.

Had he forgotten all she'd been through with his niece, or not understood how special it was to her? Not recognized Mina would never, ever do anything to harm the little girl?

She'd thought she'd been hurt before, but somehow this was bigger, more painful than even the loss of her hand. And she wasn't sure how she was going to face Kiah, after how he'd made her feel.

How could he have placed so much trust in her in the past, and lost confidence in her when it was a matter of life and death? Charm's life or death?

His lack of faith gutted her, made her feel hollow and bereft. Without his trust, could they even maintain the friendship they had?

And now she realized making love with him had been an even bigger mistake than she'd suspected. It had tied her to him in ways she could never truly undo.

Well, the joke was on her, wasn't it? She'd made the mistake of falling for her best friend, only to realize the relationship, even the friendship, wasn't what she'd thought. She'd always love him, but had to accept they were at the end of the road.

Grabbing some more tissue from the dispenser, she mopped at her eyes and blew her nose.

She'd put off making a decision about her future for too long, and now she had a clear direction.

There was no way she'd stay on St. Eustace and potentially see Kiah every day. If she were being brutally honest with herself, she'd been leaning heavily toward staying. She loved it here, loved being around Charm and Miss Pearl, and felt she could do a lot of good, professionally, on the island. Real work that would make an impact on those around her, and maybe even for years to come. The thought of going back to the rush and scurry of Canada hadn't held much appeal, even with the prestigious job on offer.

She was a different woman from the one who'd have jumped, just over a year ago, at the deputy chief position and worked herself into the ground to be successful at it. Now, if she did decide to take it, she had to be assured she could still maintain a healthy balance between the job and the life she knew she wanted.

There was a high probability she wouldn't even take the job at all. After all, no one needed to know whether she was going to, or not. She just had to turn down the job here, and tell them she was going back, once she'd fulfilled her obligations to the hospital.

How was she going to manage for the rest of the time she was on the island, without doing or saying something to Kiah they'd both regret? As angry as she was with him, she knew she'd get past it, but nothing would ever be the same. She'd have to hide behind a mask of friendly laughter, so as not to upset Charm, or get Miss Pearl on her case.

It all felt untenable, made her want to run away. Just

curl up somewhere alone, like she'd done after the divorce and the loss of her hand.

But that wasn't an option.

She was committed to staying on St. Eustace, at least for a little longer, and not even Kiah's foolishness was going to stop her from doing what she'd promised.

If there was one good thing about the situation, she thought, as she made her way out of the stall and over to the sink to wash her face, it was that it no doubt put paid to the physical relationship with Kiah.

She couldn't share her body with a man who couldn't trust her when the chips were down. Couldn't trust her to be a good custodian of his niece's life.

No matter what arguments her wayward libido and her breaking heart might come up with.

Bracing herself to see him again, Mina went back to Charm's room. Kiah wasn't there and Charm was asleep under Miss Pearl's watchful eyes.

The older lady got up as soon as Mina came in, and pulled her in for a hug. How was it that Miss Pearl suddenly felt frailer than she had before, as though the fright of Charm's illness had sapped the strength from her body?

"Mina, child, thank you for being there for Charm," she whispered. "And for acting so promptly. I'm so glad you were with her, although I know it must have been hard."

Mina hugged her back, thankful that at least someone appreciated what she'd done, and been through.

"It wasn't easy, but she's going to be all right, and that's the important thing."

Miss Pearl leaned back and cupped Mina's cheeks, her gaze searching.

"It is, child. It is. But you must be exhausted from all this drama and excitement. Hezekiah hasn't come back yet, and I'm going to stay with her for a while. Why don't you go and get some rest? You can come back later and sit with her, if you want."

Glad for the excuse to go, Mina nodded.

"Call me and let me know what time my shift is, and I'll come back. I'll take a cab and leave the car here, so Kiah has it to use."

"You drove yourself and Charm here?" The expression of shock on Miss Pearl's face would normally be comical, but Mina had no energy left for laughter.

"Yes. I didn't want to wait for a cab or an ambulance," she said, fishing the keys out of her bag and putting them on the table.

"Well," said Miss Pearl quietly, as Mina bent to kiss her cheek, prepared to take her leave. "What doesn't happen in a year happens in a day. You're well on your way to full recovery, and it makes my old heart glad to see it."

As Mina walked toward the door, Miss Pearl said, "Mina, do me a favor before you go?"

Mina paused, almost too weary to turn back, but doing it anyway. "Of course."

The elderly lady hesitated for an instant, and then said, slowly, "Hezekiah said he was going to get Charmaine something to eat, but I'm worried about him. Could you check on him, please?"

Tears threatened, but Mina held them back. "I saw him. I think he's okay. Just angry, I guess because of the lumbar puncture."

Miss Pearl shook her head. "No, child. That's not why he's angry." She sighed, lowering herself back into the chair. "Ever since his father died, he's taken the weight of this family onto his shoulders. That mother of his blamed him for not saving Benjamin—his father—and for everything else she could come up with. Kiah's probably blaming himself for not being here with Charm, and for putting the burden of her care onto you."

Legs suddenly weak, Mina reached out and held on to the doorjamb to hold herself up. "His mother did that? He never told me."

Miss Pearl nodded, her eyes solemn behind her glasses. "I thank God every day that Kiah turned out as well as he did, but he takes on more responsibility than he should, because of that woman and her bad ways. And when things frighten or hurt him, he gets angry, like a lot of men do. It's the only way he knows how to let it out."

And Mina knew how his mother's anger had scarred Kiah, both physically and emotionally. He'd said, more than once, when they were teens, how much he feared turning out like her, bitter and abusive.

Did he still feel that way? Get frightened by his reactions, instead of realizing they were natural and not dangerous?

Had he walked away not because he was angry with Mina, but because he fighting his inner demons, and was afraid he'd take them out on her?

There was only one way to find out.

She straightened, determination giving her back her strength.

"I'll find him, Miss Pearl, and make sure he's all right."

CHAPTER EIGHTEEN

She searched the hospital for Kiah, finally finding him pacing back and forth in the sanctuary garden behind the chapel. The sun was setting, roseate color tinting the sky and the water in the little fountain, but Kiah was clearly oblivious to it all. Head down, he walked back and forth, his hands clenched into fists, each stride taken as though he was trying to push his feet through the earth's crust.

With her new perspective, just watching him made her heart hurt. His pain was obvious in each step he took, the pallor of his face unmistakable.

Not wanting to startle him, but knowing he hadn't noticed her, Mina stepped onto the stone path and walked toward him. His head came up at the sound of her first footfall, and there, in his eyes, she saw his agony before he had a chance to mask it.

"Do you remember the professor at university who told us to make sure we took up a hobby?" she asked.

Kiah gave her a blank look, and then, blinking as though just awaking up, he nodded. "Professor Brathwaite, wasn't it?"

Mina snapped her fingers. "Yes, that's the one. Anatomy."

His brows came together. "What made you think of him?"

She shrugged, stopping at the neat little stacked-stone wall surrounding the garden and sitting on it. "I guess it was watching you marching back and forth like that. If pacing were a sport, you'd be a shoo-in for an Olympic medal."

The sound he made wasn't quite a laugh, but it was close. Then he immediately sobered. "Is Charm—?"

"She's fine. Sleeping, with Miss Pearl standing guard over her. We were worried about you. I wanted to check on you before I left."

"I'm fine." It came out a little like a growl, but then he repeated it, in a softer tone. "I'm fine. I just need some time to…"

"Decompress?"

"As good a word as any. Mina, I can't—"

She held up her hand, forestalling his words. "You can, Kiah. You can tell me what's going on in that head of yours."

His lips twisted, and he shook his head. "No, I can't. Not right now."

"Why?"

Kiah turned away, fists clenched again, and she saw the tension in the stiffness of his back, the taut line of his neck.

"Leave it, Mina. We can talk about it later."

"I think we should deal with it now."

He didn't reply, just took a couple steps away from her, as though distancing himself from the conversation.

From her.

Trying not to be hurt by that, she didn't move, although it was clear he wished she would just go away. It was up to her to get him to open up, and she wasn't sure how.

So she said the first thing that came to mind. "I was

scared, when I realized how ill Charm was, and angry. Even now, I'm still pretty angry."

He froze, his shoulders bowing, and Mina rushed into speech, before he could start taking the blame for that, too.

"I'm angry because she's ill, because no child should have to go through what she's gone through. But the one thing I'm not is angry at you. Are you angry at me?"

That brought him around to face her, and his expression was so anguished she could hardly bear it.

"No! God, Mina, I never wanted you to think that."

"Then what *are* you angry about, Kiah?"

He spun away and then back, as though he couldn't help himself.

"Everything," he said, his voice gravelly, as though he held the volume down by sheer will. "That Charm was ill, and I wasn't here to help her. That you had to be the one to make that call, and stay with her during the spinal tap. That—"

He stopped. Cursing, he turned away once more.

She got up, needing to be on her feet, caught somewhere between anger and pain—both for him. All for him.

"Don't turn away from me, Kiah. Face me and tell me the rest of it."

"Stop it, Mina."

It was a plea, but one she had to ignore. For him and, she suspected, for her, too.

"Stop what? Stop trying to be your friend, or trying to help you? Is that what you want, Kiah?"

"No." He still had his back to her and threw the word over his shoulder, as though he couldn't stop it from emerging from his throat. "I never wanted to hurt you, Mina, and yet I did, by asking you to take up a responsibility that was mine."

Moving a little closer, she said, "You didn't hurt me, Kiah, by asking that of me. I love Charm, and I was honored you'd put her care in my hands."

"But I shouldn't have."

"Why not?"

"It wasn't your burden to bear!" He almost shouted it, making Mina jump, startled. "It was mine, and I sloughed it off onto you and made you deal with it, hurting you in the process."

He stopped, and she could see his chest heaving, as though he'd run a mile, rather than been standing still.

"Is that it?" she said, infusing as much annoyance into her voice as she could, when all she wanted to do was go and hold him. "I'm this fragile little flower you have to protect from the vagaries of life?"

"You know I didn't mean it that way..."

"Really? Because that's how it sounded."

That made him face her, and she saw the anger still shimmering behind his eyes.

"I am trying to protect you. Can't you see that? I'm angry, Mina. Furious. And I just need a little time to get myself back together so I don't explode. Can you give that to me?"

"No..." She shook her head, seeing his eyes widen, as though that were the last thing he expected. "I'm your friend, and I'm here to listen to you rage, to scream with you, if that's what you want. To hug you, if you need me to. Keeping it all in won't help, Kiah. It'll only hurt."

The look he gave her was incendiary, and made the hair on the back of her neck stand up. But there was no way she was backing down.

"I don't want you to do any of those things." It sounded

as though his throat was tight, the words harsh. "I can manage this on my own."

She nodded slowly, holding back the pain of his rejection, not letting it weaken her resolve.

"So as not to take it out on anyone else?"

"Yes! Dammit Mina, just leave me to it, won't you?"

Instead of walking away, she stepped closer to him, saw the way he stiffened.

"You know you're not your mother, don't you?"

He stepped back, his head tilting away, as though she'd slapped him.

"What did you say?"

It was barely above a whisper, but he might as well have shouted it, for the emotional punch it packed.

"You're not your mother, Kiah. You don't hurt people because you're angry. You don't throw things, threaten people, lose your cool and intentionally say hurtful things. You have a temper, but you control it and, at times like this, you need to let the anger out with someone who cares, who understands and isn't afraid to stand with you while you do."

He stepped back again, the movement jerky, instinctive. She followed, keeping pace with him.

"You don't know what you're saying."

"Really?" Mina stepped even closer, so they were only a couple feet apart. "I was there, at school, when you came in with that cut on your head. You told everyone you'd fallen, but I got you to admit your mother threw a bottle at you. I asked you what you did, when that happened, and you said you locked yourself in the bathroom. You didn't hurt her back, although you could have, easily."

"Mina...don't."

Again she ignored his pleading tone, knowing it all needed to be said.

"And when you were on the football field, senior year, and the opposing player was calling you nasty names, trying to get you to fight, I saw how angry you were, but you wouldn't give in to it."

"I destroyed a garbage can." He said it as though making an important point, but she waved it off.

"After the game, outside, when it was just the two of us around. Did you hurt anyone? No, you didn't. And there was the time in university, when those two guys jumped you. You fought back, but once they were down, you walked away. You could have kicked the hell out of them, but you didn't."

"Stop."

He sounded so tired suddenly, beaten, but she wasn't sure she'd gotten through to him yet.

"I'll stop when I think you understand what I'm saying. The people who love you know the man you are. We're not afraid of your temper, and while we love how protective you are, we don't need you to feel as though you're responsible for our lives, because you're not."

She moved closer, so as to put her hand on his arm, and his muscles, already tight, hardened even further under her fingers.

"And sometimes you have to accept that someone other than you is going to do the protecting. I was glad I was the one who made the decision about Charm today, so that you didn't have to. I knew how much it would hurt you to have to agree to the lumbar puncture, how it would tear you up to see her go through it, so I did that for you, out of love."

"I don't like to see you hurting."

"I know," she said softly, raising her hand to place it

against his cheek, meeting his still-anguished gaze. "But sometimes it's inevitable, and you know that, as a human, a doctor, a man. You just have to accept it."

Turning his head to kiss her palm, he closed his eyes, and her heart ached to see him so vulnerable.

He took a deep, shuddering breath. "What am I going to do without you, when you're gone?"

Everything she felt for him swelled inside her, and she knew she had to find the courage to speak her truth, no matter the consequences.

"You don't have to find out, if you don't want to."

In a blink she found her gaze captured by his, and the tenderness of the previous moments fled before the intensity in his eyes.

But he didn't speak, didn't ask what she meant, just froze, almost as though he'd even stopped breathing.

"I love you, Kiah, more than I ever thought I could love anyone, and I want to stay here with you. But you have to decide whether you want me to, or not."

She almost stopped, too afraid to continue, but she was stronger now than she had been, and she needed him to know she accepted and loved him, just the way he was. So she inhaled and found the courage, even though her hand was shaking and her knees were watery.

"It scares me, Kiah, loving you this way. You'll never lose my friendship, but we could be so much more, and I can get past the fear because I know our lives would be better, together. I want you for my own, to help you raise Charm, even if we never have any children of our own, since that's not something you want. Be there for you through good times and bad, just like we've always been there for each other since that first day in Mrs. Nowac's class. All I want, all I need, is you."

He still hadn't moved, or spoken, so Mina rubbed his cheek lightly, savoring the warmth of his skin on her palm, then she pulled away.

"Or I can go back to Toronto, and we salvage what we can, from a distance."

It was up to him now, but she thought her heart would break when she turned to leave, and he didn't call her back.

Kiah tried to take in all the things Mina had said, as he watched her walk away, but her words swirled in his head, until he could hardly make sense of them anymore. His heart pounded, and his chest felt tight, so he could only draw shallow draughts of air into his lungs.

This was what love did to a man. Tied him in knots, scrambled his brains, left him without the wherewithal to know his head from his butt.

She'd always had this effect on him. Even when they were bantering back and forth, he'd been awestruck that Mina was his friend, that she actually liked him enough to stick around.

And from the first day they'd met, he would have done anything for her, up to and including laying down his own life.

She'd said she loved him, wanted to be with him, and then, in almost the same breath, said she was willing to leave and go back to Toronto.

The memory of her saying it slashed through the fog filling his head, even as his stomach twisted with emotions too numerous to categorize.

She'd said she was willing to give up on her dream of having a family of her own, just to be with him, but did she really mean it? He'd heard what she said—about his temper, about him not being like his mother—but did he believe it?

He wasn't sure he was willing to take the chance to find out. It terrified him to imagine himself turning into the monster he knew he was capable of becoming.

Yet, as he'd told Charm, Mina never said anything she didn't mean. She knew him, better than sometimes he knew himself. Was it possible to believe in himself the way she did?

Moreover, could he stand to lose her?

Let her go back to Toronto, taking the light and love and happiness she'd given him back with her?

Now he felt almost physically ill, and had to swallow against the burning lump that formed in his throat, and that sensation swamped all other emotions.

She was right, as she usually was. He'd let his fears rule his life, clung to the painful past instead of letting it go and living. But the fear of losing her was greater than any other, and he knew he couldn't do it.

And something else she'd said was true, too: they were better, together. Always had been, since he was twelve years old, and had first looked into those sparkling brown eyes.

She'd been there for him during the best and worst times of his life, steadfast and strong, cheering him on, lifting him up.

Mina was everything to him. She brought peace and joy into his heart, and comfort to his ragged and battered soul. He loved her more than he thought he could ever love.

Thank goodness he'd finally found the sense, and the courage, to admit it.

And he'd let her walk away thinking he didn't care enough to try to stop her.

Cursing himself for a fool, he took off after her, and finally caught up just as she was about to get into Mr. Brown's taxi, in front of the hospital's main doors.

There was so much he wanted to say, to tell her, but all he could do at that moment was call her name.

Mina turned, her eyes widening as she realized what he was about to do.

But she didn't resist when he pulled her into his arms and kissed her, as though he never planned to stop.

"Woo-ee! Wait 'til Miss Pearl hear 'bout this!"

It was the sound of Mr. Brown's hooting that finally had them breaking the kiss, but Kiah didn't let her go. Instead, he spent a moment just staring into her eyes, soaking up the love shining there.

Then he bent his head to whisper into her ear. "Now we're going to have to listen to Granny crow. She's been angling for us to get together for years."

She giggled, burying her face in his shoulder as Mr. Brown continued to tell everyone who passed by how Dr. K "grab up Dr. Mina and kiss her."

"Tell me you love me again, Mina."

He needed to hear it, even though she was trembling in his arms and holding him so tight he knew it would be forever.

"I love you, Kiah. And I always will."

"Ah, sweet girl, I love you, too."

"You all goin' have to get married, you know." When they both looked around, Mr. Brown was frowning, and had his hands on his hips. The stance and expression made him look remarkably like Granny, despite his being at least twenty years her junior. "Or Miss Pearl goin' beat you."

Kiah looked down into Mina's shining face and couldn't help grinning.

"What you say, sweet girl? We have to keep Granny happy."

She gave him a scowl, which was belied by the gleam in her eyes. "Hezekiah Langdon, if you think I'm taking that secondhand proposal, you clearly don't know me as well as you should, after all these years. Do it right, and I might say yes."

"Might? Just might?"

"If you're lucky, or unlucky, depending on how you want to look at it."

"Oh, I'm the luckiest man in the world, having you in my life and in my arms, and I know it."

Then, to the amusement and delight of everyone standing around and gawking, he sealed that statement with another long kiss.

EPILOGUE

MINA PUT HER hand on Kiah's arm, squeezing it with perhaps a little more force than was really necessary.

At least in his opinion.

"Stop glaring at that boy, Hezekiah. You're going to make him pee his pants."

She'd whispered it out of the corner of her mouth, obviously trying to be discreet. Kiah had no such reservations.

"Good. At least then I'll know *he* knows who's the boss."

"Come back inside and give them some privacy," she said, tugging him away from the back door and the veranda, where Charm and Ramesh were sitting.

"They don't need privacy. They're too young for privacy," he grumbled, even as he was letting her lead him through into the living room. "I don't know why they couldn't sit in here with us."

Mina just chuckled, and Granny gave him one of her dry looks.

"Charm is sixteen now, Kiah. You have to give her some leeway. After all, you were the one who said she could start dating at this age."

"Me? Oh, hell no. I think my plan was that she didn't

start until she was thirty. Mina begged for her, and now this is what we've got. Ramesh on the back veranda."

"But you've known Ramesh for years." Mina sank onto the couch with a heartfelt sigh, and patted the cushion beside her, until he sat down too. "And you like him."

"I *liked* Ramesh, until he started giving Charm those longing looks. Now I'm not too sure."

Mina giggled, then groaned. "Stop being such a fuddy-duddy and rub my feet for me. That operation yesterday has me aching all over."

Given a new topic to worry over, Kiah sank his teeth into it, even as he reached out and gently received the body parts that needed attention onto his lap.

"As for that, why did you think it a good idea, at seven months pregnant, to supervise a five-hour operation? Couldn't John have done that? You've been training him to take over while you're on maternity leave."

"He's good, but I need to make sure we can deliver what we say we can." She gave a little moan of appreciation when Kiah rubbed her arches. "John will do fine, and I've promised to be on call, just in case, but that hip surgery was complex, and I wanted to supervise it myself."

"Well, no more of that. You need to take better care of yourself, and our daughter."

Mina chuckled. "Aye, aye, Captain," she replied with a saucy expression on her beloved face.

Just looking at her made him content, filled his heart with joy and the kind of peace that had eluded him most of his life. This second pregnancy was unplanned, but Kiah had been elated when it happened. It wasn't ideal for Mina's health that their son, asleep in his crib, would only be seventeen months older than his sister, but Mina's prenatal checkups had been good, and he loved how happy she was.

He hadn't thought it possible, but he loved her a little more every day. Thank God he hadn't let his fears drive her away. She'd given him time and space to consider the question of children, not saying anything about it until he'd brought it up himself. This second pregnancy was, though, the last, according to Mina.

"Three is enough," she'd said, once she'd gotten over the shock, and he'd agreed, although, secretly, he wouldn't mind one more. Since he wasn't the one bearing or having to deliver the child, whether to have another or not wasn't a choice he felt qualified to make.

He heard Charm's laughter faintly, since he'd left the door open, and his attention was snagged once more.

"I wonder what's going on out there," he grumbled, wishing he could see through the walls separating them. "I'm thinking of putting cameras up around the house. For security reasons," he added quickly, when Miss Pearl gave him a withering look.

Mina started laughing so hard she held her belly, as though it hurt.

"What's so funny?" he asked, pinching her little toe.

"I was just thinking," she said, hardly able to get the words out through her continued mirth. "By the time you get over Charm growing up and dating, it will be time for this little one to start."

"Oh, mercy," he groaned, horrified by the thought. "Are you trying to make me go gray, all at once? Don't say things like that."

"And if she follows family tradition, we better start looking at any boy she meets when she's twelve, just in case."

"Yes," he agreed, chuckling with her, caught up in her amusement. "Apparently we fall in love young, and never get over it."

"Who better to fall for but your best friend?" she asked, sending him a look so full of love his heart stuttered with pleasure.

"No one, my sweet girl. No one."

* * * * *

MILLS & BOON

Coming next month

FIGHTING FOR THE TRAUMA DOC'S HEART
Rachel Dove

Michelle looked at her boss, but he was oblivious.

'So that's it?' she demanded of Andrew. 'I go abroad for four months, to help people who really need it, and then I come back and have to fight for my job, against him?' She hiked a thumb over her right shoulder at her rival.

There was a challenging look evident in Jacob's expression.

'I'm not worried. I like it here, actually, so I say bring it on. What do you say, Mich?'

Michelle stood up straight, drawing herself up to her full height. She tolerated 'Mich' from people she knew and trusted, but his use of it sent a wave of rage charging through her body.

He mirrored her actions, straightening his tie. She was five ten—more when she was out of her trainers and in a pair of heels—but she still had to look up at her suave rival.

'What do I say?' she said to both men, her arms folded to keep her from flailing them about like a child in the throes of a tantrum. She'd never give them the satisfaction. She couldn't be childish about this.

So she'd left, and the place hadn't been able to run on its own. They'd needed Jacob. But now she needed her job—her normality—back. She needed him to leave so she could burrow back into her comfortable life. That was her plan, and she didn't have a back-up. She had to be the victor in this fight. She wasn't sure she would be able to get up again if she got knocked down this time.

'Bring it on. May the best doctor win.'

'In six weeks I'll make my decision about who gets to lead the new trauma centre as head of department,' said Andrew. 'Don't let me down; I need you both at your best.'

'Six weeks of working together...' Jacob smiled, his pearly whites flashing as they caught the light. 'How ever will you resist me, let alone win?'

Michelle looked him up and down pointedly, ignoring the frisson that his sculpted body produced in the pit of her stomach.

'I'll survive, I'm sure.'

She held out her hand, and he shook it, holding it between them. The warmth from his hand pervaded her bare skin.

'We'll see, shall we? This is going to be fun.'

Continue reading
FIGHTING FOR THE TRAUMA DOC'S HEART
Rachel Dove

Available next month
www.millsandboon.co.uk

COMING SOON!

We really hope you enjoyed reading this book.
If you're looking for more romance, be sure to
head to the shops when new books are
available on

Thursday 23rd
July

To see which titles are coming soon, please visit
millsandboon.co.uk/nextmonth